Enchanted: Erotic Fairy Tales

The countess stepped inside, Peter beside her on a short rein. Katia stared at the gardener in his strange bonds. To see the bandages wound so tight around his thighs aroused her, and the package at his centre swelled promisingly. Could she, would she, be allowed to touch him? The thought made her shudder with excitement.

Irina handed her the leash, and for the first time she had a man under her command. He refused to look her in the eye, so she jerked the leash and demanded it, and the countess laughed.

'You do make an eager student!' she said.

The countess then lifted Peter's right arm and secured his wrist into a cuff that hung from the ceiling. She did the same with the left arm. Now he was completely helpless and at the women's mercy. Katia watched as the countess trailed a finger down the front of his bandages. The mass of crushed petals sewn inside his garment added to the already pleasing bulge. She prodded gently at the material, then cupped her hand between his thighs to determine what was padding and what flesh. How Katia longed to do the same.

'I think our holy little gardener is getting hard,' she declared, making him cringe with embarrassment. 'He obviously wants it.'

Enchanted: Erotic Fairy Tales

Janine Ashbless
Olivia Knight
Leonie Martel

BL

Published by Black Lace 2008

2 4 6 8 10 9 7 5 3 1

First published in Great Britain in 2008 by
Black Lace
Thames Wharf Studios
Rainville Road
London, W6 9HA

www.rbooks.co.uk

Addresses for companies within The Random House Group Limited can be found
at: www.randomhouse.co.uk/offices.htm

The Random House Group Limited Reg. No. 954009

A CIP catalogue record for this book is available from the British Library

ISBN 9780352341952

The Random House Group Limited supports The Forest Stewardship Council [FSC],
the leading international forest certification organisation. All our titles that are
printed on Greenpeace approved FSC certified paper carry the FSC logo.
Our paper procurement policy can be found at www.rbooks.co.uk/environment

Typeset by Palimpsest Book Production Limited, Grangemouth, Stirlingshire
Printed and bound in Great Britain by CPI Bookmarque, Croydon, CR0 4TD

Bear Skin

Janine Ashbless

Bear Skin

I first saw the bear as it came down the aisle between Travel and Biography. Perhaps the squeals of panicking shoppers should have alerted me sooner, but I was trying to find a misshelved copy of *Slowly Down the Ganges* that someone had ordered and I wasn't really tuned in to anything else. We're a big chain and the branch on Park Street is a big one too – the kind with a coffee shop at the back and piped classical music and late-night opening – but not really big enough to cope with a fully grown male grizzly. I looked up as it brushed over a rack of remaindered calendars and a squeak escaped from my lips as Labrador puppies and Rajasthani architecture and Italian vegetables spilled across the carpet under the bear's massive paws. I didn't get off my knees; I was trapped in a dead-end aisle and, besides, I don't think my legs would have worked.

The bear stopped a few paces from me and lowered its head to inhale deeply. The store lighting brought up the gloss of its thick pelt and I could see the depths of its dark eyes and the moisture on its nose. Its breath smelled of honey. 'Will you come with me then, Hazel?' it said.

My order form slipped from numb fingers. Its voice was deep and rich and masculine, with a strong Scottish lilt. 'What?' I whispered.

'You said you'd do anything to get out of this job: anything at all.'

If the blood hadn't already drained from my face I would have gone scarlet. Over the bear's shoulder I could see the peering horrified faces of customers and staff, including that of Gwen my senior manager, who treated the shop as a domain granted unto her by God. True enough, I had been complaining about my job, but only to trusted friends, and certainly not anywhere I thought I might have been overheard. Our chain is the sort that pays minimum wages but only employs graduates, so that they can bring their years of education to the challenge of shelving books in alphabetical order and coping politely with customers who are *Looking for a book, it was talked about on the radio last week, it's by Patricia someone and it's about this woman who goes to America – I think there's something about flowers in the title, but it might be fireworks or something like that, you know?* This job was driving me out of my mind, all right.

'Um,' I said, proving that my wits had already left me.

'That sort of thing gets heard, you know.' He shifted his weight from paw to paw, swinging his head. 'Will you come with me, Hazel? For a year and a day, that's all I'm asking.'

'And do what?'

'Be my true love.' His eyes were like honey too; a dark amber honey from bees that fed in northern pine forests. I felt his gaze drizzle across my skin.

'Your true love?' I became horribly aware of my body, all tender honey-glazed skin and warm flesh. Those jaws could crunch up even my bones without difficulty. 'You mean...?'

One round ear flicked. I could see the hint of a pink tongue between his lips. His breathing was heavy; I imagine the shop was far too warm for a creature with such thick fur. I wondered what else that long pelt concealed.

'Why should I?' I whispered. 'I mean, I don't know you.'

'No.'

'What's in it for me?'

'Nothing. No profit in it; only danger. No reward; only nights of my company and the risk that you might find pleasure in it.'

It helped being an animal, I reflected, to say such things in front of an audience. As for me, I blushed – but not my face only; a secret warmth blossomed down the whole length of my body.

'And I might search the whole world for a lassie bold enough to do this for me,' added the bear; 'and still not find her. Or maybe I've found her here, kneeling among the pages of other people's lives.'

I blinked. I'd never been called a *lassie* in my life. 'I need to think about it,' I said, stumbling over my words. 'Give me some time...'

A deep rumble sounded from his chest, and I couldn't tell if it was a growl or some noise of satisfaction. 'I'll come back for you then.' The aisle was too narrow for a bear to turn in so he reared up on his hind legs, paws dangling. His head was up on a level with the topmost shelves. I caught a glimpse of his cream chest and underbelly before he swung gracefully away and dropped back down on all fours. The watching faces vanished.

'Wait!' I called. He glanced back over his shoulder. 'I don't know your name.' I didn't even know if bears had names.

'It's Arailt.' As he walked away booksellers and customers scattered from his path. I started to pick myself unsteadily off the floor and was shocked to find a warmth and a slippery wetness in my knickers that had nothing to do with fear.

'You can't go with a bear,' said Lynn, pouring more sugar into her cappuccino. 'I mean, what were you even thinking of, talking to him like that?'

'In front of Gwen too.' Rosa blew onto her raspberry tea, fogging up her glasses. We were in Café Parisienne, two streets from the shop and our first port of call most evenings after finishing our shifts. 'She's livid, you know. I heard her on the phone to head office and she sounded like a wasp that's just been swatted from the jam. You can't bring a bear into her department and expect her to like it.'

'I didn't bring him.'

'Especially if you're going to talk to him about wanting to leave. You're in serious trouble, Hazel!'

'I didn't talk to him about leaving! He already knew!'

Lynn snorted. 'What sort of a name's "Arailt" anyway?'

'It's Gaelic,' I muttered.

Nikki swallowed her biscotti. 'Well, what I don't get is why he picked you.'

Looking into the mirror past her shoulder I couldn't help wondering that too. Was I so different from other junior booksellers? Did I stand out from all the other young women in the world bored with their jobs and clueless as to where they wanted to go in life? There must be millions of us. Was my hedgehog of black hair and neat body any more attractive to bears than Lynn's brown ponytail and wicked grin or Nikki's untidy bob and big boobs or Rosa's orange highlights and husky voice? *A lassie bold enough*, he'd said. I shivered. I didn't feel bold: I felt uncharacteristically cowed. Normally I'm opinionated and acerbic and ready for a giggle. Not tonight.

'He wants to lurv you,' Lynn mocked.

'He wants to do it to you bear-fashion,' Rosa chimed in. 'Wuff wuff!'

'What does a bear's prick look like, I wonder?'

'Lynn!'

'You could look it up on the Net,' I suggested, sipping my spicy chai.

'You reckon?'

'Oh yeah. Someone somewhere will have posted a picture of a grizzly-dick.'

'I've seen some grisly ones in my time,' said Nikki dryly, and we groaned.

'You think it's going to be big?' Lynn flashed me a look of delighted horror. 'Oh, Hazel – do you think it'll make up for Evan's?'

'I doubt it,' I said, wishing I'd never discussed my ex with them. I was trying to forget Evan, though it wasn't anything to do with the size of his equipment.

'He's a big boy,' she warned. 'I mean, a *big* fuzzy boy. And I bet he goes in hard. Think of the muscle on him.'

'Oh my God.' Rosa rolled her eyes. 'He'll squash her flat.'

'Her poor little pussy won't know what hit it.'

'Don't be stupid.' Nikki's voice was sharp. 'She's not going to say yes to him.'

'Of course not,' Rosa agreed. 'I mean, he is a bear. He'd just eat her as soon as he got her out of sight.'

'I agree; the whole thing's a trick. You mustn't trust him, Hazel.'

'Well,' I said, trying to be fair, 'it's not like he's a wolf. Or a fox.'

'He's still a predator though, isn't he? I mean, they do kill people, bears. They just look cuddly.'

'OK, they're dangerous,' I admitted.

'Don't even think about it: it's disgusting,' said Nikki, who is Catholic and occasionally suffers dizzying reversions to type. 'He won't even have a soul.'

For a second there was silence. Then Lynn laughed. 'It's not his soul Hazel's interested in.' She did a wriggly little dance in her seat. 'It's his ... bear necessities.'

They broke into song and shrieked with laughter all the way through the chorus, until the waiter came over to shut us up.

It was Arailt's voice, I think, that did it. The next morning as I crept downstairs in the dark to make breakfast – I have to get up stupidly early in order to get into the bathroom before my housemates, one of whom locks herself in for nearly an hour – it was his voice that I was thinking of; that deep burr and the flattened Scottish vowels. And the warmth of it, and the hint of humour, as if behind that ursine mask he was smiling. It was hard to think of him as an animal. But it was hard to think clearly at all, stood in the kitchen waiting for the toast to pop; I'd hardly slept all night, waking from a doze every half-hour or so with my heart in my mouth and a sense of impending crisis. The only way I'd been able to sleep in the end was to turn onto my stomach with my hand beneath me and masturbate myself to unconsciousness. My fantasies as I'd done it had been disturbing; starting with the memory of Arailt's warm voice, then imagining him there in the room behind me, watching my upthrust backside and my spread, quivering legs; then spiralling out of control until I was picturing him pulling back the duvet and sinking down to cover me in its stead and pushing into my eager, open sex ...

I'd come three or four times before drifting into oblivion.

Funny, but I'd pictured hands sliding between me and the mattress, cupping my breasts as he entered me. Hands, not paws.

I took my coffee back up to my room and sat on the edge of my bed. One room was all I had, and in the first steely light it looked bleak: a single bed, an old computer, a spherical plastic bowl in which my torpid goldfish, Moby, floated. The posters on the wall were all of countries I'd never visited. I shivered, then put on my coat and opened the window. My room has the advantage of overlooking the flat garage roof, and I can climb out and look over the back garden and the drop down the hill to the roofscape of Greater London. I stood clasping my mug, taking small sips and watching the watery sunrise. The grass below me was pale and lank; none of us ever mowed the lawn. It was late January and the trees stood naked against the sky. I could hear the murmur of traffic but nothing moved, all life hidden away in and between the rows of houses. Out there people were getting ready for work; they were feeding children and backing cars out onto their drives and hurrying to bus-stops and tube stations. They all, I thought, knew what they had to do with their lives. I had nothing but a job that drove me to distraction, no one to offer up my efforts to but Gwen, whose disapproval would by now be at arctic temperature, and no one to come home to at night but my goldfish. No boyfriend at the moment, no family that gave more than a passing thought to my existence, no friends except the ones I worked with, no career, no goals. That was my problem. In a world of possibilities, I had lost my way.

When I turned, Arailt was sat behind me, as if he'd been there all night. His fur was silvered with dew. I put my hand over my mouth to hold back the cry that filled my throat. Face to face once more, it was suddenly only too easy to think of him as an animal. He was enormous: even sitting back on his haunches his head was at the same height as mine. His claws were not retractable like a cat's but jutted from his paws like curved knives. I cast a covert glance between his spread thighs but long fur thwarted any glimpse there.

'Hazel.' His voice was as I remembered it and I wanted to rub its rich sweetness all over my skin. 'Are you ready to come with me then?'

I flinched from the point of decision. 'You didn't give me very long to think about it.'

'Thoughts run fast as lightning. How far did yours have to go?'

My thoughts had been round the world a dozen times and more that night and my mind was exhausted by the effort. I took a deep breath. 'Tell me: why me? Why'd you choose me, Arailt?'

'Why does anyone choose anyone?'

It seemed a fair question, if it was not simply evasion. 'Instinct,' I replied cautiously.

His mouth opened a little, revealing teeth that made the hair stand up on my neck. Then I realised he was grinning. 'And what do your instincts tell you, Hazel? What choice do you make? Are you to be my bold lassie?'

'Will I be safe? You won't hurt me?'

'I can't guarantee that. But ... if we're not suited to one another, then I promise that I will try to return you here.'

I didn't want to come back here, I realised. Even if our liaison was disastrous I didn't want to come back here, not to my rented room and my cosy, claustrophobic job. I'd do anything to get away from that. 'OK,' I whispered.

'Good.' His eyes were like polished amber. 'But there are rules.'

I was surprised; I'd assumed that he was in no position to make further demands. 'Yes?'

'From now on, you ask no questions. Whatever you see, whatever I do, however puzzled you are, you don't ask me.' His tone was gentle, almost apologetic; it took the sting out of a command that seemed wholly unfair.

'OK,' I said cautiously. There would be ways to get round that stricture if needs be, I was sure.

'The other rule is that when we love, we do it in darkness.'

It made no difference to my bewilderment and my trepidation whether I'd be able to watch or not. I shrugged helplessly. 'Fine.'

He let out a great sigh and sagged forward onto his forepaws. I wondered if he'd been as nervous as I. 'Come here then. You'll have to ride my back.'

I swallowed. 'Wait a moment.' For a second there was fire in his eyes and I nearly changed my mind. 'I have to sort out my goldfish. He can't wait a year for me.'

'Go on then.' His voice was nearly a growl. 'I'll meet you on the lawn.'

I wanted to ask if there was anything I should bring, but I couldn't. I climbed back into my room, carried Moby's tank round to Rob's door and left it by the jamb. 'Good luck,' I whispered. In the end I didn't bother to fetch anything from my room or even to lock it. If I was going to jump I was going to do it now, without looking back.

Arailt was pacing the lawn anxiously, leaving dark tracks in the dew, as I unlocked the back door. He hadn't really believed I was coming, I realised. 'It's all right,' I said, closing the door and stepping out onto the concrete path next to the sodden barbecue no one had cleared up in five months.

He swung toward me, then suddenly twisted away, rearing, as something black came fluttering in over his head. In my confusion I thought at first it was a bat, and then a wind-caught bin-bag because it was far too big for a bat. 'Leave me alone!' roared the bear, taking a swipe with his claws and snatching the object from the sky. It crumpled helplessly into the grass where he ripped it apart, and only when it was in shreds did he seem to remember me. I stood with my mouth open, aghast. The gape of his jaws had been wide enough to engulf my whole head.

'One of her Shadows,' Arailt growled, 'sent to spy on me. Don't ever let them bite you.'

I had no idea what he meant but even if I had been allowed to ask I wouldn't have been able to find my voice. I was shaking.

'I need to get you somewhere safe,' he added, looking around. 'We can't stay here. Let's go.'

It took a lot to make myself approach him. I cast a glance down at the broken Shadow and saw what looked like a swatch of shredded black leather with a blind and crumpled face. It had shed no blood as it died, and was already beginning to thin and dissolve.

'There'll be more of them about. Hurry.' He turned side-on to me and I mounted. It was like plunging into a sea of bear – the scent of him so strong; the thick, soft waves of his fur washing over my hands and thighs. I settled precariously astride his back, feeling his warmth leak into my skin and the solid bulk of his body heave beneath me. 'Hold tight,' he admonished and I gripped the coarse fur of his ruff with both hands. He plunged straight for the willows at the bottom of the garden and I threw myself face down in his pelt as their branches flashed toward my face.

Then he was running, really running, his shoulders pitching

beneath me, his breath coming in steam-engine puffs, and the wind was so cold in my face that I could not see for tears and all I could do was hold fast and pray that I would not slide off. The world fell away, blurring to grey. Though my streaming tears and the battering of his hair on my eyelids I caught occasional glimpses: a man frozen mid-stride on the edge of a pavement, a starling nailed to the air mid-flight. I swear that some time in the first few minutes we crossed all eight lanes of the M25 motorway, cutting a line through traffic that wasn't just stationary but held fast in the iron grip of a splintered moment, like Zeno's Arrow. I thought of my mother washing dishes on a Sunday evening, fallen distracted and motionless, elbow-deep in suds as she gazed out across the golf course that backed onto her house. I thought of what my broken body would look like if I slipped from Arailt's back to be smeared across the unyielding surface of reality.

The wild ride was exhilarating at first, but grew terrible. It went on until my legs clenched around Arailt's ribs went from painful to numb. It began to rain and the water drops struck my skin like stabbing tines. Only my stomach and legs were warm where they were pressed against him, while my exposed back and thighs set like ice. My mind froze too, my thoughts whipped away by a slipstream faster than any natural wind. 'I'm falling,' was all I managed to murmur as I felt myself slide off.

I awoke in a bed. For a while I lay without moving, looking at the wooden panelling of the wall, remembering a long plunge into darkness and the sensation of strong arms catching me. I felt warm again and wriggled my toes luxuriously. Then suddenly realising I was naked between the sheets, I sat up fast, clutching the covers to me.

I was in a large old-fashioned bedroom. Heavy velvet drapes blocked off the windows from floor to ceiling, and wall-lights with nasty yellow-fringed shades provided the only illumination. All the furniture was big and clunky and made of very dark wood. My gaze swept across the bed, which looked huge and solid. Of course, it occurred to me, it would have to cope with the weight of a bear.

I shivered, though the room wasn't cold. I was alone, but I was naked – that meant someone had undressed me. Given my memory of rain-sodden clothes, I wasn't outraged, but I couldn't imagine bear paws being delicate enough for such a task. Maybe he'd simply sliced them off my unconscious form with those claws, I speculated, and froze as another memory welled up from the depths – this one much fainter, almost too tenuous to be a memory at all: a terrible sensation of cold and weakness as if my whole body had turned to clay, and then a warmth between my thighs, a hot wetness as of a licking tongue and the heat spreading up my belly from it.

'Arailt?' I whispered. The only sound was the murmur of the water in the radiators. I sneaked a look under the coverlet and saw no sign of ursine kisses, but the faintest smell of honey mingled with my own scent. I blushed from head to toe.

I got up at last and padded over to the big wardrobe, my feet sinking inches into the pile of the rug. But when I opened the door – gingerly, unable not to think of B-movie corpses tumbling out – I found not my own gear but racks and shelves laden with women's clothes. I pulled out a dress at random and found it was a silver evening gown, trimmed with ostrich feathers and bearing a designer label on an inside seam. A bit garish, I thought, stuffing it back onto the rail. My next, rather more careful choice, was a crimson silk chemise, the sort you might wear as an underslip or a party dress. I shrugged into it, enjoying the cool whisper of the fabric on my skin, and paused to look at myself in the mirror on the back of the wardrobe door. For just a moment I thought I understood what Arailt saw in me; the hemline just above the knee showed off my legs and the simple flattering lines of the dress made me look straight and fit and somehow fearless, as if I had nothing to hide. My hair, battered by wind and rain, had turned from its usual moussed spikes into a tousled boyish mop. A bold lassie indeed.

Then I laughed. It was just a dress. But I kept it on as I sought in vain for a hairbrush or a pair of knickers, and then gave up and headed for the door.

The house was enormous. I realised that the moment I saw the corridor, its strip of red carpet stretching away toward an arched staircase well. It was also old, and rather badly lit by dim bulbs. The huge panel of stained glass at this end of the corridor was blank against the darkness outside. It was night already, so I'd lost a day. For a moment my courage failed me. Then I told myself that this place was just like the slightly run-down country hotels my parents used to take me to when I was small and we were still going on holiday together. I was probably somewhere in Scotland, I reasoned, thinking of Arailt's accent.

Biting the inside of my cheek, I set to work exploring the main rooms. Be bold, be bold, I told myself: he's not a fox, or a wolf. Bears are grouchy and hot-tempered and prone to solitude, but they're not *bad*, are they? I wasn't going to find a roomful of his previous victims swinging from meat-hooks ... surely.

Many of the doors were locked, in fact. Others opened onto bedrooms and bathrooms, clean and warm but apparently unused. Then as I worked my way round the lower floors I discovered sitting rooms and studies and a library – the books were all hardbacks, but several were modern, printed this year. A television room held a huge collection of films on DVD, but when I switched the screen on to look for a news channel I couldn't find an outside signal, just pale static. A dining room enclosed a vast table laid at the far end for one; I gave it an unkind look and shut the door quickly because there was something about that lonely place-setting that was chilling.

All the windows I investigated had barred interior shutters.

I feared the front door would be locked too; but when I found it, it opened easily enough – onto a black gusty night filled with the creak of trees and the hiss of rain. Not one light glimmered out there, not even the moon. I retreated into the hall, my skin covered in goose bumps from the chill.

There was a photographic print hung at the foot of the stairs and I paused to look at it. It was modern and seemed out of place in this oak-panelled pile. It was a full-length and life-sized portrait of a rather beautiful woman, framed in brushed silvery metal. Standing against a featureless white backdrop, she was so pale that she almost merged with it and with the shoulderless white dress she wore. Her hair was an arctic-blonde glissade, her irises colourless and picked out only by their dark rings, and her lips so bloodless that their shape was only a pencil sketch upon the paper of her skin. You'd think that the photograph was hopelessly over-exposed, except for the area of shadow under her mantle: that was so dark that it looked black. It was, I thought, as if she'd taken all her natural shade and colour and trapped it in that one area of her apparel. Pallid as she was, there was nothing bland about her; the expression on her face was intense and even disturbing. It was a lovely picture, I thought, but I wasn't sure I'd want to meet the model in the flesh.

Nearby I found the kitchen. That was a shock too; it was brightly lit by fluorescent strips and sumptuously appointed to modern standards. Definitely a hotel kitchen, I thought, looking at the stainless steel counters and the huge ovens. One thing that surprised me was that the hobs were all electric, not gas. I recalled that in all my wanderings I hadn't seen a single open fireplace such as I'd expect in a Victorian pile like this. I opened a cupboard at random, to be confronted by rows of jars and packets.

'Wow. Somebody shops at Fortnum and Mason.' I reached down green olives stuffed with pine nuts with one hand and white-chocolate-dipped raspberries with the other. My stomach flipped; I realised that the uneasy feeling in my belly I'd had since waking was at least partially hunger. I quickly assembled myself a truly sybaritic meal, snatching mouthfuls as I hunted out of sheer greed: swathes of Parma ham, a creamy block of some Swiss cheese, delicate smoked trout, baby tomatoes tossed in fresh basil and truffle oil, and asparagus parboiled while I broke and buttered a stick of fresh French bread. Looking for pâté or something to put on the bread I found a jar of honey and broke the seal. The wild, sweet scent took my breath away and without thinking I plunged two fingers inside and sucked the stickiness from my hand as it oozed down toward my wrist. I opened a bottle of what looked like vintage wine and poured myself a generous glass, before sitting down to eat my hoarded treasures at the bench.

Then the lights went out.

It wasn't a bulb failure. I should have known that, but I still looked for the illuminated display on the microwave. Not even those blue glimmering digits were visible in the now pitch-black kitchen: the electrics were all down. As I pushed back my stool it occurred to me that someone could have thrown the mains switch. My mouth seemed to fill with ash. I strained my hearing. Nothing stirred. Without the light I felt irrationally cold and shivers chased up and down my spine.

We do it in darkness.

I started to feel my way down the kitchen bench, and nearly screamed when my stool went over with a crash. My heart was thudding like a horse trying to kick its way through a stable door, and I pressed my hands to my breastbone. 'Oh God,' I whispered, 'please;' but even I didn't know if I was begging mercy from a higher power or from Arailt. In the end though, because it was either that or hide under a bench, I sidled toward the door, cracking it open as softly as I could.

The hall beyond was in utter blackness. I slid out, keeping my back to the wall and blinking hard as if I might be able to dispel the darkness from my eyes. It didn't work, but something new stole upon another of my senses: a thick animal reek, like wet dog.

I know I shouldn't have panicked. I knew even then that Arailt had never offered me any overt threat, but there was something about being alone in the dark with a big predator that woke such an atavistic dread that I could hardly breathe. The blood roared in my ears. He's wet, I thought: he's come in through the front door. Get away from the door quick! To my left was the dining room, and I inched my way blindly toward that, one hand on the panelling, one outstretched and dreading what it should touch.

'Hazel.' The voice came from behind me, and with it came a heavy tread. I blundered into the door and groped for the handle. 'I smell on you sunlight and grapes, sweet pork and pollen-laden bees and the dry earth beneath the grey olive groves.'

I wished I hadn't eaten the ham. Bears are carnivorous, you stupid girl! I roared inwardly, as I forced open the door and stumbled into the room beyond.

'Hazel, you remember your promise, don't you?' The floorboards creaked; he was following me. I kept going in a straight line until I bounced off a high-backed chair and whimpered. I hadn't forgotten my promise, but I could not bring myself to honour it.

'This room is wood from tropic shores and beeswax, food served half-cold and conversation served icy.' His voice was soft; he was in the doorway. I retreated hand-over-hand down the row of dining chairs. 'I cannot miss your scent in here, Hazel.'

Stumbling into the void, I grazed my hip against a sideboard and scrabbled for the connecting door into the library.

'Are you running from me?' He didn't sound angry or gloating, just a little unhappy.

Of course I wasn't running from him: how could I? I was blind and lost, navigating by luck. He never made a wrong step, moving with heavy grace between the unseen islands of furniture. I had no chance of escape. My retreat was driven solely by instinct.

'Book-dust,' he murmured. 'Printer's ink and long wet afternoons while the shrubbery drips and the river roars in its bed. You smell of books too, Hazel, but not enough to hide in here.'

I collided with a sofa and it nearly knocked my legs from under me. Gasping, I waited for the sudden rush, the hot breath, the teeth. Nothing happened.

'Your fear is sharp. I thought . . . I thought you braver than that.'

His voice was no closer. If he'd intended to catch me, I told myself, he could have done it long ago. I forced myself to straighten up, smoothing down my dress, swallowing the lump that was filling my throat. 'The dark,' I said hoarsely. 'The dark's frightening.'

'I warned you about the dark.'

'Yes. You did. It's stupid of me.' My backside was braced against the padded leather back of the sofa. 'The dark shouldn't make any difference.'

'It makes all the difference in the world.'

Not to what you're going to do to me, I thought, running my hands helplessly through my hair. 'Well, you're right. I made you a promise. Come on then.'

I heard him move into the room, his claws scraping on the polished boards then muted on the rug. I breathed deep and let the smell of him fill my nostrils. I heard the wuff of his breath in those heavy jaws and thought, better if he takes me from behind. Turning, I gripped the leather sofa-back with slippery hands and set my feet apart.

He stopped. 'Is that how you want it?'

'It's easier for you this way . . . I'd have thought.' I didn't dare admit that the desire to shield my vulnerable throat and belly was overwhelming. He didn't reply. But I felt for the first time the moist touch of his nose against the back of my knee, and then that great muzzle pushed up between thighs, lifting me onto my toes. I gasped. When my heels hit the carpet again I spread them wider, bending at the hips to push my bum out toward him, nearly choking with terror. I felt the hot gusts of his breath on my bottom. With one hand I reached behind me to pull up my flimsy skirt. Then he licked me with his great wet tongue, long enough to lap me from clit to bum-hole in a single stroke, and I cried out, unable to conceal a pleasure so shameful that it could only be confessed under cover of darkness.

Arailt uttered a low rumbling moan and then said, 'Turn round.' His voice was thick with urgency; I knew that sound.

I wanted him to lick me again. I was wet to match his mouth. I let out a sob.

'Turn *around*.'

I obeyed, tears running unseen down my face.

'Hazel . . .' He rose up suddenly and planted his forepaws to either side of my hips. His fur was damp from the rain. I flinched, shutting my eyes though it made no difference to either of us. His breath smelled of honey, as it had done the day we met.

Oh God, I moaned inwardly, my heart running riot. 'Arailt,' my lips whispered as I reached for him, plunging my hand into the soft pelt of his chest – and encountered smooth skin. For a moment I froze, speechless. Under my moving palm the fur parted as if along a seam, and I slid my hand beneath it down a hard musculature: pecs and flat breastbone, the torso of a man. I touched his forelimb and the fur fell away to disclose an elbow, a hard bicep, a shoulder. 'Oh God – What –'

Arailt's fingers covered my lips, pressing the words back. 'No questions, ever,' he whispered in my ear, his voice the bear's voice and a man's voice, the same as it always had been. Fingers, not claws or paws, I thought – and then they were withdrawn and his mouth took their place and any questions I had were stolen from my lips along with my breath as he kissed me. He tasted of honey, and of my sex. I ran my fingers along his jaw and felt stubble a week old but no fur, then down his throat and found his Adam's apple. His lips were hungry, his kisses laden with intent, but his teeth were not like shears. When he caught my bottom lip between them he drew no blood, only a leaping stab in my heart and a low cry from my throat.

Gently, he released my mouth. I passed one hand over his face. His eyelids trembled under my fingertips. He kissed the palm of my hand. 'Arailt,' I repeated as if it were a spell, a word of profound magic.

My other hand slid across his shoulder and I felt the bear-pelt finally slip from his back, heavy as sodden velvet, heavy as a bear-hide would be with skin and fat still adhering, sliding to the carpet. Underneath he was naked. Christ but he was a big man – not anything like as big as a brown bear of course, but broad-shouldered and solid with muscle. He made me feel fragile. I felt his strength as he put his arms about me and pressed up against me, his skin hot on mine. His strength – and his desire. He was immensely aroused and his erection was insistent. His lips sought me out again, needing no light. For a moment we clung together, face to face, breath mingling. 'Not too much of a disappointment, I hope?' he asked, laughter bubbling under his words.

'No.' Suddenly, out of nowhere, I began to shake.

'Don't be like that.' His hand cupped my face and encountered the wet smear of my tears. 'Hey, my Hazel; is it so bad?'

'Just a shock.' My voice was quivering too. I'd steeled myself for the bear; I'd been ready for him. I was not ready for a man. I hadn't been for months. There was an intimacy and a danger in the man's embrace that there could never be in Arailt as a bear, I realised. A bear, even a talking bear, can only treat you like meat: it takes another human being to treat you like shit.

'Oh God,' I gasped, 'oh God . . .'

'It's OK...'

Was it? Was it OK to yield to him now? I couldn't get him and the bear straight in my head. Heart racing, I ran my palm down his chest, smoothing the slight roughness of his body hair, all the way to his groin. He had a lovely big cock with a velvety foreskin, hot in my nervous hand. 'You're real!' – it came out as a hiccup and a giggle.

'Too right,' he said with fervent delight, folding his hand around mine, guiding my grip on his member up and down the shaft.

'Oh...'

He kissed me on the lips and then the throat, biting and licking the line of my neck as I offered it up to him. It didn't occur to me to be afraid of his teeth. I was lost in his kisses in moments, forgetting eventually even to stroke his prick. He didn't seem to mind; he slid to his knees before me, pulling out of my grasp and setting my bum firmly against the sofa-back. He kissed his way down over my bare shoulders as he eased aside the spaghetti-straps of my slip, and then his mouth was on my breasts and I forgot to breathe. The darkness was total but now my blind eyes were filled with crimson stars as he ate his way in honeyed kisses across my breasts, suckling at my nipples, breath hot on wet skin. I grasped his head, running my fingers through his short hair, raking the nape of his neck. The silk dress ran down my legs like cool water. Then he stooped to the taut line of my belly and he was nuzzling up against my mound and parting my thighs and I had to let go of him to grasp the leather and lean back, opening for him, almost on tiptoe. His tongue was sweet fire. He lifted my left thigh and draped it over his shoulder – all the better to eat me with.

Arailt: a stranger pressed between my thighs in the dark, his tongue taking possession of my clit and my mind. A man whose face I couldn't picture. A man I'd never even seen. I thought I'd melt on that hot, avid mouth. I thought he'd lick me away like an ice-cream. But I didn't go quietly into dissolution though I'd lost all ability to construct a sentence; my evocations were half poetry and half blasphemy and all helpless surrender, as the inky darkness turned to pulsing crimson and then the stars in my head went nova.

Almost as soon as I was done he stood, scooped me up bodily and dropped me over the sofa-back onto the padding below. Then he stepped over in one stride and descended on me, urgent now. It wasn't graceful, our coupling; in the blackness we tangled our limbs and fumbled for access, gasping and giggling and heaving until somehow I guided him into me, and after that he knew exactly what he was doing. He did it hard, just as Lynn had warned – and it was so good. I arched beneath him and bit his shoulder and urged him on with whimpering cries. I had one leg up the sofa-back and one foot on the floor and my head hanging over the side, jerking with every thrust: What after all was the value of decorum, there in the dark? What was there left, here in the dark, when all that was familiar and normal belonged to the daylight? Certainly no regret or guilt or fear any more: only his weight and the friction and the smell of our bodies and the need and the pleasure and the igniting fire of orgasm.

The fire consumed us both.

When we'd finished gasping Arailt slid from me and dropped with a thud to the carpet. 'Jesus,' he whispered, cradling his hot face on my heaving breast. 'I want to do that again.'

I dissolved into spluttering laughter.

'What's so funny?' His tone was comically offended, but he ran his hand accurately down the length of my abdomen until he could sink his fingers into my muff.

'If you can do that again I'll –' The words caught in my throat as his fingers circled my clit.

'You'll what?' Raising himself, he explored my throat and face with his lips until he found mine and planted a questioning kiss there.

'I'll be very very happy,' I said in a small voice.

He chuckled. He had a rich and deeply dirty chuckle. 'I didn't say right now. Or here.' Standing, he pulled me up. 'There's a lot more room on the bed, for a start.' He slid my arms around his neck. 'Come on, you wee slip of a thing. I'll carry you up.'

'Wee slip?' I mocked, wrapping my legs around his waist. 'Oh, the big man reckons he can carry me all the way up to bed...'

He didn't even catch his breath. 'No problem. Except...' He took my bottom lip in his teeth and tugged it gently. I moaned. His hands, which had slid under my bottom to support my weight, took a lascivious squeeze. 'Except that I might have to stop and put you over the top banister and fuck you there,' he added.

In the morning I awoke alone. That was the pattern of my time in Arailt's house; he came to me every night without fail and he was always gone in the morning. During the day I was left to amuse myself how I liked, but I had no contact with another soul and that took a lot of getting used to. I craved Arailt's presence, longing for the moment the lights went out and the draught from the front door gusted down the hall. I wanted his voice warm in my ear and the touch of his hands on my shivering skin. I needed some interaction with another sentient being. I needed jokes and argument and empathy. Most of all I needed his sexual desire; the moment he pulled me against him, the taste and the texture of his rising excitement, the appetite that brought my inchoate self into focus, there in the dark.

I was crazy for that unseen body so hard with muscle, so strong and sweet and responsive to my caresses. The way his skin yielded to my teeth, the prickle of goose flesh as I whispered up the line of his back, the jump of his shaft beneath my tongue – I was all hunger. I starved all day for him, and gorged at night. I tasted the salt of his sweat and the musk of

23

his desire, and he in turn ate every inch of me. Deprived of our sight we knew each other by taste and scent instead. There were no secrets in the dark.

I got to know Arailt's body well; what it liked, what it dreaded, what it needed. Sometimes they were the same thing. But I never got to know him. He never spoke about himself. He volunteered not one thing about his life and I bit back the forbidden questions.

It was hard finding the right rhythm to live by, to find enough to occupy my mind while he was away. I read in the library, catching up on literature I'd never had time for despite my best intentions; Dickens and Burgess, Plato and Steinbeck and Kerouac. Just because you work in a bookshop doesn't mean that you get much chance to read. I watched films on the huge plasma screen TV. I cooked, creating more and more ambitious dishes as I learned from the recipes, and I washed up after myself, but there was no other work to be done round the house; by dawn everything was tidied and swept clean and the cupboards restocked. There would be presents for me too most mornings: a new book or a DVD, a wooden puzzle or a sudoku pamphlet; once a loaded MP3 player which I seized upon eagerly. A newspaper always waited on the doormat, though no delivery boy could have made his way to that house.

I explored the exterior of the building on the second day. The house was situated in a wooded valley and the grounds were so overgrown that it was impossible to venture more than a few yards before running up against an impenetrable wall of rhododendron and holly. There were traces of a driveway, but it was almost as thickly barred by intertwining branches as the rest of the grounds. But that wasn't my greatest problem out of doors; within a few moments of my emerging a dark fluttering shape flicked over the roofline and circled down toward me. I retreated to the back door, grabbed a rake and scooped the leathery Shadow from the air on its next pass, flinging it to the mossy gravel and battering it with the rusty iron head until it stopped moving. After that I did not dare venture out without a weapon.

There were days I was restless to the point of panic. Once I went round and cut the fringes off every lampshade in the building: once I took up a tin of varnish stripper from under the kitchen sink and painted blistering graffiti down the black Victorian panelling. Arailt, if he noticed, said nothing.

The shutters on all the windows were padlocked shut, which added to the claustrophobic atmosphere of the house. No natural light made its way into any room but the hallway, and few artificial sources either. In the whole building I could not find a single match, candle, torch or any light source that did not draw its power from the mains electricity.

Gradually I learned to pace myself, to set myself goals. I asked for canvas and paints and, taking them to the old conservatory – which once I'd scrubbed the algae off the glass panes was the only room with good light – picked up the hobby I'd last indulged at college, experimenting with colour and filling the white spaces with searing abstracts. I could look up through the roof while I was painting and see rows of ragged Shadows waiting restlessly in the treetops. When spring sent armies of sparrows to bicker and shrill before the windows I went outside – armed and wary – and began to hack back the encroaching shrubbery with shears. I didn't make much headway down the smothered drive but I uncovered carpets of snowdrops and primroses and bluebells as the year unfurled, and let the light in upon them so that they flourished. The Shadows kept their distance once they found I could fight back.

As the days grew longer Arailt began to arrive before dark-fall and he'd spend time with me in animal form before, without warning, the lights would go out. I'd sit with my naked feet buried in his thick pelt and read aloud to him from my latest book. We'd watch movies together, and argue because our tastes did not coincide. He was fond of foreign-language films, particularly French ones that seemed to me unendurably slow and affected. Such an inclination didn't seem to fit with his rugby-player physique and it reduced me to giggles, but when I chided him about it one night he rose and chased me squealing through the pitch-black house until he had me cornered and then he fucked me thoroughly on the dining table, excoriating me the whole time in the filthiest French.

I experimented with different outfits from my wardrobe, and he loved to lie at my feet while I lolled in flimsy lingerie, but he never once sloughed his bear skin by daylight. Always he waited for impenetrable darkness before he laid a hand upon me. And after we'd rutted he would lie cradling me, touching my skin with his fingertips as we talked. He talked less than I did; perhaps he was naturally reticent or perhaps he'd been with people all day and was content to be silent. I had no way of telling. I could not ask. He was a good listener, particularly when he was in bear form and didn't get so distracted by my pliant body under his wicked hands. I was starved of conversation, so I chatted about anything that came into my head. I told him about my family – about my father leaving when I was twelve, and what my mother had done to drive him away. I told him anecdotes from my very ordinary life. I even told him about Evan, which made him growl. I talked about what I'd like to do in the future, about what I'd learned that day from the paper, and he'd offer the occasional opinion. I'd have liked to have heard more. I'd have liked to have asked him what he did when he was away, about where we were and what were the Shadows after and who was the woman in the portrait on the stairs, about how it was that he was a bear by day and a man by night. But by the terms of our agreement I couldn't even enquire as to whether he preferred me in red or in cream lace. I had to couch everything in terms of statements, and hope that he'd rise to my bait. Sometimes he let small things slip. Once I said, 'It's such a great kitchen,' and he replied without thinking, 'I like to cook.' But when I looked pointedly at his clumsy paws he fell silent except for a long rumble of exhaled breath.

Sometimes I picked things up without a verbal explanation. He would come in exhausted and shaken and simply fall asleep in my arms. He would arrive smelling of smoke. Once he turned up with a gash in his shoulder that had bled copiously, matting the fur all the way down his left forelimb, and I stitched the wound up with fishing line from the cupboard in the study. That was horrible, but there was no alternative so I had to do it.

He didn't say how he'd come by that injury. Like a Victorian husband, he told me nothing and expected me to accept it all. There were days when I wanted to shriek and slap him. There were days I wanted to climb on the roof and leap off the ornamental turret just for a chance of glimpsing a further horizon. I did my best to bite it all back and not betray the craziness seething beneath, but I don't think I did that good a job of it. He'd watch me ranting up and down the carpet with those dark bear eyes, saying nothing as I let it all rip about some triviality I'd seized on that day. Then later he'd tumble me into bed and we'd fuck savagely and he'd endure the bruises he got at my hands and the nail-tracks I left down his back.

I forgave him everything for the sake of that strong cock and those honey kisses and the encircling tenderness of his arms as I rested against his chest.

Then the year turned toward autumn and the days grew shorter once more. Darkness thicker than the tangled rhododendron branches seemed to press in on the house and the thick cap of cloud over the valley never lifted, sending rain drumming down for days at a time. I could feel the fear of entrapment rising like floodwater. 'I want to go back to London,' I announced one afternoon.

'What?' Arailt lifted his muzzle from my thigh.

'Just for a little while. A day or so. I want to see my friends.'

I reached out and stroked the thick fur behind his ear. 'They'll think I'm dead, you know, Arailt. They'll think you ate me up.'

His lip lifted, revealing ivory canines.

'It's not fair on them. I'd just like to . . . see them for a while. Let them know everything's OK, that I'm happy.'

'Are you?' The question was slammed down like a gauntlet.

'Yes.' I cupped the underside of his jaw. 'I don't want to leave, Arailt. I just want to see my friends for a few hours.'

He took me back to London on a grey afternoon, arriving just as the office workers started to spill out onto the street. Funny, but I hardly noticed the chill of the journey this time: perhaps whatever it was about Arailt was rubbing off on me. It was strange riding in down the familiar roads on bear-back. Most people pretended not to see us. I dismounted outside the Café Parisienne. 'I'll wait for you over at the park gate,' Arailt growled.

I hugged him, burying my face in his ruff, before tripping away into the café. They'd seen us through the window and by the time I slipped off my coat Nikki and Rosa had scurried over from our usual table and flung themselves shrieking about my neck. For several minutes we hugged and jiggled and talked all at once, while they made sure I was solid by squeezing me until I was breathless. 'Your hair looks terrible!' announced Rosa, thrilled: 'Where have you been?'

'Where's Lynn?' I countered anxiously.

'She made senior bookseller this summer. She'll be here in about ten minutes when she's finished the admin.'

I wanted to hear it all. I let them lead me to the table and we ordered drinks and I quizzed them about everything that had happened since I'd left. It was so good to be able to ask questions! Then when Lynn arrived we went through the hugging and the questions all over again. This time round I talked. I told them everything and they listened with eyes wide, squealing as I described Arailt's bedtime transformation and begging for details. I had to flap my hands and beg them to keep their voices down as they repeated my words. We ordered food. I listened voraciously to all the shop gossip they could recall. I answered question after question, sometimes laughing, sometimes solemn. Their eyes were huge. Then I sat back, tucking chips into my mouth, proud and relieved.

'So you're, like, a desperate housewife now?' said Lynn, tearing her baguette between lacquered nails.

'Oh you've changed, Hazel!' giggled Rosa.

The smile slid off my face. 'What do you mean?'

'Well, you know, you sit round all day waiting for your man to come home and give you a good seeing to,' said Lynn. 'You don't work. You don't go out. You don't see your friends. It's not like you.'

'You're a kept woman.' Rosa sniggered.

I hitched one shoulder in an uncomfortable shrug. 'I, uh . . .' But I couldn't take the sentence anywhere.

'It sounds like he's holding you a prisoner there,' Nikki said dryly.

'I am not a prisoner! I got to come back here, didn't I?'

'It's been nine months, Hazel.'

A dull flush rose up my neck. 'Sorry . . . I've just been busy.' It sounded lame and I knew it.

'Yeah. Shagging. We know.'

'He's a *great* shag,' Lynn murmured. 'Big cock. Goes for hours. We heard.'

'He should let you out more often. You should make him take you out to clubs and stuff.'

'You're not even on email any more, Hazel!'

'If he's as rich as you reckon, you should at least be getting some proper presents off him. Things you can take away when he's had his fun. Your time's nearly up, isn't it?'

I sat back hard, aghast. I'd expected them to be relieved and pleased for me and maybe, if I was being truthful, just a little bit envious of my fit and exciting lover. I hadn't expected this. 'He's a good bloke,' I muttered.

'Yeah, right. He dresses up as a bear and he'll only screw you in the pitch dark. What's he got to hide, I wonder?'

'Nothing!'

'He's probably ugly as sin.'

'Maybe he's a troll.'

'No!' I was getting defensive. 'I've ... I've had my fingers all over him; there is nothing wrong with him, believe me. He has the best body I've ever got my hands on. And his face is ... fine.' I'd touched his face often and often, but the truth was I'd never constructed a mental portrait of Arailt to call upon. It just wasn't a skill I possessed. 'Two eyes, one nose, that sort of thing. No scars. He's not missing anything.'

'So he's not fat or deformed,' Lynn sneered. 'Maybe he's old.'

'No way!'

'Or wall-eyed.'

'Maybe,' suggested Rosa, 'he has a port-wine birth-mark all across his face and he's ashamed to let you see it.'

'Maybe he's an albino. Maybe his eyes are all pink and squinty.'

I wanted to say that none of those possibilities mattered, but I couldn't. It wasn't just that I wanted him to be handsome – and oh how I wanted to be able to say that – but that I didn't want him to be something I didn't know about. 'Piss off,' I muttered feebly. 'This is my boyfriend you're talking about.'

'We're just thinking about you,' said Nikki, laying her hand on mine. 'What's he hiding, Hazel? 'Cos he's definitely hiding something.'

I stared at her.

'You should get a look at him, you know,' confided Rosa. 'When he's asleep maybe.'

'I can't. The electricity's on a timer ... or something like that.'

'Then use a torch, for God's sake.'

I bit my lips. 'There isn't one in the house.'

'Cigarette lighter? Match?'

I shook my head. I was feeling sick. 'Nothing.'

'That's . . . weird.'

'What the fuck is wrong with him?' breathed Lynn, eyes narrowed.

Rosa pulled a bunch of keys out of her handbag. Attached to the ring was a dinky little torch shorter than the length of my hand and she unsnapped it. 'Take this then.'

Numbly, I slipped it into my jeans pocket.

'Though I wouldn't go back to him at all, if I were you,' said Lynn. 'Now; what are we going to do tonight? Shall we go down to Yates's and get a round in?'

They all fell to discussing where we'd be drinking. I looked at my watch. 'I'd better nip out and tell him I'm staying over. Back in a minute.'

'Doesn't he have a phone?' Then Nikki put her hand over her mouth, giggling. 'Oh – I guess he doesn't have pockets.'

Scooping up my stuff I exited onto the dark street. The little flashlight dug into my groin as I walked the two streets to the park. Nobody was using that gate: Arailt was waiting where he'd said, laid out in a municipal flowerbed with his head on his paws. He got up quickly when he saw me approach, and something about that speed made me think he was afraid. But I couldn't be sure, of course; his expression was unreadable, because he was a bloody bear.

'Hazel?'

'It's OK,' I said, swallowing the knot in my throat. 'Let's go home.'

Three nights later I used the torch.

I swear I tried to resist the temptation; I knew I'd be betraying his trust. But I was haunted by the accusation that Arailt was hiding something. Wasn't he betraying my trust too? If there was something wrong with his face and he did not believe I could cope with it, what did that say about his opinion of me?

I think he noticed the new reserve in my lovemaking, but he said nothing.

It took me hours to pluck up enough resolve, the night I slipped the torch from under my side of the mattress. I gripped the plastic cylinder in clammy hands, wondering if Arailt was truly asleep beside me, or just pretending as I was. Only when the clock struck three downstairs did I twist the head, sending a beam of light dancing out across the bedclothes like a lighthouse beacon across a turbulent sea. Instantly I capped the bulb with my hand, and the light turned the margins of my flesh rosy red. I held my breath, waiting for some reaction from Arailt, but he lay still, breathing deep and slow. He slept on his side, facing toward me. Cautiously I parted the grid of my fingers, and let my eyes rest upon the edge of the cream silk coverlet lying across his hips and lower belly. His skin was a richer cream, the delta of hair I knew only by touch a dark brown.

I was tempted to draw down the sheet and get a look at his cock before even his face – so tempted that I was ashamed of myself. My heart was so loud in my ears I wasn't sure that I would hear if he stirred.

Slowly, with infinite care, I let the narrow beam of light move up from his hips to his chest and further. His upper arm was lumpy with muscle even when relaxed. Soft tufts of hair peeked from the crease of arm and chest, and neat sparse hair covered almost all his chest and stomach. His nipples were really dark, the colour of milk chocolate. How often had my mouth sucked on those sweets? I was transported with wonder.

The stubble on his jaw had claimed the whole of his neck almost down to the collarbone. And there at last, by the glimmer of torchlight, was Arailt's face. The lips I'd kissed so fervently. A nose that hinted at having been broken long ago. Dark brows thickest toward the centre and short brown hair that was so dense and sleek that it still had the look of fur.

He opened his eyes. He gave no warning; didn't sigh or stretch or snore. He just opened his eyes and looked straight at me, and I thought that those eyes were the thing about him that had changed least from bear-form because they were dark-honey brown still. I clamped my fingers tight over the torch bulb, capturing the light, but his hand closed accurately on my wrist even in the renewed darkness; accurately and hard. I wrenched out of his grasp and slithered away across the bed. The torch fell on the covers between us; I tried to grab it but when Arailt sat up fast I recoiled.

'Had a good look?' he demanded, his voice hoarse with wrath.

I fell off the far side of the bed, onto my knees on the floor. Arailt threw back the bedclothes and got out on his side. 'Had a good look?' he repeated. 'Like what you see? I hope so, because it's your one and only time.'

Lit from below, the muscles of his body stood out in weird relief. The dim light barely touched his face and all I could clearly see was his thighs and crotch and abdominal muscles, and the clenched knots of his fists. That was my first glimpse of the cock that had haunted my imagination for so many months, but at that moment it meant nothing to me but a rebuke. He stepped to the end of the bed and I thought he was going to come round for me, but he turned and paced up and down on his side, breathing hard, his movements jerky with frustration as he glared at me and then at the corners of the room and then back at me. 'Why?' he groaned through clenched teeth. 'Why now?'

'What have I done wrong?' I asked, then I clapped my hand over my traitor mouth. 'I'm sorry!'

His laugh was short and bitter. 'A wee bit late for that, Hazel; the damage is already done.' He swung round suddenly and struck the wall with his open palm, swearing. 'Why?' he roared. 'Why couldn't you wait? Three more bloody months, woman; that's all it would have taken!'

His anger scared the hell out of me. 'Don't shout at me!' I screamed back. 'Don't you dare fucking shout!' Arailt actually retreated a step. The fury left me in a wail: 'What have I done wrong?'

He went still for a moment, only the heave of his chest betraying his emotion. Then he dragged his hands over his head and climbed forward onto the bed, kneeling there with his thighs apart, the torch almost between them. Deep shadow defined his every contour. I could see his face clearly once more, and the glowering dark eyes with picked-out points of light like burning stars. That was nearly unbearable, because my brain could not decide whether I knew this man or not, and half my mind saw Arailt and half saw a naked and very dangerous stranger.

'Come here.' His voice was low, but sounded more like a growl than an entreaty.

I didn't move. I wanted the bear back. I clutched my arms.

Arailt closed his eyes and turned his face away. 'You had questions, didn't you? You couldn't wait for the answers.' He shook his head. 'I should never have taken you back to London,' he groaned, and behind the anger I heard his despair. After all this time I was good at reading the emotion in his voice. 'So near, and so bloody far. God, Hazel ...'

I took a tiny move toward him. 'What's happened?'

'Oh ... I gambled, and I lost.'

'On what?'

'On you, Hazel.' His eyes fixed mine. He had deep-set eyes that demanded attention. He wasn't stop-you-dead-in-the-street handsome, not at first sight. Not until you looked into those eyes. 'I'm engaged,' he said, and the words were so unexpected that it took a moment for me to catch up. 'I'm betrothed to the Queen of Shadows. Or at least that's the way she'd phrase it.' His lips narrowed. 'I was sold to her, by my family, when I was very small. And as the time of our marriage grew closer, I tried to break off the engagement.'

'I don't understand,' I whispered.

He looked at his hands. 'These things are never airtight. There's always an escape clause. In this case, if I could find another woman to love me every night for a year and a day, then the queen would give up her claim. But this woman must not love me for the sake of my face, nor for gain, nor for pity of my story. She must love me without reason and without question, simply from the boldness of her heart.' His voice was dry now, the anger withered to regret. 'One chance, Hazel.'

'Oh.'

'It was always a long shot.'

I knelt up on the edge of the bed. 'This queen – she's the woman in the picture downstairs?'

He nodded. 'She'll know by now that I've lost. She'll be on her way already.'

Across the empty expanse of the bed we faced each other; two people on our knees, naked. 'What will happen then?'

'You'll be all right. I will see to that.'

'But what will happen to you?'

'She'll take me to the house that stands East of the Sun and West of the Moon and she'll slowly . . . consume me.' Little lines of strain bloomed around his eyes when he said that, but then he shrugged and looked away. 'As she has done with others.'

'You have to stop her,' I protested.

'I can't, Hazel.'

'Someone must be able to!'

'No.' His voice had grown quiet. 'I belong to her.'

I walked forward on my knees to him and took his face in my hands. And there under my palms was the Arailt I knew. 'You belong to me,' I told him.

He touched my lips with cold fingertips. 'I wish that were true.'

'It is.' *Believe me*, I wanted to cry out. *Believe me. I never meant to betray you. Don't you understand? I didn't know. I didn't know!*

'Hazel...'

I kissed him. His lips were dry. He shivered at my touch. 'Don't go,' I whispered. 'I love you.'

He fell into my embrace with a wordless groan and for a moment I put my arms around him and held him fiercely, gripping his back, his head, his shoulders, trying to squeeze the despair from him even as my own welled up behind my eyes in great hot tears. I ran my fingers through his hair and down his neck and across his shoulders. He lifted his face and kissed me and I shut my overflowing eyes so that the taste and the touch of him, so unutterably familiar, could overwhelm my senses. I was sobbing as our lips moved together; choking on his kisses. He pulled me into his lap and as I straddled his hard thighs I was shocked to find even harder flesh rising to meet me.

'My Hazel,' he whispered, his voice unsteady.

I furled my fingers about his shaft, gasping, 'Oh, my love.' My fingers looked pale around that flushed dark flesh and the glossy head glistened with moisture beneath the sweep of my thumb. It was the first time I'd glimpsed that dewdrop of arousal seep from him, like a tear wept for his painful need. He bore me over onto the bed and buried his face in my throat, his grip fierce, his bulk inexorable. The torchlight bounced as the mattress moved beneath us. Arailt's cock was iron and his need urgent; he pushed inside me without ceremony, heaving his body onto mine. I could taste the fear in his bitter sweat as I swept my tongue across his throat. I pulled him deep into me, yielding to his desperation. This was for him; I knew that. This was so that he could take some last part of me into the shadows when he went; some taste of sunlight, some glimpse of life. He moved with an unthinking ferocity and strength, driven by blind instinct, hammering into me. I clasped the small of his back and beneath the smooth skin I felt the arch of his spine and the clench of his pumping muscles. And I watched him, for the first time, as we loved. There was enough light from that shaken torch for me to see the sheen and the shape of him as he laboured upon me: the set of his broad shoulders, the dip of his head and the strain of his neck, the dark stipple of his cheek; and though I was a hundred miles away from climax that sight nearly exploded my heart in my breast. I held onto him because that was all I could do. I held him, my bear, my lover, and urged him on, my eyes swimming with tears.

And as we fucked the Shadows came, crowding in from the corners of the room, crushing down on our tiny patch of light, rustling and creaking. Arailt was still thrusting into me when the darkness overwhelmed us and I passed into unconsciousness.

I've never had a worse awakening. I opened my eyes to grey daylight, shivering, every muscle aching from the hard and tussocky ground on which I lay. My first glimpse was of tiny trees in mesh shelters and a hawthorn hedge; dead leaves from the hedge had blown down and stuck to my soaked clothes. The roar of traffic was loud. I sat up groggily. I was wearing the same clothes I'd had on when I let Arailt steal me away nearly a year previously. Underneath me was a shabby fur coat, its upper surface the only dry patch in the whole field. Beyond the hedge a six-lane highway thundered.

I'd been, I eventually worked out, lying out in the open on a patch of ground attached to a motorway service station. When I picked up the fur coat I found it was worn and moulting, the lining torn to shreds, and if it was bearskin it retained none of its original owner's grandeur. I pulled it on, desperate for warmth, and found that it had been cut for much broader shoulders than mine. There was a rent high on the left sleeve, sewn up with fishing-line stitches.

I started to sob then.

I made my way to the service station and from there I hitched to my mum's house. I wasn't going back to my old place. My room must have been rented out long ago, and I didn't want to cast myself upon the mercy of my friends, though I was under no illusion that this was their fault. They'd been jealous and bitchy, but it was my pride that had ruined everything; my desire to prove that I'd done well for myself, that I had a lover worth boasting about.

Hitching was stupidly dangerous, but at that point I didn't care what happened to me. I think a part of me would have actually welcomed disaster; it would have seemed fitting. As it happened, none of the drivers offered me any threat and I got to my mum's just as the setting sun smeared the clouds green and yellow. Mum was standing at the back door when I walked into the kitchen, looking out across the suburban golf course that backs onto every house in the row. It was exactly the same place she'd been standing when I last walked out on her; only her clothes had changed. It was as if the years had not passed here in this quiet street.

'Hello, Hazel,' she said, surprised. 'What are you doing back?'

I told her that I'd lost my job and been dumped by my boyfriend, and she hugged me and made a fuss and poured a mug of tea. But all the time her eyes kept stealing back toward the window, and eventually she opened the back door and stood in the frame, staring out across the greens. She'd been here every night for ten years now, waiting to see him again; that man with sea-green eyes who'd strolled across the rough one summer's evening and called her to the fence and made love to her on the sweet grass of the fairway. My heart turned to glue as I saw her, my mother, yearning without ease for that man who was not a man, could not have been a man – because nobody could love a mere man so helplessly for so long on the strength of one sunset tryst, could they?

That devotion had cost her almost everything. I think my father could have forgiven a fling with a nameless stranger; a momentary madness – but not that she loved him, that man with eyes like the sea.

I left her and I went to bed in my old room, and nothing there had changed either. I spent three days in bed, weeping, my face scrunched into the damp pillow. I slept and woke and lay blankly until the tears came welling up again. When she wasn't keeping vigil Mum would bring me food and drink and would even sit with me, stroking my greasy hair as if I were her little girl again, a child with a fever. She offered no words of comfort, though; no, 'It'll be all right. You'll feel better in a while.' She couldn't, could she?

On the fourth day I got up, washed, ate and packed some things into a rucksack; the ragged old fur coat went in first and folded down surprisingly small. Mum was out at the shops when I left, and I deposited a note on the kitchen table:

To call back a straying lover: go on a Wednesday evening where you know dwarf elder to be growing, and stab your knife into the plant and let it stick there. Then go away. Go back to it at dawn when day and night divide, and go in silence, and no matter what frightful thing or man should come toward you say no word to him before you come to the plant which you marked on the previous evening. Dig out the plant, take it to a church and lay it under the altar until the sun is up high. Afterwards wash it, boil it three times in milk and drink that. It will soon be better for you.

I was lying, of course: the recipe was one for breaking a love charm, and I'd copied it from a book in Arailt's library. He'd suggested the volume after I'd described my mother's enchantment. But I was certain she wouldn't try it if she knew its real purpose. She wanted her lover back; she didn't want to stop loving.

No more than I did.

I went back into central London. Arailt had found me there

and I figured there was a chance that there would be people who knew him, or perhaps more of his kind. I booked bed and breakfast in a dingy place that called itself a backpackers' hostel. Then I walked the streets, stopping anyone I could and asking, 'Please: do you know the way to the house East of the Sun and West of the Moon?'

Nobody knew. Most people looked straight through me, or laughed and shook their heads, moving on as if pulled by a tidal current. Even the police didn't glance in my direction. It was strange that I was treated for the most part as if I were invisible, when I'd never felt more exposed. I felt like I'd been split open from throat to crotch and that my raw wound was gaping to view, pain dancing across the nerve-endings. Sometimes I would double over in the street and retch from the agony of my loss.

Hours congealed into days, and days into weeks. I went through the dregs of my savings and was living on a credit card that I knew would foreclose on me as soon as they realised that I paid nothing back. I wasn't eating much. My voice had grown hoarse from repetition of the same words, and my eyes barely focused on each new face. I fell into a twilight fugue that was more like dream than waking, more like breathing murky water than breathing air, more like bleeding softly to death than living. It was after nightfall in a street somewhere near Trafalgar Square that I first got an answer to my question.

'I know of the house,' she said, 'but I've never been.'

I clutched at her sleeve. 'Please, tell me! You know? You know the way? Please!'

The girl caught at my hand. She was taller than me and so fair that her fine short hair was like feathers off a swan, and I'd have thought it was bleached if her eyebrows hadn't been white too. There were silver piercings in those brows, and in the side of her nose and the underneath of her pale lower lip. Her eyes were silver: metallic contacts, I assumed. 'You couldn't get there,' she said. 'It's too far for you. Though my sister might know how you could do it...'

'Please, I have to –'

'You have to?' She grinned crookedly. The silver lenses made her look feral.

'I'm looking for someone –'

'Arailt. I know.'

I stared. 'You ... know?'

'Everybody knows.' Her smile was conspiratorial. 'I'll ask Urd for you, shall I?'

'Please.' My voice was no more than a whisper. I felt like someone had opened a door on the world and sucked all the air out, leaving me in vacuum.

'But you'll have to do something for me first.'

'What?'

'Come and dance with me.' She jerked her head to indicate a neon-lit door. Her hand, which had never let go of mine, squeezed.

'I'm not ...' I didn't know how to finish that sentence. Not in the mood? Not dressed for it? Not capable?

'But I am.' She tugged me across the pavement. I was able to take in that she was dressed for clubbing – her slender frame decidedly underdressed for the November night out here, anyway – in a plaid miniskirt and wet-look tube-top, before she pulled me through the doorway and down the narrow stairs within. I wanted to ask her what she knew about Arailt, but the music hit us like an assault. I actually scrunched my eyes shut.

The house in the valley had been so quiet.

In the basement lobby my guide paid for entry and slipped off my coat and rucksack. I protested, clinging to the bag and shouting over the thumping beat, but she laughed and stuffed my belongings into a locker, handing me the key. She stripped me down to my unglamorous T-shirt and I could see the sense of that because the club was warm, though I resented her commandeering hands. Then she pulled me through into the next room, right into the centre of the crowd, and began to dance. The dancefloor was really dark, lit only by strobes and tumbling lasers and flashing gels. I could smell the heat of a hundred bodies gyrating around me, sweet and humid. I stood dumbly, the only still thing in that hall, unable to move. There was no rhythm in me, though the galloping beat thudded in my spine and made my eardrums buzz.

I'd been vaguely aware that most of the dancers were female; it now dawned on me that even the ones dressed rather like men were women.

Come on: dance! mouthed my silver-blonde, inaudible over the music. I shrugged, hopeless, so she put her arms around me and pulled me snugly up against her right hip and thigh, her right breast nestling neatly between mine. She put her lips to my ear. 'My name's Verlandi,' she said, audible now. 'What's yours?'

Weird name, I thought. 'Hazel.' It felt so strange, being held that firmly by a woman. She was softer to the touch than a man, but her hands were just as importunate. She eased me into an undulating dance, our bodies moving together. I was helpless with shock. I let her press me against her grinding hip. I let her snake her tongue between my lips, and I tasted her lipstick. Her tongue was pierced through with a ball-headed stud and she teased my tongue unmercifully. *This is not me*, I thought: *I'm at home in bed with Arailt. Everything else since has just been a dream.*

Verlandi spread her fingers over my hip and rubbed her thumb across as much of my mons as she could access, her pelvis rotating in time with the beat. Her other arm held me close so that my head was filled with the scent of her perfume and her clean sweat. When I opened my mouth to protest she kissed me again, rattling her tongue-stud across my teeth. The lights flashed and the music pulsed and I found I was moving with her, seduced into the dance and then into something more.

Under my jeans my sex seemed to bloom, the petals unfurling plump and velvety as those of roses. Her thumb circled, pressing at all the right points. The pressure of her strong thigh was easing mine open. All around us other couples slithered and twisted, embracing in the strobe-light rain. Her tongue traced slow circles around my lips. Her fingers were between her tights and my jeans now, working up a heavy friction that was both comforting and disturbing, relishing the heat they'd engendered. Her right palm squeezed my bum-cheek. I groaned, but nobody could hear over the music. I pressed up against her, and nobody could tell that we weren't just cinched together in dance. Her thumb ground into my clit.

I came crying out wildly but nothing was audible, as if we were all deaf. The world spun around me in flashing points of disco light, and as it settled again I realised we were both drenched with sweat, the skin of Verlandi's shoulders pulsing with reflected light. I clung to her briefly, my breasts heaving against hers.

'Feel that?' she asked, pressing her fingers to the arterial pulse at my throat. 'Feel it, Hazel? It's still there.'

Verlandi took me riding pillion on her Ducati 999S to her sister Urd, who looked old enough to be her mother, was as dark as Verlandi was fair and resembled her in no way except for the silver eyes. Urd did not seem like the sort to wear fashion contact-lenses; she was heavyset, and her thick uncombed hair was grizzled.

'This is Arailt's girl,' said Verlandi by way of introducing me.

'Ah. The one who couldn't keep her word.'

I burned.

'She's looking to get to the house East of the Sun and West of the Moon. Can you help her?'

'I know how it used to be possible to get there, but not how this one might do it. Maybe our other sister knows. I'll take her to Skuld, for a price.'

'That'll do, won't it, Hazel?'

'What price?' I asked, dazed but finding my voice at last.

'A bit of housework.' Urd gestured around her at the book-lined walls of her study. As she went off to find the brushes and dusters Verlandi pressed something into my hand; it was my namesake, a little hazelnut.

'Break this only when you really need it,' she warned me, then slipped through the patio doors into the overgrown garden and the golden autumn afternoon that lay outside. I held the nut awhile, assessing the contents, then pushed it to the corner of my jeans pocket.

Urd set me to cleaning her house, a dark Victorian pile with many floors and windows inadequate for its depth. It reminded me a lot of Arailt's place. She didn't own a vacuum cleaner; I had to do it by hand. Every surface was cluttered with worn hardback books and curios that looked as if they belonged in a museum; flint knives and stuffed birds, Chinese vases and animal skulls, glass sculptures of sea worms and varnished pufferfish with expressions of terminal surprise. I didn't last more than a couple of hours because the total futility of the exercise was obvious from the start. I was only stirring the dust up to dance in the yellow window light and settle elsewhere. After a fit of sneezing, I sat down on an overstuffed armchair and let the tears well up to bathe my swollen eyes. I was still crying when Urd came into the room and stood with hands on her wide hips.

'Given up already?'

'I can't do it!' I sobbed angrily. 'It's impossible!'

'No. But it does take patience and effort, girl. You seem to be lacking in those.'

I burst into tears then, covering my face in my hands. 'I'm sorry,' I groaned. 'I'm no use, I know, I can't get anything right...'

'What's this – guilt? That's of no help to anyone, girl; not to you or me and certainly not to Arailt.'

At his name I choked, retching my sobs into the duster.

'I have a cure for self-pity, girl.'

'Bitch!' I spat. 'How can you –'

She slapped me across the face. Not particularly hard, though she had big hands and could probably have knocked me silly if she'd wanted to; just hard enough to leave me staring with shock. 'Watch your language,' she snapped, 'you self-indulgent child.'

I gaped. From the corner of my eye I could see the open door and it would be possible to storm out past her, though where I'd find myself if I made it out of the house I didn't really have a clue.

'That's stopped the tears, I see. Real pain's so much more satisfying on a guilty conscience than your histrionic whining, girl.'

'I've not got . . .' I stopped.

'Hmm?'

I couldn't say anything, just pant. Of course I had a guilty conscience. I just didn't like anyone else pointing my guilt out.

'Now, Hazel, if you know what's good for you, you're going to stand up and go lean over the piano in the corner there.'

'What are you going to do?' I whispered.

'Satisfy your desire for punishment.'

At the word *punishment* I flushed from head to toe. Urd smiled. For a moment we locked eyes, but hers were as slippery as mercury and I couldn't keep my gaze fixed. There was an uncomfortable warmth between my legs as well as on my struck face, as if the blow had landed there too.

'Now get up.'

I rose, my legs as wobbly as a fawn's, and went over to the baby grand piano I'd tried so vainly to dust. I could see the streaks I'd left on the polished casing.

'Drop your pants and bend over it.'

I let my jeans fall. I could smell the furniture wax as I bent at the waist and rested my chest on the old wood. My nipples were uncomfortably hard against its coolness. My bum stuck out, still clad in my cotton knickers.

'Good girl.' She came up behind me and drew my panties up tight into the crack of my bottom, exposing both cheeks. She stroked the skin with the palm of her hand and I shivered. 'Very pretty,' she said, and then smacked me hard.

I didn't squeal at the first slap, though I nearly bit my tongue in shock because the sting was sharper than I'd expected. The second blow landed on exactly the same spot and hurt more, making me clench. The third transferred to my other cheek. Each landed with an astonishingly loud crack of skin on skin; I couldn't believe she was hitting so hard without hurting herself. I felt the blood rush burning to my skin. My arse felt like it was catching fire. She was a slow smacker, working without hurry. She liked to explore my tingling skin with her fingertips between blows, savouring the heat perhaps, or my breathless whimpers of discomfort. I didn't know what was worse: the sting of the blow or the anticipation before it landed. I squirmed and bucked, tucking my cheeks away from her in fear then pushing them out just to provide her with more skin, a different target. My face was screwed up and a wail bubbled in my throat even as I ground my teeth together and refused to let it escape.

Urd stopped and ran her palm across the curve of my bum-cheeks, breathing as heavily as I did. It felt like her touch burned even as it soothed and cold shivers crawled down my thighs. My bottom was tingling with heat and felt like it was ballooning up. She cupped the gusset of my panties and I realised I was swollen down there too. She rewarded that discovery with a swat on the cotton, considerably gentler than on my padded behind but sharp enough to make me jump and yelp.

'Scream if you want to, girl,' she said, and went back to her first targets. If anything she struck harder now, and my skin was alive with armed pain receptors that exploded at such brutal slaps. This time I let the shrieks rip from my throat as my hips danced from side to side and my fattened, quivering arse shook and jounced at each smack. I ground my crotch into the hard wood as if I could burrow into the piano and hide from her.

It didn't occur to me to stand up and refuse her attentions. I drank in the pain and craved more, even as I dreaded every individual strike.

When my whole world had been reduced to a circle of fire and my tears and spit were running onto the piano, Urd paused for a second time and clasped the cotton pocket beneath my throbbing buttocks. The gusset of my panties was soaked with sweat and other, more slippery juices; so soaked that she could poke the cloth with her finger and sink it right into my slick hole. My pussy was so swollen and puffy that it filled her palm and, when she rubbed expertly over it, round and round in agonising circles, I cried a broken 'Oh!' one last time and came on her hand, burning.

'You needed that,' she whispered and I, through bubbling snotty sobs, could only agree with her.

Urd took me to their third sister in a shabby antique Rolls-Royce, and pressed a hazelnut into my hand as we walked to the door. 'Don't use it until you must, girl.'

Skuld lived in an extravagantly modern house with wooden verandas that overlooked a lakeshore. She was tall and elegantly boned, and the tiny hat she wore did not cover her cap of shining red hair, nor its black netting half-veil the quicksilver sheen of her eyes.

'This is Arialt's girl; Hazel,' said Urd. 'She has a problem with perseverance.'

'So I heard.'

'And she wishes to go to the house East of the Sun and West of the Moon.'

Skuld surveyed me coolly. 'She will get there; I see it. But not by any route I know. Perhaps the East Wind will carry her there.'

My heart, which had risen at her earlier words, crashed again.

'Take her to the East Wind then, sister.'

'Tonight I'm having a party.' That explained her slinky dress. 'If she'll help serve my guests, and do it properly without stint or slacking, then I'll take her in the morning.'

My heart seemed to shrink with dread, but I nodded.

'Good. You can be the Drinks Girl. Come in then.'

She handed me over to domestic staff, who had me scrubbed and plucked and my hair trimmed before I was fit to be costumed for the night. My dress consisted of nothing more than an apron of soft black rubber that laced at the back with cord and industrial-sized eyelets. It covered me demurely from bust to mid-thigh, but at the back a gap as broad as a hand was exposed all the way down, revealing the crack of my backside to all onlookers, my soft flesh pillowed up around the cords.

Skuld positioned me in a room by one of the patio doors, where I served drinks from behind the low bar. Skuld's guests were as eerily elegant as she was, and their almond-shaped eyes rested upon me with knowing, disdainful looks. Every time I turned to a shelf my bum-cleavage was flashed. As the night turned dark and guests spilled onto the decking to admire the summer moon and the swans upon the lake, I knew that here in my brightly lit chamber I was visible, glowing, to everyone. I bit my lip and clung to my dignity and carried on, determined that this time I would not bottle out. For the first time in days I was too busy to think of Arailt's abduction.

Then one man approached me. 'I need the toilet,' he said, slightly slurred.

'It's down the corridor, sir, on the left.' I pointed.

'No. I need a piss. You're the Drinks Girl.'

'I don't understand ...'

'You don't, do you? You're the Drinks Girl. Get on your knees.'

Cold fear slopped over me like a wave, followed by a warm flush of outrage that made the blood sing in my ears. I looked around, but there was no help anywhere. The doors were open and people were laughing and flirting outside. I knew there would be neither sympathy nor outrage from that crowd. I looked at the white suede rug. I could refuse him, I supposed. But then I wouldn't be keeping to my side of the bargain, and keeping your promise seemed to matter to these people. It might be the *only* thing that mattered to them.

I grabbed all my courage and I sank to my knees, the tight rubber sheath that smelled of talcum hobbling my movements. I opened my mouth and the man unzipped his fly and stepped closer. It didn't take long – it was the shame that I found difficult to endure, not the physical act. And he seemed satisfied with the service. But before I could find some way to rise in that constricting dress, another man stuck his head in from the veranda.

'Aha. The Drinks Girl?'

'Be my guest,' said the first.

After that there was little let-up. Between customers I stayed on my knees, too stupefied to move. Women were the worst; I got a crick in the neck from the angle I had to tilt back my head and didn't always manage to catch it all. When nature worked its course and I myself needed to find relief from my bloated belly, two men held me up over a tray of champagne glasses and when I'd filled them the entire circle of guests sipped the contents and discussed the flavour like connoisseurs, with every sign of enjoyment. I watched from under my lashes and felt a strange and reluctant pleasure, as if we were linked in a wicked communion.

I finished the evening knelt at Skuld's feet, my head resting against her knee as she sat discussing politics and absently stroking my hair. At peace, of a kind.

*   *   *

Skuld ordered a taxi in the early hours and I snatched some sleep as we drove through flat countryside. She woke me just as dawn was breaking and dropped a hazelnut into my hand. Instinctively I recoiled from the tiny object.

'Don't open it except in the utmost need,' she warned.

The East Wind lived right on the edge of London in a penthouse flat overlooking marshy country bleak with driven snow. Three hundred and sixty degrees of curved glass gave him wonderful light, even on a winter's dawn. He opened the door with a camera in his hand: a great big one trailing an electric cord that snaked away across the polished hardwood floor.

'This is Hazel,' said Skuld, and walked away.

'You have an interesting face,' said the East Wind. 'May I take some pictures?' His own face was craggy and hawkish with a long nose and thick brows, and he was casually dressed in grey T-shirt and trousers with designer logos.

'I'm looking for the house East of the Sun and West of the Moon,' I gasped.

'I know. Why?'

I was momentarily confused. 'There's a man – Arailt –'

'I know that. Why are you trying to get to him?'

I bit my lip. His scrutiny was cold but intense. 'It's my fault that he's held there. I'm to blame.' I shuffled my feet. 'That's what everyone thinks, anyway.'

'Really? Does Arailt blame you too?'

I thought about the flare of his anger, as bright as a matchstrike in that darkened bedroom and then extinguished almost as quickly – because in his heart of hearts he'd never expected me to succeed. 'No,' I said, feeling sick. Arailt's forgiveness was as unbearable as everyone else's condemnation. He'd expected so very little of me.

'Fascinating.' The East Wind lifted his camera to his eye and clicked.

'Will you take me?' I asked, my mouth dry.

'I can't. I don't go that way. But ... if you'll let me take some pictures of you I'll ask my brother the West Wind. He might be able to carry you there.'

I blinked.

'Will you?' He steered me gently to face the inner walls of his apartment. They were covered in huge blown-up photographs of women. The pictures were all monochrome and to my untrained eye extremely beautiful. I was certain from the style that he was the one who'd taken the portrait of the Queen of Shadows. They were also, despite their tasteful artiness – a curved shoulder here, a flexed back there, the stark black lines of a leather bodice on pale skin – unmistakably themed around bondage and fetishwear.

'Like that? Do you ... put them on exhibit? To the public?'

'Of course.'

As if I'd not been censured and disparaged enough. I thought of Arailt and took a deep breath. 'OK.'

He took me through to his studio, which was set up with lights and backcloths and, in one corner, a computer and a huge flat screen. Displayed on it right then was the picture he'd just taken of my face, the doubt and dismay etched around my eyes for all to see. It's not easy to confront your own face on that scale. 'Ignore the screen,' he advised me. 'Just pay attention to me. Now, if you'd care to undress ...'

He took photos swiftly and casually while I undressed, as if to get me used to the camera's intrusive eye and the pageant of images it produced. Then he got out a roll of black tape and took pictures of my bound wrists and ankles. The tape wasn't sticky on my skin but it clung to itself securely when wound multiple times. He set me in various poses, seated and then lying down. The creamy texture of my skin filled the screen. He blew on my nipples to bring them erect and the resulting close-shot, with those tight areolae perfectly rendered, surprised even me with its vulnerable beauty. He took pictures of my backside and my spread thighs and my flushed face. I couldn't stop blushing. He took pictures with and without flash, fiddling with the camera settings, absorbed in the technicalities of lighting. I found his abstraction both comforting and provoking: a man shouldn't be able to see a woman's pussy peeking between the pale curves of her thighs like that without being moved.

He taped my wrists to my ankles so that I was nearly immobile and took shots of my raised arse. The flash went off like a rain of warm kisses on my sex. I wriggled, forgetting my anxieties. He fetched something from his desk. 'Do you mind?'

It was a bullet-shaped object about the size of my thumb, the colour of haematite. I stared.

'It'll take your mind off any discomfort,' he said with a smile, slipping it between my sex-lips. I was moist to his touch. The bullet came with a remote-control; when he thumbed the button it came to life within me with a low purr, sending its vibrations right through me. I gave a little gasp.

'Too intense?' he whispered. 'No. I don't think so.'

He laid me on my side and then on my back for more photos, shooting several directly up between my quivering thighs. The vibrator hummed, provoking a thousand tiny electric shocks to my nerve-endings. My breathing was coming in a new rhythm. I twisted against my bonds, finding them frustrating, shifting my pelvis. The East Wind took shot after shot; hundreds by now, maybe into the thousands. He caught my flushed face and my parted lips and my dilated pupils. He caught the sheen on my breastbone and the first glisten of escaping moisture between my plump labia. He explored my slit with his fingers and captured the expression on my face, shooting one-handed, awkwardly, but still snatching each tiny moment from oblivion.

'Oh God,' I whispered, my eyes full of terrible, wonderful images of my own helpless surrender to desire. 'I'm going to come. Please. Please. Let me.'

'Hold on a little longer,' he whispered, opening his own trousers and releasing a stubby, immensely thick erection. He knelt over me to jerk off. It was the only time in the session that he wasn't able to take pictures as he needed both hands; one to cup his big balls and one to jack his tool. His splashes of hot, sticky semen fell copiously on my belly and tits and open lips. And as soon as he'd done he snatched up the camera again and shot like he was thrusting into me. One finger sought my sex and stirred my clit and I arched and spat and came shamelessly under the repeated thud of the flash, soaking up the light, letting him see everything and capture everything, for all time.

As I showered and dressed he sifted through the photos on the computer. 'That one, I think,' he said at last, putting it up full-sized on the screen. I looked at the low-angle shot. My right breast dominated the foreground, with my partially occluded face behind. There were pearly globs of jism melting on my nipple and the curve of my breast, but it was the expression in my eyes that really caught me; that expression of terrible need and sorrow that was almost agony – and yet somehow perfect. It was like looking into my naked soul and seeing everything that I felt for Arailt. I looked beautiful.

'Yes,' I said. 'That's the one.'

The East Wind didn't bother with a vehicle; he simply picked me and my rucksack up and stepped off the edge of the roof, whirling me westward through the sleet. We landed on a sunlit beach; on the turf of the low cliff-edge above the sand nodded clumps of daffodils.

The West Wind looked considerably younger than his brother; younger maybe than me. He had salt-tousled brown hair that hung in wet curls and he wore his wetsuit open to the waist and hanging down. His bare torso was tanned and toned and lithe. He wasn't alone; his friends sat with him on the warm sand, tins of energy-drink in hand, their surfboards propped close by. They were the only people on the beach.

'This is Hazel,' said the East Wind, drawing me into their circle. 'She wants you to take her East of the Sun and West of the Moon, brother.' Then he was gone in a swirl of dry sand.

'Why'd you want to go there?' the West Wind asked.

This one was a cocky young beggar, I thought. I stood up straighter. They were all watching me and looking amused, but it didn't matter to me any more. I wasn't ashamed. 'Because I love Arailt,' I said.

His lip curled prettily. 'You don't love him. You barely know him.'

I felt like he'd punched me in the guts. 'I know him enough.'

'Any idea what he was doing when he was out all day?'

I shook my head.

'He was out hunting.'

'Hunting what?'

'His family.'

I remembered the only words he'd ever let slip about his family: that they'd sold him to the Queen of Shadows. I remembered the smoke smell and the blood. I turned the words of the West Wind carefully over in my mind and then let them settle to the bottom of my skull. 'I see.'

'Does that make a difference to how you feel about him?'

How could it not? 'I love him,' I answered flatly.

The West Wind smiled cynically. 'You're just afraid you've blown it, Hazel. You're just scared you'll never get a chance at someone that hot again, that you'll have to settle for dross. You're scared that it'll never be that good with anyone else.'

My mouth was dry. 'That's not ... No.'

'Forget him, darling. Go home. Mourn, and recover. Fall in love properly with someone of your own sort.'

'No,' I said hoarsely. 'I love him.'

The West Wind grinned, leaning forward, elbows on his knees. 'Prove me wrong, and I'll take you to my brother. The South Wind will be able to carry you there.'

I closed my eyes for a moment, breathing deep.

'It's my best offer,' he added lightly.

'If that's what it takes, then.'

He stood with an insouciant grin. 'You'll love it, darling,' he said, slipping the top button of my shirt. 'Every inch.'

Slowly, with appreciation, he stripped off my shirt and threw it to one of his friends. Then he kissed me, his lips sweet and teasing, and while I was distracted they all closed on me. There were nearly a dozen of them, I guessed, though I hadn't actually counted. I felt their hands on my back and rump and thighs. One knelt to slip off my shoes. Fingers unhooked my bra and and tickled my spine and explored the flat curve of my belly as they eased my jeans fly down. I shut my eyes. They stripped me naked, there on the beach, under the brittle spring sunshine. I would have been cold but the breeze had dropped to nothing and my whole body was blushing under the caress of those hands. The youths murmured and chuckled with pleasure with every discovery they made. They pulled me back on my heels, all my weight resting against three spare, warm bodies, while roaming hands explored me from head to toe, tugging my nipples and delving into the crease between my thighs. When I opened my eyes it was on a blur of floppy hair, narrow chins, lean muscular arms, hairless torsos. They smelled of the sea and their fingers tasted of salt.

'Lift her,' said the West Wind gently and they grasped me all down the length of my back and arse and legs, easing my thighs open as they raised me from the earth. I felt weightless, afloat on a sea of hands. Their hard arms and chests pressed against me. I tried to focus on the West Wind himself, who stood between my parted knees. He'd peeled his wetsuit down to his thighs by now and his cock stood proud in his slim hand. His scrotum was hairless. He looked so boyishly pretty that even at that moment I felt as if it were I leading him astray, but there was nothing innocent about his eyes. 'Tell me,' he said, stroking his lustrous prick until it jerked, 'that this isn't what you really miss.' He stepped forward and pressed his flushed crown into the wet furrow that his friends had prepared for him, slipping it from clit to bum-hole and back. 'Tell me it isn't cock you want, darling.' He shifted his hips and slid into me with a slight grunt. His friends were breathing hard, watching, fascinated. 'Arailt's cock,' he growled, working his own deeper with measured thrusts, pressing up to me till I felt his fat charged balls on my cheeks. Each plunge lifted and dropped me in their hands, like a wave. 'A big cock.' He found my clit with his thumb. 'My big cock. Feels good doesn't it? Just as good. That's what you want isn't it? You enjoying that? You feeling that right inside you? You taking it as deep as you can, darling, oh yes, taking it good and proper now aren't you? Oh yes, I like to hear that; you tell it like it is.'

If he said more than that I didn't hear him. I was too busy making noises of my own. I came with my head thrown back and jammed between two hard male stomachs. They shoved fingers down my throat as I thrashed, as if to feel my cries.

Afterwards they laid me on the sand and took it in turn to stuff their pricks between my lips and unload. They were young; some couldn't hold out that long and spurted on my breasts and thighs. I regretted every one of the salt sea-spume ejaculations that I didn't get to taste, but I rubbed them into my skin and licked my fingers and opened my mouth and my thighs for more. They had the vigour of youth too; several came back for seconds. The West Wind kept claim on my sex though; working me with fingers when he was resting. I was so wet I could hear the squelch of juices as he thrust.

I was encrusted with sand by the time we were done, my hair in sticky disarray, my limbs heavy as if I'd swum for miles.

'Are you sure you still love him?' the West Wind asked, sweet and low, his lips brushing mine.

'Yes,' I whispered. 'Yes.'

* * *

The South Wind lived on the shore too, in a white modernist house that overlooked a stretch of shingle. It might have been Brighton; I saw no signposts as we swept in over the sea but there was a forlorn pier.

'You've brought me a girl?' he asked, putting his hands in his pockets. 'You know I don't do girls any more.' He looked like a roadie from a band that had been touring for too many decades; he carried a paunch and a goatee and his sandy-ginger hair was long at the back and non-existent on top.

'This is Arailt's girl.'

'Ah. I see.' He looked me in the eye for the first time and nodded.

'Hazel,' added the West Wind, as he slipped back out through the door.

'Righty-ho.' The South Wind chewed his lip as we stood in confusion. 'Do you want a bit of pizza then, Hazel?'

There was a big bowl of salad on the table by the sofa arm and the remnants of a fifteen-inch pizza next to it. 'No thanks.' I wasn't hungry. I'd lost track of when I'd last eaten properly, my mind a dreamlike confusion of seasons and sunsets and dawns. I was drunk on time and high on unreality. 'I need to get to the house East of the Sun and West of the Moon.'

'So I hear.' He sat down on the sofa. 'Can I ask why?'

'Arailt's there,' I said. 'I love him.'

He accepted that without a flicker, but his next words turned me cold. 'Are you sure he loves you?'

'No one's ever sure of that,' was my answer, delivered with pain. I remembered our last, hurried conversation. There hadn't been time to ask the right questions, or to say everything we'd needed to say. 'But ... yes. I think so.'

'You think so?'

God, it had been such a mess at the end; anger and desire and fear all mixed up. 'I screwed up,' I admitted in a low voice. 'I got him recaptured, yes. But I don't think he blamed me.'

'But could he love you after that? That's the question, isn't it?'

I couldn't answer, my throat was suddenly so swollen. I blinked hard.

The South Wind sighed. 'Well, I can't take you there anyway, Hazel. But my brother might be able to.'

I managed to swallow. 'The West Wind said you could!'

'He was mistaken. The North Wind's the strongest of us all; the only one strong enough to carry you that far.'

'OK.' I steeled myself. He wasn't actually ugly, just terribly unfashionable. 'What do you want?'

He shrugged. 'You got a nice backside, for a girl.'

I put the rucksack down and, kicking off my shoes, started to undo my buttons.

'Uh . . . turn around.'

I turned my back on him and pulled down jeans and pants to my ankles in one motion, offering a flash of pussy in one last protest. I hooked my socks off with my toes.

'You can leave your top on. Come over here and sit on my lap.'

I obeyed, facing out from him, which suited us both. He ran his hands over my cheeks. 'Nice.'

It did feel nice, his caresses. I tried to relax.

'Did Arailt ever fuck you in the ass?' he murmured. He used the American pronunciation and slipped his finger down my cleft to touch the opening in question. I clenched instantly.

'No.' The inquiry felt incredibly intrusive.

'Why not?' His fingertip tickled the tight bud.

'I don't know . . . He's too big . . . you know.'

The South Wind chuckled. 'I could get my whole hand up here, to the wrist.' As I broke out in a sweat he patted my bum reassuringly. 'Not today, mind. It'd take practice, of course.'

I shivered. He felt the slight relaxation in my muscles.

'Get your feet up here on the cushions, Hazel.'

One at a time I lifted them awkwardly, so that I was kneeling rather than sitting astride his legs. He pushed his thighs apart.

'Now, head down. That's right.'

Carefully he lowered me so that my elbows were on the floor between his suede loafers. I slid my knees back on the cushions, feet in the air. Now I was lying face down, legs agape, my arse and snatch spread in his lap for his inspection. I felt the blood starting to fill my head. His carpet was gritty.

'Good girl.' He picked up a bottle of olive oil from next to the salad bowl; I heard a noise like a kiss as he uncorked it. 'Extra virgin,' he sighed as he started to drizzle the green oil down the crack of my arse.

'Oh,' I whispered. He started to get hard under me then. The oil felt cold and smelt peppery. It coated my anus and ran down into my warm sex, tickling. When he directed the narrow stream directly over the eye of my bottom I flushed to the tips of my fingers.

'It's going to be a little messy.' He used the fingers of both hands to massage my crack and my arse. He slipped one finger into me easily, using the oil to lubricate the delicate tissues. I squirmed, unable to understand how he could want to touch me in there. It was dirty. It was the worst, the least attractive part of me. How could he want that? How could he find pleasure in it?

But I was finding pleasure. My body sang with sensation; the fullness, the slickness, the way he glided inside and out. He got a finger in from each side and worked me to dilation with circular strokes, relaxing the reluctant ring of muscle. Lightning flickered up and down my spine. He stooped to blow gently on my hole and I felt the cool whisper of air on tissues that had never been exposed before. I could feel *so much*: my anus was more sensitive to the touch than my vulva, and the discovery all but horrified me.

Then he released his cock from his pants, letting it slap stiffly against my sex as he went back to work on my arse. I ground my clit against its hard root. He had four fingers inside me now, churning deep. I wanted to suck him in. I was gasping. I was wide open.

'Up,' he said, and stooped to lift me. The headrush nearly knocked me out even before he impaled me straight on his stiff cock and my anus took him deep with terror and joy. I grabbed his knee to steady myself as he thrust up into me, over and over. He groaned as he approached his crisis, slapping up wildly against my jiggling bum, and I plunged my fingers into the slush of olive oil between my thighs and matched him groan for groan as he shot his spunk into me, my sphincter clenching and pulling and pulsing around his prick in little spasming muscular dances of delight.

As I lay back pillowed on his stomach and felt his cock slip from me in an ooze of spent seed, the South Wind panted, 'What – what an ass – Oh that's a marvellous sweet asshole, Hazel.'

'Oh yes,' I agreed.

The North Wind lived alone, in a broch on a barren Scottish hillside. He did no more than glance up when we came in and then went back to staring out of the unglazed window at the bronzy heather.

'This is the girl we heard about,' said the South Wind, patting me on the shoulder. 'Arailt's girl.'

'She's wasting her time.'

'She needs you, brother. You're the only one who can take her East of the Sun and West of the Moon.' He departed.

Dust lay on every surface of the dreary room. I looked around, but the only feature of interest was the North Wind himself; tall and lean with scarred cheeks and black hair like washed silk. He wore a waxed trailrider's coat and a white silk scarf: dressed for the outdoors though seated in his carved armchair with his long legs stretched out before him, and showing no intention of ever moving.

'Why should I take you?' His voice was weary; a declaration of indifference.

'Because I broke my word to Arailt,' I said, 'and now I'm going to rescue him.' And that was the truth of it; I was going to rescue my bear. Not because I felt guilty or because I loved him or because I needed to prove myself worthy of him – although all those things were true – but because it was my task. I was taking responsibility for what had happened. I was taking it: just as I might take anything else of worth and claim it and defend it against those who'd wrest it from me. Even Arailt hadn't let me take it; he'd kept it for himself for as long as he was able. But he was now helpless and the responsibility was mine.

The North Wind looked up then, frowning. 'You'll take on the Queen of Shadows?'

'Yes.'

'Then you're a brave lass. But I can't help you.'

For a moment I was stunned. 'You what?'

'Get out, Arailt's girl. You're wasting your time here. I cannot help you.'

'But you're the only one who can take me –'

'I can't take you anywhere. There's no compact between us.'

'Compact?'

'I can't carry you until you have first given me something of value in exchange. And what could you possibly offer to me?'

Oh, I thought as understanding dawned; I know that rule. 'There's the usual price, I suppose.'

His face pulled briefly into a grimace. 'In a thousand years, Arailt's girl, I've been stirred by neither woman nor man however much I might desire it. What makes you think that you can release me?'

'Hazel,' I told him, stepping forward. 'My name's Hazel.' Through my mind danced images of all that I'd learned, from Arailt and from others. The sensation of skin on skin in darkness.

The intimate knowledge of every part of a body mediated by touch not sight. The stinging piquancy of pain mixed with pleasure. The tremulous sensitivity to be found at the anal portal. The strength that comes from self-discipline. The rush of surrender. The peace in submission. The fear of the unknown, and the joy of recognition.

I took the scarf from his neck as he sat and covered his eyes, knotting the silk at the back of his skull. 'And you will take what I have to give you,' I told him.

The house East of the Sun and West of the Moon stood on rolling white hills under deep twilight. I thought at first, as we scudded in low and fast over the pallid swells, that the terrain was covered in snow. Then, as the North Wind let me slip from his arms and my feet found gritty purchase, that it was sand dunes that I stood on. Only when I crouched and my hand found crystalline dust and the withered body of a starfish hard as cardboard did I realise that it was salt: so much salt that it were as if all the seas of the world had desiccated instantly to create the white billows.

'I can't take you further,' gasped the North Wind, doubled up with his hands braced on his knees. He'd carried me so far and so fast that I'd watched the moon roll by beneath my feet like a silver ball. 'Her house is over there. I wish you well, Hazel.'

I thanked him, then I set off in the direction he'd indicated. The susurration of the dunes and the crunch of my footfalls were my only accompaniment. The air was bitter and so dry it took effort to blink. I passed the desiccated corpse of a basking shark half exposed in the salt, its huge mouth set in an empty scream. Then I crested a wave and the house of the Queen of Shadows rose up before me, glittering like Vegas in shimmering pinks and blues. It was difficult to make out its outline because the lights were never still, but closer I found the first outpost of the building; a great thick slab of glass thrust up out of the salt. Within the glass lights danced and as I looked closer I saw traffic signals and car headlamps and the neon flicker of advertising hoardings. The images illuminated my skin faintly when I laid a hand to the glass.

As I pressed on the glass structures became more common and their configurations more complex, until I could make out what seemed to be the entrance to a building composed entirely of those slabs, fractured images flowing and glimmering on a thousand surfaces. Then from the gateway spilled something that was shadow, not light. It slid across the dunes toward me, elongating as it went, appearing on crests and disappearing into hollows. I had no means of defence and nowhere to run so I stood my ground. When it was almost at my feet the Shadow paused and reared up out of the salt to stand in front of me, its outline manlike. Against the aurora background it looked pitch black.

'What are you doing here, girl?' It spoke in familiar tones: the voice of my ex Evan. For a moment the shock struck me mute. 'Well?'

'Do you know who I am?' I asked, my own voice wobbly.

'A nothing. An object used then discarded. A leftover.'

'I'm Hazel.' I closed my fist over three small items in my pocket. 'Tell your queen that I've come to trade and that she wants to see me. '

'And *you* want to deal with the Queen of Shadows? You're playing out of your league, little girl. Arailt won't protect you now.'

I clenched my jaw. 'Tell her. I have something she will want. Tell her that.'

'Follow.'

The Shadow slid back to the ground and began to retreat. I hurried after it, kicking up salt, breathless. As I reached the steps something white appeared in the doorway; a tall slender woman. It was her; the one from the portrait. White as salt, I thought: white as neon – but under her mantle of white fur black shadows hung and chittered. The Shadow shaped as Evan slid back to her feet and vanished into a fold of her long dress.

'Well?' Her face was even colder than it had looked in the photo, though just as beautiful.

I pulled out the first hazelnut, the one given me by Verlandi. 'I came to trade.'

'Why else would a tramp like you turn up on my step? What do you offer?'

'In here, a dress.'

'Why should that interest me?'

'This dress is woven of moonlight reflected upon the sea of humanity's dreams. If you were to wear it you'd be the desire of anyone who looked upon you: that's its power. No one could resist you.'

She cocked her head. 'Show me.'

I broke the nut open between my fingers and drew out the shimmering dress. It took my breath away just to look at it. I had no idea if the Queen of Shadows had breath to lose.

'Name your price.'

'A night with your husband, Arailt.'

She almost smiled. 'You miss him, do you?'

I could safely admit to that.

'For that dress, though there are no nights here you may have ample time with Arailt. Much good may it do you.' She took the garment from my hands and turned away. 'Follow me.'

'Wait.'

I felt her cold gaze like a slap.

'You haven't seen what else I have to trade.' I drew out the second nut, Urd's gift.

'Well?'

'Shoes to go with the dress.' I weighed the nut in my palm. 'It's not enough to be desired. Any whore can be desirable. You want to be envied. These shoes are cut from the skin of the Lamia herself and will make you envied by every woman that sees you; that's their power.' I opened the nut and displayed the shoes within. In colour they matched the dress; they were striking and cutting-edge stylish and flaunted a designer name on the insoles that changed as I tilted them. 'You want these shoes.'

'Name your price, tramp.'

I took a deep breath. 'I want your word –'

'My word? How dare you.'

'Your word,' I said, holding my ground even though those pale eyes seemed to burn me. 'The shoes are mine to give, or not. I want your word that if Arailt chooses to leave with me, you will let him go free.'

Cold calculation stirred in her face. 'You have my word that if he is fool enough to choose you then I will release him.'

Not good, I thought; there was something going on. But it would have to do. I handed over the shoes. Then I followed her into the house East of the Sun and West of the Moon.

There were no rooms within, or at least none that I could make out; just endless interlocking corridors of glass, of shadow and flickering image, in which walls and doorways could barely be told from each other and no visual map could be constructed in the head. After a few minutes panicked attempt to remember our route I realised it was hopeless. I blundered blindly after the Queen of Shadows, the only solid figure in a world of overlapping ghosts. She led me to the only piece of furnishing I saw in that place; a bed made of glass. White sheets spilled over its edges and my eyes seized gratefully upon the plain colour.

'I'll leave you,' said the queen. 'Enjoy.'

Clammy with trepidation I approached the bed. There lay Arailt flat on his back, eyes closed. A sheet covered him to the chest. He didn't stir. For a second I wondered if he was still alive, and then I saw the shallow rise and fall of his ribcage. Gently I whispered his name as my hand found his warm, naked shoulder. 'Wake up. Wake up, love.'

He didn't move.

I called louder. I shook his arm. I stroked his face, discovering stubble that had turned softer with length, almost a beard now. Nothing worked. I bent over him and kissed his lips, unable to think of any other cure for an enchanted sleep. I got not the slightest response.

Confused, at my wits end, I pulled down the sheet to bare him. There were bruises all over him; reddish stains like the love bites that grace the necks of teenagers – except that at the centre of each bruise was a puncture mark. And he'd lost weight, I thought; he seemed somehow diminished, lying there sunk into the bedding. His face looked gaunter than I recalled. I was seized with the horrible fear that this wasn't Arailt at all, that it was a trick of the queen's. After all, I barely knew him by sight and now the recognition I'd felt at first glance seemed flimsy and fading. Dumping my rucksack I bent over the bed and shut my eyes, brushing my face against his chest and stomach, recalling the sensory map of his body I'd constructed in the dark. I crawled up and down his body. His skin smelled like warm baked bread, his thighs sweeter, his pubic thatch sharper, the musk of his armpits unmistakably Arailt's. I kissed him, and began to cry hot bitter tears.

I lost it for a while then, overwhelmed by frustration and fear. I smacked my fist down on his chest and wept on his face and bit him – not hard enough to draw blood but enough to leave crescent teethmarks in the skin on his ribs. He stirred a little at that, his breathing troubled, and I struck him across the face with my palm and screamed at him. His head rocked but the red imprint of my hand was my only reward. 'Please,' I begged, covering his body with mine and wrapping my arms tight around him, my face buried in his neck. He murmured under his breath and slept on.

I had no magic to counter hers. Nothing to save the man I loved.

Gradually my fury leaked away into despair and at length

I sat up, straddling his thighs, my broken breathing the loudest sound in that room. I stroked the face I'd abused. Even unconscious he stirred my greed. I looked down at his body helpless beneath mine and then at his flaccid penis. I blinked. Soft it might be, but I could swear it was fuller than the last time I'd looked.

Of course men do get erections in their sleep.

I didn't really think about what I did next. I just unzipped my flies and slipped my hand inside my knickers, gathering the moisture from within. Then I pushed those fingers into Arailt's mouth, brushing the tip of his tongue before wiping my perfume over his lips. He shifted almost imperceptibly beneath me, his breath coming in warm gusts. Encouraged, I wriggled down between his legs, flattening myself against the bed. I started on his thighs with soft wet kisses, then took each of his balls in turn into my mouth and felt them roll beneath the loose skin. I licked his scrotum until the sac tightened to wrinkles and then I moved up to his cock. His response was slower than normal, but I wasn't in any hurry. This might be my last time after all. And he did respond; thickening and hardening and pushing further and further into my mouth. I tasted his salt.

God, I love his prick. The West Wind was right about that. I love the hardness and the imperious pride of it, the way it moves like a living animal with a will all of its own, the way it butts my hand and nudges my lips and jerks to get my attention. I love the fact it won't take no for an answer. I love the strange symbiosis Arailt has with this incorrigible demanding creature, his attitude half arrogant and half shamefaced and all delight.

When his cock was stiff enough to stand proud of his belly I released it just long enough to pull off my denims and straddle him again. His brow was creased now, his chest rising and falling swiftly. As I sank down on his length he squirmed and arched his shoulders. I circled his nipples with my fingertips, playing with the hair on his chest while at the same time gripping him inwardly. Then I smoothed my hands down the length of his torso to his hips and I reached behind me to gently heft and stroke his balls. They were carried high and full now.

Arailt's lips parted as he drew air deeper into his lungs.

'Yes,' I whispered. He filled me as he had done every night for months, almost uncomfortably thick in the first moments and as hard as wood. I used my thighs to rise and sink upon him, relinquishing the inches and then taking possession once again. It was going to be hard work for me: he didn't thrust, he didn't support me with his hands or encourage me with teasing touches upon my clit, and I didn't dare touch myself in case I lost concentration. I had to rely on the strength of my thighs and my will to carry me through, pumping him with each swoop and rotation of my hips. I felt my juices begin to flow as I grew accustomed to his girth. I saw his stomach grow taut and his chest expand as the tension built in him; he seemed to be breathing in but not breathing out.

I was really slick now, each descent tugging the threads of pleasure connecting cunt and clit. I could take him deeper without discomfort, right to the root, and each intrusion seemed to rearrange my insides. When I felt his pelvis move beneath me for the first time like a pulse I nearly lost control. I wanted to touch myself. I wanted to thrust down on his impaling cock and batter my clit until he broke my spine. His thighs between my legs were hard not just with muscle but with tension. There was a glaze on his chest and sweat in the dark ringlets of his crotch and a flush on his throat. He arched, groaning, and as he started finally to thrust Arailt's eyes came open in a blank stare, seeing but not seeing, fixed on my face but a thousand miles away. Then with a thick cry he came, reaching out in his extremity to grab my hips with heavy hands, and that touch even though it was nowhere near my clit still set me off and we came together, as one.

As above, so below.

If sex isn't a form of magic then nothing is.

He blinked, still quivering with the spasms that possessed him, still pulsing into me. 'Hazel,' he groaned. As I fell on him lips found lips and hands found faces and we spoke each other's names like prayers, our breath mingling.

Eventually he sat up, his arms around me as I straddled his lap. 'How did you find me?' he asked in wonder.

'I had help. From a lot of people.'

Arailt smiled. 'My brave Hazel,' he whispered as his lips danced over mine.

'She's a common little tramp,' said the Queen of Shadows from over his shoulder.

In one motion Arailt pushed me off his lap onto the bed, turning to interpose himself between the two of us. His instinctive protectiveness made my heart thump. 'Leave her,' he warned. 'She's not yours.'

'On the contrary, the slut and I have a deal.' The queen's face was Botox-inscrutable but her eyes flashed. All around her massed her Shadows; they hung from the glass ceiling and crawled across the floor at her feet and peeked from under the hem of her cloak. They whispered their excitement in dry creaking voices and leered from crumpled faces like burnt paper.

'You promised a night with him,' I said, my throat dry. She was wearing the dress and the shoes under her fur mantle. The shimmering fabric framed glimpses of her glacial skin; she was stunning beyond words.

'I said ample time and clearly you've had that.' Her voice was the only expressive thing about her and sharp with poison. 'Now for the second part of our bargain. Time to choose, Arailt.'

'Choose?'

I could hardly look at her. She was magnificent. I was only too aware of my dowdiness and of how plain I was in comparison to her. I was knelt up on the bed with my socks and shirt still on, and my bare thighs and exposed bush were only pitiful.

'A free choice between the two of us. That's what she paid for with the earnings she made from her whoring.'

Arailt looked between us as if not quite sure he believed what he'd heard. I felt sick.

'Go on, Arailt. Mortal or immortal: drab or queen.'

'No contest,' he said darkly, his eyes lingering on her as every man's must but his hands drifting over the bruises on his torso. The Shadows had surrounded the bed by now, like a tide rising about a tiny island.

She quivered. 'But be aware: if you choose her then you go free, as she wanted.' She eased aside the deep cleavage of her dress and the Shadow that had been clinging to her left breast took flight and fluttered away to join the others. I caught a brief glimpse of a pallid nipple, sticky with saliva. 'And before you step out of this house my Shadows will pierce her to the marrow and drink her to a dry husk.'

'What?' I whispered, a spark of fire waking in my chest.

The queen's glance was razor-edged with triumph. 'You asked free passage for him, not for yourself. You should be more careful when you bargain.'

'Bitch,' I squeaked.

'Now choose, Arailt. Will you buy your freedom at that cost?'

Arailt said nothing. His face was setting into a mask as hard and cold as hers; for the first time I could see a resemblance between them: a closeness of type.

'Choose!'

My denim jeans were soft beneath my hands. The Shadows overhung us like a wave about to crash.

'If I chose you it'd be on the promise that you'd let Hazel go free and safe,' he said hoarsely. 'And that you'll give her passage home.'

'That would be acceptable.'

He took a deep breath.

'No,' I said, and I broke open the last of the hazelnuts from my pocket; the gift of Skuld. The world went black. The Shadows as one began to scream in voices like dying babies, like tearing skin. Their queen screamed like a woman having her entrails ripped out. I grabbed onto Arailt's warm and naked body in the dark and clung to him as the wave fell at last, tearing at us both. But it had no solidity; as fragile as scorched paper, the Shadows beat themselves on our bodies and fell away to ash. At last even the voice of the queen was still. We sat holding one another in absolute blackness, absolute silence. I could hear the rush of my own blood in my ears.

'What is this?' Arailt asked softly.

'This is a piece of the darkness from before time,' I said. 'Before the first suns were lit. Before there was light. And without light there cannot be any shadows.'

'Ah.' We sat in silence for a while longer. Then Arailt spoke up again. 'Do you know the way out, Hazel?'

'No.' I slid off the bed and groped along the floor for my rucksack. I could see not the faintest glimmer of movement even when I passed my hand in front of my face. 'But you can find it. You don't need to see.' I extracted the mangy fur coat and pressed it into his hands. It smelled of mothballs and charity shops, but when Arailt pulled it on a warm wave of bear fur and honey filled my lungs. I felt him slip to the floor beside me, changing shape. He breathed a great wuff of relief and laughed deep in his chest.

'Get up then, my Hazel. I choose you.'

'Hold on.' I groped for my jeans again and stuffed my legs into them, not bothering about my knickers that formed a knot wedged down one leg. In the blackness I could only find one shoe so I abandoned the search and mounted Arailt's broad back, gripping his thick fur.

'Hold tight,' he said, and set off into the darkness, nose to the floor, sniffing as he went. He followed the trail of my passage back through all the winding maze that was the house East of the Sun and West of the Moon, through unseen doorways and past blind alleys and through snaking switch-back corridors until I heard the crunch of sand beneath his paws and we emerged suddenly onto the salt dunes under twilight. Neither moon nor sun stood overhead, and behind us was a wall of darkness. Just as the first stabs of joy entered my heart there came from that darkness an ululating wail: a noise of grief and fury and hate. It was close, and closing.

'She's followed us!' I gasped. 'Hurry! Run!'

'No.' Arailt half-rose to his hind legs, shrugging me off. Then, turning, he launched himself back into the darkness with a roar. I scrambled to my feet. Somewhere within the black pall the bear's roar and the wailing met. There was a horrible noise for a brief time, followed by silence. Then Arailt came lumbering out once more. There was white stuff on his long claws and heavy jaws; a liquid I at first assumed had to be cream. Then I realised that even her blood had been colourless.

Arailt eyed me, head down and breathing heavily.

I ran up and flung my arms around the thick ruff of his neck.

'My bold lassie,' he growled, pressing his broad head against me. 'Now ride.'

I descended from his back in the doorway of the bookshop on Park Street. I was a bit surprised to find myself there and looked about me; it was well into the deep hours of the night and the street was deserted. A light dusting of snow lay on the ground – less than an inch, and it would be gone by morning unless it froze.

'Is it Christmas?' I asked. It was strange seeing snow in the middle of the city like this. It seemed to remove all the shadows from the night world.

Arailt stood up on two legs and threw off the bear shape. It was the first time I'd ever seen him do that. He was naked beneath, of course. He knotted the ragged skin about his waist so that it hung like a furry ankle-length kilt. 'It's February,' he said with a glance at the stars overhead. 'The year is up.' He brushed the frost from the hair flopping over my face. 'And every night for over a year you've loved me without reason and . . . *almost* without question.'

The best thing about seeing Arailt's human face was recognising the twinkle in his eye. For a moment we simply smiled at each other. Then we sobered and I felt the first flutter of fear. He touched my cheek softly.

'You don't have to stop now, you know.'

'Are you sure?' I whispered.

There was a strange light, a yearning, in his eyes. 'I promise.'

I laid my hand on his breastbone, taking a deep breath. 'Good. Because I don't think I'd be able to.'

Gently he drew me against him and we kissed. In the cold street that kiss burned its way right through me and warmed me from top to toe. I was gasping by the time we broke for air.

'Shall we go indoors?' I suggested. Another look made me add, 'And, you know, maybe get you some clothes?' He was, in his bearskin skirt, technically covered up enough to appear in public. But there's something irreducibly indecent about a big half-naked bloke, barefoot in the snow and grinning.

'I don't need clothes just yet,' he said, backing me up against the marble side of the shop doorway. 'Not for this.' His hands were on the front of my jeans working the buttons and zip, round the back on my suddenly bared bum lifting me clean off the ground, and all at once I was pinned between his hard warm body and the cold stone and he was frantically working to part my thighs. My own hands were on his chest, his hips, then up through the gaps in his kilt finding heat and hard muscle and eagerness. Part of me was aware that there was a security camera overhead and this was all going on tape for the staff to see tomorrow, but I didn't care. Not with his honeyed mouth on mine and his cock slipping into me, and my sex and head full of fire and my hands on his wonderful, warm, bare skin.

The Three Riddles

Olivia Knight

The Three Riddles

The Engagement

Everyone wanted to explain the love between Pearl and Thomas. Some said the elves had sprinkled love-dust on them. Others said – the king's brilliant daughter and the Champion of Minotha, where's the magic in that? Still others said they slotted together so well that they must have known each other since the sun and moon first fell in love. It's usual that a young couple thinks no one's ever loved like them – it's rare that the rest of the world secretly agrees.

Their intimacy irked people. The other knights told Thomas he was wrapped around the princess's little finger. The king's counsellors argued that the knight had too much sway with the princess. Everyone watched the mercurial princess with her steady knight and shook their heads – she'd lead him a dance then break his heart, they told each other. In truth, everyone who saw them together pined for their own true love – some still had the person but not the love, some the love and not the person, but Pearl and Thomas had both.

They lay together on her bed in the small hours, the heavy curtains drawn around them, staring up at the patterned canopy and playing with each other's fingers. On the ledge behind them, a tallow candle hissed, dying, and the shadows of their hands jumped on the far curtain.

'When did you first know you loved me?' he asked.

'When you first rode through the gatehouse.'

He turned on his side, his sinewy thigh resting on her softer leg. 'Then you just loved me for my looks.'

She giggled. 'Not at all – you were covered in armour. No – I think maybe when I saw you practising – or that dinner – or maybe on the wall-walk, when you pointed out which direction your home was . . . I don't know. Maybe when you took over my sword training.'

'Did you already love me when I kissed you?'

'Could you taste love on my lips?'

His hand swam down her bare skin. 'I think so. Sweet as honey.'

'What about you?' She turned to face him, his burly body making her feel as small as a wren. 'When did you first know you loved me?'

He touched her breast, her chin, her lips. His eyes, rich brown and deep as wells, drank her up. 'When I was born.'

She laughed again. 'But I wasn't born yet!'

'I still knew.' He smiled the way she loved most – assured and knowing, as if he understood the world's secrets and was amused by them. 'And then when I was ten years old, a page in my uncle's manor, I suddenly stood stock-still and thought – today, my true love came into the world. And my uncle hit me on the head for not pouring his wine.'

'Liar . . .'

'Heart's truth.' He kissed her slowly. Their bodies had moved together, lithe and lively, while the candle had burnt down, but already she melted again to his kiss. Between them, his shaft wavered and extended.

'They gossip about us in the court, you know,' she said.

He grimaced. 'What do they say?'

'That I'm too flighty and you're too phlegmatic, that we'll never last.'

'They're just jealous, then.' He rolled onto his back and she snuggled over him, resting on one elbow, tracing his features.

'And that I boss you around.'

His face softened. 'I'd do anything for you.'

'But I don't boss you.'

'No . . . You know what I think? Lie next to me, look up.' The bed's wooden roof was lined with quilt, embroidered with the royal insignia of Kwestriminotha. Hundreds of years ago, Kwestria's symbol had been a gold circle with a silver centre and Minotha's a blue circle with a green centre. Since the union, they had come together as two curving teardrops forming a new circle. 'That's what we're like,' he said, mimicking the shape in the air. 'In a way, we're identical. And we fit together perfectly.'

He knew her mouth was twitching naughtily before he saw it. He pinned her to the bed, hefty and powerful above her. His eyes intensified; the candle flared, sputtered, and died. In the dark he said, 'I love you,' and his shaft nudged between her thighs. Her hands ran up the swell of his biceps, down the sides of his broad back, and grasped his hips as she opened to him. He slid easily back inside her, back where he belonged, and drove in and out, unhurriedly, until her whimpers like birdsong mixed with true birdsong and pale light shone between the drapes. Then, knowing he must leave her bed soon, he thrust faster so that she screamed his name and babbled with love. He held back while she arched, convulsed, and gripped, then he pulled out at the last moment as bliss ripped the cream from his cock, spattering her belly. Breathless and captivated, half smiling, they gazed at each other in the gloom and her fingers drew mandalas on her stomach with his juice.

Alvey Castle perched on a crag above the port, three sides rising from the cliffs while the other two gave onto rocky terrain behind it. Her father's rooms in the south-east tower, like hers in the south, were protected on either side by the sheer cliff-face. While hers overlooked the sea, however, his fronted the port below where the two great rivers, the Toan and the Lan, ran together in the gorge. They sliced a silver V through the country, dividing Kwestria in the west from Minotha in the east. Like this, the king said, he lived on Kwestrian soil but stared always at the bluff of Minotha.

As she closed the door behind her, the heavy wall-hangings and layers of rugs muted the residual buzz of castle life. 'You wanted to see me, Daddy.'

King Jarod sat at a long table covered with maps, sealed documents and scrolls. He was scowling at a piece of paper and took a few moments to glance up. His daughter wore a heavy gold gown, encrusted with glittering glass and white embroidery, its train extending a yard behind her and the sleeves drooping to the floor. A wide ruff kept her head high and a gilt coronet held her hair back from her face. He blinked, surprised.

'Nice outfit.'

'It's Thursday, remember?'

'Ah – of course.' He sighed, leaning back in his chair.

'So what is it? I still have a queue of petitioners from the great hall to the gatehouse. Anything serious?'

'I need you to translate.' He pushed across the paper which he'd been examining so ferociously. 'It's in Udian.'

She grinned. 'And your Udian's rusted overnight? I can take the little legal matters off your back, Daddy, but this is really pushing into your dotage!'

'No, Pearl – this one's in code. My Udian isn't good enough to decode and translate simultaneously.'

'Oh.' She sobered as she picked up the paper. One hand fiddled at the back of her neck, under the trailing curls and diamond pins, to unfasten the ruff. 'Intercepted?'

'On the border between Udia and Tarpash.'

'Right.' Her good humour vanished. The narrow marshy country of Tarpash provided only two things: excellent horses, and a buffer zone between Udia and Cantaland. It was always allied to one or the other, but currently to Cantaland. Secret messages with Udia boded ill. She took the paper and a quill to a smaller table by the window. For an hour, paper rustled, parchment crackled, and their pens scratched. Pearl sighed and muttered to herself as she tried out different options, all of which refused to yield clean text.

'I need more time,' said Pearl eventually. She tugged a cord sharply. A few minutes later her lady-in-waiting, Shanon, hurried in breathlessly.

'Our apologies to the petitioners but we won't be able to see any more today ...' She paused, considering how far some had travelled. 'We'll open court again tomorrow morning. Can you see that anyone who needs accommodation is quartered?'

'Difficult?' asked her father as Shanon left. 'Have you –' He broke off, hacking.

'I don't like that cough,' she said.

'Funny, it's not your throat it's tickling,' he retorted, in a croak.

The long summer day faded. Ships settled in their docks, barges were lashed upriver, and the port lights danced over empty black water. Pearl kept scribbling as she ate one-handed from a plate of grilled quail. She licked her fingers clean and just stopped herself from wiping them on the formal gown.

'Hanky, Daddy?'

She caught it from the air, wiping her fingers and mouth.

'This is the advantage of hunting clothes – they don't show up grease. OK, are you ready?' She swung around in her chair. King Jarod folded his hands expectantly.

'According to this, Cantaland's raising an army of knights.'

'And Tarpash is nervous.'

'Enough to change alliances, it seems. Udia wants them to raid and steal back all the horses they can. And Udia also wants safe passage across Tarpash.'

The king poured them each some wine and stood by the window, swirling his glass reflectively. 'If Udia gets Cantaland ... It's all getting too unbalanced, Pearl. We've just been holding it together, distracting them, dangling your hand at both countries, but that's not enough any more. We need to –'

'No! It's out of the question.'

He looked at her sharply. In the dull firelight, her beauty had turned stern.

'You're not pregnant, are you?'

She shook her head.

'Am I offering our foreign friends a virgin bride?' His mouth twitched in amusement. 'The Udians are very strict about that sort of thing.'

'As if I needed more reason not to marry an Udian!'

'Cantaland, then?' He tossed her a picture of a fair-haired, pale-eyed teenager staring into the middle distance. 'The youngest prince.'

She eyed it disdainfully. 'Why bear a child, when I can just marry one?'

'Seriously, Pearl. We must consider the question.'

'What's there to consider? If we marry Cantaland, we're at war with Udia. If we marry Udia, vice versa. Tarpash is too weak to consider. We can flirt with both, we can even get engaged to both, but we can't marry both. It's impossible.'

He leaned against the wall, studying her. 'And this masterful analysis wouldn't have anything to do with Sir Thomas, would it?'

She flushed. 'We've always defended ourselves. We don't need allies!'

'If Cantaland's expanding its army –'

'Sir Thomas could beat their best knight one-handed!'

'Yes, I know. Your lover's a great fighter. But can our second-best knight beat their second-best knight? And the third and the fourth? I say we need Udia.'

'And I say Udia would be our doom.' She met his glare stubbornly.

'Is this the princess or the woman talking?'

'Both.' She flung her hair back. 'The princess says Udia would never marry us and accept us as equals. They'll never think a queen is equal to a king. To them, marrying us would be like adopting us.'

Jarod pursed his lips reflectively – there was a kernel of truth in her argument. 'And what does the woman say?'

'That I'll spend my entire life serving this country – but I'll do it with the man I love at my side.'

The king sighed. 'There's only one man who can change your mind about anything, and it's not me.' He spread his hands. 'Very well. But something has to be done.'

She pulled her chair forward. 'They'll attack in the spring, before the rain softens the marshes. So midwinter, we invite everyone here, for an engagement ball – they'll all come, because they'll all still be hoping for marriage. We make sure all their best tacticians are on the guest list.'

'Fill our castle with vipers?'

'Keep the vipers in our sight. You and I will have six months to draw up trade agreements so labyrinthine that by the end of it no one can *afford* to attack each other. We get them all signed on the sly . . .'

Her father was shaking his head. 'I still think Udia. And you know, if you marry, you and Sir Thomas can still –'

'His pride wouldn't stand it!'

'And he's not the only proud one,' observed Jarod wryly. 'Fine. Not even the king can stand against your combined wills – let's hope our enemies can't, either.'

When Pearl reached her rooms, her ladies-in-waiting scrambled to their feet, blinking back sleep. Pearl's eyes swept the room.

'The fire needs rebuilding,' she said peremptorily. 'And wine – maybe spiced wine – I don't know, something strong. And more candles. Lots of light.' She clasped her hands so tightly that her rings dug into the soft flesh between her fingers. 'And send for Sir Thomas.'

The three women headed for the door, but the princess interrupted. 'No – Elaine and Fern, you go. Shanon, how do I look?'

Shanon was soft-featured, with the dark hair common to

Minothans. Since she came to court, she'd gained roly-poly hips and bosom, but her pretty plump face belied a will of steel.

'Your hair needs fixing,' she said. 'And there's ink on your lips.'

Pearl licked a finger and rubbed it roughly over her mouth as she sat. 'Quick then – my hair!'

'Is something wrong?' asked Shanon, tugging the curls back under their pins.

'No – well, yes – some affairs of state – all isn't as it should be in the world,' said Pearl distractedly.

'No,' agreed Shanon. 'Fate will soon go off course, if we're not careful.'

'What? What have you heard?'

'Too many people are ignoring the elves. How can we find our fate if they don't guide us?'

'Oh!' Pearl laughed in relief; for a moment, she'd feared that alarm was spreading.

'You may laugh,' said Shanon stiffly. 'But the elves are the guardians of fate and they guide our country. We ignore them at our peril. There.' She patted the final curl into place.

Pearl turned, smiling. 'I wonder, if the elves guide the country, why they never have the occasional word with its rulers? Somehow, they only ever appear to common folk ... Why is that, do you think?'

'I'm sure I don't know.' Shanon's face hardened and the princess decided not to tease her about her superstitions.

When the room was tidied and candles glowed on every ledge, Pearl paced restlessly. The window drapes were tied open to the warm summer night, displaying the open sea. The high moon cut a silver swathe across the waves and salty air gusted through the windows. A knock at the door made her jump, but it was only Elaine with the wine. Pearl poured a glass and drank it in one swallow, grateful for the strong brandy mixed in. Elaine and Shanon exchanged puzzled glances as the princess polished the lip mark off the silver with her sleeve and fidgeted with the goblets, arranging them. She started at another knock on the door and quickly sat.

'Sir Thomas of Minotha,' announced Fern. He stepped in, casually dressed in blue hose with a doublet thrown over his linen shirt, his thick black hair tousled with sleep under his cloth cap. He looked around in surprise. Pearl bit her lip.

'You may leave us,' she said breathlessly to her ladies-in-waiting.

Thomas bowed. 'Your royal highness.'

'Oh, don't . . .'

He smiled broadly as he pulled up a chair opposite her. 'Well, it is a bit formal. I don't think I've ever seen this table cleared of papers before.' He smoothed his hand across it.

Her hand shook as she poured the wine with careful concentration. 'I hope I didn't wake you,' she said politely.

'I'd rather sleep in your bed than mine – even if it means I don't sleep.'

'I did wake you, then – but it couldn't – I couldn't – wait.'

She slid his glass over, avoiding his eyes. She felt as if a dozen trapped falcons were beating their wings inside her.

'What is it?' he asked quietly. His heart was turning to lead. 'Look at me.'

She glanced up, like a frightened hare. 'It's – I have – I'd like to make a proposal,' she finished all in a rush.

He watched her impassively. He'd always known the chances of marriage were slim – and known, too, that he'd reject the suggestion she was about to make. He'd have her or not, but never watch another man go to her bed and stay on as her paramour.

'Go on,' he said steadily. 'What is it?'

'It's – it's a proposal.' She waited, but he didn't react. 'I'm proposing. Only I don't know how.'

He stared at her. Shyly, she met his gaze. His hard look faded as his eyes widened, soft and brown. His Adam's apple bobbed. 'You're kidding.'

She shook her head. It might have been the candlelight, but his eyes seemed to glisten.

'This is why you're so nervous?'

She nodded, unable to speak with that naked love and disbelief on his face.

'Come here.' He opened his arms and she abandoned her chair for his lap, where she nestled with one hand furled against his sturdy neck. 'I was worried,' he whispered into her curls. 'I thought I was going to lose you.'

'Never,' she said fiercely.

He kissed her, long and deep, one strong hand at the small of her back and the other drifting up the scratchy, ornamental bodice. As his fingers drifted over her cleavage, she mewed and he smiled. Her breasts were ever the chink in her armour.

'If we're engaged, does that mean I don't have to pull out?' His hand slid into the soft space, pressing the mounds on either side. 'It's practically my duty not to, now.'

'I'm the princess, not a heifer,' she retorted, fighting to push him away. 'You don't have to get me up the spout to know it's worth marrying me. Honestly, you Minothans...'

He was stronger; she knew her struggles were useless. The more she wrestled, the more she giggled, and the weaker she grew. He trapped her back against his chest, her arms at her sides, and his hand cupped her breast inside her dress. Through her skirt, she could feel him protruding in his hose. His index finger circling her nipple, he said softly, 'I'm going to make you the happiest woman alive.'

'I know...'

'I mean right now.'

She shivered, wiggling back against him, and he yelped. 'The glass on your dress!'

'We can take it off.'

Still holding her breast, he unthreaded the ribbon at her back. The bodice fell loose and he lifted her to her feet to unhook her skirt. When she stood in just her shift, he tugged her back to her perch. Her nipples jutted hard through the silk, against his palms.

'I didn't mean I wanted to get you pregnant,' he said against her neck, breathless. Their hips squirmed, manoeuvring his hard shaft closer to her lips through the cloth. 'I don't care if my bride has the world's flattest stomach – I just want to come inside you. To feel – you – gripping me tight – while I – come.'

'We must wait.' Her breath was rising. 'Till winter – at least – I need my wits about me ...'

His powerful arm lifted her in the air as he scooped her shift above her waist. She raised her arms, obediently, and his hands slithered over her bare breasts as he slid the flimsy garment off. He touched the curls at her lap and her skin dimpled with shivers.

'Are you cold?'

'No,' she squeaked, but he scooped her up anyway and carried her to the fireside, laying her down on the soft fleece.

'My beauty ... my princess,' he purred.

'My knight,' she said proudly.

He knelt, taking first one nipple then the other into his mouth. His hands roamed her haunches and bare stomach. His calloused palms were on her inner thighs, parting her legs. She moaned his name and ran her hands through his hair as he crouched lower; his hands raised her hips, lifting her to his mouth, and when his tongue found her bead, she cried out. He was submerging her in a dreamworld of firelight, soft wool and delicate probing. The sensations ran like filigree around her limbs, her body melting and diffusing. She lost all sense of parts, of her own shape even. There was a centre, hot soft and exquisite, and a rippling cloud into which the shining threads ran, lighting it up like torches in the mist. It grew brighter, into hot sunshine, and all she needed to do was bask. The heat was flooding her skin. The brilliant centre exploded slowly, blinding her. Sweet and fierce, it washed over her, and the long thin sound in the distance was her own crooning.

His tongue kept twirling as his finger penetrated her. When she opened her eyes, her desire was already rising again, but more wakeful now, and hungrier.

'Thomas,' she said hoarsely, lifting her head. His eyes met hers while he kept licking. 'I love you.' Her head fell back; her hips rose. More thickness was rubbing inside her now – her eyes fluttered open to see him kneeling upright, one hand still pushing into her, the other pulling down his hose. His cock leapt free. Her hand found it, massaging its buttery hardness, and his muscular thighs trembled.

'Make love to me.'

'Yes.'

He picked her up to kneel, her lips on his forehead, while he guided the tip of his cock into her. She swayed when its bulk bore in and he caught her.

'Not hurting?'

'No.'

She lowered herself slowly, groaning as her soft walls gave way. His arms wrapped tightly around her waist; gravity forced the last few inches in. Impaled, she jerked helplessly and sobbed onto his shoulder. He hoisted her up and down his length, until need gave her new strength and she rode him, slower then faster then slower. The thrusts made her half-delirious, but seeing his face stripped and vulnerable with passion tore her heart open. She cried uncontrollably, because she realised he'd always been holding a small part of himself back, against the day she married someone else, and it had stung him to the core. And now he was completely exposed to her and she loved him unbearably – the gloss of his chest with its soft skin overlying firm muscles, the width of his shoulders, the tilt of his head, his thick eyebrows, the bulge of his cheeks when he smiled, the breadth of his jaw and its dark stubble, every strand of his black hair. She loved everything and it terrified her.

He yelled out and she gave herself up entirely. Then neither were in control, both bucking and wild and clutching each other. With a terrible effort, he wrenched himself out of her, pushing in his hand instead to feel her clenching around it as his cock spurted over her breasts. They collapsed together, tears still rolling down her face.

'Don't cry, sweetheart, why are you crying?'

'Because we love each other so much, and I'm afraid.'

He cradled her close and they fell together into exhausted sleep.

Deep in wintertime, snow lay patchy on the coast and thick on the plains behind Alvey Castle. The rivers inland froze over every night and the trade barges crept slower than ever, splinters of ice floating in their wake. The Udian duke, Kardan, rode with his retinue through the border mountains and overland across Kwestria. The sky was layered grey with cloud, the snowy ground bluing, when he drew up on the crest of a hill. In the distance trotted a group of riders and he pulled out his spyglass. His advisor, reining in next to him, did likewise.

'A hunting party – royals?'

'Nobility, at least,' said Stefan, scanning them. 'I don't see the king. Oh, look – that little brat from Cantaland is here.'

'Is his nursemaid with him?'

Stefan laughed.

'Who's that girl in the grey breeches, with the fur hat – that uppity one, riding like she owns the place?'

Stefan shifted his glass. 'Ah – I rather think she does. That's the princess.' He glanced at the narrow-faced duke, who was peering with new interest.

Her skin was pale, but her cheeks brightly flushed from the cold, and her long hair slapped smoothly against her back as she rode. Kardan angled the glass to study her body in its close-fitting hunting outfit and grunted in satisfaction. 'Perhaps marriage won't be such a hardship,' he said, tucking his spyglass back in his saddlebag. 'I was afraid I might also need a little present from my aunt to help things along.'

'Your aunt gives me the creeps.'

Kardan ignored him. 'And these girls really have no qualms about not waiting for the wedding ring?'

'No, my lord. In some parts of the country, I believe a few good fucks beforehand are practically *de rigueur*.'

'And the men actually still marry them, afterwards?' Kardan wrinkled his fine nose in distaste.

'A custom you will also have to observe – she *is* the princess. But at least you'll have an entertaining engagement.'

Kardan scowled. 'I hope she's not already having an entertaining engagement. You know how I feel about soiled goods.'

'What – that you like to visit them regularly for a modest sum?'

'Watch your mouth! This is my future bride.'

Stefan shrugged, unabashed. 'So give her presents and pretend it's payment. There have to be worse prices for a kingdom than an experienced rider in your bed.'

Looking thoughtful, Kardan returned the spyglass to his eye.

The princess rode next to Sir Thomas of Minotha. On her other side, Prince Gilbert of Cantaland struggled to keep his horse level with theirs. He was even younger than his picture had shown him, without the first hint of fluff on his chin.

'A skill in the hunt shows the mark of a good leader,' he piped up. 'Your skill, your highness, is clearly without question.'

Pearl battled to keep a straight face. For an hour now, the boy had valiantly produced a string of inane compliments.

'And we haven't seen even a hare yet,' said Thomas, po-faced. 'Your keen judgement does you credit, Prince Gilbert.'

'Don't tease,' mumbled Pearl from the side of her mouth as the boy-prince, flattered, elaborated on his theme. Both pressed their lips tightly shut, fighting laughter.

His panegyric was abruptly cut short as a donkey careered into view, its small rider flailing at it with a stick and yelling.

'Wolves!' cried the child frantically. 'A pack of 'em – Reid village – the grown-ups're holding 'em off – me mam's bleeding...'

The riders wheeled around, Pearl and Sir Thomas streaking into the lead. She dug her knees in, leaning forward, as she unslung her bow and slipped the string into the arrow-notch.

'Sword's better,' said Thomas, speeding alongside her. 'Arrow shots will only make them angry.'

She flashed him a grin. 'With your shooting, maybe. Mine will kill them.'

They heard the shouts before they leapt over the hilltop and the hamlet came into view against the tree-line. A dozen people, three of them very old, were lashing out with axes and chairs, their children cowering behind them. A woman was splayed on the ground, her throat torn open, a streak of brilliant blood on the snow where she'd been dragged back. The wolves wove back and forth, watchful. Pearl's quick eye counted eleven animals, their sides hollow with starvation, their jaws snapping murder. Four went down with arrows in their sides before Thomas had finished bellowing, 'Quick – out of the way!' to the villagers on whom their horses were bearing down. His sword flashed and swung down, spraying wolf-blood as it arced back through the air.

Pearl had her own sword out now, her horse dodging and dancing as she stabbed downwards. A huge matted thing leapt at her leg. Flinging his sword into his left hand, Thomas gutted it mid-air and, as the jaws closed on her ankle, it died leaving nothing but a bleeding scrape. Pearl slashed at the snarling animals still rising toward her like a wave of stinking fur and teeth. Her horse reared, whinnying in terror, one hoof cracking a wolf's skull. As it bucked again, Pearl was thrown – Thomas yanked her up by the scruff of her jacket, hauling her onto his lap. She swung her foot over the horse's head, her riding boot kicking hard against the upper teeth of one of the beasts. She swore violently as the incisor pierced her sole, but the animal had fallen back for a moment. Four remained, snarling and slinking from side to side. Pearl's horse had fled.

'Where the hell are the other hunters?' said Pearl angrily.

'This lot aren't going to give up,' said Thomas grimly. 'You're right-hand, I'm left.'

'I can fight left-handed too –'

'Not like I can. On my count, we look behind us – sword ready? One – two – three.'

They twisted around, heard the claws scrabbling on the snow, and spun back with undercuts. Pearl grunted with effort as the wolf's heavy body slid down her sword, and flung it loose. Thomas's sword whirred, spraying them both with blood – she slashed once more, straight through the eyes of her attacker, and its howl of pain rang hideously through the snow. She thrust down into its belly, heard the hiss of expelled air, and then only silence, people crying, and hoof beats.

Thomas turned his horse. The rest of the party were cresting the hill.

'Don't bother hurrying,' yelled Pearl. 'We'll just take the pack on single-handed!'

'Shh,' whispered Thomas, wrapping his arm over her, gripping her tightly. 'Shh, it's over.'

She wiped her face and found her hand drenched in blood. She twisted to look at Thomas, also spattered in crimson, and he saw the terror in her eyes. She was shaking violently against him.

'You see, Prince Gilbert?' he called. 'You were right! The princess is a hunter without parallel!'

His embrace held her upright as she slackened against him.

* * *

Late that night, the door's creak woke Pearl. Her eyes flew open. Heavy tapestries hung at every window, blotting out all moonlight, and thick drapes shrouded the bed. Her hand moved quietly to the truckle bed under her own and found her swordhilt. She twitched the curtain to one side – only dying embers lit the room, but against them a slim silhouette, on tiptoe, was just discernible. It approached. Sighing inwardly, she let go of the sword.

'Princess Pearl,' declaimed the shadow squeakily. 'Too long have I lain awake with longing for you – as you have surely done for me.' The separation between each word suggested he'd learnt them by heart. He opened the drape, fumbling for her in the dark. She rolled her eyes, wondering how to send him away without wounding his pride too badly. To her astonishment, he was already climbing in beside her.

'Do not be afraid, fairest of women! It is only my excessive love that brings me here, where I may demonstrate it more fully.' His small body wiggled closer.

On the other side, Thomas raised his head with interest.

'I don't think the princess is afraid, Prince Gilbert,' he said gravely.

The prince screamed, sitting bolt upright.

'All the same,' he went on, in a fatherly tone, 'when you want to seduce a woman, it's always advisable to check the bed for other suitors first. Otherwise, you put her in a very awkward position, you see.'

Pearl forced the bedcovers into her mouth to muffle her laughter. Gilbert leaped off the bed, babbling, 'My lord knight – Sir Thomas – I had no idea . . .'

'No idea of what?' Thomas's voice was harder. 'That the princess was engaged – the very reason for your invitation to Kwestriminotha? Now get back to your own bed and leave us to ours – unless you want to take me on in single combat?'

As the door slammed behind the terrified prince, Pearl doubled over in guffaws. 'Oh, that poor child!'

'He's lucky he's a child,' said Thomas, smiling despite himself. 'If he'd been a man, I wouldn't have been so kind.'

'And I'd have used the sword in my hand.'

They snuggled back into each other's warmth and Thomas sighed. 'You said they'd all still be hoping for marriage. I just didn't expect them to be so bloody obvious about it.'

'It doesn't bother me,' said Pearl tiredly. 'What worries me is the trade agreements.'

'Still haggling?'

'Mmhmm . . . if they're not signed, our whole plan falls apart. I'd depended so much on Daddy doing the negotiations.'

'He's no better?' asked Thomas softly.

'No better and no hope.' Pearl's voice cracked and she rolled closer into the bulwark of her lover's body. 'It's all we can do to hide that he's dying.'

The Necklace

Pearl sat rigidly as Fern twisted strands of hair into fine plaits, while the servants ran back and forth at Shanon's instructions. Elaine nervously held up a cluster of holly, the berries brilliant in the dark green leaves.

'The witch hazel's not in flower, so I thought we could make a wreath of...' She trailed into silence before Pearl's disbelieving stare.

'With a yellow dress? Red, yellow and green – whose colours are those, Elaine?'

'Cantaland's,' stammered the lady-in-waiting. She was close to tears. 'But your highness – I can't *make* it bloom...'

Pearl swore. 'Do I have a green dress, Shanon? That's a Minothan colour, at least.'

'No, your highness – but you do have the red one, with the silver edging.'

'Fine. Red for love, then. And the holly wreath.'

'I thought red was for blood.' Thomas strolled in, still scruffy and sweaty from his morning's sword practice. His linen shirt sleeves were rolled up and his hose mud-stained. 'Or for anger.' He winked at Pearl and her eyes softened.

'You're not dressed for the ball yet?'

'My squire's polishing my armour so fiercely you'll see your own pretty face in it all night.' He glanced at the overladen table. 'Are all these our presents? Can we play at guessing?'

'You should know better, Sir Thomas,' said Shanon reprovingly. 'It's bad luck to know the giver.'

Fern looped the last plait into a stiff curl.

'Go get yourself ready now, Fern,' said Shanon. 'I'll get your dress, your highness.'

Thomas's face lit up. 'Are you naked under that sheet?'

Pearl giggled and, as the two ladies left the room, flashed it open. He'd barely glimpsed her breasts, the crease of her waist and the tuft of curls before it was demurely closed again and Shanon brought in the red gown. Thomas turned back to the table to hide the hardness lifting his shirt-tails and, trailing her sheet, Pearl joined him.

'What's this?' She lifted a piece of tabby-woven linen, embroidered with script inside a floral border. 'A poem?'

Shanon dropped the gown. 'Your highness – that's the elves' pattern!'

'Oh, really?' Pearl cast an amused glance at her whey-faced lady. 'Let's see what the elves have to say to us, then...' She read out loud.

May the gold and the white, the green and the blue,
Receive in their bed a new lease.
May the union seal forever the two
In loyalty, conquest and peace.
May she always be vain of the colours of home
Before she is vain of her own.
May he always forgive and his pride never roam
In anger, away and alone.

'Very pretty, Shanon.' She laughed. 'But your embroidery's better than your poetry.'

'I didn't make it! It's a riddle from the elves. Look at the pattern – Sir Thomas, you're Minothan, tell her!' Shanon was outraged.

Thomas smiled. 'It *is* the elves' pattern – every Minothan knows it well.' He winked.

'Well, then, let's decipher our riddle. "The gold and the white" – that must be Kwestria – "the green and the blue", that's Minotha. "Their bed", I'm Kwestrian and you're Minothan, so that must be our bed – the union... now whatever can that mean?' She sniggered.

'Your highness should dress,' said Shannon tightly.

Pearl dropped the sheet and Thomas turned away hurriedly.

'These elves know you well,' he said over his shoulder. 'They warn you against vanity.'

'And you against pride and stubbornness,' she retorted, 'so they know us both. Careful, Shanon – your brooch is undone.'

'Yes, your highness.' Shanon went on pulling the laces tight over Pearl's bosom.

'Aren't you going to close it?'

'I'd rather not.'

'What? You could prick someone.'

Shanon shrugged implacably. 'I was asked to leave it open.'

'Who on earth by?'

'The elves,' she said quietly.

'Oh, for goodness sake!' snapped Pearl. Thomas chuckled.

Shanon raised her head, eyes flashing. 'Your highness may make fun of my beliefs, but Sir Thomas of Minotha should know better. The way a scarf is draped –'

'May change the world's course,' completed Thomas. 'We won't tease you any more, Shanon, it's good to follow the old ways.'

'As should you,' said Shanon sternly, turning away.

Thomas looked back at Pearl, now fully dressed, who shrugged.

'Your necklace.' Shanon held out a gold chain with an enamel pendant in yellow, white, blue and green.

'I can't wear that with red! Thomas, there was a red choker among the presents – can you see it?'

He held up a thick band of glittering rubies, tiny diamonds between them throwing rainbows.

'Oh, it's perfect,' she breathed. 'And the diamonds will pick up the silver exactly.'

'Your highness!' cried Shanon. 'The poem says the colours of home!'

'Don't be ridiculous, I won't be mismatched for your old wives' tales. Thomas, give me the choker.'

He hesitated and Shanon thrust the gold chain into her hand, saying, 'You must wear it!'

Angry, Pearl flung it across the room. 'And I would if your precious little elves had made the witch hazel flower and I was in my yellow dress! I'm a princess, not a country-girl with one piece of jewellery that she wears with every outfit! I am a princess and I will damn well look the part!'

She stopped, aware of their stares. 'I'm sorry,' she said stiffly. 'I have more important things than superstitions on my mind right now. And they weigh heavily.'

She breathed deeply to force the anxiety from her face. Taking the choker from Thomas's unresisting hand, she hooked it around her neck and kissed him. 'Go and dress, my love. Your armour should be shiny by now. And Shanon, get someone to fetch me a glass of wine.'

At the ball, Pearl's tension didn't ease. Rather, it manifested itself as an arrogance that even Thomas found insupportable. When she flirted with Prince Gilbert, drawing him out of his mortified silence, Thomas said in a low voice, 'Don't – you're encouraging him.'

'So what?' she retorted, quietly. 'He's a boy, now, but he'll be a prince to reckon with one day – I'd rather he remembered me flirting than throwing him out of my bed.'

'I'd rather he stopped trying to get in your bed,' muttered Thomas, but she'd turned the beam of her attention onto Kardan, the thin-faced Udian duke. She kept pressing her guests to drink more of the lovely Kwestrian wine and as their faces turned redder, they leered and joked more suggestively with her. She only wet her lips in her own wine – she was giddy enough with the attention, feeding off her admirers.

At the end of the evening, she gave Thomas a look of pure hard triumph.

'Now we'll see how my negotiations go,' she crowed softly.

'Would your father approve?'

Her eyes flared with angry pain. 'My father is *dying*. I must secure his kingdom's safety. Don't wait up for me.'

He lay waiting anyway, watching the shadows until the candle died, then listening to the last whispers of the fire. The door creaked slowly and shut again. He heard her struggling to undo her dress and he stared up at the dark canopy. Her behaviour had upset him and he felt the pain hardening like stone. Was the Queen Pearl going to be cold and supercilious, like this? *She has a lot to bear right now,* he reminded himself. *The loss, the responsibility – no wonder she hides her softness.* He got up.

'Let me help you with that.'

By candlelight he unknotted the ribbons, front and back. He avoided looking at her still-haughty face.

'Any luck?'

'A little – not enough yet.'

He carried the candle to the ledge behind their bed and she sat up next to him.

'You haven't told me exactly what you're trying to do. Am I allowed to know?'

'Of course. We want to control the supply of war goods, firstly – so that Udia's metal and Cantaland's timber pass through us, but no one would sign that straight and simple, so we're detouring everything through the lesser goods. Well, I say lesser, but that's the second stage, introducing luxuries that people won't want to live without, eventually that will put brakes on the war machines.'

He frowned, not following. 'So what are you arranging with Udia?'

'Their metal for wine, timber and wool.'

'But we have metal –'

'Obviously! But I've told them our mines are almost dead, and they're happy to get the timber from us instead of Cantaland.'

'Do we have enough? The Minothan forests are sacred...'

'We're getting it from Cantaland, along with extra sheep, and giving them metal, fruit, brandy...'

'But we have plenty of sheep –'

'That's not the point! It's midwinter, they can't see our flocks, I've said they're plagued. And that's our excuse for not selling them salt, we'll supposedly need it to salt our slaughtered stock.'

'Why aren't we selling them salt?'

'So they have to get it from Udia, in exchange for silk – I've had all the Udian guests put in silk-lined beds, so they get a feel for it. This way, those two are trading, but we control Cantaland's metal supply. Plus, if Udia wants to invade us, they'll need timber.'

'But if we're selling it to them...?'

'Honestly, Thomas!' she snapped, flinging herself down to sleep. 'That's what "control" means!'

He paused, mastering his own anger. 'Don't be impatient. I'm just asking.'

'Well, you're being deliberately stupid.' She rolled on her side. 'I need to sleep.'

He curled to spoon around her, but she lay unresponsive in his arms. When he tried to kiss her neck, his lips met the cold stone of the choker.

'You're still wearing your jewels,' he whispered.

'It doesn't *matter*,' she mumbled. 'Let me sleep.'

The next night, Pearl stole in even later. The fire had been rebuilt and Thomas was sitting at the table in his hose and shirt. She stopped in confusion. He looked up at her, then back at his goblet of wine.

'How did it go?' he asked blandly.

'Quite well, I think.' She started walking past him, but he caught her wrist.

'And you do your negotiations alone? Why not let your father's counsellors help you?'

'Those old men?' She laughed scornfully. 'They can't even follow my thinking! Lord Payden's the only one with any grasp, and he's in bed with lockjaw – thanks to Shanon's stupid brooch.'

'So you work alone.' He still held her arm.

'Yes.'

'And how does that involve kissing Duke Kardan?'

Her face whitened. Recovering quickly, she snatched her hand away and folded her arms. 'So you followed me.'

His hands shook as he cupped the goblet. 'Under the circumstances, I think I did right.'

To hide her trembling, she strode toward the fire. His eyes met hers, accusing and pleading at the same time. Her face tightened.

'Well, Pearl?' His voice was tense. 'You're my fiancée – I think I have a right to ask.'

She looked away as he approached. His hand fluttered, as if to take hers, then sank again. 'My love ... please.'

'I will be queen – the kingdom comes first – I will do what I have to do for my kingdom.'

'For your kingdom,' he echoed, disbelievingly. He could still see how her body had yielded against Kardan's, her face lifting, their mouths meeting – then the kiss had gone on and on, their hands groping through each other's clothes. It hadn't looked like self-sacrifice. Even the memory made bile rise in his throat, however many times he'd washed it back down with wine.

'Yes!'

'And how far are you prepared to go – *for your kingdom*?'

Her slap stung him across the cheek and mouth. His body tensed as if to pounce, but he didn't move. His eyes bored into her. Turning, he lifted his doublet from the table and shrugged it on.

'I won't see you tomorrow,' he said. 'I think I need to be alone.'

He left. She looked numbly at the hand that had hit him, then stared unseeing at the empty room, trying to feel what had happened. Absent-mindedly, she stroked the rubies at her throat.

She unrolled the treaty again on the table in Kardan's room. If Thomas knew she was here, she thought – but she hadn't seen Thomas all day. She could sort that out later; this took precedence. Kardan was reclining elegantly in his chair, one eyebrow half raised in amusement.

'I had thought eighteen gallons of wine,' she said, 'but we can change that. How much of our sweet wine will it take to persuade you?' She was struggling to concentrate. Since she'd stepped warily into his room, lust had tingled unbearably in her.

He leaned forward slowly and her eyes rose to meet his.

'I don't think I'll need much persuasion.'

She flinched; he laughed.

'But as for your treaty – no. I see what you're after, my clever little princess.'

'What?' she said, feigning innocence.

He shook his head, smiling. 'Peace, of course. The same as us. But your little plan won't work. It's too late, Cantaland's already too strong. Why do you think they sent that baby of a prince? They want you to think they want marriage – but they don't need you on their side, any more than they need Tarpash.'

Her throat dried with shock, as she realised he was right and she was a fool. Prince Gilbert's suit was laughable – why hadn't she seen through that?

'We also want peace,' he murmured. 'If Cantaland gets Kwestriminotha...'

'We can stand against them,' she said tightly.

'Against all their knights, Princess? And what about your people, on the Minothan border? They're only safe while Cantaland looks west, to us.'

She smoothed out the useless treaty. 'What do you want?' she asked quietly.

He lifted her hand and pressed his lips to it. 'As duke – an alliance. As Kardan ...' He let the words float, unfinished, in the air. His mouth drew her finger in and lapped deftly around it.

'An alliance,' she repeated, her throat dry.

His tongue touched the soft web of skin between her fingers. 'Cantaland grows strong. They raise knights like soldiers. Already, they're turning against Tarpash.' His voice was low and hypnotic as he recapitulated. At each phrase, his lips parted, brushing her hand, sucking lightly. Between the shivers of sensation and inexorable flow of his words, she was mesmerised.

She stayed where she was, staring at the table, when he relinquished her hand and walked around to stand behind her. His hands rested on her shoulders, warm and slender.

'Your intelligence hasn't failed you,' he said. 'You saw clearly – for peace, we need balance. But Cantaland is too strong. In the opposite scale, we need both our countries.' His hands slid over the swell of her breasts, under her gown, cupping her. Her nipples stiffened. His fingers caught them, rolling and pinching until she whimpered out loud.

'Peace,' he said insistently.

'Yes,' she croaked.

With one movement, he tore her gown open, ripping the bodice and her shift, laying her breasts bare. He swung her chair around, kneeling to her level as his hands groped her roughly.

'I think, my princess, you have met your match.'

'Duke ...' she began. He grasped the waist of her skirts and yanked hard, his delicate hands surprisingly strong. She was naked, only the tattered bodice still hanging over her shoulders. His hand folded possessively over her mons.

'We are natural rulers, you and I,' he said. 'We do what we must for the world. We can't afford the softness other people enjoy – but I think we can still enjoy some things.'

His hand twisted, one finger pushing into her. She reeled, rocking instinctively onto it, as he shoved two fingers into her wetness, urging her on dispassionately.

This is madness, said her mind coldly, *and it must stop*, but her hips bucked. Again, her lack of emotion struck her. She felt nothing for this Kardan. Any grief or anguish for Thomas, which surely she must be feeling, was locked away. Only her body responded and she was grateful – at least, while this burning lust gripped her, she wasn't completely numb. She clenched around him, rubbing back, fighting toward orgasm, but he whipped his hand away and hauled her to her feet. The last shreds of her clothes fell off her and his throat rasped in hungry admiration. He laid her on the table, lifting her legs so her heels tucked against her bum. Her legs splayed to his hand which returned to shove in and out. Gripping her heels, her knees wide apart, she rolled her head back, striving for satisfaction against his fingers. Dimly, she was aware of him undoing his own clothes, but she let the lust blind and deafen her to everything else – it was so close now, so close, she would come and it would all end . . . He stopped, and she yelped.

One hand pressed inside her thigh, her skin quickening to his warmth. His other hand guided his narrow cock into her and she closed her eyes, not wanting to see its unfamiliar shape, but hungry to feel. His first thrust pushed her backwards along the table and he dragged her closer to him. He leant over her, his face level with her rigid nipples, and began to pump. With each shove, his balls slapped lightly against her. He grabbed her shoulder, to tug her against him, and clasped her breasts, watching how she grew wilder with each rough squeeze.

'Yes, Princess,' he said hoarsely. He yanked her to him, as deep as he could go, and lay hard over her, forcing her to be still. His lips parted hers and drew long kisses from her. As their tongues meshed, he could feel her secret places clutching around him. He groaned, sinking down to her throat, maddened by her naked breasts on his chest. He wanted to fling himself savagely – but this first time, at least, it was imperative that he pleased her. He licked the choker and the skin of her neck below it, as she squealed.

'You like my gift, then,' he said. 'I'm glad – it suits you.'

'It was from you?' she gasped.

'Oh, yes,' he said, 'my aunt made it specially,' and his hips began to move again, gliding, gradual, making her moan, then speeding up, and at last slamming while she screamed under him. With her arms flung behind her, her breasts pointed skywards.

'On my breasts,' she gasped, twisting and pointing them. 'Come on my breasts.'

His lust trebled – her request was dirty, sluttish, and excited him beyond all control. He gave a few last thrusts then yanked out, spraying deliciously all over her shameless tits.

The sky was fading from black to dark Prussian blue when she returned to her rooms, holding the ruined bodice closed. A shape stirred in the darkness and stood. Thomas's familiar bulk was silhouetted against the window.

'Pearl.' His voice was rough from sobbing. 'My love – what have you done?'

She stood frozen, waiting for the prick of tears, but her eyes were dry and her face immobile.

'Did you get what you wanted?' he asked bitterly. 'Are your precious treaties signed?' She could hear he was still crying.

'No,' she said distantly. 'It won't work. I must marry the duke.'

'No!' It was more like an animal's cry of pain than a word.

She wished he would leave before the growing light showed him the state of her clothes.

'You can't!' His voice cracked.

'It's for the kingdom,' she said dully and walked through to sit on her bed. None of the curtains were drawn and the fire had long since died. Bleak, chilly dawn crept through the glass.

He knelt at her feet, his features more discernible now. His cheeks shone, wet; black bruises lay under his eyes; his mouth twisted in misery. Her fingers remembered his tousled hair, but she didn't slide them into it. As he registered the frayed edges of her bodice, he cried harder, but didn't speak a word of blame – only, 'Pearl, my darling – what's happened to us?'

My heart is like the sky, she thought. *White and cold.*

'Won't you even speak to me?' he pleaded, his hands on her knees.

'I don't see what there is to say.'

For a while, he just looked at her. Then he backed off, his face working. 'How about "I'm sorry"?'

She registered a terrible pang, but so far away that it was only a faint echo. Nevertheless, it raised a flicker of guilt and she surged with anger – what else could she do?

'I am a princess,' she said harshly. 'I don't say sorry. I do my duty for the kingdom.'

His fists curled as he turned his shoulders away. 'So this is the end of it, of all our love? Just like that?'

'I'm marrying the duke, I must, but we can still –'

'Never!' he shouted. 'I'll never share you. I'll take you back, even now –' his voice was breaking again, between rage and grief '– I would die for you, but I won't share you. Pearl, please . . .'

'You don't understand what a kingdom requires!'

His muscles bunched. He stared hard at her, trying to see through this new stranger to his true love, feeling his wrath grow as her words echoed in his head.

'Then I quit my service to the kingdom,' he ground out at last. He walked out of her rooms, out to the stables, and then rode out of the castle, angry and alone.

'Daddy,' whispered Pearl, kneeling at his bed. The sleepless night had left her head dull. The stuffy warmth of his bedroom made her eyelids droop, but his hand was cool. 'I've done something. Something irreparable.'

He stirred and his wandering eyes found her. His hand gripped hers weakly. 'My little Pearl.'

'I'm marrying Udia.'

'That's nice,' he murmured. 'Who's Udia?'

She laid her forehead against his arm, so he wouldn't see her despair.

King Jarod died a few days after the new engagement was announced, leaving his daughter, now queen, to make her own marriage negotiations.

The queen's ladies sat in the outer room, listening in silence to the raised voices within. Outside, the snow was dwindling and in the green clumps of exposed grass snowdrops bobbed and waved their drooping heads. Elaine and Fern embroidered; Shanon worked at the queen's table, sorting documents and tallying costs. Something metal struck a wall and clattered onto the ground. The three women shared a glance. Pearl and Kardan's relationship was punctuated by screams – sometimes of passion, sometimes of rage.

'How *dare* you?' Pearl's voice screeched. 'I am *queen*!'

'And I will be your king and you will obey me,' roared Kardan.

Wearing only her shift, she drew herself up to her full height, her eyes glinting as hard as the diamonds at her throat, nesting between the rubies. Her nose curled with disdain. 'You will never be king,' she said witheringly. 'Oh, we can fight the terms till the sun grows old, but I will never set an Udian king on the throne of Kwestriminotha. Really, Kardan, are you so stupid?'

He stared, stunned. 'You never intend to marry me?'

'Oh, I'll marry you, I'll even bear little half-Udian heirs, but you'll wear a consort crown or nothing. This kingdom is mine.' Despite her anger, she cursed her impetuous words – that bargaining chip had been useful.

He stalked across the room, grabbed her arms, and shoved her back against the wall. 'I won't be ruled by a woman.'

She strained back from his face. 'You will be ruled by the queen,' she said contemptuously.

'Queen?' He barked with laughter and pushed his groin against hers. 'You're nothing but my whore.'

She wrestled to get free, feeling her blood rise as their bodies rubbed. His shaft bulged in his tights and he forced her hand down onto it.

'Only a whore fucks men so freely.' Trapped in his hand, her fingers were dragged up and down his stiffening cock and his breath came faster.

She felt the answering heat between her own legs, but said coldly, 'And that comment is just another reason you'll never be king.'

'You'll do what I want in the end.' He spun her around, her face flat against the hanging tapestry, and lifted her shift. 'You always do.'

His fingers scrabbled between her slick lips, checking her wetness, then the hard tip of his cock pushed in. As he stabbed into her, he wrenched the wide-necked shift down to her elbows, pinning her arms at her sides. The stiff tapestry chafed her cheek and breasts as his jerks rubbed her against the wall. He groped her bottom, slithering inside her – she was dripping, as always.

'My whore . . .' Thinking of her like that always made him hotter and he repeated the words for his own pleasure. He twisted her away from the wall; she half fell, just catching herself with her trapped arms. With her legs together, bent over in front of him, she was tighter and he groaned as he drove back in. Crouched on the ground, Pearl felt him slamming deep into her, his hips smacking her bottom, and thought of nothing but the sensations rising relentlessly. Let him think he was using her, let him think he would get his way with her throne as he did with her body. Her heart was steel, but her lust for him burnt. A finger dug into her anus and she gasped with fierce pleasure, doubly penetrated.

'Filthy whore,' he moaned, galloping against her, racing to his peak, but she was there ahead of him, clawing at the ground and squealing, then whipping away so that he sprayed on her back. He bellowed with fury, trying to plunge back in, but the last of it was already spurting helplessly. He knew her trick, now – she wouldn't let him get her pregnant. Some day, he promised himself, he would tie her down and take her at his leisure, jetting inside her, drenching her womb with his spunk. She was already dressing while he still knelt, his cock dribbling, and cold rage rose. It was no use marrying her, now. Without the throne, the whole thing was pointless. He'd say nothing, he'd get more pleasure from her yet, but he needed a new plan.

'I have to go to Udia,' he said, standing.

She shrugged indifferently and he fought the urge to slap her. This joke of an engagement must go on a little longer. It was time to visit his aunt.

'I'll be gone for some months,' he said.

'Fine.'

As she opened the door, the three ladies turned hastily back to their work.

'Your majesty,' said Shanon, 'you're wanted in Lord Payden's rooms.'

Pearl sat on a stool, leafing through papers. A few servants hovered, waiting to clean out the room, and the counsellor who'd sent for her stood by the door with the guards. Chill wind gusted through the room, rifling at the pages, carrying away the sour smell of death. Lord Payden's emaciated corpse had already been carried away.

She glanced up. 'Lord Elmer, will you send for my head lady-in-waiting?'

She'd planned to hold the funeral tomorrow – now the body would be flung to the sharks or dumped in a ditch. She toyed with the idea of putting his head on a spike, as they had in the old days, but that was too barbarous and the flesh would stink. She returned her eyes to the papers in her hand, but stared through them at her own thoughts. Shanon's soft cough broke her reverie.

'Can we have the room?' said Pearl.

As it emptied, she looked up at her lady. 'Lord Payden died this morning, Shanon. He died of lockjaw, I suppose, but in the end of starvation – we couldn't get any food into him. It was a horrible, very painful death, and he was one of my most trusted counsellors. He was in charge of trade, you know.'

'Yes, your majesty.' Shanon was impassive, but her face whitened.

'It was your brooch that infected him. Did you know that?'
The woman nodded.

'And under his body, they found these.' She waved the sheaf of papers. 'Dated the very day he fell ill. These are letters for Cantaland, Shanon – meant for Prince Gilbert's retinue to carry, I imagine. In here, he agrees to rig the border checks on the trade barges from Cantaland. Hidden in the hull, under the deck, there were going to be soldiers. Sneaking in, sailing down into Alvey Port, right into the heart of the country.'

She studied Shanon's shocked face carefully. 'Did you know he was planning this?'

'No.'

'Thanks to your brooch, we've escaped an invasion.'

'Thanks to the elves, ma'am,' she replied.

Pearl nodded thoughtfully and looked out the window. Lord

Payden's rooms were in the same tower that hers had been, before she moved to the royal rooms fronting the port. She stood and leaned on the sill, overlooking the restless sea, remembering how she'd teased Shanon that day. *The last day of my happiness*, she thought, and she tugged restlessly at the necklace around her throat.

'How do the elves speak to you, Shanon?'

'Different ways, ma'am. They can give a sign, a pointer, with their pattern in the dust or flour or snow or anything. Or leave riddles. Or just a thought, but a strong one. Sometimes they speak to me.'

'You see them?' Pearl found she could believe in the message, now, but not in the elves themselves.

'No – it's like someone whispers in my ear. They don't like to be seen. Your majesty . . .' Shanon hesitated.

'Yes?'

'I didn't think you wanted me to speak about the elves, but I have a request.'

'Go on.'

'They said I should bring my little brother here, from Minotha. Rian.'

Watching the white flecks of kittiwakes swoop and dive into the wide sea, Pearl smiled to herself. When Shanon had first arrived, all she'd talked about was Rian; no doubt, she still missed him.

'If you want your brother, he's welcome at my court, Shanon,' she said indulgently, turning around. Shanon's smile lit up her own heart, then Pearl faltered, quickly downcast again. Doing someone a kindness felt so sweet. When had she last been kind? She fidgeted with her choker, thinking how apt the name was; it always seemed to sit on her windpipe, lately, suffocating her.

Midsummer had passed before Kardan returned to Alvey Castle. By then, Pearl was too busy to argue the terms of their marriage – trouble was brewing in the country. For the first time in twenty generations, the union between Kwestria and Minotha was teetering. She and Kardan used each other quickly and roughly in bed, then went about their separate business.

In the great hall, she sat on the throne with the counsellors ranged in a semi-circle on their chairs. She wore her full royal regalia, from the crown to the sword strapped at her side. Until she had their trust and they hers, formality would remind them of her rank. Everyone was shouting and she slammed her hand on the throne arm for silence.

'Lord Elmer – you first.'

'Your majesty,' said Elmer, 'all the reports say the same thing – a man is travelling from place to place, persuading the Minothans that you only care about Kwestria. The way you threw over Sir Thomas is considered the final proof.'

'If the union breaks, our enemies can eat us in chunk-sized pieces,' said Hudson.

'But Thomas is one Minothan – not the whole of Minotha,' said the queen.

Lord Sheldon cut in. 'You underestimate how popular he is in his own country. The Minothans trust him. If it comes to the crunch, they'll follow him, not you – all this trouble shows that.'

'He's trying to start an uprising against you,' said Lord Royce angrily. 'You must issue a death warrant!'

Her eyes glittered. '"Must", Royce?'

'Your majesty would be *well advised*, then,' he said sardonically, folding his arms.

She seethed, but breathed deeply – they mustn't see her lose control. When she spoke, it was in measured tones. 'I will not believe that Sir Thomas is the one inciting all this trouble. I know him well, my lords, and there is no man on earth more honourable. He is not a traitor.'

'Blind as a love-sick puppy,' muttered Elmer.

'I beg your pardon?' She leapt to her feet, enraged.

He stared at her defiantly. 'You may think you know your erstwhile knight, your majesty – but we're men, and know men. And no man takes kindly to being cuckolded, thrown over in public, and replaced while his bed is still warm!'

'You presume, my lord!' she spat out. 'My bed is none of your business.'

'On the contrary, *your majesty*,' said Royce, 'the disorder of your bed is what's created this mess.'

Her cheeks turned bright red as she stared at him. 'My lord,' she began softly, her eyes narrowing.

The slide door opened and she turned sharply to see Shanon.

'We're in council!' roared Royce. 'Get out!'

Pearl held up her hand to silence him, facing Shanon. 'I hope this is important,' she said quietly to her lady.

'Yes, ma'am,' said Shanon, with a hostile glance at the counsellors. 'The elves told me to come, ma'am – my brother's arrived – he's with me.' She pushed forward a boy on the cusp of puberty. He shrank back against his sister before the imperious queen.

Lord Sheldon, sitting closest to them, had caught her words and threw his hands up in disgust. 'The elves!' he snarled. 'You'll listen to the elves before you hear your own advisers, I suppose.'

'This boy has just come from Minotha,' said Pearl slowly. 'Tell me, Rian, do you know anything about the stranger who tells people I don't love Minotha?'

He nodded, wide-eyed, then added, 'I've seen him, your royal . . . queen . . . highness . . . majesty.'

She smiled for the first time that day. ' "Your majesty" will do.'

Elmer leant forward. 'What did he look like, boy?'

'Um – he was tall – he had black hair.' He looked up at his sister for support as the lords grumbled in disgust.

'That's every man in Minotha,' growled Sheldon.

'Please, your majesty, I can draw him.'

'He's good, your majesty,' said Shanon, proudly. 'When he draws a wren, you can hear it sing.'

'Very well.' She led him to the table on the side and he leant over, scribbling, while the lords sat restlessly.

Wine was brought in and the men walked around, stretching their legs. Pearl stood apart, watching her counsellors keenly. Royce, Elmer and Sheldon were the most troublesome. She trusted and respected Elmer; she must punish his disrespect, but keep him. The other two had to go. The remaining four – Lyall, Maitland, Hudson and Camron – were apparently biding their time to find where the power really lay. She smiled grimly. If they thought her counsellors would rule her, they were mistaken.

Rian looked over from the table, wordlessly. Pearl crossed to his side and glanced down. Her blood cooled in her veins. The boy was gifted. On the paper, so alive that he might breathe, was Kardan.

'Bring Kardan,' she said flatly, to Shanon. 'Tell him – we need his advice, in council. Thank you, Rian. You can go.'

She turned to the lords, who were drifting back to their chairs, and held up the picture.

'You will say nothing when he is brought in,' she informed them. 'You are witnesses, only.'

As they waited, her thoughts ran over everything that had passed between Kardan and her, wondering if this had always been his plan, if their whole engagement had been a ruse to weaken Kwestriminotha. The more she thought, the more the choker tightened around her throat. Visceral memories of sex swamped her. When Kardan walked in, she nodded breathlessly to the guards waiting at the door and they fell into step behind him.

'So the queen finds she needs a king at last,' said Kardan complacently.

She regarded him as coldly as she could, her heart hammering. The guards took hold of his arms.

'What's this?' he demanded.

'You're a traitor,' she said hoarsely. She put her hand on her sword hilt. The choker constricted; she grabbed it, fighting for breath, and he laughed scornfully.

'You won't harm me. You're my thing. My plaything, my little whore.'

She tried to think of his betrayal, but her mind swam with him penetrating her. The counsellors watched, aghast, as she staggered toward him like a drunkard, her hands clutching her choker.

Kardan smiled knowingly. 'As long as you wear that, you're mine,' he said in Udian. 'You don't have the will to take it off.'

'You – underestimate – my – will,' she rasped. Close enough to smell his skin, she was light-headed with lust and asphyxiation.

He was chuckling as he pulled his arms from the guards' grip and slid them around her waist. The choker eased when she laid her body against his and she drew deep, grateful breaths.

'Feels good, doesn't it?' he murmured. His cock was stirring against her. The room was silent, the onlookers tense and bewildered. She strove to think of something which would give her strength, some concrete talisman against the spell which held her. Thomas was a blur – the castle, a shell – the country, just land – then her mind landed on the mandala. The two teardrops interlocked; in the gold, a drop of silver, and in the blue, a drop of green. His hands roamed her back and rump, guiding her to nest his erection between her thighs. Lust swelled. She fixed the mandala in her vision as her hand ran up his chest, down his arm, and onto her sword-hilt. As she stepped back and swirled around, she drew the sword in one fluid movement and completed the circle with its blade raised and level, running smoothly across his neck. He staggered back, clutching the wound, his eyes agape. He tried to speak, but blood hissed and bubbled at his throat. The choker strangled her like a noose. She could neither breathe nor utter a word, but she stepped back neatly as Thomas had taught her and ran the duke through. His wild eyes stared down at the new wound. When she pulled the sword out, he fell, and she stamped hard on his heart. Blood sprayed through both cuts; his eyes rolled up. As his head fell back, the choker fell open and tumbled off, its curse broken. Her sword tip on the ground, her dress splashed with Kardan's blood, she looked up at her counsellors.

'Remember this,' she said. 'This is how I deal with traitors.'

The Tangled Path

> Return to the path you lost.
> Give up what you love and seek
> Alone and before the frost.
>
> Then look for the craftsman swift,
> Protect the defenceless weak,
> And honour the humble gift.
>
> If all you can find's a dearth
> Of hope and the sky turns bleak,
> Then follow the tangled path.

Autumn tore at Pearl's heart. The trees turning to russet and crimson, the sharp smell of apples in the orchard, the chilly mists – each change engulfed her mind with memories of Thomas. Since ridding herself of the enchanted necklace, everything she should have felt over the last nine months was crunched into a single day, then at night she dreamt of him, and as she woke the pain rushed back. Five times a day, her eyes glossed with tears, but she let no one see her cry. In the evenings, she retreated gratefully to her rooms, where she didn't need to hide her true face. She curled up on the window sill in the dark, her forehead against the cold glass, and alone with her black grief she watched the lights of the port. A knock came at the door, then Shanon's low voice.

'Come in,' said Pearl, wiping her face and taking a gulp of wine.

Shanon began lighting the candles.

'No – with the light, I'll only see my own face in the window – I want to watch for messengers.'

'When they come, they'll come to you,' said Shanon firmly, holding the flame to another wick.

The princess sighed. She'd sent messengers to every town in Minotha and when they didn't return, sent armed men after them – but no one came back. Could Thomas be so angry that he imprisoned her men, or killed them? Even if his only reply were a curse, that would be no more than she deserved – and easier to bear than these empty days of hope souring. Uninvited, a memory smacked through her: on a black and orange night like this, Thomas and she had watched the sea through the candlelight reflections and he'd recited an old Minothan love story.

She waited until the sudden nausea passed, then said, 'Where's the riddle? I must check it.'

'Surely you have it by heart.'

'Yes, but – oh god, what have I done?' She pulled her hands to her mouth, her knees drawn up to her chin. 'What if I've misinterpreted it? All I want is Thomas – I see him everywhere, in everything, every face is his, every song the minstrels sing seems to be about him, so of course I think the riddle's about him! Why is it so cryptic, dammit! Why don't they just tell me what to do?'

'Some say that knowing your fate will change it.'

'But not knowing, I could ruin everything – all I see is what I want to see!'

'That doesn't mean it's wrong.'

'But it could be – the second line – *give up what you love –*'

'*What*, not *who* you love. Your majesty, we've been through this so many times.'

'Yes.' She emptied her goblet and refilled it, ignoring Shanon's reproving glance.

'You can't drown your sorrows.'

'I know.' Pearl grimaced wryly. 'They've learnt to swim.' She took a long sip anyway.

'Ma'am – it's no use following half the riddle.'

'Oh, not that old song again! This is no time for the queen to go galloping off on a wild goose chase.'

'If that's how you see it.' Shanon shrugged and turned away to sort through the papers. Just as her father had relied on her to pick up the excess work, so Pearl had come to rely on Shanon.

'I'm the queen – I can't risk my life and my kingdom! Maybe if I took an armed guard . . .'

'The riddle says alone. But if it's not important, marry Cantaland and have done.'

Pearl stared, shocked at her rudeness. The advice, though, was as sound as ever. She believed in the riddle or she didn't; all or nothing. This compromise wasn't working. She closed her despairing eyes and shielded them. *How much am I prepared to risk for Thomas?* she wondered, and knew the answer: every life in the kingdom, including her own.

'You do understand the political situation, Shanon,' she said levelly.

'Of course, ma'am. We believe Cantaland's armed and ready to move, Udia wants to avenge their duke, and the silence from Minotha's borders bodes ill.'

'And you still think I should go?'

'I still trust the elves' advice, yes. But you've left it very late to go before the frost.'

Pearl leant back thoughtfully. As her breath misted the glass, she traced the mandala on it and spoke slowly. 'I'm three counsellors short, what with Payden's death, and retiring Sheldon and Royce. And I find I'm tired of only hearing men's opinions – it suited my father, but not me.' She met Shanon's eyes and smiled faintly. 'Lady Shanon, this is long overdue. Will you join my council?'

* * *

Damp clung to the walls of the great hall, the huge fire only making the air sticky. The five lords were scowling; only Shanon remained serenely indifferent.

'Our only hope is to marry Cantaland,' said Lord Camron.

'Udia isn't so strong yet. We can hold them off,' said Queen Pearl from her throne.

'Not with Cantaland snapping at our heels! We can't fight both.' Camron folded his arms angrily, looking around for agreement.

'And we need an heir,' said Hudson. 'The sooner the better.'

'Then we'd better not look to Cantaland,' Pearl replied smoothly. 'Prince Gilbert won't be ripe for a few years yet.'

'So we find someone who is!'

Shanon's clear voice cut in calmly, speaking – apparently – to the air. 'Her royal majesty is not a brood mare to be put under the first available stallion.'

'I meant no disrespect,' said Hudson stiffly, glaring sideways at the lady.

'I have reached a conclusion.' Pearl gripped the arms of her throne. 'Sending messengers out for Sir Thomas has proved pointless.'

'Thank the heavens!' exclaimed Elmer.

Pearl continued as if he hadn't spoken. 'I've decided I must follow the riddle wholly or not at all.'

'Not at all would be a favourite,' Elmer muttered.

Her lips whitened with anger. 'Tomorrow, before the frost comes, I leave to look for him myself.'

Elmer exploded out of his chair. 'You must be mad!'

'Lord Elmer!' she cried sharply.

'You've thrown over one fiancé, killed the other, and now you want the first one back? And while you chase your lovers the kingdom must rot?'

'*Lord Elmer.*' She rose, hand on her sword-hilt, her eyes icy. 'Either your mind wanders so badly that you don't know what you're saying, or you're deliberately speaking like a traitorous dog.' With a hiss of metal, she half drew the sword. He was silent. 'You served my father well. For his memory, I'm loath to kill you. But one more word of insolence and I *will* overcome my reluctance and I will gut you where you stand.'

He sank back into his seat. She sheathed her sword but rested her hand on it as she stared them all down.

'Make no mistake. My men have their instructions. One whisper of insurrection while I'm gone and the culprit will be locked in irons to await my pleasure. Kardan died an easy death when I stamped on his heart. I won't be so kind if one of my own people betrays me.' She scanned their faces as she spoke. Elmer's lips compressed in grudging admiration that the princess had stopped play-acting and become queen. Hudson, Camron and Maitland paled.

'You three' – she pointed them out – 'are under house arrest until my return. While I'm gone, my seal and my authority go to my most trusted advisor, Lady Shanon. She'll act for me and disobeying her will be the same as disobeying me – punishable by death. In the case of war, Lord Elmer will command my armies.' She turned to face him. 'You proved your worth in my father's time. Now prove it in mine.'

As the lords left, three under armed guard, she gestured for Shanon to stay, and sat slowly.

'I threatened them to judge their reactions – I've never been so sorry to be right.' She looked at her lady. 'Are you sure you can stand up to Lord Elmer?'

Shanon suppressed a smile. 'Your majesty – I can stand up to my queen.'

Pearl laughed shortly, without humour. 'Is your queen so terrifying, then?'

'Yes,' said Shanon frankly. 'So I'm well prepared for Elmer.'

Pearl's fingers fumbled in the sharp cold as she dressed in Shanon's clothes and tied a woollen scarf over her hair. Until she knew the situation in Minotha, she'd keep her identity hidden. In the courtyard, the ground was hard and dawn light sparkled on the icy walls. The horse's breath misted. Pearl's heart sank at the sight of the frost, but she mounted without a word.

The ferry took her across the mouth of the joint rivers, her face hidden under the scarf, and she rode up the zigzagging cliff road into Minotha. At the top, she looked back at Alvey Castle, rosy in the sunrise, its flag dangling slackly on its pole, then cantered on, following the road blindly. Neither she nor Shanon had solved the second verse – 'the craftsman swift' could be anyone, anywhere – so she headed for Thomas's estate. Perhaps someone on the way would know about an unusually fast artisan.

Winding downwards through the great pines, the cold deepened and dampened. Condensation dripped from the needles and on every side the bare trunks repeated, sparse and disorientating, into a white haze. The horse's hooves thudded rhythmically. Branches creaked as their sap slowed. Her neck prickled as if someone were watching her – she turned sharply in her seat, but the road and woods were empty. Again and again she spun, only to find herself alone, until she decided that just checking had unnerved her. Nevertheless, her hand found the comforting hilt of her sword, hidden in her skirt. She couldn't imagine Thomas hurting or holding her messengers – something else might have picked them off, one by one.

At dusk, the road forked and she turned right, down toward the coastline and the nearest village. She saw it flickering between the tree trunks, dour and uninviting without lights burning or people moving. Nearer, she saw why. The houses stood roofless and charred, the mud dark with ash. Not a soul stirred. Picking her way down the deserted streets, she came to a small square. Her face contorted. Bodies were heaped high in a blackened mess, the flesh of their faces burnt away to expose grinning teeth. She shook with rage. *These are my people*, she thought, her jaw taut. In the last twilight, she searched the ground for tracks and the houses for clues, but what the fire hadn't eaten the rain had washed away. She rode back up the mountains and camped in the forest.

After that, she avoided the roads, weaving her horse between trees on the uneven slopes. The crab-apples and sour berries that grew along the coast were shrivelled to bitter nubs; she remembered Thomas saying that after the autumn equinox, the goblins pissed on the fruit. She saw few animals – only old fumets from the small Minothan deer, a handful of squirrels, and the occasional bird overhead. Under a rotting log, she found a nest of milk snakes banded dark red and white. She slashed them with her blade and tied them on a stick over a small fire. The meat was tender and buttery after days of hunger and she sucked it greedily off the bone – then hesitated, embarrassed, with that same persistent feeling of someone watching her.

Every settlement she passed along the coastline had been torched, the people piled and burned. Sickened, she turned inland and as she rode her heart screamed. Her subjects looked to her for protection; how could she not know what was happening to her own country? And where was Sir Thomas, the Champion of Minotha, while the corpses of his people were stacked in huge pyres?

The mountainous forests of Minotha formed a crescent around the country and the queen rode up through the mountains for several days, then down toward the fertile plains at the centre. In the distance, a small town nestled at the base of the slope by a river, smoke rising from its chimneys. As she approached, her heart sank. Rooftops, not hearth fires, were burning. Figures moved between the houses. Her eyes narrow with hatred, she assessed them – twenty, perhaps thirty – too many to take on in attack, but she could pick them off by stealth. She edged closer. They were too small for soldiers – one wore some kind of robe – then the robed one picked up another of the figures and she blinked, realising they were not the enemy but the survivors. She spurred her horse on, straightening in the saddle.

'I'm your friend!' she yelled as they scattered, terrified. She galloped over and leaped off her horse, her sword at the ready. 'What's happened here? Who's done this?'

Women and children stared blankly at her, their clothes torn and their faces bruised.

'You don't know?' said a woman. She shook her head in amazement. 'But Cantaland's overrun the whole country.'

'Cantaland!' Pearl stared at her in horror. 'This far south? Already? But why has no one told the queen?'

One of the other women laughed roughly. 'That bitch? As if she cares about Minotha!'

'But Kwestria will defend you –'

'Where are they then?' she yelled. She flung her arm to point at the ruined buildings. 'My husband, my sons, are murdered and burned. We sent warning, we sent word, but where's our queen now? She doesn't give a shit about Minotha, she proved that when she murdered our Champion!'

'*Murdered* him?' said Pearl, dumbfounded.

'Just like she killed the duke! Or didn't you hear about that either?'

'Yes – but the duke was a traitor – she didn't kill Sir Thomas!'

'Where is he then? He wouldn't leave us to our deaths like she does. No, she's killed him all right. Kwestria will never help us and we can't fight these knights.'

'Our only hope now is if Udia comes to protect us,' put in the first woman bitterly. 'They hate the Cantas as much as we do.'

Pearl stepped back, appalled. 'No – this isn't right – I can't . . .' Breathing fast, she pushed her hand into her horse's mane, holding it tight.

'Where have you been, not to know?'

'In – in the forest,' said Pearl. She let Shanon's lilting accent creep into her voice, fearing to sound Kwestrian.

'Ha! Looking for the elves, eh? But they've abandoned us just like Kwestria.' The woman spat on the ground.

Pearl looked from the desolate houses, their last flames mixing with the sunset, to the plains, then to the group of survivors. 'Are any of you trained to fight?'

They shook their heads. 'Those who were – they're already – there were too many.'

'The soldiers might return.' She thought of her maps; this part of Minotha had no forts or keeps. 'You can't stay here – there are caves in the mountains. Come.'

As they walked, distrustful glances fell on Pearl and when they arrived, the women avoided her, busying themselves over the children. She tethered her horse and left with her bow and arrow. A brace of wood pigeons softened their suspicions.

'The children will eat, at least,' muttered one of the women.

'It was all I could find,' said Pearl, pained at not having caught enough for everyone. 'The woods are bare.'

'Soldiers will do that to a country,' the woman said gruffly. She had an axe, its handle blackened but useable, and she began to split wood with surprising efficiency.

Pearl sat on a rock, hunched against the cold, watching her. 'You're good at that.'

'My husband's a boat maker. *Was* a boat maker,' she amended.

'I'm sorry,' whispered Pearl.

The woman spun around, her hand on her hip. 'Are you a Canta?' she demanded. 'Then don't apologise!' She wiped her face roughly and went on axing the wood. 'This is all the queen's fault.'

'The queen's,' echoed Pearl distantly.

'She should've kept faith with the Champion.'

'Yes. She should've.'

'And if she hadn't murdered that duke, Cantaland would never have attacked us. All we can hope is that Udia takes us over, instead.'

'Why do you keep talking about Udia?'

The woman gripped a log, splintering it for kindling. 'Something one of the soldiers said,' she muttered. 'Something about not leaving anything for Udia to rule over when they got here. We're feeble without Kwestria, but Udia's strong.'

'But how would they be better? They treat their women like cattle!'

'Better cattle than dead or raped,' she said bluntly.

Pearl blanched, looking with newly horrified eyes at the women quietly cradling their children or each other.

'What's your name, anyway?'

'Shanon,' said Pearl quickly.

'Not married, eh? Well, none of us are married any more. I guess I'm Widow Swift now.' She stuck her hand out. As Pearl shook it, the realisation ran like ice through her veins.

'Your husband – he was called Swift . . .'

'Kole Swift.' Her mouth twisted painfully. 'As fine a craftsman as ever there was. The world won't see the likes of him again.'

Pearl barely slept that night, curled on the bare rock. The fires were out, to hide their presence, and she lay staring into the dark, listening to the muffled sobs around her. She should have defended them. She should ride back to Kwestria for reinforcements – no, first she should follow the fresh tracks and see how many they'd be fighting, then go back – and while she did, what about the other towns in their path? Her sword-work would be valuable, her archery more so. A message, then – but they'd sent messengers. None had arrived; her own hadn't returned. She had to go back.

She turned over restlessly, the stone digging into her hips. Shanon would tell her to keep following the riddle, but she'd left it too late and the craftsman was dead. What about the rest? She recited it in her mind until she fell into a brief, disturbed sleep. She was shaken awake near dawn.

'Hush – hush!'

She stared at Widow Swift, crouching over her. 'Wha–?'

'You were shouting in your sleep – "Thomas, Thomas."' She touched Pearl's hair pityingly, the first gentleness she'd shown. 'Is that your young man's name?'

Pearl's mouth contorted. Unable to speak, she eventually shrugged.

Misunderstanding her uncertainty, the woman stroked her hair again. 'No news is good news, they say. He might yet be alive.'

Pearl closed her eyes as her stomach heaved. Disobeying the first riddle had cost her her true love and Kardan his life. Her delay over the second had killed all these people. If Thomas should be dead, because of her proud scepticism ... She stumbled out of the cave, gagging. As she knelt, wiping her mouth and shaking, she made up her mind. Doing things her way was causing untold damage. She'd obey the elves.

Leaving the survivors to their hideout, she followed the soldiers' tracks. The ground was pinched with cold and bare of snow, making the hoof marks faint, but she guessed that about fifty men rode together. She had only twenty arrows. *Protect the defenceless weak*, she reminded herself. If she brought some down without getting caught, she could get her arrows back from the bodies. If Thomas were riding with her, they could take on an army ... Her lips compressed.

The soldiers had moved east, alongside the forest, but wheeled slowly northwards with it. She frowned, puzzled. Something was amiss – something besides the wholesale destruction of her people. The southern coastal villages had been attacked before this last one, but Cantaland lay to the north. Why would they sneak down through the whole of Minotha then wreak destruction as they combed backwards?

On the coast, they'd killed everyone, but in the last town they'd spared the women and children. Why? She stopped her horse, staring at the ground, then slid off to crouch low. Her fingers traced the imprint of a horseshoe. Cantaland was low-lying and often muddy; their horseshoes were studded, to keep the animals from slipping. This print was smooth. Cold prickling ran over her skin. Colours could be changed, even armour, but no Canta knight would exchange his own battle-trained horse for another. She heard a rustle behind her and leapt to her feet, spinning and drawing her sword. The grassy knolls and dells, with their isolated humps of bushes, stood silent. No bird hopped out or flew up into the sky. It was a snake or a beetle, she told herself. She'd be grateful to eat either right now, but the soldiers were still riding.

Late in the day, she reached an oak grove on the forest's edge, the grass around it crumpled and torn. On her hands and knees, she rifled through the broken stems and found crumbs, then a mouthful of rough bread. She gobbled it, her jaw spasming with hunger as she tasted the honey and salt. This was Udian bread: she remembered Kardan complaining how bitter and bland the Kwestriminothan bread was. It was Udian soldiers who had slept here, had eaten here, and were now a full day's ride ahead. She stood fast, then swayed, grabbing her horse for support as the world blackened and whitened. Without eating, she'd never have the strength to catch up or fight them when she did. When her vision returned, her eyes raked the landscape. An eagle circled, poised to dive, and beneath it, less than a stone's throw from her, a squirrel crouched in terror. Her arrow was notched in a second; her mouth watered at the thought of the plump rodent roasting. She hesitated. *Protect the defenceless weak. So who's the defenceless weak now? The people who'll die if I can't save them? Me, starving and faint? The eagle, desperate for its meal? Or the squirrel, who could keep us all alive?* She had her bow and arrow, the eagle its claws. The squirrel had nothing. She tilted her arrow and as the bird swooped, claws straining, she knocked it out of the sky. The squirrel streaked past her, into the oak grove, and she sank. Eagle flesh was tough and rank, but it would do. When her strength came back, she'd fetch it. The squirrel was bounding back toward her and stopped, tame as a falcon, by her foot. With two neat paws, it removed the acorn from its mouth and chittered.

'You're welcome,' said Pearl ruefully. 'Though I think you'd have been the better meal.'

It presented the acorn in outstretched arms.

'Thank you, but I don't eat acorns.'

It withdrew the acorn for a moment, studied it gravely, then held it out again.

Honour the humble gift, thought Pearl bitterly, and opened her hand. The squirrel dropped its offering in her palm and squeaked.

'Thank you,' she said sadly as it scurried away.

No one was here to see her. With the acorn clenched in her fist, she folded her arms around her knees, dropped her head, and let despair wash over her. Even well-fed and at full strength, even trained by Thomas, how could she take on an army of fifty or more knights? Her plan was blind arrogance, nothing more. They'd slaughter her in minutes; if she brought down ten, forty would still remain to murder her people. Whatever she did now, people would die for what she'd already done. She raised her head, white and drawn with desolation, dry-eyed. Banks of slate cloud darkened the plains, as bleak and cheerless as her own heart.

She struggled to her feet, waited for the light-headedness to pass, and leaned heavily on her horse while she unbuckled its saddle. She lay against it, staring into the forest where a disused track was overgrown with brambles and tangleweed, leading into the darkness. *If all you can find's a dearth of hope* . . . She pushed the acorn into her pocket, pulled the saddle tight again, heaved herself up, and spurred the horse forward.

It pulled back disdainfully from the tangled path. Slumped on its back, she dug her knees in.

'Everything I've tried to do has ruined people's lives, or ended them,' she told it. 'So we're doing what the elves say, even if it makes as much sense as a silk shield.'

She woke on the ground, curled against the warm flanks of her horse kneeling beside her, still in its saddle. The tree canopy was dense, dull green, holding back the faint daylight. She rubbed her face against the horse's neck and pushed her hand under the saddle to loosen it.

'Sorry, you,' she murmured.

'And so you should be!' said a thin voice.

She jumped to her feet, her sword ready, swaying as her vision wavered.

'Treating the beast like that – it hasn't had a good day's grazing since you started.'

'Who are you? Where are you? Show yourself!' she commanded.

From a tall clump of ferns, a small creature stalked forward, goat-like and grinning. Its feet were cloven, its haunches shaped like an animal's and its body covered in hair, but it walked upright, arms akimbo. Its eyes were human-shaped and golden as a cat's; its ears started off in ordinary lobes, then rose above its head to end in sharp points.

'You can put your sword away.' It sang more than spoke. 'Who'll take you to the elves if you skewer me?'

She stared. 'Is that where the path leads – to the elves?' she demanded.

'More or less, in a way, round and about,' it trilled.

'Are *you* an elf?'

That tickled it into a fit of musical giggles. 'An elf! Me!' It capered from side to side, finishing in an extravagant bow. 'I am their humble servant, and your lowly guide through the living maze.' It stood up again, its head level with her waist.

She sheathed her sword. 'Lead the way, then.'

A grin split its ugly face and it shook its head. 'Oh, no. I can't *show* you the way.'

'Then how are you a guide?' she asked, irritated.

'In this way and that. I'll give you the odd prod.' To prove his words, he dug his finger hard into her ribs. 'Now which way do you want to go?'

'I guess I'll follow the path,' she muttered. 'There's only one.'

She turned her back and led the horse forward. She set a fast pace, pushing against her own tiredness, but the creature danced alongside her effortlessly. He wouldn't let her ride the horse, insisting that animals were free in the forest, and when she wanted to shoot a woodpecker for food, he screamed in horror. He led her instead to a sheltered stream where the horse and she could drink, and showed her soft white berries growing on the bank. They looked unhealthy, spongy as fungus, and tasted like dry flour, but they eased her hunger pangs. When he led her back to the path, it was forked.

'This isn't the same place!' she said angrily.

He shrugged. 'Find your way.'

Neither was more tangled than the other, so she chose the steeper path, reasoning that it would lead deeper into the mountains. That night, snuggled close to her horse, she thought of Thomas. *He's alive*, she told herself. *I'd feel it if he were dead. He's out there somewhere, real and breathing, my love, next to me but for the distance between us.* The thought was obscurely comforting and her face softened.

The creature pinched her sharply. 'Dreaming of Thomas?' he leered. 'Thinking he still wants you, after the duke's shoved his thing inside you every which way?'

She gritted her teeth, ignoring him. He curled up next to her, big-eyed.

'Oh, Thomas,' he whispered mockingly, 'my true love, I'm so sorry I spread my legs for Kardan every time he dropped his trousers, and now that I've killed him will you take me back? You see, I'm one lover short of a good fuck.'

To her humiliation, Pearl began to cry, swearing and slapping at him through her tears. His mood transformed instantly. Small and lithe, he darted between her flailing arms and curled on her lap, cradling her head remorsefully and caressing her hair with his little hands.

'I'm sorry,' he keened, 'I was cruel, I didn't mean to hurt you, I'll help you, you'll find him, it wasn't your fault, it was the necklace ... Shh ...' He kept soothing her until she nestled back down and drifted off to sleep.

The next day, he was true to his word. He stroked her hand as they walked, looking up at her with anxious pity. The path branched more often now, and every time he tugged her to show the direction.

'We've been here before,' she protested. 'I recognise that horse chestnut, the moss on its trunk – see that fungi on it, like shelves?'

'No, no, don't worry, I'll take you to him, I know he loves you,' he assured her.

She caught her breath. 'You've seen him?'

'Oh *yes* – and he's so handsome, so big and strong. This way, now.'

'He is, isn't he?' She smiled faintly, her heart swelling. 'I haven't asked you your name.'

'You can call me Puki. Now this way.'

He pulled her down another path and she stopped short. Its dim green twilight gave way to the sudden gold of a clearing. Even from a distance, she knew his shape instantly – knew, even, from the set of his shoulders, that he was deep in thought, his face stern. She dropped the horse's reins and ran.

'Thomas!'

He looked up, confused and remote, then joy dawned and he held his arms out to her. Almost crying, she flung herself into them – but instead of his warm chest and neck, she smacked into rough bark, grazing her face and falling back. Where she had seen Thomas, a tree stood, two branches roughly resembling arms. Shrieking giggles echoed behind her.

'Yeah, right,' wailed Puki in hysterics, 'like he's been hanging around in a clearing the whole time! Yeah, that's Thomas all through!'

'You bastard!' she howled, lunging for his throat. He ducked neatly and pranced around her in circles as she grabbed for him, chortling as if they were playing tag. At last she gave up and folded onto the grass.

'I hate you.'

His hand touched her hair. 'I'm sorry,' he said gravely. 'But I had to prove it to you, that I can't show you the way.'

'You *offered*.'

'You accepted,' he retorted. 'But come – shh, we will find him, we will, I promise. Come on, get up, that's it ...'

That night, Puki built them a rough tent while she took the horse to the stream. If Puki ate or drank, she never saw it. While the horse slurped, she scooped water into her own mouth and splashed her face. She opened her wet eyes to see a reflection fluttering in the running water. Her heart turned over as she raised her face. Thomas stood on the other side, his arms folded. His face was hard.

'Thomas ...' she whispered, pleading and frightened.

He shook his head slowly, though his throat tightened. 'These are my woods. You're not Minothan. You shouldn't be here.'

'But – I've been looking for you – Thomas ...'

'Well. Here I am. You found me, well done. You can go now.'

'But we need you!' Quickly, she described what she'd seen, but he interrupted her angrily.

'And what did you expect, Pearl? You made an alliance with Udia then killed their envoy! It's too late to fight back now, the country's overrun. A good queen would surrender before any more of her people died.'

Her eyes filled with tears. 'I will, if you think so. But Thomas, please.' She held out her hand across the stream. '*I need you.*'

His mouth twisted, but his eyes darkened. 'And you had me,' he said, 'and you threw me away. No, Pearl. Fix your kingdom if you can, but you can't fix what you did to us.'

'Please.' She began to sob, still on her knees. 'I'm so sorry – please.'

His eyes were wet. He shook his head. 'Never. You'll never have my heart – not any more. I wish I could love you again. But I can't.'

She doubled over, crying; the acorn fell from her pocket and she caught it. The horse whickered, raising its head. She looked up: Thomas was gone. The muddy bank didn't even bear his footprints. It was just another illusion, she thought, her heart sinking. But wherever he is, he must surely hate me that much. Sadly, she traced her way back to the makeshift camp where Puki was enthusiastically building a fire.

'Don't bother,' she said dully. 'It's no use trying to find him. We must go back. I have to surrender.'

'No!' he cried in dismay.

'It's no use, Puki. Come on.'

Dejected, he looked at the leaping flames he'd nurtured to life. 'All right,' he said reluctantly. 'But in the morning – I've made you a bed and a fire, get some rest and warmth, at least.'

She had no spirit left for argument. She curled up on the dry moss he'd scooped together under the leafy tent and lay watching the fire, heartsick, while he played his pipes. The melody yearned, soothing and lilting like a promise, and she drifted into sleep.

When she woke, only embers glowed. Thomas was crouched over her, shaking her gently. As she opened her mouth, he covered it with his hand.

'Shh – don't wake Puki. Pearl, you have to get away from him!'

'You're not here,' she said. 'You're just an illusion.'

'I'm not – you have to believe me! He's lying to you, tricking you, he'll get you lost and leave you here. Trust me!'

He looked so real, from the reassuring breadth of his shoulders to his dark brown eyes full of concern and love. Hesitantly, she put her hand to his face and felt the rough stubble.

'I'm so sorry,' she said tearfully. 'How can you ever forgive –'

He wrapped his arms fiercely around her, lifting her against his chest. 'Darling, it's OK, I know – it's not your fault, it was the spell – oh, my poor baby.'

She clung to him, still struggling to believe he was real though she could feel his warmth and smell his familiar skin. 'You're not a dream?'

'No.' He held her tighter. 'They trapped me here – I would never have abandoned you like that – but we'll get out together. Oh, darling, I love you, you came to find me.' His mouth found hers, she could taste his tears on his lips, feel the familiar way he turned his head to kiss deeper, and it was him.

'We'll never be apart again,' he said.

Her hands slid through his thick black hair as their mouths met more eagerly. His hands were sliding over her, gripping, as if to reassure himself she was really there.

'We must leave before dawn,' he panted.

'Before dawn,' she agreed, and they sank together onto the moss mattress. His hand slipped inside her bodice, over her breast, and she cried out softly. The night was still thick black and she fumbled hastily, untying the ribbons. When she guided his hands to her bared breasts, he moaned in ecstasy, rolling onto her, rubbing his cheeks against them. He was heavy, the ground hard under the moss, but if he'd crushed her she would have died willingly. Over and over, she stroked his arms, his large back, his hair, his neck, remembering his shape and finding it even more perfect than her memories. He pulled his own shirt open, laying his bare chest on hers.

'We'll go soon,' he said, 'I just – god, I want to kiss you, hold you . . .'

They whispered each other's names between kisses, fearful and tender, and their bodies moved cautiously against each other's through their clothes. This was how they'd lain long ago, before they'd ever made love, learning each other and terrified and desperate with longing. He pressed between her thighs, hard, and she wailed quietly. He held her close; his hand found its way under her skirt. She shivered as it crept up her thighs, she pleaded as he stroked her lips, and then one finger sank smoothly into her, parting soft flesh, probing, and her whole body pulsed around it. He bent over her face, kissing her, and only those twin connections existed: his lips on hers; his hand in her. He was moving so slowly; she wanted to linger forever and couldn't wait another moment.

'Please . . .'

'You want me?'

'*Yes* – always, forever.' She thrust her hands into her skirts to pull them up and got tangled in her pocket. As she fumbled, her fingers closed on the acorn. His solid weight vanished, but little fingers still scrabbled inside her. With a scream of disgust, she threw Puki off her.

'You filthy beast! You animal! You traitor!' she screeched. Her body still ached helplessly; her heart ripped. Puki was cowering, sulky.

'You liked it,' he said defiantly.

'I thought it was *Thomas*!'

'You could still think it's Thomas,' he said lasciviously, creeping forward.

'No!' She scrambled away. 'I only want Thomas if it's really him! Not a tree, not a dream, and not *you*!'

His eyes narrowed. 'Be careful what you wish for, especially in the land of elves. Are you sure?'

'Yes!'

'Even if it means you'll never see or touch him again?'

She faltered. Cold dawn was breaking, pale and gloomy under the forest's ceiling. Her heart stilled. 'Never?'

Puki raised his eyebrows.

She stared through him. 'Have I read it all wrong? All along – should I have given him up? And all those people are dead. Oh, god...' She grabbed his narrow shoulders, shaking him violently. 'You have to take me to the elves! I don't know what to do any more!'

He wrested himself free. 'Fat lot of good it would do you,' he said rudely. 'If you can't tell the truth apart from your own wishes and fears, how can the elves help you?'

'But I'm going the right way – I'm on the tangled path...?'

He laughed scornfully. 'You think this is the only tangled path in your kingdom? You don't know up from down, lady.'

'You're lying.' She stood, ripping his leaf canopy, and dusted the moss off her skirts. 'That's all you've done from the start.'

'Besides encourage you, and feed you, and keep you going, you mean? Besides protect you since you laid foot in Minotha?'

'That was *you* following me?'

'Yup. Keeping you safe, getting you here. How do you think you got through and none of the messengers can? Or did you just think you're so clever, perfect little Pearl, Daddy's princess? It was me, leading them astray, clearing your way.'

'But for *what*? You won't guide me! You know how to get to the elves, don't you?'

'Yes,' he said smugly, wriggling back against the bed.

Pure fury rose. 'Then why won't you tell me the way?'

'I don't know it.'

'But you just *said* –'

'Are you stupid as well as ugly? I told you, it's a *living maze*. You can't learn the route, it changes! You have to learn *how* to navigate it.'

She spun around, scrutinising the forest. There, rooted and

solid, was the same old horse chestnut with its moss and fungus. 'It's following me?'

He crossed his legs, his hands behind his head. 'It must like you. Maybe if Thomas liked you that much, he'd follow you too.'

'I'm through with you,' she said softly. The sword rasped out of its sheath as she advanced on him.

His eyes were saucers. 'I'm sorry,' he gibbered, shrinking back. 'He loves you, he worships you . . .'

'I'm tired of your lies. And trying to rape the queen is treason.' She lunged with her sword and it sank through him without resistance.

He grinned up at her, put his thumb on his nose, and waved his fingers. 'Ha-ha, tricked you!'

She pulled the sword back; it came away clean.

'You have to want to kill me,' he said, smirking. 'And as I'm your only hope of finding Thomas, you don't want to. Q.E.D.' He gestured with a flourish at his unharmed body. 'Want to stab me some more? Will it make you feel better? Go on, stick the sword in, make a grand gesture, vow you'll give up forever! *Yoo-hoo! Thomas! Pearl thinks you're dea-ad! She thinks you ha-ate her! She's giving up and going ho-ome!*'

Incensed, she swept the sword through his torso and he clapped his hands in glee. 'Oops! I'm not dead! Still hoping, eh?'

The blade whistled through his neck, stabbed into his heart, and slashed at his limbs, while he danced and mocked. When she finally halted, panting with exertion, he fell quiet. She sheathed her sword. The forest's silence resumed, full of faint rustles, drips, and distant birdsong. Puki regarded her solemnly, his hands clasped at his waist.

'The only way you'll stop hoping is if you stick that sword in your own heart,' he said quietly. His face cracked in a grin. 'So which way shall we go today? I'm sure the tree would like a walk.'

She sat down, her hand in her pocket, turning the acorn over. Her thumb ran over its rough cap and smooth nut. Puki was all truth and lies, changeable as the mazy forest, but this was real and consistent. When she touched this, she knew the truth.

'Don't despair,' said Puki tenderly, leaning over her. 'Deep in his heart, you're still his one true love.'

She gripped the acorn hard. 'I don't know that and nor do you,' she said harshly. 'All I know is that in *my* heart, he's *my* true love.'

She let go of the acorn. In the distance, between the trees, she saw Thomas. He didn't smile, but his eyes clasped hers. She touched the acorn; he flickered out of sight. *It's a maze*, she thought, and headed in the opposite direction.

For days they wandered, Pearl leading the way and choosing the tangents. She grew accustomed to Puki's irritating presence. His hurtful comments became background noise; they stung, but she no longer reacted. When he pinched her with his sharp small fingers, she winced, but said nothing. One morning, he collapsed in a ball and refused to go further. She scooped him up in her arms, shocked at his thin frailty. Tenderness wrenched her.

'Never let me go,' he whispered, pitifully.

'I will, though,' she said. 'When I find Thomas.'

'No!' He wound his furry little arms around her neck, but by evening, he was back to his old tricks.

Whenever she wasn't touching the acorn, she saw Thomas – at a distance through the trees, at the end of one path in a fork, right in front of her and laying a warm hand on her face. She tied the acorn on a ribbon around her neck so it hung between her breasts, always against her skin, but sometimes longing overcame her and she moved it just for the painful joy of seeing his face. Even when he cursed her, wounded and unforgiving, she was grateful to be near him.

'We must be going in circles,' she told Puki one night.

'We've been walking so long. The Minothan forests aren't that big.'

He stopped whittling to goggle at her. 'We're not in Minotha! These are the elf-lands.'

'But if we'd left Minotha . . .'

'We didn't. We strayed. And you said I didn't guide you – pfft! What do you think?' He held up his finished carving, the stick shaped into a crude likeness of Thomas with a monstrous phallus. He sniggered. 'Now you can dream of him properly.'

She took the toy and threw it in the fire. 'I don't want dreams. I want Thomas.'

'You think I don't see you, moving the acorn so you can pretend to see him? Oh, Thomas . . .' He twiddled his nipples through his fur and she turned her back, disgusted.

Every time she saw the same wretched horse chestnut with its familiar fungi, she remembered what Puki had said: routes were useless in a living maze; she must learn how to navigate it. Perhaps if she gave up completely, that would win him back – but she couldn't believe that, and she could no more relinquish hope than fly. Puki had shown her that. She strained to remember every titbit of advice Puki had let fall. As if he knew what she was about, he pinched and prodded her until she swore in pain.

'Pretty, ladylike words,' he said. 'Thomas would be *so* proud.'

'You're evil,' she said shakily.

'So stab me. Oh – I forgot, you can't! Ha-ha!'

She held the acorn tight, pretending to sleep until she heard his soft snores. The night was utterly dark and she was alone. *This is the truth*, she thought. *Thomas isn't here and he may never love me again. I could love him forever and not have him back.* The quest itself had seemed a grand, noble thing: the indomitable queen, sacrificing everything, fighting against all odds for her true love – but was she his? Might he be happier with someone less relentlessly arrogant? *I love him, but that's*

just a fact, nothing to be proud of. And after all, who wouldn't?
He owed her nothing, not even curses to salve her conscience.
She owed him the heart she'd mangled, an irredeemable
debt.

She looked directly up into the crown of the horse chestnut.
Its large five-fingered leaves hung around her like a protecting
veil. The curving branches held their candles of white flowers
aloft in the dim moonlight, as if the winter were only a dream.
She had traced circles and spirals on the ground, doubled back
on herself, ventured in every conceivable direction, without
success. She'd tried to keep track of where she'd been so that
she didn't go there again, but every time it returned to this:
not knowing what to do, staring at the horse chestnut. She
studied the fungus, curving bowl-like on the underside and
flat as a plate above, growing at intervals up and around the
trunk, like shelves – no. Like stairs.

*If I climbed up, I would see where I am – and then I'd know
where to go.*

Cautiously, she peered over her shoulder: Puki slept, deeply.
She rose. Hesitantly, she put a foot on the first fungus, waiting
for the spongy stuff to break, but it took her weight. Her fingers
wiggled into the crevices of the horse chestnut's scaly trunk.
She clung close as she edged around, upwards. The first fork
came at two or three times her height; already, the ground was
unnervingly far. She gazed upwards into the tree. Surely, at its
crest, all she would see was a sea of tree tops, leaves in the
moonlight, glimmering and obdurate. She climbed, anyway.
When handholds were lacking, she braced her back against
one bough and her feet against another, walking her way
upwards to the next sturdy branch. The patch of ground where
she had lain with her dark thoughts had dwindled into the
distance below; from here, Puki's little sleeping body was so
small as to be invisible.

The branches were thinning; they creaked and waved with
her weight. She hugged the tree tightly. Through the gnarled

tangle, she could still see the ground and the thought haunted her that she might, suddenly, let go – who, after all, was to say she wouldn't? Her feet balanced perilously on a narrow branch. She pressed her lips, then her face, against the bough she clutched.

'Whatever is required of me,' she said, as if it could hear.

'Even if it's your life?'

They stood around her on every side, poised lightly all over the tree, bows drawn and aimed at her heart. Their matted hair flew out in great clouds, stuck through with feathers and dry leaves. Within that wildness, their faces were incongruously perfect. They stared, unsmiling and stony. All of them wore plain shifts the colour of peeled wood, the sleeves and hems bordered with glossy leaves. Her own dress was shabby and vulgar in comparison.

'Well?'

Despite her fear, she raised her chin and addressed them formally. 'I am Queen Vale Pearl Margherite of Kwestriminotha –'

Around her, bow-strings tightened. 'You're no queen here,' said one, with icy anger. 'You hardly deserve the name of Pearl. Higher!' Its arrowhead jerked upwards.

She scrambled on. Around her, the elves swarmed up as lightly as if it were the ground, their arrows always directed toward her. She kept going until one of them pointed along a branch. It looked too narrow to take her weight and she quaked. *Must I fall to my death, for disobeying them?* She turned pleadingly, but the cold fury in its eyes made her obey. As she crawled, the branch rose to tangle with the crowns of other trees, making a supporting lattice. As far above the forest floor as the parapets of Alvey Castle from the sea, the elves darted around their wooden web, leaping fearlessly over wide gaps and settling in the crooks of branches or on their length, swinging their legs. She clung, terrified, to her swaying branch. Ahead of her, in the spreading fork of a beech, sat the elf-king, a wreath of copper-coloured beech leaves around his head. She felt as small as Puki, looking at him. The elf who'd directed her bowed and presented her as 'the girl who won't be guided by anything but her own arrogance'.

The king's eyes speared her and she looked down, ashamed.

'Can you even begin to understand what you've done?' His voice resonated, shaking the tree she hung onto. 'We are the guardians of fate. But you thought you knew better – you! Who can't see the consequences of even one of your actions!' His scorn slashed through her. 'Thanks to you, the whole fabric of fate is creaking with strain. The further it goes off course, the harder to realign it. It was so simple – one tiny act – and for that, a man's heart broke, another man died. And still, you wouldn't listen to us! Now whole towns are laid to waste, whole countries teeter.'

'Please,' she said, anguished. 'Tell me what to do.'

'We can only tell you as much of the future as we see – which is more than you can. But the present, we know. Cantaland isn't your enemy, they have no army, these are Udia's lies.'

'But Lord Payden –'

'Would have made Cantaland your enemy, but for Shanon. The lady is wiser than the queen. We can give you one more riddle, one last chance to put fate back on its course, but the cost might be higher than you think.'

She quailed. 'Not Thomas's life,' she breathed.

The king smiled in grim approval. 'Not Thomas's. Here is your riddle.'

The Island

You will follow the path of the setting sun
To the eye where the waters will never run,
To your grief succumbing, protecting none.

Leaving the forest, the path broadened steadily. When it opened into an avenue and cold sunlight fell between the trees, she mounted her horse, certain the elf-lands were behind her. Puki had vanished, melting back into the bushes without a farewell or a last cruel word. Half-blinded by the setting sun after so long in the greenish gloom, she reached the forest's edge where it gave way to a broad, fast-running river. This was the north-western tip of the forest crescent, where the river Lan crossed from Cantaland into Minotha, at the beginning of its long journey down to Alvey Port. The last sunlight rippled across the water. Tying her clothes and weapons to the horse's back, she led it into the river. Her toes cramped with cold. She plunged in, gasping; the current tugged them downstream and before they were halfway across she was clinging to the horse's mane with numb hands. On the opposite shore, the gravel river bed cut her frozen feet like knives. Shivering violently, she struggled back into her clothes – damp, but not soaked – and built a fire.

The weather worsened as she rode. Kwestria was sheltered by the mountains bordering Udia, Minotha by its forests, but the delta land between the two great rivers was a wasteland across which howling gales drove snow and sleet. She found field mouse burrows and yanked them from hibernation to sudden death. All the time she was travelling, she meditated on the elves' words, both the riddle and the warnings. The first line was self-evident, although she wondered why they didn't just say 'go west'. The second line was opaque, but might turn out to be as plain as 'the craftsman swift' had been. 'Protecting none': her first duty as queen was the well-being of her subjects. Perhaps, after all her mistakes, she had forfeited that right. They might live longer without her doomed attempts to protect them. 'To your grief succumbing': she was willing, but unable, to grieve. The heartsick remorse, yearning, and hope had left her numb, as though it were too big to feel. She just kept riding, to the limits of her and her mount's endurance, collecting wood when she found it, building fires, sleeping, and waking to ride again.

She hoped to find a barge on the Toan, to avoid another chilling swim, but the river lay empty in either direction. Driftwood bobbed in the ice on the water's edge. Now Swift's teaching or tools would have proved useful, she realised glumly. She found a log to help keep her afloat, tied her things on the horse's back, and wrapped the reins tightly around her hand. It neighed angrily and reared when she tried to lead it into the freezing water until, yelling and beating it, she drove it in. The powerful flow swept them away. The horse flailed desperately, dragging her behind it; again and again, she went under, but at last it found its footing on the far side and galloped out, towing her screaming over the rough ground. It stopped abruptly, whickering, and she pulled herself upright. Bruised and shuddering with cold, she could hardly move – but she had to get warm. She wrapped her soaked clothes around her. Away from the waterline, she found a dead bush and pulled off twigs for kindling at its base. When she discovered her tinder was damp, she could have cried. Instead, she gritted her teeth against the pain and rubbed the wood until it smouldered, then sparked at a dried leaf, and finally the kindling began to burn.

For two days, she couldn't move beyond finding more wood,

drying it out around the fire and adding it. The horse grudgingly drew near her again. *Protecting none*, she thought dourly – *I have to eat*. She tapped its vein with an arrow tip and pressed her mouth to the hole, gulping the rich blood. With a scrap of fabric torn from her dress and clay from the river, she plastered over the wound.

The next morning, she was strong enough to ride and turned her horse toward the mountains. In their lee, the icy wind dropped and the scrubby growth of the plains thickened into leafless bushes and trees. At night, she noted which peak the sun dropped behind, then headed toward that the next day until the sun descended again. The way steepened, then turned into cliffs and rocky paths that a goat or a person could climb, but not a horse. The half bowl at the cliff's base was sheltered, with a small waterfall tumbling through it and wild grass, and she turned the horse loose. Before she left, she wrapped her arms around its strong neck and pressed her nose into its mane.

'I'm sorry for everything,' she said. 'Thank you.'

She looked up at the cliff then back across Kwestria. Somewhere over that distance was her own castle, with roaring fires, tables of food, hot water, clean clothes ... She began to climb. Perhaps she would just keep travelling, forever westwards, with no destination – but no. They'd said 'to the eye'. She would arrive somewhere, at something, someday.

The sun set a hair's breadth further north each day; midwinter must have passed while she wandered in the elf-lands. She hesitated over whether to continue westwards, then shrugged and followed it. She was through with knowing better than the elves. Deep in the mountains now, she kept rigorously to her course, even when it meant scaling one side and clambering down the other side of a peak around which she could have easily detoured.

One morning, she crested a mountain as the sun broke into the valley below. She winced, shielding her eyes from the blinding sparkle, and through her fingers looked again. The slopes cradled a massive oval tarn; at its centre lay an island dense with green trees. From where she stood, it formed a perfect eye, with the isle as iris. Euphoria rose as the sun's thin warmth fell on her back.

By mid-afternoon, she'd reached the stony bank. No reeds broke out of the sides and no algae clung to the rocks. She watched for fish and frogs, but nothing stirred the dead depths of the water. She'd assumed evergreens gave the island its foliage, but she could see now the luxuriant crowns of decid-uous trees, their branches lush with leaves, although ice still crusted the tarn's edge where she stood. As she watched, a bird flew down, trailing spray as it landed. It reared up, flapping wildly and shrieking. Appalled, Pearl watched its feathers smoke where the water had splashed. It managed to rise out, its legs eaten away, but its wings were riddled with holes now and it fell back into the dreadful water where it squawked hideously, was still, and melted away.

As the ripples faded, Pearl sank to her knees. This was the end, then. Even if she survived another icy drenching, she couldn't swim in this water. She began to cry – not fighting it and wiping away the trickling tears as she had at the castle, or in humiliated rage at Puki's teasing, but in absolute grief. She cried for the villages of dead, heaped and burned, for each corpse that had been a living person whom she was bound to protect. She cried for the massacred men of the towns and the women, raped while their husbands' bodies still burned. She cried for the union of Kwestria and Minotha, now broken, the mandala shattered. Most of all, she cried for her sweet strong Thomas, who'd been the pivot of her life, whom she'd watched indifferently while he begged her to save their love, whose lion's heart she'd torn apart, who would never even know how bitterly she regretted everything she'd done. She was bowed over, tears pouring from her eyes into the murderous water, unable to stop as wave after wave of sorrow crashed over her.

The sun crept behind the mountains again. The dull red on the far peaks drained. The light paled and turned blue. Splashing sounds broke through her sad reverie. She lifted her head to see a flock of geese descending on the tarn, shaking the water over their feathers. None of them shrieked as the other bird had and when they rose, wheeling around, their bodies were whole. Her fingertips broke the water – it was cold, but nothing more, the poison neutralised by her tears. She rose, her eyes on the island, calculating distance as she unslung her bow and quiver, unstrapped her sword, and pulled off her bedraggled gown. She weighed the sword in one hand and reluctantly set it down. To swim so far in such cold, she couldn't take the extra weight. She lingered on the side as the darkening air shivered over her bare skin – perhaps she should wait till daylight, make a good fire, get some sleep first – then she dived.

The cold burned like fire over her naked body and ran over her breasts until her nipples felt like hard pebbles that might snap off. She streaked through the water, her legs kicking furiously, her arms spinning like a windmill. The exertion would keep her blood beating fast. Halfway across she was already weakening. She spun onto her back, letting her arms rest while her legs propelled her. The air nipped at her wet skin, even harsher than the lake. When her legs tired, she waved her arms through the water, then turned again, swimming hard.

Her feet couldn't feel the lake floor by the island, but when she didn't sink, she reasoned she must be standing. She waded toward the shore, stumbling like a cripple – then recoiled, falling back. Pacing the shingle in the moonlight, snarling, was a wolf. She watched it warily. She couldn't feel the cold any more; instead, a delicious warmth crept through her, and by that she knew she had to get out immediately or freeze to death. It was bigger than the wolves she and Thomas had killed, its back massive, its fur gleaming silver but for a long dark marking on its hind leg. Its sides, however, were sunken: clearly, little food had reached its island – until now, she thought wryly. Her sword and arrows were on the far bank; she'd never make it back. Its eyes shone, watching her, as she swam backwards and around to find another way onto the island. Her limbs barely answered her orders as she crawled onto the rocks, away from the shingle. The night breeze lapped at her skin, soft and warm, smelling of apples, and in the distance oak trees waved their incongruous summer leaves. She clapped her hand to her mouth, stifling her whimpers as feeling returned to her legs. With a bound, the wolf appeared on the rocks. She leaped up and ran for the trees. Halfway there, her legs gave way; she sprawled on the soft turf, scrambled up, ran, and tumbled again. Scrabbling backwards on her bum and hands, she watched the wolf weaving toward her, taller than she was sitting. Her hand closed on a branch. She remembered Thomas teaching her to feint. Her heart hammering, she looked behind her for the count of two, then brought the branch around as hard as she could – it swept through empty air, her fingers lost their grip, and it flew away. The wolf hadn't moved. Without looking away, she groped in the grass for another weapon. Her hand closed on a rock and she tugged weakly, unable to loosen it. The beast crept closer. She found a smaller stone and threw it, but it fell short.

Protecting none, she thought despairingly, as its hard eyes studied her. *I can't even protect myself*. If all that would bring fate back onto its course now was her death, so be it: all her attempts to evade fate had made everything worse for those she loved, from Thomas to her people. The world would run more smoothly without her in it. She fell back as the wolf leapt, its lips pulled up and its teeth bared. It smelt fiercely of musk, its weight bearing down on her. She didn't struggle when its jaw closed around her neck but, despite her resolve, she screamed as its incisors pierced her skin. It was slurping and guzzling; she lay terrified, praying it would kill her before eating her. As its muzzle knocked at her chin, she realised it wasn't tearing her throat open, but lapping at the wounds its sharp teeth had already made. Its tongue pressed, powerful and soft at once, over and over, slurping at her blood.

It drew back, standing over her, its eyes meeting hers. Bewildered, she stared back as it drew itself up on its hind legs and howled. Its silver fur shimmered, hardening; the marking on its hind leg elongated and pulled away from its body; then an armoured knight stood over her, a sword at his side, pulling off his helmet and falling to his knees. She lay dumb, unable to move.

'My love,' he cried, cradling her head, touching the gash in her neck, 'I've wounded you – oh god, say I haven't killed you . . . Darling! My Pearl!'

She stirred weakly and murmured, 'Thomas – my love,' and was still.

Warmth soaked into her skin. All she could see was golden light. Floating in the heat, she felt something smooth and wet running over her. Her eyelids flickered open to a summery meadow, dappled with oak-leaf shadows and thick sunlight. On a spit over a blazing fire, a plucked goose roasted. Thomas was kneeling over her, dipping a scrap of cloth into his upturned helmet by the fire, and rubbing it gently over her cuts.

'Am I dead?' she asked.

He smiled, tears standing in his eyes. 'No, my love.'

She blinked in confusion, too weak and too full of bewildered joy to speak.

'Shh – rest,' he said.

He fed her morsels of goose until he judged her weakened stomach could take no more, then she drifted back into deep sleep. For several days, she glided in and out of consciousness, while Thomas nurtured her, washed her wounds, lifted her to eat, helped her sip water, then soothed her back to sleep.

She opened her eyes, placid with drowsiness, but clear-headed. In the breaking light, she saw Thomas asleep next to her, solemn in repose. His armour lay beyond him; he was bare-chested in only his hose. She realised she was wearing his linen shirt and when she rubbed her nose over it, she smelt his skin. Her heart clenched. She watched how his eyelids curved, how his chest swelled and fell, how black stubble overlay his chin and jaw, running down onto his sturdy neck. Had she ever simply slept next to him, instead of sitting awake all night to marvel at his beauty? Her hand traced the scab on her neck. It had taken so little of her blood to cure him; she would have willingly given it all. He deserved life more than she did.

His eyes were open, dark brown and still. She looked into them, her thoughts beating like drums through her heart.

'You should have killed me – or let me die. Not cured me.' Her voice was husky with disuse.

He shook his head slowly.

'The necklace was enchanted,' she continued. 'I shouldn't have put it on, I should have listened to the riddle, it's all my fault –'

'It's my fault.' She'd forgotten how deep his voice was. How could she have remembered his face so clearly and not his voice? 'I didn't listen to the riddle, I stormed out.'

'But I betrayed you –'

'I abandoned you – I left you to your enchantment, and you rescued me from mine.' His hand touched her arm, warm through the thin linen.

They lay gazing, enraptured as mother and baby by each other's eyes. Sunlight crept over their bodies, reddish-orange, lemon-yellow, and finally bright gold. In the distance, the mountain slopes were still clumped with snow, the trees leafless, but on the island summer endured. Quietly, with incomplete sentences, they told each other everything that had happened in the year of their separation. When he heard how she'd killed Kardan, Thomas compressed his lips grimly.

'I shouldn't be glad of any man's death,' he said, 'but I am of his.'

He told her how, when he left the castle, he'd been so blinded by his own tears – then his story was interrupted, because the thought of him crying wrenched her unbearably; she threw her arms around his neck and kissed his cheeks, his eyes, until he stopped her with his mouth and they both shook at the soft pressure of each other's lips – blinded by his own tears, he'd walked straight into the sorceress's trap. Before he could even draw his sword, his hand was a paw. Since then, he'd been in wolf form on the island, rung around with its poisonous waters, alone with his thoughts.

'I should have known you better,' he said. 'I said I'd die for you – but I couldn't even stay with you when you needed me most.'

'It wouldn't have been pretty.' She winced, thinking of the abusive, shrieking climaxes she and Kardan had wrung from each other's bodies. 'I'm glad you didn't see that.'

'I could have helped you.'

She nodded slowly, then a thought struck her. 'If you could think – here – when I came onto the island, did you know who I was?'

He looked down. Very low, he said, 'Yes,' and sighed. 'Yes and no. I was part-wolf, part-me, but I knew you were Pearl, and I wanted to hurt you, I wanted to rip your throat out. Only – when I saw what I'd done –'

Her fingers intertwined with his and when their eyes met again, it was with full consciousness of what each had done. She still believed the gravest fault was hers; perhaps he still blamed himself most.

'Will it heal?' He touched the scab at her throat.

'Will this?' She laid her hand over his heart.

'Will this?' He put his hand over her heart, on the curve of her breast. Her eyes blackened as they dilated. The side of his finger touched her nipple through the fabric. It hardened instantly. 'What about this?' he asked softly.

'Um . . .' She swallowed hard. Breath fought through her constricted throat to say, 'I've dreamt – of you – so much.'

He shifted closer to her on the grass, uncertainly. 'Is the reality as good as the dream?'

'Much better.' Her arm slid over his back, shaping around the packed muscles, his shoulder blades, the curve of his spine. 'It's real, for a start.'

'Yes.' He pulled her against him. She undulated so her thighs pressed on his, her stomach against his, her breasts flattening hard against his chest. Their mouths met and opened; their tongues dipped. He tasted warm and mellow, recognisable as home but startling, too. Dreams and memories, in or out of the elvish land, never held this wealth of detail – his exact flavour, the stubble grazing her chin, the precise shape of his chest against her breasts, how his fingers caught her at the waist and tugged her closer, the stifled gasp at the back of his throat as their hips collided.

He moaned 'Pearl,' and she strained closer in his arms. Despite the rising fever, it felt so fragile, as if they hardly dared presume. She trembled when he lifted the shirt off her; her eyes skated shyly away when he pulled off his hose and were then drawn back, mesmerised. She knew his cock so well, she thought, as her palm closed over it; soft and gentle between his legs or standing swollen and tall like it did now, beautiful in her hand. She curled over to kiss it. He was whimpering before her lips brushed the tip. When she nibbled the skin that strained to hold him in, he cried out, half sitting; she closed her mouth around it, rapt, drawing it deeper, and he fell back again, shouting her name. All the love she couldn't put into words was in her lips and tongue gliding over him, her hand furling around him. She was coiled, suckling, lost to everything but love and the magnificence of him, until he pulled her away, gasping, 'No more – I want you.'

She swam up his body to kiss him, but halfway there was distracted by his small tight nipple and fastened onto it. He nearly wept as sensation bolted through him; his hips bucked for her, desperately.

'My love, please,' he implored. He lifted her over him, using all his strength for the one thing he wanted. Her rapacious mouth found his, drowning him with kisses. The head of his cock, guided by his hand, swept between her slick lips. Instinctively, he jerked upwards. Both yelped in thrilled shock. He was just caught inside her. She raised herself on her arms, so their eyes could fasten on each other's and not a moment of the experience be lost. Very slowly, she began to sink down; his hips began to rise. Their pupils enlarged. Their eyes widened. Their lips parted. Their breath stopped, then came in shuddering gasps. He was deep inside her; she was wrapped around him; it was the most astonishing, enthralling thing in the world.

They couldn't, and didn't need to, speak. They barely moved. She pulsed around him; he throbbed inside her. They stared, hypnotised, into each other's eyes. Together, they moved, just for the delicious bliss of feeling the other's sliding skin. Seeing the ecstasy spasm over his face, she rocked more deliberately. The thrill of giving him that stoppered her throat. Under her, stronger than her, he pushed upwards and her breath broke out in a wail. He thrust until she capsized and he rolled onto her, crushing her. His eyes never left hers, watching intently, thick with love, as he plunged in and out. She arched, clinging to him, and it wasn't the bright white light of orgasm, like a pinpoint exploding, but a crashing wave of amber that submerged her and held her under, while wave after wave followed, and all the time she was staring at his rich brown eyes gazing back. His cries came louder, joining hers, and her legs wrapped tightly around his hips, holding him deep inside as he flung his head back and roared. His cock, leaping within her, carried her with him.

The snow was melting as they rode back through Kwestria, sharing her horse until they bought another at an isolated farmstead. Anxious for the kingdom, Pearl wanted to gallop as fast as they could, but Thomas insisted on a steadier pace. Both she and her horse were still weak, he said; if things were as bad as she feared, they should both be ready to fight when they arrived – which meant eating well, resting properly, and rebuilding her strength. Her eyes flashed, her mouth opened to argue, then she laughed.

'You're right!'

He raised his eyebrows, amused. 'Don't sound so surprised.'

They made camp each day in mid-afternoon, long before she was tired. As her sword-master, however, he wasn't so gentle. Without his training, her technique had slackened, and he let her know it. He disarmed her repeatedly and flung her to the ground, his sword-tip at her throat or her breast. Then, 'Up,' he'd say curtly, and they'd start over.

Winded from her latest fall, she looked up the length of the sword, up his arm, to his stern, shining face. 'You know,' she gasped, 'you asked me once when I first fell in love with you.'

'Uh-huh.' His blade was cold on her collarbone.

'I think it was the first time you ever knocked me down like this. I wasn't used to being manhandled. Or bested at anything.' Her eyes softened. 'I love it. I love you.'

He tossed his sword aside and threw himself onto her, kissing and grappling wildly. They rolled, wrestling and laughing, until her skirt was up, his hose was down, and they were surging against each other, thighs tangled and mouths clasped.

'I love you,' he yelled, as he lunged wildly into her. She rose up to meet him, clinging tight and wailing at the feel of him spurting inside her.

Morning and night, they couldn't leave each other alone. The wonder of being in love and together was too over-whelming, and everything that couldn't be put into words demanded expression somehow. Even when they stopped to drink from a stream, they'd end up sprawled on the wet bank together, breathless and giggling with joy, touching each other's faces with dirt-stained fingers.

'Do you know how beautiful you are?' he murmured.

She looked at him incredulously. 'With matted hair, covered in sweat, in a filthy ripped dress, on my back in the mud?'

'Perfect.' He kissed her lovingly. 'But maybe we should spruce you up a bit before we reach Alvey.'

The villages and farms surrounding the castle were deserted of both people and animals. Worried, they spurred their horses onward, and as the castle hove into view, so did their answer. In the fading light, the port was red with Udian ships; the two sides of the castle not on sheer cliff were thick with soldiers.

Pearl blazed with rage. Her fingers tightened on the reins. 'How *dare* they!' she hissed. 'Udia doesn't have the strength to take us on – they'll be laid to waste –'

Thomas cut her short, his face grim. 'Not Udia alone. Look more closely at the soldiers – there, the ones at the back . . .'

She caught her breath, whitening. At the rear of the siege, less obvious than the red by twilight, were the greens and blues of Minotha. Rather than defending their queen's castle, they were attacking it alongside Udia.

'Let's go,' she said harshly, but Thomas laid his hand on her arm.

'They haven't finished their siege towers, we can wait a night. For this, we need to be seen. And if we're going to regain our troops, we must look the part.'

Together, they rode back to the abandoned farms they'd passed. That night, Queen Pearl sat on a rough wooden stool at the fireside, sewing in the poor light, while Sir Thomas of Minotha scrubbed her clothes in the washtub. With patient, gentle fingers, he untangled the snarls in her hair thread by thread, until he could comb through it. Both washed in a metal tub by the fire and he poured cups of water over her hair until it ran clean and smooth across her back. While she resumed her needlework, he shone his armour. The night was black, the dawn near, when they crawled tiredly under the scratchy blankets on the straw mattress. Exhausted, they reached for each other anyway. They kissed gently, side by side, moving only to help him slide into her then lying next to each other again, rocking back and forth.

'We should sleep,' she moaned, but her hips pressed closer to his, squeezing him hard.

'Yes,' he said, cupping her buttocks to draw her closer still.

They stayed entwined, murmuring and rubbing in tiny movements tightly against each other. Every time she cried out violently, he held her close, straining against him, and kept on grinding slowly.

'Do you never lose control?' she gasped, reeling, slithering.

'It's hanging – by a thread,' he answered, strangled.

'Come for me ... come inside me ...'

'God – Pearl!' he cried out. He thrust hard, throwing her onto her back, and slammed into her. In the first, dim light she could see his arm muscles standing with strain, his broad chest towering over her, his beautiful face torn with happiness, as he bucked and bellowed.

When they lay, panting, next to each other again, he stroked her cheek and chuckled deep in his chest. 'It's time to get up already. I never did get any sleep in your bed.'

They dressed painstakingly. Pearl's dress, washed and mended, would look better from a distance than it did close up. Thomas brushed out her hair again, so it fell shining over her shoulders, and in lieu of a crown they wove a witch hazel wreath. Each of them carried a pole, to which her careful sewing was fastened. His armour gleamed. As he mounted his horse, pleasure rippled through her at the sight of the magnificent knight, his helmet under his arm, his head raised high. To think that she had his love – that he shared her bed ... She straddled her own horse, prouder than she'd ever been to ride next to him.

They timed their arrival carefully. At mid-morning, the soldiers were ready for battle, the finished siege towers wheeling into position, and the sun hitting the ridge onto which they rode. The defenders saw them first, glittering in the sunlight, and a shout went up – then the attackers turned. Pearl and Thomas reared their horses, the hooves pawing at the air, and he roared across the valley in his strong voice.

'Minothans!'

He held his pole aloft and let the rippling wind unfurl Minotha's standard in green and blue.

'I am Sir Thomas of Minotha, your Champion!' he bellowed. A wild cheer went up from the Minothan soldiers, their swords beating on their shields. 'Udia held me prisoner – but Kwestria has rescued me!'

Pearl lifted her pole and the yellow and white standard fluttered in the wind. He clasped her hand firmly in his and lifted their arms above their heads.

'Will you fight with your Champion?'

They roared their approval.

'Then kill the Udians who captured me! Fight for the queen who rescued me!'

Both drew their swords and held them up as Pearl shouted, 'Kwestrians – this is your queen! To me!'

'Minothans!' shouted Thomas. 'We fight with Kwestria!'

As they charged down the hillside together, Pearl grinned at him. 'Spectacular enough?'

'I bloody hope so!' he retorted.

Before they had reached the encampment, they saw the Minothans turning and slashing at the Udian soldiers, as the Kwestrians poured out of the castle behind them. Then they were in the thick of the battle, surrounded by red uniforms, their horses wheeling and their swords spinning. Grateful for Thomas's training, Pearl stabbed and slashed swiftly, every gout of blood and severed limb a victory for her love and a vengeance for what they had endured. With their allies against them, the Udians were badly outnumbered, and before her bloodlust was slaked, she was surrounded by her own soldiers, the last of the Udians scattering. A scream came behind her; she spun. An Udian soldier, his dagger still raised toward her, was spitted on Thomas's sword.

'My Queen,' said Thomas, kicking the man off his blade.

Her eyes glowed. 'My King.'

The People in the Garden

Leonie Martel

The People in the Garden

Prologue

'You, who have withstood exorcisms by bishops, who knows neither fear nor remorse...you, who rides on night's black horse through our dark and sacred woods, take this offering from a loyal servant, I beseech you.'

In the inky depths of her eyes, the stars danced and burned. The spirit of the demon was already in her as she prepared to make the sacrifice. A colourless beam of moonlight shimmered in a black sky – a cold sight that makes people draw their blankets close around them on chill evenings and give thanks they aren't out in the forest.

Over a blouse of white linen she wore a long pointed corselet, intricately laced and embroidered with strings of black pearls. A skirt of garnet-coloured velvet hung beneath. The oval shape of her face hung stark in the night garden, pallid from the imperial savagery that ran through her blood. Her looks would not make one think of love but of murder – for she was a beauty born of the inexhaustible springs of darkness. And her hands, with their delicate white skin, did not look capable of the evil they were about to do.

She stood rooted, as if grown from the mysterious earth, the smoke of belladonna leaves gathering about her as she called to the moon.

'Oh pale, destructive star, this wound shall not heal. Feed and make strong my beautiful garden. Bring it once more to glory. Deliver me into greatness!'

1

There had been no sleep on the journey. The carriage that bore the orphaned Katia to the Manor Malinovsky had rattled some twelve hours through rural backwaters over uneven tracks. Any respite from the commotion of horse-drawn travel was to be found only in stillness, on solid ground; in a solid bed, even better. At the outset, the countryside had been soft and tranquil, corn swaying in the breeze, sloping vineyards, an occasional inn offering food. Yet further on, toward Szathmar, the terrain had changed, the arable land giving way to a wilder, less cultivated soil; the blue forest with its black earth and prowling, carnivorous creatures drew closer. Here in the woods prowled wolves, lynxes, foxes and martens – beasts that were brown in summer and white in winter. In the distance, the Carpathian Mountains formed an imposing relief against the sky, their jagged peaks lilac in the wispy-clouded half-light of early evening. This prospect was Katia's destination.

Despite the comfort of her cashmere blanket, the young chestnut-haired beauty had not been able to escape into the unconsciousness her mind and body craved. The roiling, jerking movements of the carriage prevented it, the turbulence coaxing her lustrous mane from its coil. She ached to stretch, to be out of her travelling clothes and in a hot bath infused with reviving lavender salts. Would she know such an agreeable convenience at her imminent employ? Even her eyes were tired, pricked by the tears of apprehension over many hours. Although she felt compelled to burst into sobs at the unfairness of her circumstances, she'd fought against her emotions the entire day. It wouldn't do to display weakness to Magda, the manor's housekeeper who had accompanied her for the duration of the journey.

Life had become so harsh and regimented of late. There would be no return to the young ladies' academy in Vienna to continue her studies in art, music and languages; instead she was faced with a lifetime of servitude among rough types. Already the coachmen's vulgar tongue had appalled her. How could fate have struck such a cruel blow?

Magda sat opposite, concentrating on her embroidery, but her senses were alert to everything around her, her eyes flicking up at the slightest jolt of the coach. A lifetime of hard work had been etched into the woman's constitution and she seemed unperturbed by the discomforts of the journey. Sturdy old Magda would know nothing of the society Katia had expected to soon be part of: the salons and concerts she'd been invited to attend, promenading at spa towns, showing off her parasols and pretty dresses. She did not look the sort to lend a compassionate ear to the complaints of a soft young girl from the town. Despite this, the woman seemed good-hearted enough. When they'd stopped at a coaching inn for lunch, she had traded jokes with the heavily moustached proprietor, and ensured her charge was properly fed.

Katia had smiled politely, but she'd struggled to understand them, as they spoke rapidly in the regional dialect. There had been whispered exchanges and sudden peals of laughter that made her feel self-conscious – especially when the beefy proprietor turned his attentions on her. Katia had been glad for Magda's presence in those moments.

She clutched her precious green velour bag close to her as the carriage bumped and swerved along its endless passage. At times she found herself stroking it in her lap like a small mute pet, which offered a modicum of security, but still she felt terribly alone, as persistent pangs of grief nagged at her. In the bag were a few treasures of her parents' memory that she had been allowed to keep: some of her mother's costume jewellery; cameo portraits of her father and brothers; *billets doux* decorated with pressed flowers; the sacred heart memento of her first communion.

Dear Mother and Father, why did they have to take that holiday? It was a futile question and she'd asked it a thousand times. Katia knew the reason full well. Her mother had always dreamed of ocean travel. Growing up in a land-locked nation, the prospect of a sea voyage had been a tempting novelty. Dear Mother had been overjoyed when Father announced he had tickets for the maiden voyage of the *Magyar Empress*. Yet how could they have ignored the warnings of the storm? She cursed the captain and his foolhardy bravado for leaving dock, yet her scolding breath was impotent and too long after the fact, as the captain also went down with his vessel. Her mother and father had just sat down to dinner when a forty-foot wave crashed into the starboard side of the ship. There had been a few survivors out of the four hundred on board, but Mr and Mrs Ludovice had not been in that lucky minority.

That was three months ago. And what was the future to hold, now that Uncle Istvan had stepped in to take control of her affairs? How Katia loathed that snake! She had hoped he would have found it in his heart to maintain the upkeep of her fees at the academy – but this was not to be. His finances were shadowy and didn't allow for the drain on earnings her father's steady salary had afforded. Yet Katia suspected he had cut himself a handsome slice of her parents' effects. It wasn't long after their deaths that he was frequenting the finest gentlemen's outfitters in town. With his silver-topped cane, satin-lined cape and top hat, he easily charmed the solicitors into believing he was the person best placed to secure a future for his orphaned niece. Her younger brothers' education was treated as the priority, and money was released to continue their places at boarding school – to get them off his hands. But Katia, well, he had enterprising plans for her: she would be found a position in a handsome house of the nobility. She would even earn a modest wage. What better start in life for a young woman than to learn the routine of a bustling manor house?

The solicitors had applauded the idea – the handsome lunches he'd treated them to no doubt bringing them around to his way of thinking. So, within two months of her parents' death, Uncle Istvan presented her to the Countess Malinovsky at the imperial chambers in town, where interviews were being conducted for the position of maid at her manor. In an attempt to sabotage the interview, she had protested her ignorance of service, telling the countess she had never cooked anything more adventurous than goulash, and that she couldn't sew to save her life. But this woman, with her porcelain complexion and elegant carriage, had not seemed at all troubled by this. In fact, she laughed – a feminine, ringing laugh that brushed aside Katia's inexperience as unimportant. More pertinent to her engagement was how she responded to the selection of uniforms the countess had brought with her. She had been asked to model a variety of corsets and finely made under-garments, which Katia found highly irregular but a strangely exciting aspect to the interview. The outfits were beautiful, and she felt instantly more grown up and confident wearing them.

But the meeting had left her with confused emotions. The familiarity between Uncle Istvan and the noblewoman was a mystery. Where had he made her acquaintance, kissing her hand like that and bringing her gifts? She quizzed him about their friendship on the journey home that day, but he brushed her questioning aside with a laugh, a flurry of his gloved hand, and some flippant remark about mixing in the right company. It seemed he had picked up the manners of his imperial friend. She gained no further insight into the unlikely friendship and was troubled by a nagging sense that she had been sold into servitude by her own flesh and blood. Istvan had only ever been attentive and charming, yet he was a rogue and a bounder, she knew that much.

The early evening sun streamed across the gardens, illuminating the dark figure of the Countess Irina Malinovsky. In a beaded, blood-red gown trimmed with weasel fur, her dark, waist-length hair piled on top of her head, she patrolled the grounds, inspecting her plants for signs of improvement. It had become an obsession these recent months. How she wanted to see once again the riot of colour that used to be the pride of the manor. Her beloved rose garden that a mere five years ago was the talk of the province was now a sorry spectacle. She brushed a hand against the stem of an azalea, only to send its petals cascading to the ground. The slightest tremble denuded her plants of their colour, whilst by a cruel irony the bramble and bracken grew vigorous, more suffocating than ever.

'I honour you, yet still I wait and suffer the shame of failure as you mock me,' she hissed through gritted teeth. 'I, Malinovsky, whose forefathers vanquished the Turk, I shall not be denied!'

She clenched her fists in frustration. Her dark mischief had so far yielded no reversal of fortune. No parchment etched in the blood of a black hen nor talisman fashioned from the bones of forest litter had restored the former glory to her garden. She stood by the sundial and sighed, her long, black-polished fingernails scratching at the stone. For years the countess had bred roses no one else in the kingdom could match for hue or scent – deep violet, perfect black, and the palest azure blue: undreamed-of colours defying the limitations of their species. Horticulturists would travel for days to visit the famous gardens, bringing with them gifts of fine wines, silver trinkets and the delicate pastries from Vienna that Irina loved.

Now all that was gone. Now no one came calling from the royal household to collect rose tinctures to take back to the king and queen. Irina missed the profusion of rare colour, and she longed to smell the heady fragrance that wafted across the lawns on summer evenings. But most of all she missed being Mistress of the Roses.

To her husband and the staff she had spoken of problems with the soil – too lime-ridden, too chalky, too dry. There'd not been enough rainfall, or too harsh a sun, too late in the year. Speculation came thick and fast: local farmers scratched their heads and mumbled about birds eating the buds, while the village folk spoke of the manor not working in tandem with the lunar cycle – that pruning during the dark side of the moon withered the crop.

But the countess knew the real reason her gardens had failed. The book had foretold of it. That unhallowed object which had gathered dust in the tower for some 150 years told the story. A monstrous history was repeating itself. The Beast had returned and, until he got what he wanted, a blight would visit the gardens, just as Darvulia had predicted. Darvulia ... that name from her childhood, muttered as a warning from adults to behave, eat properly and not be given over to dreaminess, lest she end up mad, incarcerated in the tower like her ancestor. Neither parent had ever spoken of the book before they died. Had they even read it? It seemed unlikely. To them she was the ancestor best forgotten, her scribblings the worthless outpourings of a lunatic. Yet the more Irina had learned of this mysterious woman, the more she recognised herself. Childless and given to nighttime wanderings, this great aunt of her great-great-grandmother had conjured ancient divinities in the primitive temples that had fallen to dust in the mountain ranges overlooking Szathmar. She had breathed life back into the old gods and had written of it as her birthright. She was not mad. She was a sorceress.

Irina had not told her husband of the prophecy. He was immersed in his own adventures, amusing himself with the photographic arts and trips to Paris; he had little interest in the gardens and she had little interest in his opinions – the manor was *her* inheritance. But things had taken a more serious turn of late and people were searching for reasons and solutions. The blight on the rose garden had this harvest spread to the vegetable plot. Potatoes, beans, beetroot, apples, pears, plums – there had been a noticeable diminution in their size and quantity. The manor had always been self-sufficient. Word would spread that all was not well in the Malinovsky household, reducing their position in the realm.

Irina was wary of the local villagers; their ears were pricked for any hint of scandal and their tongues easily loosened with rumours. Did they know the story of the Beast? No one had ever spoken directly of it but Irina had retired the old gardener the previous year when he'd mumbled a veiled accusation of witchcraft. Had he been spying on her, seen her dancing sky-clad in the bower? She wasn't taking any chances. The slightest whisper of ancient practices in the imperial home would spread like wildfire, alerting the pious miseries of the village who spoke about decency and Christian virtue. She would eat her fur stole, head and all, before she allowed those black crows on the premises.

The countess's blood had long simmered with primal passions. The woodland crones had taught her as a young girl that she was not as others, that her bloodline was powerful and could be venomous; that she was touched with the wolf's sense, the fox's cunning, the sparrowhawk's keenness.

'Know thou wert born of no earthly seed,' they said, 'that thou camest forth on the dew of the henbane.'

It had been the same in Szathmar for as far back as anyone could reach – the old powers were destined to run through the veins of a chosen one. And in the countess they found imperial measure. The crones initiated her into their magic. They taught her of the herbs that induced trances and where belladonna grew in solitude, in a halo of blue-violet.

As a teenager she had been scolded for bringing martens'

heads into the house – misguided experiments in fertility that saw her banished to her room for days. Strange moods and tempers had consumed her. On the threshold of womanhood she had fallen under the spell of the moon, which brought melancholy humour but also vivid, corrupt illusions that inflamed her and made her irresistible. She had practised love spells and fashioned talismans that drew admirers, and she had dazzled her family with her skills at horticulture, keeping secret the sorcery she used to bring such rare colour to the gardens.

Wilder and wilder, by her eighteenth year she had gone over to the ancient folklore in total, offering magical refrains to the spirits of the trees, cavorting dances learned from gypsies. Her parents had threatened to disown her, so she'd learned to practise her craft in secret, lest she risk losing her inheritance.

Once married, she'd tried to leave behind the ancient ways, convinced the modern era her husband embraced would usher away the power of the old gods. Yet the pull had grown even stronger in recent years. And one night, that *walpurgisnacht* of her thirty-fifth year, she had been seized by the urgency of the calling and had raced under midnight's shroud to the woods, where the sorceresses of the forest had welcomed her back.

As she patrolled her withered gardens, past the flowerbeds bordered with rosemary and lavender, she didn't feel like a woman at the height of her powers, but the rewards of her most secret and potent magic had yet to manifest results. She teemed with the expectancy of what would transpire come the Naming Day – All Hallows' Eve. Her master was so dreadful and mighty. He had come to claim his dominion, to seek a new bride, as Darvulia's book had foretold, and he had made his presence known in the ways all male creatures express their potency. In the sheltered bower near the summerhouse, in the blue night of midsummer's eve just three months past, she had fallen before him. And his presence was so powerful she had found herself speaking in tongues like a savage from the darkest lands.

And what had happened in those delirious moments had left her with the knowledge she was not alone in her realm. She did not have complete privilege to the beauty of the gardens. Indeed, she did not have any privilege at all. All that blossomed and rioted into glorious being was his. It was his to give life to, and his to destroy. And even though she had been frozen by his terrifying presence, she had wanted him, and wanted to serve him totally.

Darvulia had been right. His inhuman majesty was primal and all-powerful. He would restore her reputation. Yet the countess was impatient. She was the custodian of her ancestor's legacy, and she would not see her powers diminished. A bride he would have.

She walked through the rose garden and down to the summerhouse, where she sat and watched the evening sunlight sparkle on the lake. The new girl was due to arrive soon – the pretty maid she had hired to replace the other one, just gone. She looked perfect. The count would be silly with desire for her, no doubt. Although he craved the whip across his backside over traditional bedroom congress, Irina would need to keep a close eye on how things developed. The girl would need to remain intact, whatever else went on.

It amused her to engage assistance in the disciplining of her husband; it took her mind off her troubles. Some of the girls she had invited to their bedchamber had been hopeless, and had run shrieking from the house in a matter of days. But this new one, this Katia, showed promise. She had about her a certain haughtiness that augured well. With this thought in her mind, she left the summerhouse and returned to the manor. She wanted to be ready for her arrival.

The coach persisted through the final stages of its journey as Katia brooded on her family and her future. The horses settled into a steady rhythm along a long, exceptionally straight track, either side of which lay dense woodland, the taller trees over-arching on both sides to form an arboreal tunnel into which the carriage was drawn. It should have been a moment for contemplation of the beauty of nature, leaves perfect in their hues of late summer. Instead, a rush of dread filled Katia's senses – a sharp premonition of the isolation she might feel as a girl from the town with barely any grounding in the customs of rural life.

She was wise to be wary. For this was the realm of shadows and shapes and dark smoky dwellings, where creatures howled in the night and the interior of the woods was as unknowable and perilous as an uncharted cave. And for the past few miles, certain trees had taken on a sinister twist, their branches offering gnarled invitations to enter their realm. In the bark of the silver birches were knots of wood that formed the kind of tree-faces she remembered seeing as a child. They scared her then, and they scared her now. Startled eyes and mouths were imprinted there as if rooted, mute witnesses to some enormous terror. She pulled her fur collar closer around her neck and was glad not to be walking this route.

As alien to her as was the untamed and perplexing land-scape, was also the prospect of service. She was on the precipice of drudgery in a place where it would be impossible to find the fashionable items she had recently introduced to her ward-robe. Thank goodness she had been allowed to bring some personal belongings with her. She prayed the three deep leather suitcases and hatboxes strapped to the roof of the carriage had not been unduly battered.

They came to a fork in the track, the carriage slowing to turn right, and finally the perimeter walls of the manor came into view. The house itself wasn't yet visible, but the length of the wall ran out of sight in both directions. An unscalable iron gate was fixed into two moss-covered columns forming the entrance to the grounds, upon which stood the statues of two proud deer, as if surveying the boundaries for intruders. This threshold left visitors in no doubt as to the grandeur of the establishment, and the importance of its owners.

The coach slowed to a stop, the horses snorting, as Magda lowered the window and shouted to the gatekeeper to hurry with assistance. A strong scent of wood smoke drifted into the carriage through the open window, and a dampness unknown in the town in late summer rolled out of the forest. Katia had heard how harsh the winters were in these parts, and she would be glad of her furs. She prayed her employers would be kind; that she wouldn't want for the basic things such as food and warmth and occasionally being allowed to wear her own clothes.

There was some more shouting and the gates were heaved back by a shaven-headed ox of a man wearing a leather apron and sturdy boots. At closer range, Katia noticed the gate was inset with metalwork carvings of boars' and wolves' heads, and a large circular centrepiece that bore some kind of demonic face. She had heard this province, famous for its vineyards and flowers, was also known for its primitive beliefs. There had been a marked absence of churches on the second half of the journey and she hoped there would be a chapel at the manor. Her parents would have wanted her to continue attending Mass.

The final stretch of the journey was in motion. As they rounded the long driveway, through the grounds, another world came into view: a vista of nature tamed and manicured. There was even a lake, with two bridges modelled in the Venetian style. Katia was awe-struck. Over the far side of the lawn, the sun picked out the top of a summerhouse, its pinnacle gleaming white. Her heart lifted. For a few moments, her qualms were forgotten, and the grip on her velour bag loosened. The manor and its estate were beautiful and vast; she had known nothing of its glory when she had been selected for the position. She felt her pulse race and her breath quicken with anticipation and relief. To think that she would be living here, among all this beauty. Maybe it didn't matter so much that she wouldn't be returning to the academy. It looked civilised. There may even be someone here who could help her practise her French.

The twilight glow of the waning sun brought her hair to a rich chestnut, and she fancied for the briefest instant she was Lady of this establishment; that her parents had bequeathed the place to her as a surprise legacy. Foolish reveries, for she was brought sharply to reality by Magda's earthy announcement.

'We'll be fortunate to get supper tonight, it being Sunday and all. Lucky if the cook has set aside some stew and cake. Out of sight and out of mind, that's the way the kitchen operates here. Mind you, you look like you could do with feeding up, my girl.'

She slapped a leathery hand on Katia's leg. So, this was not to be Katia's castle. This was not her magic kingdom. She was staff – and would be treated as nothing more than a lowly servant at the beck and call of the Count and Countess Malinovsky for however many years it pleased them. She smiled weakly at the housekeeper.

'We'll do best to get those cases of yours in without fuss,' she said, cocking her thumb toward the roof of the carriage. 'I can't imagine what the countess will think of a servant bringing so much baggage with her. And hatboxes too. Anyone would think you'd been to Vienna or Paris, with all those fancies.'

Katia was swift to stipulate the terms her Uncle had agreed with the countess – she had been allowed a larger quantity of belongings than staff were usually entitled, on account of her bereavement and her being so young.

'Yes, dear, that's as maybe. But all the same the mistress doesn't like untidiness. We'll haul it up to your quarters quickly as we can. It's my job to see you are presented to her at nine o'clock, after supper and before her bath. We can't be having any laboured unpacking and whatnot.'

Magda pushed open the door of the coach and leaped from the vehicle in one bound, ignoring the driver's assistance, as if to mark her unaided arrival on home ground. Her brown boots crunched solidly on the gravel as she strode toward the side of the building, rummaging in her bag for her large, jangling set of keys. Katia, in contrast, gingerly eased herself into the open air, her footfall as precarious as a young deer's, as she took the driver's hand. He bowed his head and breathed a liquor-tainted 'Miss' at her as she alighted, and Katia wondered how much firewater he had imbibed during the journey. No matter, she had arrived safely and her mood was lifted now she had seen the manor.

For the next few minutes, with Magda's help, the driver and his mate unstrapped the cases and set to work ferrying them into the servants' entrance at the side of the house. Katia craned her neck to look up at the windows, to see if she could catch a glimpse of the count or countess.

'We'll put a stop to that staring, missy,' Magda puffed in her ear as she heaved another case down from the roof. 'We don't want dreamers below stairs.'

'Sorry,' Katia said. 'I never thought the manor would be so beautiful.'

'You'll get used to it soon enough when you're running about at their beck and call, black-leading the grate of a morning and fetching eggs from the coop. You be sure to help with these bags. Anyone would think *I'm* your blessed servant!'

The countess was seated on a high-backed chair by the window of the drawing room, fastidiously repairing the cuffs of her favourite black satin day dress.

'It would appear our new help has arrived,' she announced calmly to her husband, standing up to get a better view of the carriage and its disembarking cargo.

As was customary at this hour, Count Nikolai was reclining on his purple chaise longue, smoking and reading the newspaper, a glass of red wine and a crystal decanter at his side.

'Is she as delicious as you described?' he asked.

'She's as comely and well-fashioned as one would expect of a pampered miss from the city. She holds herself quite regally. She has the slender waist and fine bosom of a young woman at the threshold of adventure.'

The lure was too great for Nikolai to merely be given commentary. He had to get a glimpse of this girl of whom his wife had spoken so temptingly. He came to stand beside the countess, leaning on the window seat for an unimpaired view.

'She has about her a certain dreaminess not uncommon in females her age,' he said, 'as yet unaccustomed to the urgency of adult desires.'

'That will come,' said the countess. 'Think how she will be brought to life once she has a whip in her hand. I can barely wait to witness the transformation.'

She leant back onto the embroidered waistcoat of her husband, her eyes closing in rapture.

'It's always so thrilling to see the vitality of the newly corrupted,' he whispered. 'But we must have patience. I beg you not to alarm her too early with too severe a sport. Remember the other girl?'

'Do you think I'm a fool? I have learned my lesson,' said Irina. 'This one is special. The young doe is consumed with a passion for fine clothing. Look at all those trunks she has brought with her. I could not silence her at the interview such was her enthusiasm for silks and satins. And when I had her parade in corsets, she was radiant with power.'

'Istvan will never know how indebted we are to him for arranging this convenience,' Nikolai said softly, his voice croaky with the stirrings of desire.

'I think the seven hundred crowns we paid him for his trouble might betray some element of our gratitude.'

'Yes, of course.' The count laughed. 'The old goat. His moustache positively bristled when I handed him the payment. He even made a comment about quality merchandise, as if the girl were no more flesh and blood than a Turkey carpet or a consignment of glazed fruits.'

'A transaction neatly executed,' said the countess.

'Do you think we can get her to parade for us tonight?' asked Nikolai, his blue eyes glinting mischief, his fingers pulling at his immaculately waxed moustache.

'Now who is being eager? We do not want her fleeing because you have alarmed her with your unseemly advances. She'll need encouragement, coaxing, to mould her to our image.'

'In that case, may I take some token from you now?' he asked, bowing before his wife. 'For I fear I may not be able to contain myself. I burn for her already.'

Nikolai seized his wife's hand and placed it at his centre. She gripped him and felt him throb.

'I shall grant you fifteen minutes,' she announced coldly, yet with a hint of a smile playing at her lips. She glanced at the ormolu clock on the mantelpiece to note the time. 'But tonight I do not feel disposed to tolerate the evidence of your sins. You shall contain yourself in your strap.'

Swiftly, Nikolai went to the bureau drawer and took out the satin sheath his wife had fashioned for him to wear at moments like these. With trembling fingers he unfastened his breeches and slid the silken garment over his length. The device fastened at the small of his back and sat snugly in the crevice of his buttocks, holding him firmly in place. Its interior was lined with satin that afforded him an exquisite chafing and, once his breeches were securely refastened, he was contained and provoked to the peak of madness.

He knelt down once more, his expression imploring the countess to allow him access to her most secret treasure. She sat primly on the high-backed chair, parted her legs – encased in soft kid-leather boots, button-fastened to her knees – and lifted the hem of her full skirts. For the next twelve minutes, her husband was softly enveloped under a swathe of organza.

2

At ten minutes to nine, Katia stood pensive in the kitchen as Magda tied the lace straps of a white cotton apron in a bow at her back. The bib of the apron was pinned halfway over Katia's ripe bust, which sat snugly in the low-cut square neckline of a long-sleeved fitted black tunic. A white lace-trimmed cap was fastened to her head. On her feet she wore polished black ankle boots with small heels that put a slight tremble in her walk.

She was exhausted, but grateful for having been allowed to bathe after the long journey. She had soaked her travel-weary body in the deepest bath she'd ever seen – and mercifully there had been lavender salts to soften the water. In the simmering, soporific liquid, she had almost dozed off, but the urgency of meeting the count and countess kept leaping into her mind to prevent a surrender to slumber.

'The countess and her husband are very particular about manners,' said Magda, applying quick strokes of a large silver-backed brush to Katia's hair. 'You are to address the countess as "your ladyship" or "my lady". The gentleman is, of course . . .'

' "Your lordship" and "my lord"?' Katia ventured.

'That's right. You shouldn't do too badly. Not like some of the slovenly girls we've had here. You should please the pair of them handsomely, I should think.'

'What exactly are to be my duties?' Katia asked.

'Her ladyship will explain all that, but they will be the usual ones of a maid, I'm sure. Cook can always use help in the kitchen. I dare say you'll lend a hand to Peter – he's the gardener and responsible for the veg we grow here. Mind you, he's got his work cut out these days. The harvest isn't looking too bountiful this year. It's a real problem, so it is.'

Katia knew nothing about vegetables and harvests, so she looked around the room as Magda continued to fuss over her hair. It was very different from the cosy modern kitchen of her family home. The manor was ancient, built in the fifteenth century, and the flagstoned floor and thick walls were not the greatest conductors of heat. But the huge wood-burning cooking range threw out wonderful warmth, and Katia imagined the staff would congregate here most often in the winter.

A pan of stewing fruit bubbled on the stove and the autumnal smell of cinnamon and cloves hung in the air. Casserole dishes and pots and pans were stacked on thick wooden shelves, whilst ladles, whisks and giant aluminium spoons hung from a metal pole suspended from the ceiling. And from the walls hung ropes of garlic, sprigs of herbs and bags of onions. In an alcove next to the cooker, a chunky ginger cat lay coiled on a cushion atop a wooden spice cabinet. Katia's parents had kept a Siamese cat with a velvet collar, more elegant than this mouser, but she was glad all the same to see domestic animal life and his presence made her smile.

Magda was back to talking about the routine, and Katia was alerted to pay attention.

'Of course, there are fires to be lit early of a morning and all manner of dusting and washing to do.'

'This house is so big, there must be tons of sheets and counterpanes to wash and iron.'

'Don't we know it! Her ladyship likes the finest Egyptian cotton, too, and regularly changed. We'll have you pulling your weight, even though there's not much of it. Now, come along. It's time for your meeting.'

Katia followed Magda out of the kitchen and into an anteroom used for storing bags of salt, corn and tinder wood. On one side were windows looking out onto the grounds, now in darkness. She longed to explore the gardens, but there would be time aplenty for that. Now she must pay attention. Oh goodness, she hoped everything would be all right. They went through a low, curtained doorway that opened onto a corridor lit with gas lamps that led to the main part of the house. A thick oak door at the end of the corridor was the portal that opened onto the vast hall. It was Katia's first glimpse of its baronial splendour.

Ancient history was embedded in the fabric of the building. The walls were painted russet red and heraldic blue, on which appeared repeated motifs of leaping deer, boxing hares and cranes in flight. Here and there were little gold shields, some featuring the same image of the boars' heads she'd noticed on the main gates.

From the ceiling hung giant tapestries featuring hunting scenes, and as her eye followed the trajectory of the wide staircase she became aware of several huge oil paintings of former nobles who once had claim to this vast and splendid house. She had never been anywhere like it. Even the music academy she had visited with her family was not as grand as this. She spied two suits of armour on the upstairs landing and wondered if any battles or swordfights had taken place there. Would the count be of knightly descent? A military man, perhaps, hardened from his land's endless war with the Turks.

Magda's no-nonsense practicality broke through her thoughts: 'Plenty of time for gawping. Let's get you properly introduced.'

Magda strode across the hall and knocked on the door at the left-hand side of the staircase.

'Come in,' answered an imperious female voice.

As Magda opened the door, a blast of warmth welcomed them. A fully banked-up fire roasted orange and yellow in an ornately tiled fireplace. It was that which drew Katia's attention first, although she was also distinctly aware of the tall gentleman who stood in front of it. Her eyes flickered over him just long enough to see he was immaculately presented. Yet he wasn't the only handsome thing in the lavish, wood-panelled room. The place was resplendent with fine objects and luxurious furniture – chaises longues, sumptuous velvet chairs and tasselled footstools, huge ceramic pots with palms growing out of them, lacquered screens and thick oriental carpets. A chandelier of black and red crystals formed a mesmerising centrepiece in the ceiling, and it was to this that Katia fixed her gaze.

'Miss Katia, your ladyship. Just as you wanted her.'

'Thank you, Magda, that'll be all,' said the countess.

With a rustle of skirts, the housekeeper vanished, and Katia was alone with the couple. She bowed her head and curtseyed. And felt the atmosphere instantly change.

'Good evening, your ladyship, my lord,' she offered.

'Stand up straight, my dear. Let's get a good look at you,' the countess said haughtily.

Katia breathed in deeply to effect a ramrod-straight back and what she felt was elegant deportment.

'There's no need to freeze like a statue,' the countess said. 'You're not on military parade.' Then she asked suddenly, 'Do you like animals?'

'Oh yes, my lady,' Katia replied immediately, softening her pose, her eyes lighting up. She was conscious of the count in his fine tailoring regarding her sudden enthusiasm, aware of a smile registering beneath his moustache. As yet he hadn't uttered a word.

The countess moved fluidly across the room toward the window. She went behind the heavy, golden velvet curtains for a moment then emerged holding something shielded with a purple scarf. With a graceful sweep she was back, standing in front of her. This animal was no cat or dog.

'What do you think it is?' asked the countess, testing her.

'I should hope it is a little songbird, my lady.'

'No, you are quite wrong.' The countess remained still, impassive.

'Please, your ladyship, I hope it isn't something frightful,' Katia said, seized with the horror that she might be expected to handle some giant insect – even worse, a spider. Although she had been in the presence of the countess for only a few minutes, she sensed the woman possessed some eccentricities.

'We don't think he's frightful,' said the countess. 'We think he's quite the charming little gentleman. Say hello to Mr Lautrec!'

With the theatrical gesture of a magician, she removed the scarf to reveal a most unexpected sight. Sitting in her left hand was a lizard. Katia moved closer. She had no fear of reptiles; she'd barely given their existence a second thought.

On close inspection she saw that the creature had not been left as nature intended. The light from the chandelier was dancing in dazzling colours around them, refracted by jewels of different hues. These were not to be found in rings on the countess's fingers, but were embedded into the lizard's body – a couple of emeralds, a large topaz, a ruby.

'Isn't he a darling? Nikolai picked him up in Paris a couple of weeks ago. Would you like to hold him?'

Katia tentatively put out her hands to receive the delicate tread of the lizard's feet. She lightly traced a finger over the jewels. It really was a most unique gift and she was pleased to see the creature didn't seem hindered by its accessories.

'He's charming,' she said. 'I've never seen anything like it.'

'An expression one exclaims with monotonous regularity in Paris.' The count had spoken. He was advancing toward her. 'The city of a thousand rare delights.'

Paris. She had hoped to visit Paris after graduating from the academy. Now that opportunity was dashed. But this was no time for regrets. She turned her attention back to the reptile.

'He's very friendly, for a cold-blooded animal,' said the count.

'He's particularly partial to intimate contact with pretty ladies, despite his size. Apparently the sensation of his little feet over one's naked flesh is quite exhilarating.'

What a thing to say! Katia thought. Yet, once aired, it was difficult not to imagine the sensation. She glanced shyly at the count, biting her lip with embarrassment at what he had just said.

'You can take him to your room tonight,' he said softly, his eyebrows lifting as he came closer toward her.

'Oh no, I really don't think that's necessary,' said Katia, lowering her eyes and feeling the heat of him next to her.

'Please . . . look, he likes you,' the count insisted, slowly trailing a finger from her collarbone to her waist. It sent a shiver of excitement coursing through her skin. 'He can keep you company on your first night.'

Thinking it would be rude to refuse yet startled by the count's familiarity, she accepted his offer, wishing it was him who would be keeping her company. She was then invited to sit down while the countess ran through the list of daily, weekly and monthly tasks that would form the bulk of her duties. She stressed the importance of the various uniforms Katia would be required to wear. There was the standard black and white issue for serving meals and cleaning, but on occasion she would be expected to dress in other outfits, which the countess duly presented. Draped over the back of one of the chairs was an elaborate corset. It came with accessories – a black, feathered mask and long silk opera gloves. With this attire, she would be expected to wear long riding boots and her hair would be worn up. Katia couldn't imagine what event would require these garments – perhaps a fancy-dress ball – but the countess was as enigmatic in her explanation as she had been at the interview. She wondered if any of the other staff were requested to dress this way. She couldn't imagine Magda or the cook squeezing their beefy arms into those slender gloves.

Although her ladyship cut an imposing figure, Katia got the

sense she and the count were trading private jokes, watching for her reactions. A number of knowing but strangely forced smiles flashed between them, and the emphasis they put on words like 'discipline' and 'favour' alarmed her a little, but in a strange way she felt privileged. Perhaps she could learn much about sophisticated life from this couple.

The countess explained the layout of the manor and the rules pertaining to where she could and could not wander. The room at the top of the tower was absolutely out of bounds, it being the countess's private study. Similarly, the library was the sole domain of the count. Both rooms remained locked at all times and there was no spare key for either. There was a wine cellar and also a family vault, the thought of which brought a shiver to Katia's bones.

Things could be a lot worse. Her own room was well maintained, if somewhat isolated, situated at the back of the house. It was cold, with a tiny fireplace that would struggle to heat the room, and the ceiling was low, yet the window afforded a magnificent view of the grounds. For a moment, if she forced the circumstances of her employment out of her mind, she could still imagine she was the Lady of the Manor.

She retired that night, carrying all her uniforms with her, her head a riot of emotions. The count had taken every opportunity to stand close to her, even to touch her, and his wife hadn't seemed in the least perturbed. How unusual they were. What must it be like to have a worldly man such as the count desiring you, embracing you, undressing you? Katia wondered, aware that his subtle caresses had brought her to a heated anxiety. In recent months she had been dwelling often on feelings that used to confuse her but now made her feel excited and warm. The slightest attention from a handsome man would lead her to spend hours pondering what she realised were indelicate thoughts, yet they were too arousing to banish. She would do well to put such things out of her mind now, she reminded herself, yet Nikolai was so handsome.

She was allowed to take a drink of hot milk to bed with her, to ease her rest in unfamiliar surroundings. She was even grateful for the company of the lizard. He was very tame. She bundled herself in bed beneath a giant bearskin rug, and let the little reptile crawl up her arms and over her chest, remembering what the count had told her. She stared into his jewels, mesmerised by the colours. With flashes of blue and green light flickering behind her eyes, and her head full of strange new desires, it wasn't long before she drifted into sleep.

3

Katia's first couple of weeks passed by in a blur of domestic obligations as she struggled to adjust to life at the manor. There was no longer time for her beloved music practice, and she fell into bed each night weary and aching with the shock of using muscles she'd never previously known she had. She was made to chop wood, scrub floors, wind the mangle and carry great loads of washing around the house. Her days began early, as she presented herself to Magda at 6 a.m., before knuckling down to laundry work and polishing the silver, as well as fire-lighting and kitchen assistance. By 8 a.m. each day she had swept the grates and prepared the fires in the drawing room, bathrooms and dining rooms.

She was trained to serve the Malinovskys at table and bring them beverages throughout the day: roasted coffee, delicate teas from the Orient, massala wines at dessert, and port or brandy for his lordship, as he read late into the night or returned from one of his walks. She was always just a little bit excited to bring the count his port, as this usually meant he was alone and would fix his attentions on her. He had already inquired about her parents, and Katia had been very glad of the opportunity to let it be known that she was, in fact, a young lady, and if not for her misfortune would not be in service at all but would be graduating from the academy. His lordship had responded with kindness and they ventured to converse, albeit tentatively, in French. He was so polite – unlike the remote and frosty countess – and Katia wondered as to the details of their marriage. They seemed to occupy different ends of the house.

She was sure to present an immaculate appearance, as the countess had instructed, and her reflection pleased her as she caught sight of it in the many mirrors of the house as she went about her business. The imperial couple was greatly taken by their own likeness, being both good-looking and fastidiously groomed. The countess was attended to each morning and early evening by a personal hairdresser, a fragrant gentleman from Italy who liked to fuss over his mistress's coiffure. He would brush the imperial tresses, treat them with hot oils and lotions, adorn them with beaded caps, and fashion elaborate styles with tortoiseshell combs and jewelled pins. All the while he would be reciting news of the latest fashions, and how the *signora* would be the *bellisima de fiesta* in Milan and Venice. In fact, the countess had a whole room devoted solely to her hairdressing, where the endless dyeing, curling and combing went on, and it was no wonder, thought Katia, that the count invested so much time in his library.

It was midday, the fires were roaring and the breakfast things cleared away as Katia ascended the staircase, her arms piled with fresh laundry. Changing the bed linen and washing the countless embroidered coverings that draped across the backs of chairs or on which plant pots or stuffed creatures stood would be a never-ending task. She turned the corner at the top of the stairs, to make her way to the linen cupboard, and it was as she approached the master bedroom that she heard the dreadful sound. It wasn't what she could call familiar, as she had witnessed something like it only three or four times in her young life, yet it was instantly recognisable as the exertions of punishment. Someone – surely it couldn't be the count – was being beaten. She froze on the landing and clenched the clean linen to her breast, breathing in the scent of the cotton lotion, as if to protect herself from whatever unsavoury commotion was occurring not ten yards from where she stood.

She tiptoed further toward the source of the noise. The bedroom door was ajar. The count was bent over a velvet stool;

his jacket was off but he remained clothed about his lower person. The countess was wearing a long grey dress, cinched in at the waist by a narrow corselet. Her hair was coiled on top of her head. In her hand she brandished a vicious quirt, and brought it down repeatedly upon the count's backside. His lordship was being whipped on his buttocks! Katia didn't know what to think or how to react to this unexpected vision. Was this something religious? Perhaps the Malinovskys were seeking penance through harsh physical discipline. But that didn't fit with their sumptuous lifestyle. There was no evidence that the couple was suited to anything other than luxury. Katia remained transfixed, longing to witness his intimate flesh being reddened. It was a lustful curiosity, and she felt ashamed at how it excited her.

'What were you looking at?' the countess demanded of her husband.

'Only rare and beautiful pictures, my love.'

'Nonsense!' she shouted. 'You were ogling filth.'

'Then beat me for it,' he said. 'Whip me like a dog.'

As the countess lashed her husband's buttocks, Katia found herself rocking softly back and forth with each movement. Gradually, imperceptibly, the motion loosened the bottle of linen lotion she had folded into the laundry. By the time she felt the bottle slide against her arm, it was already too late, and it fell to the floor with a heavy thud.

The countess spun around, whip in hand, a terrifying energy lighting her eyes.

'Oh, your ladyship!' cried Katia. 'I do beg your pardon. I was just coming to change the bed linen and I, I wasn't sure, I thought...'

'Stop stammering, girl, and come here. It's time you learned something about the count. The handsome imperial count, who rides in carriages and wears monogrammed dressing gowns. I present him to you in all his glory.'

With that she lashed him once more across his seat.

'Now get up,' she ordered him. 'Get up and show yourself. Show what condition you are in.'

The count raised himself unsteadily and turned to face Katia.

Her eyes flew to the middle of his body, as there, unmistakably, was evidence of his arousal. Katia had never before seen such a rude sight and her hand flew to her mouth in shock. The girls at the academy had giggled about erections, usually when a carriage horse distended itself, but this was the first time she had been faced with the reality of a gentleman in such a condition.

'Impressive, I'm sure you'll agree,' said Irina. 'Although he struggles to keep it decent, hidden from the gaze of ladies. Very fond of taking it out in the library, though, aren't you, my dear?' she said to her husband, caressing his face with the crop. 'Perhaps you'd like to show it to our lovely new maid.'

'Would you like that?' he croaked, humbled in the presence of the two beautiful women.

'Er, yes, I suppose so,' Katia replied, unsure of how to behave in this most irregular circumstance, despite the fact that a new kind of excitement had taken hold of her with an irresistible force.

'Well then, what are you waiting for? Unbutton yourself for the girl.'

The count did as he was told, and the sight filled Katia's senses with a rush of energy. Her mouth was dry and she felt weak and hot between her legs. She yearned to grab at herself, as she had learned from her racier friends at school.

Not daring to blink, lest she miss something, she stared wide-eyed at the count's hands, as he fumbled to reveal himself. When he did, it was huge and erect and eager. Instinctively she licked her lips, wondering what was going to happen.

'Delightful, isn't he?' said the countess. 'Although so lacking in discipline. He would touch himself all day if he could. Poring over those disgraceful pictures.'

She brandished a selection of photographic prints, laying them out on the dressing table for Katia to get a clear view. The images were truly shocking. Two women were pleasuring each other with carved phalluses whilst a man gripped himself. The only photographic images she had seen had been of landscapes, stately homes, the king and queen. To think that people would abuse this marvellous invention for such debased reasons!

'Show our maid what you do,' ordered the countess.

'I take myself in hand, like this,' he said, grasping his impressive size and moving his hand up and down. 'I've done it under the dining table a couple of times, when you've served me at dinner. I like to think one day I'll plunder your pretty cunt.'

Katia exclaimed her shock at such foul language coming from a gentleman, although it was uttered so softly as to sound like a secret.

'See what a hound he is,' said the countess. 'Now put that laundry down and come closer. You are to learn something essential to your instruction.'

Cautiously, Katia approached the couple, uncertain of what indignity she would have to endure. The countess handed her the crop.

'Time to get acquainted with this,' she said. 'Cruelty is an art. And best administered on the flesh of a man such as he.' She pointed at her husband. 'Do you know what torments he endures for his ultimate pleasure?' she asked.

Katia shook her head, unable to speculate what these might be. She could not imagine how people came to such depravity of their own volition.

The countess continued: 'He denies himself the natural position of a married man, preferring instead to be thrashed as he brings himself to his crisis. He doesn't perform his marital duty, for he has to be submissive at all times.'

Katia wasn't entirely sure what the countess was speaking about, but she suspected her words alluded to practices she'd never dared imagine. It wasn't the romance she had dreamed of – the tender lovemaking she had yearned to know with a handsome soldier. These people were decidedly corrupt. She would write to Uncle Istvan that night and have him collect her as soon as possible. She couldn't remain in such an ungodly household, could she? These people were of noble birth; what on earth had happened to make them like this?

'Please have her whip me,' the count begged his wife, toying with himself unashamedly. 'Her presence alone is bringing me to such inflammation.'

'You hear him?' the countess demanded. 'You hear how he needs you? Then get to it!'

Nikolai knelt down once more, clutching the sides of the footstool and offering his posterior.

'I think this time we'll have him bare,' said Irina. 'Unbutton your breeches and offer yourself.'

He did so, lifting his cambric shirt to reveal the meaty globes of his buttocks as he once again bent over. Katia was appalled, wondering if her dear father had ever proffered himself thus for her mother. She shook the image from her mind, yet at the same time felt herself strangely breathless. The whole incident was alarming, especially for the presence of another woman – a woman seemingly as perverse as the worst of men in that she was encouraging this outrage. It was as if Katia had walked into a room in a brothel rather than the master bedroom of her esteemed employers.

She stared down at the count's arse-cheeks, curiously compelled to grab at them. Instead, she trailed the end of the crop across his skin and tapped lightly, finding herself unable to lash at him without instruction.

'That's no good, girl. He'll not be punished that way. Lay into him. Do you not think he deserves it, poring over those disgraceful photographs?'

Yes, this did seem a terrible dereliction of marital fidelity. Yes, he was a lecherous count. Yes, he did deserve to be whipped.

So it was that she raised her arm and set about bringing the crop down onto his buttocks, her eyes widening as the flesh turned pink, then red, as the count squirmed beneath her touch.

'Oh, you glorious, beautiful little bitch,' he cried. 'Continue like that and I will spend into my hand. How I wish it were your sweet little cunt, you lovely girl.'

'Stop. Stop touching yourself!' ordered the countess. She came up close to Katia, and spoke to her urgently. 'This is the moment where you can have him do whatever bidding you like. See how desperate he is. This is where a woman can enjoy complete power over a man. Learn it well, and learn the way to make a man beg. Go on, make him do something demeaning for you.'

Katia's mind raced as she thought of a fitting task to make him perform. She could barely think straight for the brazen and filthy language that was echoing in her ears.

'Crawl to the dressing table,' she said. 'Fetch me a handkerchief in your mouth.'

The countess laughed and both women watched, eyes glinting, as his lordship carried out the order. He returned with it between his teeth and sat before them, eyes pleading for more instructions.

'Take off the shirt, I want him completely naked,' said Katia, energised by the unexpected power of her position.

With the handkerchief still in his mouth, the count removed his shirt and sat before her.

'Show me, then, what it is you do alone, looking at those pictures.'

The count laid the handkerchief on the floor and once more took himself into his hand.

'I have been sinful,' he said. 'I need to feel the kiss of the whip.'

He went onto all fours, intermittently using one hand to touch himself as Katia worked the crop deeper into his flesh, reddening him to an angry hue. Her sex was swollen beneath her uniform, and her breath was quick and shallow, as the desire to touch herself increased with every swing of the lash. Under her long striped gown and thick stockings she was covered in perspiration. Her glossy chestnut hair had fallen out of its binding and swung about her shoulders.

'Oh God,' she cried, as she watched Nikolai move his hand with increased speed. What on earth was she witnessing? What had she allowed herself to be drawn into? These sensations that were so foreign to her, yet so very scintillating, did all women feel them?

Katia felt Irina's gaze on her; she, more than the count, was the focus of this imposing woman's intense concentration. Then something happened that she could not have foreseen. The countess stilled Katia's hand and seized her breasts. And Katia liked it. Her hair was taken into a clench and she was pulled close to the countess's body as the woman drove her tongue into her mouth. Katia, in her aroused state, yielded to the assault, and allowed complete access to her body. The countess spun her around and unlaced the dress, stripping her without tenderness, to reveal her naked but for her knickers and thick woollen stockings.

Nikolai ushered himself closer, so his head was positioned between Katia's thighs. He frantically worked at himself as he rubbed his face against the soft skin of her belly.

'I beg of you to reveal yourself to me,' he implored, his hands slowly working themselves up her legs to tenderly caress the satin of her knickers.

Katia knew she should forbid it, forbid all that was happening to her, yet these sensations were a revelation. She had never before felt so excited or alive. She caressed her own breasts, stroked her hair, luxuriated in the moment and lost herself to erotic abandon. The countess came behind her and slid her arms beneath hers, holding her in a clench, stilling her, allowing the count to get a firm grasp on Katia's backside and legs.

Katia watched, horrified but quiescent to the count's actions, as he peeled her undergarments down her legs, stopping to inhale deeply of her scent as he did so. Her face flamed with embarrassment, that a man, a stranger, even one of noble position, could have such intimate access to her. Her undergarments slithered down her legs and she helpfully stepped out of them, then watched, speechless, as he brought them to his face. Katia knew how pungent they must be, infused with her aroma. He inhaled while he touched himself, pumping the thick length of his manhood. She could not take her eyes off the glistening succulence; she wanted closer access, yet she dare not be so presumptuous. Whatever was occurring, the countess was most definitely in charge, and Katia knew she would not take too kindly to a maid making a grab for her husband's penis.

Still, the sight of the count in his erect state had awoken a need she would have to satisfy somehow. She could see the tight package of his ballsac being pulled and stretched as the count continued to rub at himself. Then, oh goodness, he offered to do what she dare not ask, yet in her darkest thoughts longed for. His tongue went to the downy thatch between her legs, and probed until he found the source of her joy.

Katia moaned and writhed, held fast by the countess, who she knew was also aroused, as she could feel the older woman's heart beating, squashed to her back, and feel her ragged breath warm against her ear. Could she know her ultimate moment in the presence of not one but two people? Such exposure was unthinkable, yet she could not pull away.

The movement of the count's tongue on her was like nothing else, its pace maddeningly slow at one point, building her impending climax. Her desire was an impacted device that threatened to explode so violently she didn't know what to do. Yet from some new, shameful part of her suddenly came the need to cry out obscenities, as the count worked his mouth and his hand.

'Oh make me cream myself, sir,' she cried, her forehead now

beaded with perspiration. 'I'll spend over your face if you don't stop.'

'What a little slut!' laughed the countess. 'Neither of you has any control. I should punish you both.' Despite this, she pulled at Katia's nipples, only increasing her desperate need to push herself to the limit, to say things she'd never previously thought of, let alone expressed to another.

'Oh yes. Please lick me. Bring me to my climax,' she urged breathlessly, never before knowing such a fire between her legs.

And, with a few final strokes of his tongue and tickles of his moustache, Katia was tipping over into a dazzling abyss, writhing in the arms of the countess, her sex throbbing and disgorging the fragrant juices of her adolescence over the face of the count.

It was too much for him.

'Oh, this is it,' he cried, throwing his head back. 'I am going to do it for you. You are to be my mistress as I spend for you. I cannot contain myself. I am going to let it fly and you must watch.'

Her eyes widened as a vision of bizarre undoing erupted before her. For there, in broad daylight, his lordship the count was ejaculating and staring her full in the eyes as he did so. The white cream shot from him with such force that she wanted to catch it all over herself. Some of it splashed against her legs but, appallingly, she realised that she craved to know this spectacle in her face.

She collapsed to the floor, pulling her discarded clothes around her in a gesture that attempted to regain some dignity, but this was futile. To think this bizarre and depraved situation had been her first sexual encounter! It was a very long way from what she had imagined would occur, being courted by a handsome beau. She was still intact, of course, although unsure of how long that condition could be preserved. Since her very first night at the manor a powerful force had taken hold of her. Even though her work was hard and dull, her imagination had come alive with adult desires that made her feel radiant.

She brushed her dishevelled hair from her face and started dressing. The count was in similar disarray. With his thick dark hair falling about his face, he looked rakish, and his eyes sparkled. Once trousered, he walked over to Katia and planted a kiss on her full lips.

'Thank you, sweetheart,' he said. 'You brought me off so beautifully with your sweet little cunt on my face.'

It was shocking language, yet again expressed so tenderly, and Katia found herself touched by his gesture. He didn't have to thank her; he could have been every inch the brute, like so many men of his position. Yet she realised she wanted more from him – full congress and the end of her maiden status. At that moment she would have been grateful even for a brute.

'That'll be all,' Irina cut in. 'You may leave now.'

What would be left for the countess? Katia wondered. She hadn't removed a single item of her complicated clothing, nor laid a hand upon herself. How did she get her pleasure? Perhaps time would reveal the answer to this mystery. She could not imagine how she would return to serving the couple without thinking of the depravities they had shared. Would this happen again? Might it become a regular thing?

Hurriedly dressed, and ill-groomed, Katia exited the room to make her way to the bathroom. As she hurried along the landing, she rounded the corner and literally bumped into Magda.

'There you are. I've been looking for you all over. Goodness me, you look dishevelled. Anyway, cook wants an errand running. We're out of supplies and someone has to go to the next village. You'll find a basket in the kitchen. Don't dawdle. We need the vegetables for supper.'

Walking ten miles was the last thing Katia felt like doing, but such was her lot in life now. Still, it would give her time to reflect on what had just happened. If only she could meet someone like the count she could take for her own. She had never considered that a man of such importance would want to humble and humiliate himself like that. She'd always imagined an important man would want to overpower a woman. And that thing he had done between her legs . . . it was shocking yet wonderful. To think a man and a woman could play such games. Oh, to know that again!

4

So it was that Katia found herself, her woollen cloak around her, crossing the grounds, preparing to cut through the forest and daydreaming about Nikolai.

With her basket and list in hand she traversed the lawns and was heading for the drive when she heard a thud and someone yelling at her to get out of the way. She spun around to see, barely two yards away, a freshly landed arrow in a straw-filled target.

'If I wasn't so good a shot, you might have been in the pot tonight.'

It was Peter, the gardener, running to retrieve his flights.

Katia froze as he advanced toward her, his tanned physique on display despite a recent drop in temperature. Around his forearm was a leather guard and across his bare chest the strap that held his quiver.

'Archery? I thought you were the gardener,' she said.

'Gardener ... hunter ... everything. If I can't grow the food, I'm going to have to catch it,' he replied.

'Same reason I'm being sent to the village. To get these supplies.'

Peter took the list from her hand.

'Potatoes, onions, tomatoes. Apparently, last year the pantry was full of the manor's own produce. Now we have to buy it. Breaks my heart.'

Katia took in the image of the young gardener, his firm chest and curled blond hair, and saw him in a new light. She'd barely given him a moment's thought when the cook had introduced him the previous week. Now she saw him as a man – a virile man with strong arms and thighs. She wondered if the countess had some kind of claim over this handsome son of the soil, getting from him what her husband didn't provide. She remained flushed from her experience in the bedroom, and the notion crossed her mind that Peter might guess what she had just been doing. No one else could tell, could they?

'And I suppose you are expected to go to the second village,' said Peter.

'Yes. It's a good ten miles, I hear, although quicker if I go through the woods. Cook has given me directions.'

'The woods?' He sounded alarmed. 'You must let me accompany you. How they expect you to go alone I cannot imagine.'

Katia was touched by the young man's concern. He had a soft expression and kind eyes. Yet there was also a sadness about him; a haunted look she couldn't comprehend. Maybe he too had suffered a loss.

He put on his jacket and they walked together to the main gates. Spotting the ox-featured gatekeeper, Peter ushered Katia through a gap in the undergrowth.

'Best not to let Auroch see us leave together. People too easily jump to conclusions in this place,' he said.

They found their way to the exterior of the grounds and started the long walk. Katia attempted to follow the cook's directions but Peter knew a short cut, and before long they were crunching through the autumn leaf-fall and were deep in the forest.

'What do you think of the manor?' he asked.

'It's beautiful,' she said. 'The gardens are astounding.'

'But what about the count and countess?' he continued. 'Do you not find their behaviour odd? She is barren, obviously. Ten years married and no children. And her vanity is legendary.'

No stranger to the looking-glass herself, Katia couldn't share his scorn for self-admiration.

'Well, I suppose they're a little eccentric,' she offered. 'There seems to be many locked rooms and hiding places. The countess disappears for hours every day in the tower and I cannot imagine how she occupies herself. She seems pensive, a little cold, but I suppose that's what all noblewomen are like.'

'Until the disappearances are solved, we're all under suspicion,' said Peter.

'What disappearances?' she asked, feeling suddenly vulnerable as the squawk of a crow rang out over the tall thin trees. Katia felt her heartbeat increase. The combination of unfamiliar company and the sudden noise set the downy hair of her slender arms standing upright.

'Oh, it's nothing important, according to the countess,' said Peter, with a note of sarcasm. 'But in the past year three girls have gone missing from local villages and their mothers are sick with worry. It's all the local people speak of; that and the curse. Some even think the two are linked, that something evil has awoken in these parts.'

'Oh Peter, stop it!' Katia said, her hand flying to her face. 'You don't think it's true, do you? Oh goodness, I was meant to be studying music in Vienna and now I'm in this backwater where girls go missing, and I'm walking miles to buy potatoes.'

'I don't mean to frighten you,' said Peter, placing his hands on her shoulders. 'I want to warn you. Promise you'll keep your windows locked at night. Don't enter the woods alone.'

The gardener's touch was so welcome to her already aroused body that Katia felt herself pressed up against him before she had time to correct her behaviour. She was ready for a man's embrace, awakened by her experience with the count, and the smell of Peter's skin intoxicated her senses. She wanted to kiss him passionately but before she could make a move the leaves fluttered around them and the first droplets of rain began to splash upon their heads. There was no time to explore this new, unexpected attraction. The rain grew heavier so that in a matter of seconds they were running for shelter. They found it in a small cave covered with moss, where they stood and watched the heavens' downpour pound upon the rocks.

While they waited for the storm to subside, Peter made no move to continue their physical contact. Instead he spoke of how he would restore the manor gardens to their former glory. He talked of soil enrichment, cultivating new strains of flowers so the scent of the night-stocks would rival any roses ever grown there, and vowed that the hollyhocks would grow as tall as gateposts. By the time the downpour had slowed to a drizzle, Katia was happy to move on, their initial clinch seemingly forgotten, surrendered to Peter's speech of how he would put right all that was wrong in the garden.

By the time they arrived at the village she had learned how Peter had worked the earth with his father since childhood. The land was in his blood, he said. The harvest was the most important time of year, what he lived for, yet this season he had been denied that satisfaction. The wealth of an estate could be measured by the health of its crops, and the failure of the Malinovsky gardens hung heavy around his heart.

'I am a practical man from a family of practical men,' he said, 'but God has deserted the countess and her gardens. I believe only His power will restore it.'

With that, he crossed himself, and Katia was reminded how she had barely given her own faith a moment's thought since arriving at the manor. How could she take confession now – admit to indignities in which she'd so willingly participated? She was no longer innocent yet, instead of feeling shame, she burned with excitement to know more of adult life.

They found the farmer's shop and, their basket loaded with supplies, they stopped for food in a dark, low-ceilinged inn decorated with the red and black flags of the region. Dried bunches of herbs hung from the beams, and over the serving hatch a gnarled root was prominent.

'What's that?' asked Katia, as they sat on the dark wooden benches.

'The mandragora,' said Peter. 'Plucked from under the gibbet at moonlight, it is said to protect against evil.'

'Sounds primitive,' said Katia.

'Such thinking is strong here. The mindset in these remote parts trails the civilised world by some three hundred years. Just look around you. These people are full of superstitions.'

Katia scanned the room. Paintings adorned the walls, featuring fantastical beasts – griffins and winged dogs, and eagles with lethal talons. In one picture, a group of hand-maidens was making an offering to Isten, the god of the forest.

Suddenly, a sour-faced woman in a grubby apron was at their table.

'What'll it be?' she asked

'The goulash – two bowls,' replied Peter.

The woman peered at him up close, her piggy eyes narrowing in her fleshy pink face.

'You're Laszlo's boy, ain't ya? Taken up recent at the manor?'

'That's right.'

The woman walked away, and began wiping tables. 'Sorry, there's no food here,' she mumbled into the fleshy rolls of her neck.

'Please,' said Katia. 'We've been walking all morning. We're famished.'

'Can't help you. Sorry.'

With a gruff face she waddled back to the kitchens. Peter and Katia could see the steaming pan of soup on the stove and slices of bread piled on the chopping board. Katia leaped to her feet and apprehended the woman, grabbing her by the arm.

'You do have food. What's that in that pot, then, if it's not stew?'

She spun round, astonished at being touched by a stranger.

'Foolish girl! Who do you think you are? This food is for the good folk of this village. Honest folk.'

'We haven't done anything wrong. We have money. Look!' Katia retrieved her purse and brandished a coin. 'We work at the manor. Why won't you serve us?'

'You answer to her . . . that fiend . . . we don't want her nor her likes in here. Don't care what money you have. You'll not find anyone round here who'll have you sup in their house.'

The woman folded her meaty arms across her chest, as if to put a final bar on the conversation.

'I'll have you know I answer only to God,' said Peter. 'Too many people around here speak of fiends and nonsense. They'd do well to read the Good Book.'

'We have our ways and customs, I'll grant you,' the woman said. 'But them's not her ways. There'll be no good come to that place, nor no one in it while that woman is there.'

'You're speaking rubbish, woman,' said Peter. 'We're not "of her kind", as you put it. We do honest jobs. Why be so mean-spirited with your kitchen?'

'I'll not sup with the devil, nor the devil's own,' she grumbled. 'I'll not risk catching the blight you've got.'

'The soil just needs regenerating, that's all,' said Peter, keen to allay fears and rumours.

'Tis a curse. Nothing else for it.'

When her two sons appeared from the back of the inn, silent and thickset, Katia was relieved Peter did not push the argument. There was no budging this woman's opinion and she didn't want trouble.

'Come on, Katia,' said Peter, and they both made for the door under the glare of the burly young men. 'Bet your soup's rotten anyway,' he called back as they left.

They trudged back up the hill toward the forest with empty stomachs, Peter carrying the basket. A wind had got up, and leaves swirled around their legs as they bolstered themselves against the breeze. *These people are truly backward*, thought

Katia, homesick for the little tea-shops of her home town; for the bustle and exuberance of the city and the trappings of the modern world. She had expected the area would be remote, but all this talk of the devil and curses was ridiculous. The Malinovskys were unusual and vain but they weren't evil, surely. Those girls who had disappeared ... they'd probably fled to the town, if they had any sense!

Peter remained silent, lost in his thoughts, while Katia daydreamed about her former life. With neither of them concentrating on the track, they soon lost sight of the path and found themselves in a wooded valley littered with leaves and fallen branches, high banks each side of them. As Peter tried to get his bearings, the wind whistled through the trees and Katia thought she could hear the sound of chanting. She placed her hand on Peter's arm and cocked her head. There it was again – a mournful incantation accompanied by murmuring lower notes, similar to the recitals one hears in a monastery.

'Quick, over here,' whispered Peter, grabbing Katia and pulling her behind the trunk of a felled tree. The chanting grew louder, and then, across the top of the ridge, a procession of figures in long robes made their way toward a dip in the gulley and stopped, bending down to pick at the ground.

'Who are they, and what are they doing?' asked Katia.

'Witches, gathering roots and leaves,' whispered Peter, 'for their ungodly purposes. Look, see this,' he said, pointing at a small plant with a black flower, 'that's belladonna, deadly nightshade. Here is also hemlock and colchicum, from which poultices can be made to heal wounds but these crones will ground them up to summon spirits. Maybe Ordog himself.' He spat on the ground.

'Ordog?'

'The dark beast of these parts. One legend says he rides the forests four times a year, when the veil between our world and the wood world is lifted. Ordog, Isten ... belief in them is strong here, kept alive by the antics of foolish people.'

'I wonder if *they* get served at the inn,' pondered Katia.

'Oh, very likely. Those who masquerade as the most pious are often the most energetic worshippers of demons. Nothing is what it seems.'

'But Peter, you don't believe in these superstitions, do you?' she asked, affecting as feminine an intonation to her voice as she could muster. She wished for Peter to respond to her. Crouched down, her skirt was hitched up her legs, and she hoped he might notice her desirability, lay his strong hands on her ... but it was not to be.

'My head tells me no ... yet I've seen things in these woods I cannot explain. I'm sure to have my Bible with me at all times.'

They watched the sorceresses gathering their plants, continuing their incantations. After a few moments they huddled together and emptied their individual handfuls into a jute bag. Then they joined hands and began walking round and around in a circle, offering their thanks to the spirits of the trees. They looked harmless enough to Katia but Peter's expression was frozen into a stern look of ill-regard. After a few minutes of ritualised walking around, they made their way up the steep bank and out of sight.

Peter and Katia scrambled up the other side and, once they got a wider perspective on the landscape, they were able to find their bearings. They stayed to the path and, two hours later, emerged tired and hungry on the straight track along which the coach had first brought Katia to the manor.

Szathmar really was a strange place. She imagined how Uncle Istvan would laugh to hear the talk of devils and demons. He could not have known how backward the local people were, otherwise he would surely have never banished his only niece to the region.

They cut through the undergrowth to avoid Auroch and crunched up the driveway, where a severe, almost spectral figure waited for them outside the main door of the manor. The countess was not in a good mood.

'See how many petals have fallen since you choose to do women's work all day!' the countess barked at the gardener as he walked up to her, clutching the basket of vegetables. She released a handful of rose petals to the ground. From the expression on Peter's face, Katia could tell he too was scared of this savage woman.

'You –' she pointed at Katia '– take those vegetables inside. Later on I may let you observe how much of a man Peter is.'

'Please, don't drag her into this,' he begged. 'She doesn't need to see –'

'She'll see whatever I choose her to see,' Irina replied. 'And she's seen quite a lot already today, haven't you, my dear?'

Katia silently pleaded the countess wouldn't be specific. Thankfully she turned her venom on Peter.

'Tell me, what kind of a man is it that spends his life tending flowers and shopping for vegetables? Where is your claim to masculine prowess?'

'My prowess is found in worship, my lady,' said Peter, his head hanging in surrender. 'For God is my commander.'

'Pah!' she spat. 'A fat lot of good he'll do you. Still, at least your faith makes you humble. With the extra showering of rose petals we've had today I do believe your humiliation garment may be finished. You have two hours before you present yourself to me at sundown.'

The gardener slunk away and as she watched him go, Katia was decidedly intrigued. A humiliation garment? Could it be that the strapping gardener was going to be punished? Would her ladyship take the whip to him as she had her husband? Despite her better nature, Katia found this a thrilling prospect, and she went to the kitchen in search of food and something to take her mind off these strange new desires.

* * *

A perfect stillness hung over the estate, punctuated only by the occasional cry of a peacock and the sound of the countess's boots as she walked up the path of the walled garden. She wore a long, teal-blue satin dress with a high collar. The bristling pelt of a forest beast sat about her shoulders, clasped by a decorative enamel brooch. Her dark luxuriant hair was plaited and looped around her ears and upon her head sat a blue velvet cap from which protruded a heron's plume.

This evening she teemed with a wickedness that brought a smirk to her imperial lips. For over her shoulder she trailed a leash, her finger casually looped through its leather handle. Behind her, making tiny baby steps – for the bandages that bound him were tight around his thighs – was Peter, attached to the leash by means of a collar that sat around his neck. His chest was covered by his leather jerkin yet his feet were bare, as befitted a slave.

The gardener had proved to be really irritating, with his talk of God and his miracle fertilisers that yielded nothing, and would continue to yield nothing as she knew whose law ruled here. Still, it amused her to have fun with him. What possible resonance could his dusty Middle Eastern prophet have in her ancient land of forests and wolves?

Irina was anxious for contact with her master. Her latest translation of an obscure paragraph in Darvulia's book had charged her with excitement: 'Dedicate the orgasm of a maiden or follower of the Nazarene cult to his unearthly majesty to swiftly know his pleasure' it said. She had clapped her hands in glee, for here she had both! Surely it wouldn't be long before her gardens were restored to bloom.

'I have a special treat for you this evening,' she said to Peter. 'Pretty Katia is waiting for us in the summerhouse. Isn't that lovely?'

Peter could only moan his protest, for he was gagged with one of the countess's silk scarves. The look on his face when she had called Giulio to her dressing room to have him tie it had been a picture. The popinjay hairdresser had shrieked his hilarity at the incongruous spectacle of the normally rugged groundsman bound in the tightest undergarments.

Cocooned and silenced, he presented an image of humbled manhood, his strength useless against the countess's bonds. To struggle and rebel would see his dismissal, and he feared that more than the cruel torment of his perverse mistress.

Unconcerned with his opinion, the countess made her way down the sloping lawn, Peter hobbling behind her, toward the octagonal wooden structure that stood bandstand-proud at the edge of the lake. And there was Katia, kitted out as the countess had requested in riding boots and a low-cut dress that hugged her young figure to its most voluptuous advantage. She wore long satin opera gloves and about her neck a velvet choker with a dazzling jewel at her throat. The girl really had been a very good choice.

Peter throbbed in his bonds at the sight of the two women. As much as he struggled to fight the desires surfacing in his body, he was powerless to prevent the onset of an erection. Ironic though it was, the tightness of the bandages only made his embarrassment more pronounced, for stitched inside the swaddling were hundreds of rose petals, their silken touch caressing him like an angel's breath. Twice before he had been made to demean himself in front of the countess, but to have to endure God only knows what humiliation in front of her and the maid was really too much. He hung his head but knew his fate was already written.

Katia stood wide-eyed with expectation. The countess had summoned her soon after she'd retreated to the kitchen. Relieved from scrubbing carrots, she had been taken to the countess's dressing room and there, in front of the count, had been stripped and made to dress in this provocative outfit. The count had run his hands all over her, sliding his fingers between her legs, but only briefly, as the countess had more urgent business than her husband's titillation. He would get what she allowed, when she allowed – no more and no less. As soon as Katia saw herself in the mirror she beamed with delight. This new way of dressing made her feel potent and confident, and she was beginning to understand the effect it had on men.

She had been told to wait in the summerhouse, where the countess would entertain them both with a little theatre. And now, here she was and, good to her word, she had brought the gardener to her for punishment practice. She had felt uncomfortable when the countess had suddenly started talking to her as if she were one of her friends, sharing female secrets, but right now she felt elated as she trailed the tendrils of a multi-thonged lash through her hands. In the shaded interior of the summerhouse, not visible from the manor, the three of them were quite secluded.

The countess stepped inside, Peter beside her on a short rein. Katia stared at the gardener in his strange bonds. To see the bandages wound so tight around his thighs aroused her, and the package at his centre swelled promisingly. Could she, would she, be allowed to touch him? The thought made her shudder with excitement.

Irina handed her the leash, and for the first time she had a man under her command. He refused to look her in the eye, so she jerked the leash and demanded it, and the countess laughed.

'You do make an eager student!' she said.

The countess then lifted Peter's right arm and secured his wrist into a cuff that hung from the ceiling. She did the same with the left arm. Now he was completely helpless and at the women's mercy. Katia watched as the countess trailed a finger down the front of his bandages. The mass of crushed petals sewn inside his garment added to the already pleasing bulge. She prodded gently at the material, then cupped her hand between his thighs to determine what was padding and what flesh. How Katia longed to do the same.

'I think our holy little gardener is getting hard,' she declared, making him cringe with embarrassment. 'He obviously wants it.'

He moaned into his gag. In a gesture of kindness, she untied it and let him speak.

'Please . . . I need to . . . can you . . . ?' he croaked.

'I need, I want,' she mocked. 'I thought your religion forbade such unseemliness. Today you are going to partake in a little experiment. We need to see how much of a man you are. You are going to learn strength through humiliation.' She walked around him, back and forth, her high heels clicking on the concrete, before pressing her soft bosom into his back.

Katia watched him twitch with excitement as the countess ran her hands over his shoulders, arms and pectorals.

'You really have been most diligent, fashioning this garment for our pleasure. We want you bound and corrected, unable to touch yourself. Isn't that right?' She looked at Katia, pressing her hand once more on the swelling. Peter pushed against it, crazy for any touch.

'Tell me what you feel,' Katia said sweetly. 'Do those petals feel soft, silky, like something else? Tell me what they feel like.'

'They feel like . . . a woman,' he said quietly.

'Oh, do be more specific,' snapped the countess.

'Like a female sex.'

'That's right. And what would you like to do to that sex? Plunge into it, feel the sleek joy of its comfort?'

'Please, I need release. I'm a Christian but I am still a man.'

He sounded as if he was about to weep.

'I think he needs a reminder of his position,' said Irina. 'Come here,' she said to Katia. 'You'll help him remember, won't you?'

Katia could not bear to be denied the touch of a man any longer. Peter wasn't nobility; he was betrothed to no one.

She need not wait for the countess's approval to lay her hands upon him. It would be her first time, and she ached between her legs for the knowledge. This was no time to be hesitant. She stepped forward, stretched out a gloved hand and, like Irina, cupped it over his bulge. Heavens! It felt enormous, this live thing that offered so much promise. What was she to do with it?

She didn't need to wonder, for Peter began thrusting against her hand and she felt the full measure of him, the length and girth making her breathless. One day, hopefully very soon, she would take something like this into herself.

'Does it feel nice?' she asked, struggling to add an icy tone to her voice, as the countess had instructed.

'Of course it feels nice. You witches, why do you torture me so?' he pleaded.

Katia didn't take too kindly to being called a witch. To get her revenge she would add to his plight. She recalled the obscene words the count had used on her – their power.

'You need to use your imagination, Peter,' she said. 'I want you to imagine those petals are my silky cunt. You can thrust up hard against them, into my tight virgin sex.'

Peter flashed her a look of absolute shock, his eyes glinting with shame at this unexpectedly sordid development, as Katia leaned forward to suck on his nipples. She began licking him all over, insinuating her body against his, all the while rubbing him as he pushed against her hand.

'Good Christ, woman, do you want me to demean myself so totally that I spend inside these bonds?' he said. 'You don't know what you are doing, God forgive you, you must be under the influence of some drug or demon.'

He twisted and writhed in an attempt to escape her ministrations but it was futile. The exquisite feelings were too strong.

Katia was almost breathless with arousal. She had forgotten she was supposed to be whipping him and had given herself over to purely wanton physical contact – the contact she had been denied earlier in the woods. But it would be a shame if he ejaculated into the rose petals. She so badly longed to see it happen like the count's eruption that morning.

'Stop!' shouted the countess. 'He is so desperate this will all be over too soon.'

Katia released herself from the bound man and stood back to get her breath. It was completely unthinkable, but she had to touch herself. She was flooded with the juices of arousal, swollen and needy for something inside her. She was so far gone down the path of indecency she didn't care that the countess was watching. It was Peter and his manhood that was uppermost in her sights. She took the handle of the lash and rubbed it on herself. It felt good. Would she dare to bring herself to a climax in front of these people? In the case of the countess, the second time that day?

The countess was impatient. She walked over to Katia and snatched the object from her. The rounded end of the handle shone with her juices. She immediately thrust it under Peter's nose, then demanded he suck on it. Katia was bereft yet mesmerised by the blatant perversity of this woman. As he sucked, he swelled again, and she once more reached out to feel him in his confines. He moaned and writhed, jerking his hips against the air.

'You are both ready,' announced the countess. 'Overripe virgins on the brink of your debauchery.'

With this she took the lash and cracked it against Peter's back, her teeth showing pointed and white, her eyes sparkling as if she were possessed. He flinched but remained hard. Then, to his and Katia's surprise, the countess retrieved a small knife from her bag and began to slice at the bandages. Peter suddenly became contrite, thanking her over and over until Katia wanted to strike him for his obsequiousness. But she watched transfixed as the bonds slowly unravelled, discharging the rose petals to the floor. Finally, finally, he was revealed, as red and angry about his person as she'd imagined. Now he was naked from the waist down, at once priapic and vulnerable. There was only one thing she wanted to do, and she looked to the countess for permission.

She gave her consent, and Katia was immediately privileged with the sensation of her first touch of his velvety penis, hard in her grasp. It felt wonderful, yet still she craved more intimate contact. Tentatively she knelt down and brought her mouth to him.

He groaned and writhed as the countess issued forth her opinion.

'You are both insatiable for the rewards of the flesh. No half measures here. I want to see your complete undoing – both of you.'

Katia marvelled at how the woman was able to conduct this depravity without recourse to touching herself. She wielded the lash against Peter's buttocks, looking glorious in her satin dress, but he barely flinched. The stings didn't dampen his condition, and as Katia slid the full length of him into her mouth he thrust against her, obviously desperate for his release. She was enthralled by the novelty, pausing occasionally to rub his balls or stare at the live thing in her hand and giggle.

The countess was lashing at Peter, hissing all kinds of obscenities whilst he was muttering barely intelligible things that Katia perceived to be filthy expressions. So much for his piety!

She had quickly learned how to use one hand to work him, while the other went between her legs. As his movements became more urgent she withdrew, ordering, 'Tell me what is happening, what you are about to do.'

She wanted to hear it from his lips, for this would bring her own crisis.

'I'm about to . . . I can't stop, oh, oh,' muttered Peter.

'Say it!' she demanded.

'I'm going to ejaculate, to do it all over your face.'

With her new-found sensitivity to the ways of men, she was aware of a rush inside his flesh and then the magical white cream was jetting out, its target true to prediction. The moment was so divine that she too began to pulse in her silken undergarments, her cries soft but her heart pounding as she sank into a blissful oblivion. She faintly noticed the countess making some curious noises of her own. Her arms were outstretched as if in worship, her eyes rolled back into her head. She registered briefly that she seemed to be uttering some kind of incantation – like the ones she'd heard in the woods, but she was too lost in her own pleasure to care. She noted that ecstasy sounded very like worship, and for a second she was reminded again of her faith but she banished it to the back of her mind.

After a few moments of readjustment, the countess snapped the fastenings on Peter's manacles and the two women walked silently back to the house fully dressed, leaving the naked, wilted gardener to fend for himself.

5

Someone was calling her name. It was difficult to pinpoint which direction it was coming from – there was no one in the room. It had to be from outside, although it sounded too clearly pronounced, too melodic, to be a shout. Her instinct told her the voice was female but the overriding sense was that it was otherworldly, as if some creature was trying to form a human pitch. She knew instinctively that she should go to the window. Wrapped in the bearskin she felt her way in the dark and pulled back the curtains. Below, the garden was shrouded in a mist that ebbed and flowed like the rhythm of the ocean. And there was her name again. Maybe someone needed her to fetch something. Maybe it was one of the staff, locked out and freezing. She had to find out.

She lit her oil lamp, wrapped a massive velvet cloak around her, and made her way down the narrow flight of stone steps and along the corridor, into the kitchen. The ginger cat fled from his seat and darted under a cupboard, his eyes fixed upon her like two yellow marbles in the dark.

She could still hear her name, yet curiously the pitch sounded the same, as if she were no nearer the source. She opened the door to the anteroom, held the lamp at head height, and peered through the window, into the darkness. There, on the lawn, was the figure of a girl – dark-haired, like her, of the same age or thereabouts. She was clad in the most extra-ordinary clothes for the time of night. More than anything, her dress resembled a wedding gown – cream silk and pearl-beaded. On her head was a garland of flowers. She was beckoning and smiling.

'Wait!' cried Katia, tapping on the window. 'Stay there, I'm coming out.'

Without any recourse to the practicalities of what this person wanted, Katia went immediately to the kitchen door. Whoever it was out there, they must be freezing. Where could they have come from? Outside her breath was foggy in the chill air as she called hello. She looked around to locate the girl but she was already taking off at high speed – barefoot, she noticed – across the lawn.

'Stop, wait,' Katia called after her, slowed down by the heavy cloak and by carrying the oil lamp. 'What do you want?' It was something of an imposition to be woken by this person and then ignored as she tried to help.

In a moment, Katia was following the pale glow of the girl's dress into the rose garden. What possible reason could there be for such behaviour at this time of night? Was there some kind of an emergency? Why was no one else about? It occurred to her that she should rouse Magda, but she was already a good way across the grounds by this point and in the slipstream of her quarry. She would call on the help of others once she discovered exactly what was afoot. She kept thinking she saw figures moving out of the corner of her eye – shadowy shapes that changed form, from dog, to human, and back to dog again. Then they were gone, as if lifted up into the trees.

For a moment she stood spellbound, panting, the oil lamp the only tangible thing she had to hold on to. Her bed felt a long way away. She crooked her head back to observe the rustling leaves above and around her. The poplars and yews were swaying, bowing in unison, as if orchestrated by some great composer. The clouds flitted across the black sky, borne along by a swift breeze. She had never seen clouds move that fast before. Something was not right. An acuteness electrified her senses. She was spinning, everything was hazy, and once more she heard her name being called – this time echoed by the cries of nocturnal birds, the owls and nightjars. Then, before she knew what was happening, she felt a force – something struck her full in the face, and the girl was standing not six inches from her. How did she appear so suddenly? Katia had just seen her flit away some ten yards in the distance. And now here she was – curious. She appeared luminous, a golden shimmering light around her, as if she were standing in sunlight, yet they were in the pitch-black night. Her features were intangible yet all too familiar. For it seemed that Katia was looking at herself. This girl was identical in build and hairstyle. When she spoke, her voice seemed to come from far away.

'Hear the sounds of the night creatures,' she whispered. 'Hear their hearts beating and smell as they smell. The blood of predator and prey.'

'I cannot,' Katia replied nervously. 'Not just now ... what is it you want? Please tell me. I want to help you.'

'Their needs are endless and timeless. Hear them, just for a moment.'

The girl then touched Katia's ear, her caress so delicate, then she lightly grazed her nose with her finger, and it was as if she had at once been given access to a kingdom of extra-sensory powers. She no longer had need of the velvet cloak, and shrugged it off, lightening her bearing, now warmed and illuminated by a new blood that rushed through her veins like sweet warm honey.

The girl took her hand and, fleet of foot, they both skipped deeper into the undergrowth. And with her senses finely attuned to every smell and sound in the garden, Katia felt herself being lifted, her feet lightly skimming the grass as she was suddenly covering great distances with one bound. It felt to her as if she were swimming, her limbs languorous, stretching out to touch everything she chose – the tops of the trees, the water of the lake, the russet fur of the fox running keenly beside the summerhouse, looking up at her with flinty eyes. She could see all and sense all.

This weightlessness, this abandonment of earthly laws, filled her with a giddy delirium and she began to laugh, a wild laugh of release from the troubles of the material world. Nothing mattered. Nothing except the rapturous beauty of nature, of which she was a part. The breeze felt uncannily warm, the scent of the earth and its flowers filled her nostrils, and her eyes lit the way before her like lanterns at a bonfire party.

The girl at her side had grown as tall and slender as a young birch tree, her limbs shining, her skin flawless and luminescent.

'Come ... come with me to meet my master,' she called on the wing, in that singing voice that lulled Katia into complicity – that voice which had lured her from her bed.

'Yes, yes,' cried Katia in reply. 'Take me with you.'

And then she was moving at an impossible speed, drawn into a starburst blackness that seemed never-ending. All the while her strange friend held her tight as they flew over the tops of the trees, over the roof of the manor. After an indecipherable passing of time, they landed on soft moss, glowing emerald green and inlaid with what seemed like jewels. They were in an arboreal enclosure entwined with honeysuckle and ivy; the mists were curling around them, and Katia found it hard to keep sight of her discarnate companion. The only reference point she had was the inky dark sky, its scudding clouds, and the fragment of a waning moon. The lamp was gone, dropped somewhere on their flight over the lake.

The rules of everyday life had disappeared, shattered by a transcendent power. Katia wanted to run around the garden, announcing her joy to the world in celebration of the delights she had been allowed to see, yet she was fearful all this magic would instantly cease if she left the arbour. She sat on the moss and waited for the next instalment of this incredible night to unfold, enveloped by a warm sensuousness that ignited her consciousness.

'Who are you' said Katia, 'and where do you come from? What is happening?'

The girl's eyes burned in the dark, dazzling green like the jewels at their feet, and she flashed Katia a smile informed by an otherworldly knowledge.

'I have come to show you your destiny – the world that awaits you. He has sent me to bring you to him.'

'The count, you mean?'

The girl shook her head and laughed, a ringing laugh that reminded her of someone else – the countess. Did the Malinovskys know what was going on in their garden? Were they, too, able to transcend the physical laws of the material world like this enchanting creature that sparkled and danced in the night?

Her heart throbbed as the girl took her hand and squeezed it, then began uttering some incantation in a language of which Katia had no recognition. This reminded her of the mass she used to attend with her mother and father. She had always loved Our Lady, in her translucent white and blue robes, had prayed to her on her knees, the incense cleansing the church of evil spirits as she offered the mother of Jesus her tears and young girl's wishes.

Here, in this mossy garden, with the scent of leaf mulch and the musk of mammals that hunted the flesh of others pungent in the air, Katia inhaled deeply of the teeming nature around her. Gone was the hallowed sanctity of the church, with the marble figures that had once inspired her awe and reverence. An earthier sensuality had now made itself apparent. Here were conditions for a keener triumph – blazing, alive passions that would illuminate the path to her awakening.

She clenched her hands into the soft green carpet, entranced by the jewels, yet not wanting to wrench them from their place – their material value was irrelevant to the incomparable privileges she was being allowed this night. And just when she was beginning to feel unsure of what to do with all this beauty and fascination, she was frozen into alarm. A third presence was in the garden – bringing with it an atmosphere of total command. For this was his realm. And he had arrived, just as the girl had predicted. This was her master.

She didn't know how to respond to the vision that silently and powerfully manifested itself before them. She looked once, then twice, then stared at the emerald ground for a few moments. And when she looked back for a third time, she was facing a giant being – human in form but covered in luxuriant black fur – that stood at the end of the bower. Around him swirled the mist, so thick Katia couldn't yet see the bottom of his towering limbs. The head, similarly, was swathed in the fog, but vague features – a wild tousle of hair, the edge of the chin – were discernible. Breath flew out in urgent plumes from concealed nostrils. Katia felt her hands being pulled toward this Goliath, and she craved to run her fingers over the glorious lustre of the fur. She should have been terrified – here was an unearthly, doubtless evil being, born from God only knows what diabolical source, and she was drawn to it, to him, to his uncompromising masculine majesty.

Her insides liquefied, and she was seized by the need to go to him without her night garments, to burrow her lissome body into his muscular form. She saw his eyes now, distinctly human in their expression. And distinctly desirous of the two acolytes prostrated before him. Then, the unthinkable, as he addressed them in a voice that was dreadful, commanding.

'You have come to me of your own will, and for that you shall be rewarded. See first how I reward your escort, she who has reached out to you from our world.'

With an almighty bound he was immediately next to the two girls. In close proximity to his gigantic presence Katia trembled as she imagined the sensation of his arms around her, his powerful paws tearing the nightdress from her body, his excitement making itself evident in a shocking display of unbridled animal need. But it was not her that he chose there and then to paw at, to pull tightly into his chest. His primary consort was lifted into his grasp and thrown around each side of his huge frame, as if she were weightless. She giggled and squealed, like a giddy young girl whirled around by the first rush of love's tempestuous energy. Then he softly caught her and lay her down once more on the moss, where she assumed a position of wanton submission and the giggling stopped. Her mouth hung loose, her lips were moist, and her eyes gleamed with the intoxication of her master's attentions. And then she began to writhe a sinuous dance, like that of a handmaiden in a temple dedicated to lust. For the first time Katia was witnessing the beguiling tricks of her own sex in all their tantalising display, as practised since earliest times to ensnare man. Yet what kind of man was this? What kind of lovemaking would be possible?

She stared transfixed as the girl rolled onto her front then arched up onto all fours to present her intimacy to the Beast. And as he came closer, to cover her, she turned to face Katia.

'Can you imagine what a potion is the scent of my sex to my master? How rich my musk, how strong his need?'

Katia said nothing, but continued to watch – how could she do anything else? – for the moment of reckoning was about to occur: the revelation of how this act would be realised, and what monstrous equipment would emerge from that bestial undergrowth around his crotch.

The girl reached backwards to find her master in his exalted state, and he responded, his manhood proud and urgent, leathery and as dark as his fur. He was impressively endowed, but not of a size to be injurious to his lover. Yet the girth of him was what elicited in Katia the most dizzying curiosity. And she realised she was jealous, yet also confused; she wanted so badly to be in receipt of his attentions, yet what was she thinking and desiring? To be made to couple with this ungodly creature?

As swiftly as the morals of the civilised world flashed into her mind, they were banished by her excitement at the spectacle in front of her. By now, he had entered the girl and was setting to her with a hunger that threatened to devour her. He had begun to growl, a warning of the ferocity he could unleash if his partner changed her mind. There was no doubt that he would take whatever he wanted from the delicate girl, forcing himself into her sweet crevice until he was satisfied. Yet there was no danger of her fleeing. She was given over to him totally, bucking and rocking against his strength.

His growling increased to a roar that threw Katia back a couple of feet, startled by the all-enveloping force of the sound. It was apparent that the Beast was reaching his crisis. He was baring his teeth, the gums luridly pink in the shadow of the garden. He threw back his head and began to issue forth the sound of his tribe – the eternal lupine howl that stops all creatures in their tracks, that inspires lesser mammals to bristle with reverence for the great ruler of the forest. With the sound of his cries still ringing in the midnight air, he then launched himself more forcibly onto the back of the girl and, Katia was alarmed to see, he sank his teeth into her neck like the beast he was.

She could no longer watch without playing some part in this thrilling adventure. Tentatively she stretched out a hand and ran it along his back. His pelt shivered. His breath came rushing out of his nostrils in a rhythm that spurred her on to more vigorous stroking. His fur was glorious, and she raked it with her nails, encouraging more urgent thrusting. And then, just as Katia was settling into an almost tender communication with this creature, as if he were no more fearsome than the kitchen cat, she felt her arm becoming electrified. The animal power that surged through his loins was travelling along his spine, along her arm, and moving through her entire body.

Even if she wanted to, she was powerless to prevent the eruption of exquisite energy that then pulsed through her as she called out her own joy. With a concentrated rush, the unearthly feelings began to gather in one place, at the centre between her legs. As the sensation built stronger, distilled and pure, she could scarcely believe what was happening. For she was experiencing her most intimate moment whilst clinging onto the back of some cursed devil as it slaked its lusts within the body of no ordinary human girl.

And then she was rolling around in the earth like a vixen. She threw herself to the ground, arms entwining over her head as she shouted her crisis from the very depths of her soul. As the moment took her and she knew such wild rapture, the sound of her master howling his own release into the sky melded with her cries and, in unison, all three wanton creatures fell into the voluptuous abyss.

Katia awoke the next morning with the sense that she'd suffered a restless night. She felt she had been dreaming but, frustratingly, she couldn't recall the details. All she knew was that her body felt as if it had been taken apart and put back together with an extra sensitivity. When Magda came banging on her door at 6.30, she was shocked to find she'd overslept and was late for her duties.

She dressed hurriedly and presented herself bleary-eyed in the kitchen, where there was a commotion. Peter was there, his shame seemingly forgotten, talking excitedly of how the countess would be delighted about what had happened. Magda, the cook and a few other staff were in high spirits, and Katia was relieved that whatever had occurred was taking the attention away from her tardiness.

'Look, Katia,' said Peter, beaming. 'God has blessed us overnight.'

In his hands he brandished five roses, each one of a colour so vibrant she could scarcely believe they were real.

'The garden is blooming. It's unbelievable when only

yesterday the place was almost barren, but there it is. It's a miracle! Come and see.'

'I need to get on with the fires, Peter. I'm late this morning,' she said sheepishly, not wanting to catch his eye.

Peter looked at Magda, who immediately replied, 'Oh, go on. Just a few minutes. She'll make up the time, I'm sure.'

With this Peter took Katia by the hand and together they went into the grounds. It was a beautiful day – the early sun was radiant and the gardens were bathed in golden light. As she ran across the lawns with him she was suddenly struck with the disquieting sense she had done this before just recently – raced over this exact ground – yet with someone else. Her mind was fuzzy, but she didn't want to dampen Peter's delight. They approached the rose garden and there, in full glory, was a sight to behold in wonder – the shrubs were bountiful with perfect roses of myriad hues.

Katia stepped into the walled enclosure and surveyed the beauty. Although she knew she should be getting back to the kitchen, she was drawn to the bower, past the rose garden and further down to the lake. The scent of honeysuckle filled the air and again she was consumed by feelings she couldn't quite identify. Whether it was the heady scent of the flowers or the delicious feelings churned up by the previous day's erotic experiments, Katia couldn't say, but her arrival in the bower was accompanied by an acute awareness of her natural sensuality. She felt again those strong stirrings of sexual desire for Peter. He looked so angelic, with his curly fair hair and slightly fleshy body, that he reminded Katia of a cherub – a cherub in the rose garden. It made her giggle, and she was in a devilish mood as Peter rounded the corner and caught up with her.

Before she knew what she was doing, and with all thoughts of house rules dispatched, she made a grab for his wrist, pulling him toward her.

'I am so happy for you,' she said. 'Your talent as a gardener is obviously reaping rewards.'

She snaked an arm around his waist as her arousal increased, then wriggled her hips slightly, as she sought to inflame him once more. Oh, how she wanted him to repeat what the count had done to her! But it was not to be. In fact, Peter remained motionless, his eyes closed and his mouth set in a firm straight line.

'You are a very pretty young woman, Miss Katia, but I cannot condone your behaviour. Yesterday was unseemly and indecent. We both lost control, and I beg of you to repent.'

And with that he pushed her from him, leaving her aching with a need for contact with a man. Any man.

'You know I live by God's law. It is not right for a young woman, for any woman, to sport herself as a harlot. Why do you behave thus? I'll kindly ask you not to lay your hands upon me again.'

Katia was crestfallen. She shook her head and remained defiant. Whatever had awoken in her was not going away. If anything, she felt panicked that she might be driven mad by these new desires. She longed to see a man in his erect state again, and if Peter wouldn't oblige then she would have to find someone who would. She ran through the options but they were limited. She wasn't yet so desperate that she would proffer herself to Auroch. There was only really the count. Yet she dare not risk angering the countess. If she was thrown out of the manor, where could she go? She would be at the mercy of her uncle, and such a prospect did not appeal.

'I ask you to say a prayer with me now, here in the bower,' said Peter. 'To make up for yesterday's indecency and to thank God for His grace. Kneel down with me.'

She did what he asked, although it felt ludicrous going down on her knees before a bunch of roses. He recited the paternoster, and she mumbled the words along with him but was seized by the compulsion to utter the obscenities he had begged of her the day before. She bit her lip and suppressed a giggle. Peter said his Amen, shot her a disgusted look, made the sign of the cross and stood up.

'I don't know what kind of people the Malinovskys are, and I'm not as daft as to bite the hand that feeds, but an unwholesome atmosphere dwells in this place.' He paused and looked around him, breathing hard while Katia stayed kneeling, fixing her eyes upon his body. 'For all our sakes I intend to see it banished. May the mercy of God be upon you.'

And with that he marched off.

Katia stayed in the garden and tilted her face to the morning sun. She felt its regenerative goodness beam down upon her. She was tired, though, and didn't want to spend her day fetching and carrying, roughening her hands with manual labour, although she'd soon have to get back to Magda. But as she turned to leave, she saw a flurry of black rushing across the lawn. The countess must have awoken and heard the news.

Katia dived into the bushes to hide, fearful she would be reprimanded for shirking her chores. From the camouflage of the rhododendrons she could see the countess whirling about the gardens, shouting to the sky, terrifying in her passion. Katia had never seen her so animated.

'At last, at last!' she cried. 'The turning point has come. I am honoured once more. You have rewarded me.'

She started calling out in a dialect unknown to Katia. It appeared the woman had taken leave of her senses. Then, 'Oh master, oh master, you have come!' she called out.

All external sensory information suddenly retreated, as Katia was propelled into her own thoughts. Those words. She had heard them before, but where? Her heart and temples thudded as she crouched in the bushes. 'My master, come, meet my master.' Katia was rooted to the spot, electrified with confusion as the recollection of last night's dream gradually unfolded.

The beastly master. The spectral girl. The impossible flight over the lake. What kind of pandemonium had she been witness to? As Katia watched the countess seized by her manic triumph, all of the previous day's events crashed into her consciousness. Yet the illicit pleasures of whipping the count and taking Peter into her mouth did not concern her as much as the distinct awareness that through no conscious will of her own she had communed with something unearthly. A thing very like the creature Peter had described but with a dark mane and shining member. And worst of all she had enjoyed her experience. But who was the girl, the otherworldly waif bathed in the shining light?

This was all too ridiculous. She chewed her hand and stared hard at the flowers. Yesterday the roses were wilted and bare and this morning they bloomed in a riot of colour. How could such a thing happen? It was a blatant defiance of nature. Yet Katia knew in her soul this was not the work of God. It was a reward of some kind, but from whom, and for what reason? Was this dark being, this master, behind the garden's restoration?

What was she thinking! The wrench of her changing circumstances and the shock of hard work must have unhinged her mind. Maybe she'd been made delirious by the wine the count had allowed her before she had retired to bed. Had he laced it with laudanum to take advantage of her? Surely not, for he knew she would have willingly returned his attentions. Either her overactive imagination was getting the better of her or Peter was right and God had deserted the Malinovskys. She felt a sudden flash of remorse that she hadn't taken his prayers more seriously. What had got into her of late that she was compelled to behave so provocatively? As Irina continued to spin like a dervish, Katia vowed to uncover what was going on. Perhaps a little detective work would take her mind off her uncontrollable levels of arousal.

6

Katia passed the rest of the day in a subdued mood unable to share in the household's rejoicing. Let the staff believe in Peter's proclamation. She wasn't about to shatter their dreams, but a nagging sense of some awful truth gnawed at her soul. She went quietly about her duties, each hour bringing fresh visions of the previous night's events to startle her. She'd gone to her room to search for the oil lamp and her cloak, desperate for proof that her suspicions were foolish fears, yet neither item was there. She recollected seeing the falling flame of the lamp on its descent to the lake, of shrugging off her cloak on the lawn. If it had all been a dream, then where were they now?

She dared not whisper a word of her suspicions to anyone. In any event, Peter was ignoring her, his head held high and his expression pious. It disappointed her that he'd chosen to deny himself pleasure when she had just awoken to its joys, but his denial would be his loss. The count was still interested in her, and when she brought him his port that evening she was pleasantly surprised to find him in a talkative mood. She had recently started to pass the time of day with him during her visits to his study. She knew it was not really done for servants to converse with their superiors, but his demeanour seemed to invite it – he spent so much time alone that Katia reasoned he would be appreciative of a little late-night conversation.

'The countess must be thrilled by what's happened in the garden,' she said. 'It really is a kind of miracle.'

'Quite extraordinary, if you ask me,' he said, rustling his newspaper and betraying his fatigue with the subject. 'I've not seen her since midday. She was so overcome that she retired early.'

He put down his paper and looked at Katia.

'I really don't know how a few shrubs can be so exciting. I'm surely missing something. Now, science – that's exciting. Look at these chaps. The inventors of wireless telegraphy!'

The count beckoned Katia to look at an article in his newspaper telling of how a Russian named Popov had just demonstrated for the first time the existence of electromagnetic radio waves.

'Just think, very soon we may be able to hear our fellow countrymen speaking to us through wireless receivers. In our lifetime every decent home will have one. It's feasible that one will be able to hear a concert happening in Vienna without actually being there. The possibilities are limitless.'

She leaned over him and felt a frisson of excitement being in close proximity to this handsome and interesting man. They were completely alone, the countess at the other end of the house, and she couldn't help but run her gaze over him, checking for his arousal, wanting to lay her hands on his thighs, her senses aroused and hungry for experience.

'The world out there is taking leaps and bounds into an exciting new age, while Irina is bound to her ancestors' legacy. The gardens are beautiful, and I wouldn't be without them, but it's making her ill.'

He stopped talking for a moment and gave Katia a long appraising look.

'You seem like a sensible girl. Head on your shoulders. What do you think?'

'Sir, I'm sure it's not my place to hazard a guess. I feel so far away from all the things I love. And certain things are ... troubling me.'

She stopped, apprehensive of saying more for fear of sounding foolish. How could she speak of beasts and curses to this worldly man? She chose to let him lead the conversation.

'Oh, dear girl, you mean about yesterday? Yes, I suppose it must have been startling for you. Don't be troubled. I have certain ... what to call them ... fancies. My wife loves roses. I admire a different form of beauty – the female form. In fact, my admiration goes as far as worship.'

He stretched out an arm and Katia was rewarded with the feel of the count's hand on her buttocks. She steadied herself on his chair as her heart was beating wildly. *Let him continue, please*, she begged.

'I should very much like to worship you,' the count continued, trailing his hand down her leg, then up again. 'I should like you to stand before me in your undergarments and boots and command me to honour you.'

'I should very much like that,' she whispered in reply, in truth uncertain of how she would find the required will. He was so comfortable articulating his specific desires whilst she didn't know where to start.

'Although, her ladyship ... she would want to be there, of course. And I'm not sure if I ... I mean to say ...'

'Come on, girl, speak your mind,' encouraged the count, patting her bottom.

'She scares me, sir.'

'Oh, you don't need to be scared of Irina. She won't whip you. It's my hide she likes to tan. Men are her targets for punishment, not the fairer sex.'

'But she would want to be there, surely? I hate to think she'd catch us alone.'

The count shrugged. 'Take our little conversations in French. She doesn't know about those, does she?'

'Not unless you've told her.'

'I have not. And this could be the same. A mutual pastime she need not know about.'

'A secret, is what you are saying.'

'A man needs to have secrets,' said Nikolai, smiling and flashing his brown eyes at her.

Katia simply couldn't resist his attentions. She used to yearn for the comforts of hot chocolate on a cold day, or the gift of some trinket from her favourite shop but, awoken to the thrills of physical pleasure, she now longed for adult congress with the count. It was tragic that he happened to be husband to the most fearsome woman in the realm. And she worried that his taste for fearsome women would soon bar her from his sphere of interest. For although she was amused by games of punishment, what she craved in her most private thoughts was what the count, seemingly, could not provide – the full union of man and woman. She ached for want of it. To take that ripe and urgent flesh into her for the first time, and then again and again. She gripped the chair and bit her lip in anticipation of when this would happen, if this would happen.

'If only I could show you Paris,' he sighed. 'You would come alive among its delights.'

Katia felt both wounded and elated. To think he deemed her a worthy companion to take to the city of her dreams! Yet there was no chance of leaving the manor. Life was so cruel and yet so strangely enchanting. If only circumstances were different. She sighed and fiddled with her apron.

'I will get there one day,' she said. 'But as to what you require of me here, I scarcely know where to begin. What you did to me yesterday was, well, no man has ever touched me there, let alone what you did.'

She flushed and stammered. How could a man and woman discuss such intimacy? Even married it seemed scandalous. Yet the pleasure it had brought her – could it be so wrong?

'I am confused, sir. I have been brought up to behave as a young lady.'

'My dear, it is exactly what you should be doing. The younger the lady is when she discovers her powers, the more confident and strong will be the woman.'

He somehow made the permission to be illicit seem wise.

'Do you think you might care to do it again sometime?' she asked softly.

'I will do whatever you command of me,' he said, trailing a finger under the crease of her bottom. 'Your sweet cunt teases me constantly. You only need to ask.'

'Allow me to reflect,' she said. 'To acquaint myself with your language, that sounds so very wrong.'

'I speak honestly, the language of lust. If only Paris could be ours, just for a weekend, I would awaken you to the glories of decadence. Show you the things I've seen. Take you to parties where girls lead men around on leashes; where fine ladies are serviced by dark-skinned body slaves; where those same fine ladies strap leather phalluses to themselves and take each other; where the champagne flows and the fun doesn't end. Another life, maybe, my Katia, but your imagination can accompany you anywhere. Cultivate the interior life and you will be forever liberated.'

In the fiercely protected domain in her tower, illuminated by scores of candles, the countess sat with Darvulia's book. The day of reckoning was drawing ever nearer. A fire blazed in the grate and the light of the flames reflected off the philtres of many-coloured tinctures she had brewed for her craft. In glass jars on shelves were touchstones fashioned from the tongues of adders; there were also lumps of borax, formed in the heads of toads, for protection against plagues and blights.

Sprigs of sagebrush and henbane littered the floor, and precious round bones lay drying on them, ready to be fashioned into talismans that would ward off prying interlopers. She was counting the hours toward the Naming Day – the time she would offer up the ultimate sacrifice. Her eyes glittered with the sense of spiritual servitude she carried for her master. She felt wedded, irrevocably, to her calling; her dark powers brought to a new height by the turnaround of fortune in the garden.

The end of this month, All Hallows' Eve, would see the veil lifted and the deed done. Then glory eternal would be hers.

All afternoon and into the night she had been drawing black geometry – signs and sigils associated with her necromantic ken – in preparation for the day. Her veins flowed with the diabolical lava of her bloodline and she suppressed all thoughts of obstacles. Her master would forever reward her for this act of total worship. As she had read so many times, so Irina read again of the rite, performed that Hallows' Eve of Darvulia's fortieth year.

The young girl had been dressed in transparent bridal robes of cream lace, her budding breasts evident through the garment. A garland of ivy sat on her head of long dark hair. Bound by ropes, she had been led to the bower. The sorceresses had prepared the potion and the girl was made to drink from a goblet of beaten gold, Darvulia leading the ritual. A band of gypsy musicians had found their way to the grove, striking up their drums and stringed instruments as a fire blazed in the centre of the attendants. Belladonna leaves melded with frankincense to smoulder about their feet and the witches, already given over to the delirium of their own brews, began to dance and chant.

A Bacchanalia ensued until the garden became bathed in an unearthly blue light. Then he appeared. Irina read the passage over: 'Our black lord came to us, dreadful and mighty, crawling from the smoke, his skin glossy, his mane proud. When he saw his maiden bride his eyes burned with animal need and he reared up to display his masculinity, shining in the moonlight. At that moment I knew we had united the parallel worlds of lust and divinity.'

The next passage never ceased to inflame her with its potency, describing in detail the voluptuous congress between the Beast and his bride, as the musicians played trance-inducing tarantellas and a great roaring filled the night air. The girl was relaxed and given over to the rite as the strong fingers tore away the flimsy dress to reveal her lithe body, glowing pale in its nakedness. Darvulia and her assorted audience cheered on the master as he powered into his bride's tight young sex and she was a maiden no more. Irina became wet every time she thought of it, of his dominance, his rich seed releasing into the girl's body. How she wanted to see it for real.

There could be no error. She was charged with the task of leading a new maiden to his illustrious majesty. She had already prepared excuses for the girl's disappearance. She'd say she had caught her stealing from her dressing room – stuffing one of her jewelled caps down the back of her dress, and had been instantly dismissed. She could get the coachmen to run some false errand, so a carriage was visible in the grounds the next day. No one would dwell too long on the departure of a thieving servant. It seemed a shame to cast the girl in this ignominious light when she was such a delicious and beguiling creature, but needs must. And once the deed was done, and the master had spirited his new bride to his realm, she could relax and find her regal measure once more, rewarded with immense power from serving her dark lord.

For the following week, Katia went about her duties with diligence, doing her best to avoid encountering Irina alone. Serving the imperial couple their meals was particularly unnerving, for the woman's gaze bored right through her whilst the count's seemed to caress her. Was the countess jealous? Despite the turnaround of the garden, she seemed to be possessed by a dark mood and barely spoke. Katia was confused. Surely the woman had only encouraged her to engage in those games of punishment with her husband. How could she regard her with such accusing stares? She secretly hoped she would be invited to join them again, but the atmosphere seemed to have changed between the Malinovskys. No more wry smiles were traded; no secret jokes or plays on words.

Katia had attempted to fish for clues as to how the countess passed her time in the tower, but Magda gave little away and Peter now seemed to regard her as no more than some wanton Jezebel. It was no good asking the cook; the woman had little interest outside of baking and roasting and was practically illiterate. All that was said was that her ladyship was a talented woman who had dedicated her life to the study of plants. Katia suspected there was more to her than that, and she longed to see what secrets she kept. Her curiosity grew daily, as did her feelings for the count. Their evening assignations were the only thing that prevented her from sinking into melancholia for her previous life.

Late in the evening he would read to her of worldly events as she teased him by lifting her skirts and running her fingers over his lips after delving into herself. On one occasion he had gone as far as to fall on his knees in front of her as she scolded him for his un-gentlemanly conduct. He had taken hold of himself and asked her to recite after him the most vulgar French vocabulary, as he feverishly worked himself to his moment. And how she loved to watch him! So handsomely endowed, so mischievous, so learned. She asked if he might consider allowing her to receive his tribute over her breasts, and he said he would give it some thought, although they were always to be mindful of conducting assignations that could be covered up at a second's notice.

She found time to walk in the grounds and observe the changing season, occasionally spotting Auroch raking leaves and burning them. She was far too timid to open conversation with such a brute of a man, yet she wondered about his life. What did such a person think of all day? Had he ever known a woman? This thought made her blush, but not half as much as the persistent image of his lordship's seed spurting from his manhood, as he looked deep and adoringly into her eyes. Oh, if only she could know him properly! Feel him drive into her as the ewe felt the ram, the mare felt her stallion and all healthy female creatures felt themselves covered and entered.

The early morning sun streamed toward the windows of the manor's master bedroom. A crack in the dark oak shutters allowed the light to penetrate the room, falling on the face of the count and waking him. The space in the bed next to him was cold. Yet another day had begun where he would arise and breakfast alone. It was simply not good enough. Of course he and Irina had separate interests but he feared they were becoming estranged, and for no reason he could fathom. Her experiments in the garden seemed to have paid off; the new girl was delighting them both; the staff seemed to have cheered up. So why was his wife spending all night in her study, neglecting him and all else, it seemed, bar her confounded roses? She had become irritable and moody, despite having everything a noblewoman could wish for. Even Giulio had remarked that, 'Madame does seem rather more consumed by her garden than anything else these days.' It wasn't even possible to raise her interest in the new, lavish hairpieces he'd fashioned for her.

As he went about his ablutions, Nikolai thought of how she spent her days sleeping and her nights studying, her head stuck in books. A bibliophile himself, he understood that passion, but he would never forego the comfort of his bed to huddle over a desk all night. He felt curious and vaguely uneasy. It was time to find out exactly what his wife was up to in that tower. Did she have a lover up there? A man manacled and kept for sport? Perhaps he'd turned a blind eye for too long to Irina's more extreme cruelties. He'd never allowed himself to think too deeply about how she took her private pleasures, the bite marks he'd noticed on former serving girls. And the ones who'd disappeared.

As he applied sandalwood soap to his face, he thought back to their courting days, how her father had warned him she was not as others, even though Nikolai was a great catch for his wayward daughter, in her twenty-eighth year and still unmarried. She had frightened away all suitors before him with her fiery temper, insatiable lusts and her unwillingness to be penetrated.

Nikolai had known women of a similar inclination in Vienna and Paris – and known great pleasure at their hands. It pleased him that his wife was 'not as others'. He had married a beautiful imperial vixen, not a timid waif, and up until now their arrangement had worked wonderfully. Yet what had possessed her of recent months was casting darkness over their marriage. Even though she still attended to his needs, she was distant, brooding, almost unreachable. On one of his recent visits to Paris he had seen the great Charcot performing hypnotism on a hysterical patient, and had thought of volunteering Irina for the same treatment. But he couldn't get her to leave the manor, and that irked him too.

He stared at himself in the mirror, then took his razor to his face. How he yearned for companionship on his journeys. How wonderful it would be take Katia with him, to see her lovely young spirit come alive. This was surely an impossible dream. Yet the girl inflamed him so. Her young breasts pressed against her uniform were surely made for his hands to cup. And when she wore her long black boots under that white lace apron, well, it was more than a man could bear. He longed for her to realise the command she could have over him yet it was obvious she was begging to be undone from her virgin status. Should he be inclined toward the traditional forms of private union, such a thing would be glorious, no doubt. Just to see the expression on her sweet face, to see her cheeks made pink with arousal, to feel the honeyed vice of her sex. It *was* tempting.

He washed his face, applied wax to his moustache, cologne to his neck, and dressed for breakfast. As he descended the stairs Irina emerged through the door that led to the corridor that ran around the back of the manor. Her clothes were dusty, her face paler than usual and her eyes sunken.

'Good morning, my dear, how are you?' he asked, forcing a jolly tone.

'Tell the servants I don't want a fire lit in the bedroom for a few hours,' she grumbled, ignoring her husband's pleasantries. 'I need to sleep.'

'Most of us do that at night.'

'Curse you! I have important work to do. I am at a crucial stage in my research, I'll have you know,' she spat.

'Oh, very well,' said the count, not rising to her bait. 'Shall I order you a late luncheon – say for two o' clock?'

'All right. Until then, I'm not to be disturbed.'

'Oh, same as last night, then, and the night before, and the day before that?'

Irina shot him a furious look. Her eyes blazed venom and were illuminated by an unnerving zeal. He'd seen that look in the eyes of fanatics in the asylum when he'd been in the audience of Charcot. He knew to leave her alone. Plus, with Irina abed he could investigate the tower. He just had to find a way of getting in without a key.

Over a breakfast of eggs and fruit he concocted his plan of entry. In all the years he'd lived at the manor, he'd never attempted such a feat but he was confident he could pull it off. He beamed at Katia as she brought him his Earl Grey tea and cleared his plates.

'You look ravishing this morning,' he said, which brought a smile to her face as she blushed. 'I wonder what you must have been doing to look that radiant.'

'Working hard, sir,' she said. 'Out this morning gathering tinder.'

'Oh, I don't believe that for one minute. You've been rummaging around under that bear rug of yours, haven't you?' he teased. 'Thinking about handsome young men, I bet.'

She threw him a look of shock, as if he'd prised open her

guiltiest secret. He was in an adventurous spirit, keen to carry out his plan and enjoying a new-found sense of excitement. He leaped up from the table, planted a kiss on the top of Katia's head, and marched off to retrieve rope, climbing tools and stout boots from the old shed down by the main gates.

It was an hour later before the coast was clear for Nikolai to put his plan into action. He didn't want to alert Auroch to what he was doing, and had to wait for the gruff groundsman to go about his duties down by the lake, out of sight of the manor. By 11 a.m. Nikolai was straddled across the wall that ran around the roof, inching his way precariously toward the tower window some eighty feet up from the ground. It would be pointless trying to break down the door or steal her key. The ensuing row could prove fatal, with him on the receiving end of his wife's wrath if she thought he was spying on her. It was her greatest fear – one she had expressed to him on many occasions. She would never guess that he would bother to scale the roof, though, negotiating the jagged brickwork. But he was enjoying his challenge. It reminded him of his more daring escapades at the academy. He hadn't lost his touch. His balance and poise were impeccable. If he could just get the metal climbing hook lodged inside the sill of the tower window he could swing himself over onto the next level.

He tied the metal claw to the rope, coiled it up and swung his arm out as if throwing a discus. It landed with a dull clank against the brickwork. A further two attempts repeated the defeat. It was a narrow gap, and his aim needed total concentration. Spurred on by the novelty of his task, practice made perfect, and on the seventh swing, the claw found purchase just inside the window. He made the daring leap over the ramparts and landed on the stone balcony about eight feet beneath the window. Now all he had to do was haul his weight up to the ledge. His muscles strained, and he resolved to spend more time swimming than lying about on velvet couches. Still, he pulled himself up the rounded turret and scrabbled about with his legs until he was pivoted at the waist.

He forced the window open to its widest aperture, breathed in to make himself as flat as possible and squeezed himself through. He landed in an ungainly heap on a wooden work-bench, scattering feathers and various organic detritus about him, then jumped to the floor, dusted himself down, and took in the full measure of what surrounded him. The vision was so shocking that his breath caught in his throat. It was years since he had been in this room and the change was remark-able. Once a simple, plain room, the place now stank of musty things and the humus of animal litter. It was if he had landed in the nest of some gargantuan carnivorous bird. Fresh fox pelts were stretched across wooden frames, and the pickled eyes of various woodland creatures stared at him from glass vessels. Snakeskins lay coiled in jars, a collection of the horns of various animals were mounted along one wall and, under-neath them, differently sized eggs – whether bird or reptile he knew not. About the floor and on the workbenches were pieces of parchment with primitive markings etched on them. He scrutinised one to see, unmistakably, that blood, rather than ink, had been used. Was it from one of the unfortunate crea-tures whose skin was now curing in the dark? Or could it be from a more sinister source?

Open in a prominent place on Irina's desk was an ancient book. He carefully scanned the pages of what seemed to be half scrapbook, half diary. The handwriting was erratic, set at all angles into the vellum. Some of it ran in circles and other entries were imprinted around the edges. Dried flowers and illustra-tions graced the pages, some in a pretty arrangement, others pressed into diabolical sigils. Crude drawings had been made – of devilish beasts with giant phalluses and large-breasted women sucking upon them. Nikolai turned to the first page, which revealed the book's provenance, as the opening paragraph began: 'I, Darvulia, am wedded to the ancient divinities. I give you here my story – the story of His return.'

He recognised the name of Irina's mad ancestor. He hadn't known she had written a book. What on earth was his wife doing poring all night over this superstitious rubbish? Moreover, what ghastly experiments had she been undertaking? The shadowy history of her bloodline was eating into her soul. He feared a moment for her health, and pledged to get her away from the manor – maybe a journey to the Italian coast would work wonders. He continued to flick through the book, ever mindful he was prying into his wife's darkest secrets, and that she could burst through the door at any moment. His throat was dry with the fear of being caught but he had to read a little more. 'The Naming Day: as the rite has been handed down so today, in the year of my dark lord 1745, we give up the virgin maiden to His glory. I, Magyar noble, with the emblems of savage Scythia about me, am born of this barbarous land yet honour it, bright and shining, in my hour of triumph. For I am truly blessed to bear His scar. That I exist in the coming of his 150-year cycle, I blaze with glory. Whosoever next takes up this torch, you will be known as highborn wanton.

From whatever starry realm in which I will then dwell
I will salute you. For to know Him
is to serve Him. And I plead you serve Him well.'

The count held the book at arm's length, grateful that he lived in 1895 and not these dark times of which this poor unfortunate woman was obviously a victim, driven by primitive beliefs. Goodness, 150 years wasn't so long ago, yet so much had changed.

It was ironic that in the midst of Nikolai congratulating himself for being born to an age of reason, the sickening truth of Darvulia's soothsaying seized his consciousness. 1745 . . . 1895 . . . the 150-year cycle of the Beast. By this calculation he should be making an appearance this week. Preposterous nonsense! So this was why Irina was so distracted. She really believed her half-crazed ancestor's fantasy was real. And what was her role in this? Was it leader of some sacrifice? And who was the victim? He scanned the lines for clues. There it was: 'we give up the virgin maiden to His glory.'

Surely Irina couldn't be contemplating ... Katia? It simply wasn't possible that such hocus-pocus could be going on under his nose. Was the girl in danger? All Hallows' Eve – it was still a few days away. Thank goodness he had undertaken this sleuthing. Forewarned was forearmed. He may not be able to save his wife from madness, but he could surely protect the young woman who had so enchanted him from undergoing atrocious indignities. And there was only one way to do it.

7

Katia sat in the kitchen chopping vegetables as Magda and the cook bustled around her, speaking loudly in dialect. If only there was someone else her age, a girlfriend she could share her thoughts with. Peter was not that much older but tensions between them were such that he ignored her. It was less that she had been intimate with him in the summerhouse than that he was still shamed by her witnessing his subjugation at the hands of the countess. She'd tried to explain that even the count was in thrall to her in that way, but he'd stopped listening, saying he didn't want to hear about their depravities.

Winter was well on its way. Rising at 6 a.m. was a wrench, as the mornings were now icy cold. She had to dress hurriedly in her tiny room, sometimes under the bedclothes. It wasn't until about 9 or 10 a.m. when fires were lit and breakfasts taken that she was sufficiently warmed up to take a wash in the servants' bathroom, ferrying large jugs of steaming water from the kitchen. Even there it seemed she wasn't allowed her privacy. She was still trembling with indignation at what had occurred earlier. She had been naked in the tub, her body glistening with soap, when suddenly the countess was standing beside the bath, looking down on her. The woman had crept into the room, silent in her long grey dress, and locked the door behind her. At first Katia thought she was in trouble – maybe she had discovered her trysts with the count. She was only slightly relieved to see she was smiling. But it was a cold smile that sent a chill through her body and she had remained motionless in the water, trying her best to cover herself with her sponge.

'You know, you really are the prettiest maid we've had at the manor,' said the countess, lacing her compliment with a shot of venom. 'You have a quality about you the others didn't have. But I suppose you know that. All pretty girls of your age know the power they possess.'

Katia had protested, 'Your ladyship, I have no power. Please, can we speak once I'm dressed?'

'Feeling a little vulnerable?'

'Well, yes, I am.'

'Stand up. Let me see you in all your glory.'

When Katia hesitated the countess seized one of her nipples between her fingers and tweaked it sharply.

'Stand up, I said!'

She slowly rose from the water, the foam of the bath oil sliding down her limbs, her body wet and shining.

'Turn around.'

Katia did so, feeling horribly exposed. Was the countess going to whip her? She trembled slightly, and the countess noticed even this.

'Like a young mare,' she said, 'its flanks aquiver.'

Then came the touching, as she ran her hands proprietorially over the flare of her hips and across her breasts. It was an abuse of power, but there was something horribly arousing about being touched by a fully clothed person while she was completely naked.

The next thing, the countess was planting soft kisses on her neck, gently caressing her waist, her buttocks, and then sliding a hand between her legs. Softly, so softly, that Katia was lulled into a sensuous relaxation, imagining it was Nikolai preparing her for intimacy. But she was brought sharply out of her reverie, as Irina spun her round and seized hold of her hair, forcing her tongue into her mouth while her fingers darted between her legs.

'Do you think I haven't noticed your pathetic, coquettish little gestures in front of my husband?' she asked. 'Do you think he's really interested in you? You know nothing of the ways of adult life, you foolish little virgin. I'm going to show you what you are, and what happens to frivolous little girls.'

Katia tried to wriggle out of her grasp but the woman was so much stronger. She had hold of her hair and pulled it so hard Katia had no choice but to step out of the tub and stand squirming naked on the rush carpet. The countess steered her up against the wall, where she continued to have access to every part of her body. Her eyes were glazed over in a kind of demonic fury, her strength seemed superhuman and an intoxicating animal scent rose up from out of her dress. It was a gross imposition, but still Katia couldn't save herself from responding to the woman's lustful advances.

'You're going to come for me, you little bitch,' she hissed. 'That's what you want, isn't it? You play the innocent yet you are consumed by your own narcissism, like all spoilt young girls. Know these earthly pleasures well, my dear, for soon you must prepare yourself for paradise.'

As was typical of late, the countess was speaking in riddles. What paradise could she know, stuck in the kitchen and worked to the bone? Yet, against all rational judgement she sought the countess's fingers at the nexus of her pleasure – skilled hands that would allow no retreat into modesty. Katia closed her eyes and leaned back against the wall, imagining it was Nikolai overcome with desire for her. It was somehow less troubling to believe a man's hands were on her, especially the hands of a man she desired so ardently. And from this molestation Katia brought herself to a shattering crisis as the countess whispered obscenities in her ear. Like Peter she had been undone for the woman's craven pleasure. She'd been naïve to think she would be exempt from indignity merely because she'd dressed up and assisted in the torment of the gardener one afternoon. Now she too had been subjugated. Yet instead of it making her contrite and humble, like Peter, she seethed with indignation, nurturing the seeds of revenge that would teach her twisted tyrant a lesson. Let her call on this master. He was a figment of her warped imagination. Leaps and bounds were to be taken into the future with scientific progress. Nikolai had said so. In the future there was no place for backward superstitions.

The next day, the count retreated to his library, both to think about his discovery, and to take his mind away from it. He had recently taken possession of an exquisite monograph by an illustrator who was all the rage in Paris, and he longed to spend a leisurely couple of hours examining his prize. This artist had gone further than anyone had previously dared, conjuring scenes from Sacher-Masoch's *Venus in Furs* and salacious narratives chronicling the extremes of adult experience. He would drive himself to distraction poring over the illustrations, timing his experiment so Katia's arrival would coincide with his reaching a point of madness.

He'd crept through the kitchen late the previous night and slipped an envelope under her door containing details of the exact time he would receive her, and strict instructions as to what she must wear and do. If he was going to partake of the common form of intercourse, then at least it must be dressed to his liking. He hadn't spelled out his intentions – there was no point alarming the girl. He would make it a surprise for her, as he knew how much she craved him. It was only natural, he told himself.

It was 11 a.m. Irina would sleep until at least 1.30. He had half an hour to prepare for the experience. He hoped he would be able to do the deed. It had been over ten years since he'd last plundered a woman. If the girl was fabulous enough in her costume, everything should progress to its natural conclusion. He opened the book. Here was the human form, male and female, bound and whipped and ecstatic – in close up and as set pieces. The sensual curvature of the bodies, the detail of the tightly laced clothing, the sheen of perspiration that covered the flesh, the emotion that emanated from the models' expressions – all was remarkably naturalistic. It seemed the touch of genius had graced these drawings; an intuition that proved their creator was as much an enthusiast as his audience. Not even the new science of photography could capture what this talented master had brought to life.

He leafed carefully through the pages, the close-up plates inflaming him most swiftly. Close-up 1: The long leather skirt of a cruel mistress is swished aside to reveal a shaven mound. A whip is coiled around her gloved hand. Close-up 2: Her fingers part herself to show a glistening fold of intimate flesh, made wet with desire. Close-up 3: The abject humiliation of one who has become her toilet, as he lies beneath the stream pouring over his face. Close-up 4: The mistress's hand is between her legs and her gloved fingers are damp with her moisture. Close-up 5: She's laughing, her face radiant with cruel joy. The tendrils of the whip are stretched taut across her lap.

How he longed to be in that lap – to be kept longing for the unnameable delights of woman. To be allowed only the smallest token from her: the lick of her finger, moist with her juice; her soft manicured foot to kiss. He was hard and he remained transfixed by the images that sought to bring him to rapture. He laid a hand on his tumescence and ached to know his dreamy eruption. He couldn't stop looking at the second picture; to be that close to the most private aspect of a woman was a greedy, guilty intoxicant and, as he imagined the humiliation, he pushed harder against his hand, harder still, his mind ablaze with scandalous images. He must not allow himself skin-on-skin contact; he would remain contained but fully erect to bursting point. Could he stand the torture? With too much movement he might go off. It had happened before, in a bordello in Buda. The mistress there had a compulsion to watch bound slaves ejaculate into their trousers as she whipped their buttocks. If the girl sat astride his face, the very same thing could happen here today, in the library. That would be a disaster. But it gave him an idea for how she would be deflowered. He didn't want her adopting a submissive position and he certainly wasn't about to grind around on top of her like a common oaf.

He took his desperate need to even greater heights, as he turned the pages to reveal sketches of women in tight lacing, their breasts bulging over the leather, the nipples hard. He had to contain himself until Katia came to find him. Oh, exquisite torture, the blissful ache of tainted desire!

Katia flitted through the kitchen, a cloak concealing her elaborate costume, a basket on her arm, presenting the appearance of someone going mushroom gathering. But it was to a far more thrilling and less wholesome assignation that she was headed. Her instructions had arrived late. The envelope that had been slid under her door, albeit silently, had woken her. There was a connection between her and Nikolai – she was able to sense him before she saw him, as if her body was electrified by his presence, every cell awakened to sensual possibilities. Their rehearsals for the preliminaries of lovemaking had been conducted in his study to a point where she needed only to hear his voice to be aroused. And now, for the first time, she was to be received in the library – his sanctuary. It was very early in the day to be engaging in covert behaviour but she was willing to risk it. She'd ached too long between her legs for his touch. She'd seen the size of him and had imagined over too many sleepless nights what paradise could be unleashed, if he only followed the natural course of his desires.

Tentatively, she knocked on the library door.

The sound of a key in the lock, then Nikolai was in front of her, his eyes glinting mischief.

'Ten more minutes and you may have found me in a most indecorous state,' he whispered. 'Good lord, I have never been so hard.'

He seized her hand, pulled her into the room, and locked the door behind them. Katia registered shock at the sight of him. Contained in his trousers, his condition seemed even ruder than had he been bare. He pulled her over to a spacious three-seater settee made of leather. On one of the cushions lay a book of explicitly adult illustrations and Katia could not take her eyes from it. The costume she wore could have been taken from its pages. This was no time to be coy; the count wanted her to be stern with him, to force him to take pleasure at her bidding. She'd thought carefully about what to say and the ease with which she scolded him surprised her.

'Sit down,' she ordered. 'Left to your own devices, it seems you are unable to keep your mind on more studious matters for longer than a moment. It seems it is not merely enough to stare at these depraved images, you want also to engage in the behaviour they show. Well, it's time you were taught the consequences of your sinful thinking.'

With this, she whisked the cloak from her shoulders to reveal the full glory of her outfit. A black uniform dress had been slashed mid-way at her thighs, under which she wore a starched white blouse buttoned to the neck. Her legs were encased in leather riding boots under which were black woollen stockings tied over the knees with satin ribbons. Her waist was cinched by a purple and black corselet. Only a small amount of the soft creamy flesh of her thighs was exposed, but it was tantalising in comparison to the galvanising quality of her clothes.

Nikolai sat under her gaze, touching himself through the material of his trousers. This sight was a source of fascination to her, and the moisture that gathered at her sex was slick and copious. Over the soft apex of her treasure was pressed the finest silk of a pair of undergarments that were, even on her slender body, tight. Over that taut fabric was yet another, looser pair of satin knickers, split between the legs to allow access to the glories underneath. The combination was sure to drive her lover crazy in his task – and indeed the constriction pressed up against the nub of her pleasure was emboldening her mood.

The dual knickers arrangement had been her idea and now she was gorgeously swollen.

'Turn around,' she ordered, 'and kneel on the floor. You will be whipped.'

He pressed his face into the leather of the Chesterfield as Katia took a thin rattan switch from the table and sliced the air a couple of times to introduce him to the sound of his punishment. Then, the thrilling moment, as she brought the implement into stinging contact with the seat of his trousers. She meted out a measured ten strokes, requiring his thanks at each blow. They were both careful not to make too much noise and this quiet punishment made the practice seem all the more daring. The desire that flowed through Katia's body as she lashed the count transcended all previous arousal. The thrill of the power combined with the delicious feeling of her sex chafing against the silk made her understand for the first time how it must feel for Nikolai, iron-hard and not allowed release.

But the inevitable was upon them. As he turned around, he released himself from his trousers and she allowed him only the briefest contact with his manhood before commanding him to leave it alone. He leaned up against the sofa as she straddled him, knelt upright. She could feel the heat radiating from herself, aware his face was inches from her sex.

'Touch it,' she said, and he moved his hand to between her legs.

'You madden me,' he cried. 'I cannot feel your skin yet you are soaking through the satin. The scent of you is intoxicating.'

His staff glistened with unstoppable dew. It sought its natural target and curved toward it. She could bear it no longer, so she seized hold of his staff, rubbing it across the essential zone of her desire. She had never known a hunger like it. The need to be filled occupied her, mind, body and soul. And, from the expression on Nikolai's face, it seemed he too needed to explore what had previously been forbidden.

She remembered the one great thing that had changed her life and set her on course to this sexual awakening – the feel of his mouth upon her. When the countess had dressed her for the punishing of Peter, he had been allowed to run his hands all over her, and then she had wanted to take their contact further but, under the eyes of his stern wife, it hadn't been possible. All those nights of wanting and now, finally, the moment was imminent. It was bold, it was brazen, it was unthinkable behaviour only a few weeks ago. Katia found herself inching closer to the count's face. She could see he was becoming increasingly excited and, as his hands strayed naturally toward himself, she brought the cruellest prohibition to bear by grasping his wrists and pinning them to the sofa. He slid down a few inches until he was flat on his back and then – the queening glory as she spread the aromatic heaven of her arousal over his face.

Her constriction was maddening both of them, and after a few moments he ripped his way past her flimsy defences. He was supposed to wait for orders, but it didn't work out as they had planned. Stripped of her undergarments, yet fully stockinged and booted, her young body was too tempting a prospect for even the most servile of lovers. He was priapic, desperate, reckless. He'd had enough of the teasing and had enough of spending years under his wife's orders. In one moment he reversed their positions and, in their scrabble for joy, Katia landed in a seated position on the sofa. He grabbed her firmly by the hips. It was what she'd dreamed of from the moment she'd laid eyes on him. He positioned her at the edge of the seat, knelt back and looked her in the eyes.

'Are you ready, sweet girl?' he asked.

She could only nod her assent.

His fingers were inside her, twisting in her juices, then rubbed over his face.

His hand clasped around his penis, and he rubbed it up and down over the zone of her pleasure. All the while he kept eye contact, telling her what was going to happen.

'Spend for me,' he whispered. 'Use my hardness before I fuck you. Make yourself come all over my cock, you beautiful dirty girl.'

His language, and the stark realisation of what she was doing, and with whom she was doing it, was too much for her young mind. She could feel the molten sensations gathering – the sparking and fizzing of her aroused body preparing for the explosion. She ran her hands down her thighs and over her uniformed body. She tensed and began to tremble as Nikolai, maddeningly, held away from her just a little. The all-consuming need to rush toward paradise overruled all other thoughts.

She pressed herself against him, grabbing hold of him and demanding he continue his vigorous ministrations.

'Oh yes, yes, bring me to my climax,' she hissed. 'Watch me do it, then take me. I'm coming for you, sir.'

As she bit her hand to prevent herself creating a commotion, she felt her sex constrict and throb with the blissful truth of her climax.

Nikolai appeared to be a man transformed. He perspired and his heart was racing. This was it. There was no going back. As Katia's most intimate flesh was still pulsing, swollen by her moment, he lunged inside her. Now here was the point of her undoing. Finally, after all those years wondering and giggling with her friends, after all those days spent in heated anxiety, desperate to know what the feel of a man would be like, here he was – her first. His ample length filled her, yet she felt no pain. Her desire had moistened her to receive his most urgent thrusts. Back and forth she rocked at the edge of the sofa. Back and forth, impaled on Count Nikolai's manhood.

She observed his face, the tension in his neck, and she relished the strength of his arms as he gripped her slender body. She could tell the fact she was still clothed was driving him to a greater urgency. It felt so forbidden, so thrilling, but it was to be a brief coupling. The potency of the situation was too much for the count.

'Oh, my sweet girl,' he panted. 'I'm unable to hold back a moment longer.'

'Tell me, tell me what you are to do,' she said.

'I'm going to spend in your sex, fill you with it.'

His expression turned dark, and it was as if he had forgotten his preferred submissive position. So she gathered her confidence and allowed herself to spur him on with what she knew was disgraceful vocabulary, but it felt so naughtily thrilling and pertinent to the situation, that she couldn't help herself. She writhed beneath him like a young harlot.

'I'll make you do it, sir,' she said. 'Make you come in my cunt. Ooh, it feels so good, just give it to me. Make it happen inside me.'

Her words inflamed him to greater and greater heights, but it was the sight of her running her tongue over her full pink lips while looking him in the eyes that was the final push. With a strangled cry, he pressed her tightly against the sofa and then drove into her like a man possessed. His strength and size was everything she had wished for, and she tipped over into a realm of lascivious joy. All feelings dissipated except the blissful culmination of their mutual desires. It was happening; the count was coming inside her. No longer a maiden, she was now initiated into the pleasures of adult congress and she beamed with delight. This reality overwhelmed her and sent her mind spinning, but the consequences of their activity were to bring another form of crisis to the manor. Someone else was preparing for ecstasy. A hundred and fifty years of waiting were about to come to an end.

8

The storm began late that afternoon. By the same time next day – the last day of October – it still hadn't abated. The sky had darkened with an ominous conviction, as if it would never again be blue; giant gunmetal clouds blocked out all light and the colour was sucked out of the garden. The rains lashed against the windows and a tempest swirled around the manor, sending great draughts into the corridors and extinguishing the flames of the oil lamps. The tapestries in the hall swayed and creaked on their fastenings and a whistling wind blew against the doors and billowed the curtains.

Everyone's mood was affected. Magda and the cook were especially grumpy, Giulio flopped listlessly in his quarters and the count remained locked in his library, unavailable to anyone. Peter and Auroch sat brooding by the kitchen range, occasionally pacing the room and rearranging the supplies in the anteroom, but both were surly and leaden. Only two people remained animated despite the weather. Katia refused to allow the storm to dampen her joy. She had shaken off years of wanting and dreaming, and could now replay her very real experiences with the count over and over in her mind. This only served to drive her to a state of perpetual arousal, and her body was moving more sensuously, even as she went about her normal tasks. Her hips swayed as she walked and she kept finding her fingers in her mouth for no reason other than to suck upon something flesh.

The countess charged about the manor and its grounds as if powered by the electricity of the storm. With her heavy black skirts lifted she ran around the lawns, her head thrown back in laughter. She would intermittently return to the house drenched, her eyes blazing with a supernatural fervour and her hair cascading about her in long dark tendrils. The shutters clapped and banged against the windows of her quarters. To anyone who happened to pass she made bold, egotistical declarations: she held nature in her power; all the creatures of the forest would heed her call. The kitchen staff muttered amongst themselves, and Magda was the only one to humour her mistress's megalomania.

Katia tried her best to avoid her, but the woman sought her out in the drawing room as she was sweeping the grate ready to light the evening fire.

'I'll need you for something later, my ripe little virgin,' said Irina, disparagingly, nudging Katia's hip with the toe of her boot as she knelt by the hearth. 'Something very special. Make sure you come to my room at 9 p.m.'

If only she knew, thought Katia, that insult no longer applies. But she could allow herself only the briefest triumph, as the terror of Irina discovering what she'd done had consumed her in waves since the act had been committed. She flushed pink and felt sick when she considered the consequences that could befall her. Most of all she feared that Nikolai, in a moment of weakness, would confess his sin – as was his wont in their curious and twisted relationship. She'd made him promise not to breathe a word to his wife, and he'd emphatically assured her he'd rather cut out his own heart, but still, human emotions were fragile and nothing was ever certain.

The day darkened into night and the hour arrived for Katia to present herself in the countess's quarters. Apprehension pounded in her veins; she feared the woman's unpredictability could easily spill over into a terrifying mania with herself on the receiving end of an appalling cruelty, but there was nothing to be done. An order was an order. So when Katia was greeted by a smiling countess, the epitome of charm and grace, seated calmly in her Regency chair, she was instantly taken aback.

She certainly didn't look like a woman about to fly into a jealous rage.

'You are not to question me, and you are not to protest at any point,' the countess began quietly. 'I want you to undress and put on these garments.'

She indicated a diaphanous beaded dress and veil that lay prepared on the bed. It certainly wasn't suitable attire for a winter's evening, but Katia knew better than to object. As she disrobed, the countess paced around the room, watching her, her gaze as intrusive and lupine as ever.

'That's it, everything off. Not even your underthings are to remain.'

Katia stood naked and vulnerable as the countess came closer and released her hair to fall softly about her shoulders.

'There we are – just as nature likes it,' said Irina. 'You do make a beautiful spectacle. Now, put on the dress.'

Katia stepped into the garment and felt it mould to her body. Despite her curious predicament, it felt thrilling to be denuded of her underwear beneath the dress. A pair of matching shoes accompanied the costume, and then the countess put the veil on Katia's head. When she was attired to the woman's liking, she presented the large oval mirror in front of her and asked her to reflect on her image.

'I look like a bride,' said Katia, a note of curiosity in her voice. It felt disquieting to be dressed for marriage when there was no guests, no church and, most pertinently, no groom.

'And indeed that is what you are, in a way, just for this evening. We are going to perform a little theatre, and you must be dressed for the part.'

The woman really had lost her mind, thought Katia, resigned to the fact that she would have to play along until such point as the countess tired of it. She sighed. What a very perplexing and unconventional employment this was.

Next, the countess had her hand and was leading her out of the room and along the top corridor to the back of the house. She walked in front holding an oil lamp, a large set of keys clipped to her belt. Katia was then led upstairs, to a part of the house she'd never been to – a small landing at the very top of the building upon which sat a wooden chest. The countess moved the furniture aside to reveal a small door. She took one of the keys from her chain and unlocked it. Was she really to squeeze through here, follow this crazed woman on her twisted errand? She had no choice, for the countess's familiar, unnerving strength was overpowering and, before Katia could protest, she found herself on the other side of the door, at the top of a flight of cold stone steps that curled around the edge of the house. It must have been the far turret in the top right-hand corner of the building. Where would it lead?

She felt very alone and longed for the normality of her former life. If only Nikolai had sent her some token, some small indication their meeting had been important to him, she wouldn't feel so bad. As it was, she felt miserable; she wished that the countess would be seized by a violent torment and collapse, never to awaken. No chance of that, though, as she pulled Katia down the steps, round and around in her satin shoes until another door appeared, and that too was unlocked.

Before Katia could beat a hasty retreat, a bed of straw and two lengths of heavy chain greeted her. It was a cell, no doubt used by Irina's ancestors to chain up prisoners for torture.

'No, no, what have I done?' pleaded Katia, suddenly fearful that this theatre would become all too real. What if no one else knew of this room? Was she to be left here, to slowly starve and die?

'It's for your preparation,' replied the countess. 'It is not what you have done, but what you are about to do. I told you that you were chosen. Now be a good girl and let me take care of you. Here, you must drink this.'

An open bottle of wine sat on the cold stone floor. Irina

poured a large measure into a golden beaker and handed it to Katia. 'This will help you to relax,' she said.

'I don't want to relax. I want to go home. What do you want from me? Why am I dressed like this?' she pleaded, frantic. She wanted no part of the countess's 'care'.

'Shhh,' said Irina, putting down the wine. 'I can see you need a little persuasion.' Switching her soothing voice to her usual harsh rattle, she grabbed Katia's arms and struggled to get her wrists into the cuffs attached to the chains. Katia writhed and twisted to free herself from Irina's grasp but it was futile; she was no match for the woman's strength. She sank to the straw, dishevelled in her costume, her mind racing for ways to outwit this tyrant. There were few options open to her but one was to scream. She expected fear would give power to her voice. In fact the reverse happened, and her desperation manifested itself as little more than a squeak.

'Poor Katia,' said Irina. 'Why not calm yourself by the light of the moon and this wine?'

An arrow slit in the stonework revealed the moon was fat, and a beam of pale light streamed into the cell. She felt anything but calm, realising with a sickening horror that full moon on All Hallows' Eve was not a date the countess would allow to pass unmarked.

'Drink,' she once again urged, and Katia shook her head defiantly.

'Drink, you little bitch!' spat the countess, seizing Katia's nose and pulling her head back so her mouth instinctively fell open. She poured the garnet liquid down her throat. Katia spat it out, some of the wine staining her dress, and Irina slapped her smartly across the face.

'Do you know how lucky you are?' she spat in her ear. 'You ungrateful little hussy. Don't you dare sully this dress, or I'll leave you here forever, do you hear me? Now drink!'

There was no escaping the order and Katia reluctantly allowed the smooth red alcohol to pass her lips. It tasted wonderful, infused with spices, and although she tried to fight its effects, she felt her limbs relaxing, relaxing, then she was sinking, sinking, then into sleep.

In the forest surrounding the manor, a group of women had gathered in preparation for the auspicious night. Each of them had drunk of the brew that had served them and their kind in their diabolical purposes for hundreds of years. They chanted about their fire, and beat upon drums whose skins reverberated with the ancient rhythms that brought about their trance. Their commotion was not the only sound in the woods, for the wolves of Szathmar were awake and howling, alive to the presence that called all beasts to the party.

The birch trees glowed pale against the deep blue of the sky, now cleared of clouds after the storm to reveal the winter stars burning in their mysterious glory at such an unfathomable distance from the earth. The sorceresses chanted their haunting melody, smiling at each other. Soon it would be time to proceed to the bower. Their highborn wanton would bring the girl ready to be given to their master. How lucky they were to be witness to the ceremony. Each of them had secretly longed to be bride of the Beast herself, but as each was in the twilight of her autumn, such thoughts were poignant. Yet participation in the great rite was itself an honour – an act that would bestow great power into the earth and their spells.

A coach and four hurtled through the darkness, bearing its occupants toward the manor. They hadn't dared stop en route for fear of raising curiosity in the villages. Istvan Hideg stood to make a fortune and he glowed with the sense of his own malevolent genius. Once word had got around the jaded gentlemen at his club that a spectacle to rival the wildest orgy of a Parisian bordello would be occurring at the Malinovsky manor on All Hallows' Eve, he had been inundated with whispered requests to facilitate attendance. He had never felt so important, regaling them with tales of how even the Marquis de Sade would be shocked to see this Bacchanalia, were he still alive. The countess was the most lustful libertine in the realm. A select audience would witness a young girl given over to such erotic delirium that they would be restored to the vigour of their youth for the rest of their lives. The lure was too tempting for five of his club members to resist, and the money Istvan had collected promised to keep him in luxury for the next year.

Irina had not replied to his recent letters – no doubt she was embarrassed by her moment of weakness when they'd last met. Her extraordinary claims had inflamed him that evening before Katia's interview, and had set his mind reeling. Like all followers of the left-hand path he was open-minded to a little deviance. Yet the sorcery of which she'd spoken was in another league to his and his friends' salon-bound experiments. She had taken far too much laudanum that night and he suspected she'd regretted her loose tongue. But even so, to speak of conjuring Ordog himself to present him with a bride was the darkest magic he'd ever heard. Its attempt was an event he was not going to miss.

In the woodshed, Nikolai loaded his pistol by the light of the moon. The weapon brought him confidence. He planned to fire it into the air, to scatter those howling crones back from whence they came and leave Katia alone, should this stupidity get out of hand. He was more determined than ever that his wife would be found a place in a sanitorium. He knew doctors in Vienna that would arrange it; it would be done without delay, once this confounded business was over with. He'd searched the manor since dusk for his wife and for Katia. There had been no evidence of life from her blessed tower and the kitchen staff was no help, as usual. He should have kept them in his sights.

He'd prowled the grounds in the dark, searching for clues

until he realised his best method would be to lie in wait. The ceremony was due to happen in the bower. He would allow them their foolery until it became dangerous, then he'd spring out and put a stop to their nonsense once and for all. He was glad of his bearskin coat and hat. He fancied himself as the military man he never was, hiding out in the dark, preparing to ambush the foe. But of one thing he was certain: he would be the only beast in the woods that night.

She returned to consciousness in a dusty chamber, and the slab on which she lay was cold beneath her body. She fought to remember what had happened. How many hours had she been out? She tried to sit up but her body did not respond to her brain's signal. The day's events swam into her mind, but whatever drug she had been administered prevented clarity of thought. Still she wore the beaded dress and the veil. Oh yes, the wedding...the countess's stupid game. And here she was in a crypt surrounded by several dead Malinovskys and one still vitally alive.

The countess loomed over her. Her eyes and lips were painted and her hair was wild about her shoulders. She had on a glittering emerald-green dress that would not have been out of place at the opera. On her head she wore a crown made of beaten gold that had been carved into the shape of a wolf's head at the front, with real emeralds for eyes and a tongue made of rubies.

'You wake for your naming day,' said the countess, her voice of the most sinister timbre.

'You will not say anything, for your opinions do not matter. My master awaits and he comes with great expectation.'

Despite her foggy head, it didn't take long for Katia to realise what was at stake. She thought back to her dream. It had in fact been a premonition. If only she had protected herself. If only she had prayed and kept her faith; had trusted Peter and not made a mockery of his beliefs. She had been distracted and overwhelmed by her awakening sexuality – but did she have to be given up to the Beast for her sins? Had she been that bad? She began to recite her Hail Marys. If only she'd kept her rosary. If only Istvan had paid for her to stay at the academy. If only mother and father hadn't died...

The countess laughed. 'Do you think that feeble gibberish can do you any good? You stupid girl, can you not see how blessed you are? You have been chosen. His power has brought you here and it is no more possible to prevent this consummation than it is to stop the tide of the ocean. You will know an eternal bliss as his consort. There is nothing you can do. The time has come ... Auroch!'

The giant shaven-headed frame of the gatekeeper filled the doorway. If she was powerless against the countess, there was no chance of fighting this gargantuan rustic lummox for freedom. With one swift movement he lifted her from the slab and threw her over his shoulder. With Irina leading the way, a flaming torch in her hand, Katia was carried down the corridor toward the back exit of the manor. Once in the garden, under cover and hidden from anyone's sight, Auroch put her down. She made a wobbly and very reluctant bride. To follow the original rite, her hands were bound with rope, the countess reciting an incantation in the old language. The trees swayed and sighed and the garden was alive with activity as Auroch pulled on the rope and the three figures made their way toward the lake. Owls and foxes called into the night – their cries answered by the wolf and the nightjar – and the faint sound of drumming grew louder as they headed for the bower.

The arbour had been adorned with autumnal fruits and satin streamers coloured orange, red and green. Rosehip and honeysuckle were entwined into the latticework, and lanterns swung from the branches of the hazel trees, lighting up the garden. The lawned area at the end of the bower had been given over to some kind of bonfire party. A cauldron was heating over the flames and people were drinking from it.

Some looked aristocratic, whilst others were local peasants, old women barefoot, lost in the persistent rhythm of their drums.

As the countess entered the area, the drumming slowed to a less frenetic rhythm and all bowed down before her. She took up position at one end of the gathering, where the lawn sloped upwards. One of the old women handed her a shining sword. The countess lifted it above her head, the smoke from the fire encircling her. The emerald eyes of the wolf's head crown penetrated the dark. Her presence was all-powerful, and everyone in the garden froze as she began her summoning speech.

'I, Malinovsky, descended from the Siebenburger, who took their emblems from savage Scythia. I, born of the seven shields of Szathmar, shall breathe life back into this land,' she cried.

She then recited numerous verses of ancient dialect, naming and thanking all the demons she had brought forth down the years to aid her sorcery.

'As Darvulia honoured you last, so shall I honour you now. Master, your years of waiting are at an end. This Naming Day, this unhallowed night, is yours. Come claim your bride!'

Auroch led Katia through the bower as the drumming started up again at a furious pace. The aristocrats gasped as they beheld the young maiden, beautiful in her transparent dress, her breasts and sex clearly visible. Katia's mind swam. Her vision was blurred but the heat of the bonfire was welcome. Was she going to be made to couple with some man dressed in a beast costume? Was it Auroch? She shivered at the thought, but her mind was soon taken over by the drumming. Where was Nikolai? If only he would come and rescue her. She should have felt panicked, yet she was still affected by the herbal concoction she'd drunk earlier, and she kept lapsing into a semi-swoon, partially aware she was the focus of erotic contemplation, and partially excited by that fact.

Someone scooped a cup into the cauldron and held it to her

mouth. She drank willingly, as her thirst was extreme and the excitement of the crowd intoxicating. From that moment forward, all she was aware of were people shedding clothes, dancing around the fire, the drumming and the countess, spectacular in her emerald dress, calling out litanies in worship of the gods of the forest as the fire blazed.

'Dziewanna, Artemis to the barbarian hordes, princess of the Saxon Iris. Isten, great master and spirit of the woodland. Ordog, in your magnificence, come, come ...'

A smoky blue light emanated from the end of the bower. Crouched in the undergrowth, Nikolai had not yet witnessed anything that instilled fear into his soul or concern for Katia. From what he could see, she was swaying her lissome body against the guests, allowing them to freely run their hands over her, responding to their touch by sometimes falling to the grass and writhing in pleasure until someone picked her up and the dancing began once more. He had to hand it to his wife – she had concocted some impressive prestidigitation this evening.

But now something was happening. A great roar went up around the trees, causing flocks of roosting birds to take flight. It couldn't be ... it wasn't possible. At the end of the bower the light was blocked by a great shadow, a dark shape towering over the arbour. Nikolai held fast to his pistol, ready to fire in the event of danger. He needed to be absolutely sure this creature was not some villager dressed in a circus costume. He skirted around the edges and took cover in a rhododendron bush that flanked the lawn.

A roar went up again, bear-like and fearsome. The dark shape stood upright then fell onto all fours. Its eyes glowed yellow in the dark and its teeth were bared, jaws slavering. With one giant leap it was on the lawn, its haunches slinky, its great paws padding its way around the fire. The lawns glowed a dazzling emerald colour, the same as the countess's dress.

Amidst the grass, jewels shone and, whilst the throng of people retreated to the edges of the lawn, one man in a silken cape and top hat fell onto his knees, scrabbling at the ground, trying to pull the jewels from the grass. He looked strangely familiar. Istvan? It couldn't be.

A frenzy of shouting and screaming went up as the Beast fell upon the caped figure and cuffed him around the head so he was knocked unconscious into the shrubbery. Irina stood before the dark and terrifying creature, her arms outstretched, offering praise to her master. Auroch had pulled the rope in tight and led Katia to stand before the Beast.

If he lived to be a thousand years old, Nikolai would never manage to understand what reason-defying forces had brought this abomination to life. He swallowed hard, trying his best to summon the required courage he'd need to charge the area and fire the ancient firearm. Still the sorceresses kept the beat with their drums; all bar Auroch and the countess had been transported to a condition of hysteria or delirium.

'Oh master,' cried the countess, 'you have served me with your powers, made right all that was wrong. See what I give you this night. Your wait is over. Come claim your bride.'

The dark shape reared up and a plaintive howl began to rise. Around them, all the wolves of the region cried out in reply.

Katia, her eyes glazed, walked willingly toward the creature. Nikolai, his pistol drawn, stealthily approached the scene. The countess took the sword and sliced the transparent robe from Katia's body, making her naked. Katia fell to her knees, running her hands up the furred legs of the Beast. Instinctively she felt for its pizzle and the excitement in the gathered audience was palpable as they witnessed the beautiful young woman attending to the demon. Nikolai tried as best he could, but he was powerless to prevent an illicit flame of arousal coursing around his loins at the sight of the maid wrapping her lips around the creature's penis. Suddenly he was as erect as the Beast, and he couldn't prevent himself from grabbing hold of himself in the time-honoured fashion.

Katia turned her body round and faced the countess, her sex displayed to the demon. The guests all filed to the other end of the lawn, some tripping over in their frenzy to get a better view. With one movement, the Beast was suddenly covering her, and the sight of its jet-black fur against her pale, slender body was truly extraordinary. It pumped its hindquarters into her tender flesh, as its teeth sunk into the back of her neck. The expression on her face was one of rapture as the countess paced around the activity, hissing 'yes, yes,' in an increasingly excited pitch.

Nikolai held his own tumescence, rubbing it in short bursts as his eyes fed on the scene. Nothing in the bordellos of Vienna or Paris had matched this spectacle for the extremes of erotic experience. He knew it was wrong, but he couldn't prevent himself from taking his indulgence further, further. He could see the pink of Katia's sex tightening around the leathery member of the Beast. It was too much – a once in a lifetime opportunity. He squeezed at himself but his attempts to stem the flow of his seed were futile, and it gushed up the stem of his penis to erupt in a delicious creamy flow over his hand. He cried his filthy joy into the night, his pistol abandoned to the ground.

But there was a sudden commotion. The creature had taken leave of Katia and was advancing toward the countess, its bestial arousal still evident, shining like its teeth in the glow of the flames. All eyes were upon it, until a spectral figure appeared at the end of the lawn – a ghostly girl who seemed to radiate a pure white light.

'Be still,' she cried in her melodic voice, 'for the hour has come.'

She glided over to Katia, touching her briefly and instantly waking her from her trance.

'You,' Katia managed to say. 'My dream...'

Nikolai sensed a crucial moment had arrived, and he cautiously stepped onto the lawn.

'You were the chosen one,' the girl said to Katia, 'as I was too, so long ago. But you cannot live in our world. You are a maiden no longer.'

'What trickery is this?' cried the countess. 'She is the sacrifice! Your enchantment drew her to the bower.'

'Yes,' said the girl, 'she was a maiden then, but is no longer. He can take only one who is unsullied to his kingdom. And the rite must be fulfilled tonight.'

The audience was agog. In the midst of the excitement, the count ran to Katia, covering her with his bearskin coat. She threw herself at him, shivering, coming round from her hypnosis, asking, 'What have I done?' over and over.

The count hushed her, as they crouched down, transfixed, observing the countess's panic.

'Take *me*, take *me*,' cried one of the crones, rushing forward to prostrate herself before her master.

She was ignored, and her fellow sorceresses pulled her back to their huddle. The Beast reared up, grotesque in his impatience.

'There is one here tonight,' said the girl, her arms growing long, stretching above her head, 'who is to be the chosen.'

She threw out an arm, her finger extended, pointing at the countess.

'It's you!'

'No, I am mistress of the gardens. I cannot be consort to the Beast! I will know my reward on earth. My ancestors have written of it.'

She stood her ground but she was trembling.

The girl was shaking her head. 'Are you not pure, intact, still virgin?'

'Yes, but ...'

The audience was aghast, the countess noticeably vulnerable. But then, the noise of a crowd was apparent from the other side of the grounds. Flaming torches were visible and a shout rose over the trees. Suddenly there was panic, as a mob burst into the bower, led by Peter, the gardener.

'Unholy demons, degenerates!' he cried, as the aristocrats and crones fled the scene in all directions, sensing the mob's taste for vengeance. Nikolai and Katia knew to look scared, so they would not be a target of the crowd's wrath. The Beast turned around to face them, snarling and roaring, crouched low. One fired a pistol at it, but it made no mark. The spectral girl laughed her singing laugh and shot up into the air, her face transformed into a hideous condition. Some village rustic shot at her, and she let loose a wailing scream at such a pitch that the crowd dropped their tools and covered their ears. Impossible to injure, the Beast and his consort showed no fear, and they leaped and danced around their enemy. A priest entered the fray, and the Beast launched its jaws into his side, then severed the head with one blow of its mighty paw.

Peter was advancing on the countess, reciting the Lord's Prayer and holding a crucifix in front of him.

'You fool!' she cried, taking up her sword. 'You dare deny me my power!' With one slice she knocked the cross from his hand and came for him, cutting through the air with her weapon. He backed away, shrieking when he saw what had happened to the priest, then ran from the scene.

'So much for your exorcism!' she laughed. 'To think you can defeat me, consort of the Beast, with your pathetic prayers.'

Ordog sprang upright once more and Nikolai and Katia watched transfixed, holding onto each other in a desperate clinch as the countess ran to him, then slid her hand into his.

'Take your bride to her kingdom!' she cried. 'Let us leave all fools behind!'

A cloud of blue smoke went up, then a wind of such ferocity that the head of the priest took off, bouncing across the lawn to land in the lake with a splash. The Beast and the countess were gone, vanished into the ether. The spectral girl floated down just briefly, her face again beautiful. Before returning to the dark, she touched Katia about the face, as she had that night of her first enchantment.

'Goodbye, my beauty,' she sang. 'Don't forget me.'

And in a matter of minutes all was quiet except for the sound of a groaning man staggering out of the bushes, a battered top hat in his hand.

'Did I miss something?' he said.

'Istvan!' shouted Katia and Nikolai in unison. He had time only to look at his pocket watch, before Nikolai punched him squarely in the face, knocking him back into unconsciousness.

Epilogue

Springtime at the manor was beautiful. The cherry trees blossomed in a profusion of white and pink and the peacocks displayed their fans on lawns bathed in sunlight. Mrs Katia Kovach threw open the shutters of her bedroom to greet the new day. Her laughter rang around the room as her husband entered, wearing one of her hats.

'Are you ready, my dear?' he asked. He'd reverted to his original family name, since his former wife had disappeared.

'Why yes. The cases are packed.'

'You don't need to bring too many costumes with you. Once we're settled in Paris we can send for our remaining possessions.'

'Of course.'

'Our coach is waiting.'

As the newly married count and countess climbed into their carriage, the staff came to wave them *bon voyage*.

'The new family will be arriving later this week,' Katia said to Magda as the coachmen waited for her to step inside. 'They're very nice. They'll bring children to the manor – new life, a new start.'

'We wish you every happiness,' said the sturdy housekeeper, clasping her hands. 'I do believe we've turned the corner of our ill fortune.'

'Yes, Magda, so do I,' said Katia, as they both looked out over the grounds at the gardens in bud.

As Katia slammed the coach door shut, she glanced up at the tower. The sun was strong, and she blinked to focus her eyes. Something was glowing there. A white shape. Was it waving?

Katia sat back in her seat and looked at Nikolai, resplendent in his finery.

He said something, but she couldn't hear him. All she could hear was a singing, melodic voice reverberating around the carriage: 'Don't forget me.'

LOOK OUT FOR THE ALL-NEW BLACK LACE BOOKS – AVAILABLE NOW!

WILDWOOD
Janine Ashbless
ISBN 978 0 352 34194 5

Avril Shearing is a landscape gardener brought in to reclaim an overgrown woodland for the handsome and manipulative Michael Deverick. But among the trees lurks a tribe of environmental activists determined to stop anyone getting in, led by the enigmatic Ash who regards Michael as his mortal enemy. Avril soon discovers that on the Kester Estate nothing is as it seems. Creatures that belong in dreams or in nightmares emerge after dark to prowl the grounds, and hidden in the heart of the wood is something so important that people will kill, or die for it. Ash and Michael become locked in a deadly battle for the Wildwood – and for Avril herself.

ODALISQUE
Fleur Reynolds
ISBN 978 0 352 34193 8

Set against a backdrop of sophisticated elegance, a tale of family intrigue, forbidden passions and depraved secrets unfolds. Beautiful but scheming, successful designer Auralie plots to bring about the downfall of her virtuous cousin, Jeanine. Recently widowed, but still young and glamorous, Jeanine finds her passions being rekindled by Auralie's husband. But she is playing into Auralie's hands – vindictive hands that drag Jeanine into a world of erotic depravity. Why are the cousins locked into this sexual feud? And what is the purpose of Jeanine's mysterious Confessor, and his sordid underground sect?

To be published in September 2008

THE STALLION
Georgina Brown
ISBN 978 0 352 34199 0

The world of showjumping is as steamy as it is competitive. Ambitious young rider Penny Bennett enters into a wager with her oldest rival and friend, Ariadne. Penny intends to gain the sponsorship and the very personal attention of showjumping's biggest impresario, Alister Beaumont. The prize is Ariadne's thoroughbred stallion, guaranteed to bring Penny money and success.
Beaumont's riding school is not all it seems, however. Firstly there's the weird relationship between Alister and his cigar-smoking sister. Then the bizarre clothes they want Penny to wear. In an atmosphere of unbridled kinkiness, Penny is determined to win the wager and discover the truth about Beaumont's strange hobbies.

IN TOO DEEP
Portia Da Costa
ISBN 978 0 352 34197 6

Librarian Gwendolyne Price begins to find indecent proposals and sexy stories in her suggestion box. Shocked that they seem to be tailored specifically to her own deepest sexual fantasies, she enters a tantalising relationship with a man she's never met. But pretty soon, erotic letters and toe-curlingly sensual emails just aren't enough. She has to meet her mysterious correspondent in the flesh.

Black Lace Booklist

Information is correct at time of printing. To avoid disappointment, check availability before ordering. Go to www.black-lace-books.com.
All books are priced £7.99 unless another price is given.

BLACK LACE BOOKS WITH A CONTEMPORARY SETTING

☐ THE ANGELS' SHARE Maya Hess	ISBN 978 0 352 34043 6	
☐ ASKING FOR TROUBLE Kristina Lloyd	ISBN 978 0 352 33362 9	
☐ BLACK LIPSTICK KISSES Monica Belle	ISBN 978 0 352 33885 3	£6.99
☐ THE BLUE GUIDE Carrie Williams	ISBN 978 0 352 34132 7	
☐ THE BOSS Monica Belle	ISBN 978 0 352 34088 7	
☐ BOUND IN BLUE Monica Belle	ISBN 978 0 352 34012 2	
☐ CAMPAIGN HEAT Gabrielle Marcola	ISBN 978 0 352 33941 6	
☐ CAT SCRATCH FEVER Sophie Mouette	ISBN 978 0 352 34021 4	
☐ CHILLI HEAT Carrie Williams	ISBN 978 0 352 34178 5	
☐ CIRCUS EXCITE Nikki Magennis	ISBN 978 0 352 34033 7	
☐ CLUB CRÈME Primula Bond	ISBN 978 0 352 33907 2	£6.99
☐ CONFESSIONAL Judith Roycroft	ISBN 978 0 352 33421 3	
☐ CONTINUUM Portia Da Costa	ISBN 978 0 352 33120 5	
☐ DANGEROUS CONSEQUENCES Pamela Rochford	ISBN 978 0 352 33185 4	
☐ DARK DESIGNS Madelynne Ellis	ISBN 978 0 352 34075 7	
☐ THE DEVIL INSIDE Portia Da Costa	ISBN 978 0 352 32993 6	
☐ EQUAL OPPORTUNITIES Mathilde Madden	ISBN 978 0 352 34070 2	
☐ FIRE AND ICE Laura Hamilton	ISBN 978 0 352 33486 2	
☐ GONE WILD Maria Eppie	ISBN 978 0 352 33670 5	
☐ HOTBED Portia Da Costa	ISBN 978 0 352 33614 9	
☐ IN PURSUIT OF ANNA Natasha Rostova	ISBN 978 0 352 34060 3	
☐ IN THE FLESH Emma Holly	ISBN 978 0 352 34117 4	
☐ LEARNING TO LOVE IT Alison Tyler	ISBN 978 0 352 33535 7	
☐ MAD ABOUT THE BOY Mathilde Madden	ISBN 978 0 352 34001 6	
☐ MAKE YOU A MAN Anna Clare	ISBN 978 0 352 34006 1	
☐ MAN HUNT Cathleen Ross	ISBN 978 0 352 33583 8	
☐ THE MASTER OF SHILDEN Lucinda Carrington	ISBN 978 0 352 33140 3	
☐ MIXED DOUBLES Zoe le Verdier	ISBN 978 0 352 33312 4	£6.99
☐ MIXED SIGNALS Anna Clare	ISBN 978 0 352 33889 1	£6.99
☐ MS BEHAVIOUR Mini Lee	ISBN 978 0 352 33962 1	
☐ PACKING HEAT Karina Moore	ISBN 978 0 352 33356 8	£6.99

❏ PAGAN HEAT Monica Belle — ISBN 978 0 352 33974 4

❏ PEEP SHOW Mathilde Madden — ISBN 978 0 352 33924 9

❏ THE POWER GAME Carrera Devonshire — ISBN 978 0 352 33990 4

❏ THE PRIVATE UNDOING OF A PUBLIC SERVANT — ISBN 978 0 352 34066 5
    Leonie Martel

❏ RUDE AWAKENING Pamela Kyle — ISBN 978 0 352 33036 9

❏ SAUCE FOR THE GOOSE Mary Rose Maxwell — ISBN 978 0 352 33492 3

❏ SPLIT Kristina Lloyd — ISBN 978 0 352 34154 9

❏ STELLA DOES HOLLYWOOD Stella Black — ISBN 978 0 352 33588 3

❏ THE STRANGER Portia Da Costa — ISBN 978 0 352 33211 0

❏ SUITE SEVENTEEN Portia Da Costa — ISBN 978 0 352 34109 9

❏ TONGUE IN CHEEK Tabitha Flyte — ISBN 978 0 352 33484 8

❏ THE TOP OF HER GAME Emma Holly — ISBN 978 0 352 34116 7

❏ UNNATURAL SELECTION Alaine Hood — ISBN 978 0 352 33963 8

❏ VELVET GLOVE Emma Holly — ISBN 978 0 352 34115 0

❏ VILLAGE OF SECRETS Mercedes Kelly — ISBN 978 0 352 33344 5

❏ WILD BY NATURE Monica Belle — ISBN 978 0 352 33915 7 — £6.99

❏ WILD CARD Madeline Moore — ISBN 978 0 352 34038 2

❏ WING OF MADNESS Mae Nixon — ISBN 978 0 352 34099 3

BLACK LACE BOOKS WITH AN HISTORICAL SETTING

❏ THE BARBARIAN GEISHA Charlotte Royal — ISBN 978 0 352 33267 7

❏ BARBARIAN PRIZE Deanna Ashford — ISBN 978 0 352 34017 7

❏ THE CAPTIVATION Natasha Rostova — ISBN 978 0 352 33234 9

❏ DARKER THAN LOVE Kristina Lloyd — ISBN 978 0 352 33279 0

❏ WILD KINGDOM Deanna Ashford — ISBN 978 0 352 33549 4

❏ DIVINE TORMENT Janine Ashbless — ISBN 978 0 352 33719 1

❏ FRENCH MANNERS Olivia Christie — ISBN 978 0 352 33214 1

❏ LORD WRAXALL'S FANCY Anna Lieff Saxby — ISBN 978 0 352 33080 2

❏ NICOLE'S REVENGE Lisette Allen — ISBN 978 0 352 29984 4

❏ THE SENSES BEJEWELLED Cleo Cordell — ISBN 978 0 352 32904 2 — £6.99

❏ THE SOCIETY OF SIN Sian Lacey Taylder — ISBN 978 0 352 34080 1

❏ TEMPLAR PRIZE Deanna Ashford — ISBN 978 0 352 34137 2

❏ UNDRESSING THE DEVIL Angel Strand — ISBN 978 0 352 33938 6

BLACK LACE BOOKS WITH A PARANORMAL THEME

❏ BRIGHT FIRE Maya Hess — ISBN 978 0 352 34104 4

❏ BURNING BRIGHT Janine Ashbless — ISBN 978 0 352 34085 6

❑ CRUEL ENCHANTMENT Janine Ashbless ISBN 978 0 352 33483 1
❑ FLOOD Anna Clare ISBN 978 0 352 34094 8
❑ GOTHIC BLUE Portia Da Costa ISBN 978 0 352 33075 8
❑ GOTHIC HEAT Portia Da Costa ISBN 978 0 352 34170 9
❑ PHANTASMAGORIA Madelynne Ellis ISBN 978 0 352 34168 6
❑ THE PRIDE Edie Bingham ISBN 978 0 352 33997 3
❑ THE SILVER CAGE Mathilde Madden ISBN 978 0 352 34165 5
❑ THE SILVER COLLAR Mathilde Madden ISBN 978 0 352 34141 9
❑ THE SILVER CROWN Mathilde Madden ISBN 978 0 352 34157 0
❑ THE TEN VISIONS Olivia Knight ISBN 978 0 352 34119 8

BLACK LACE ANTHOLOGIES

❑ BLACK LACE QUICKIES 1 Various ISBN 978 0 352 34126 6 £2.99
❑ BLACK LACE QUICKIES 2 Various ISBN 978 0 352 34127 3 £2.99
❑ BLACK LACE QUICKIES 3 Various ISBN 978 0 352 34128 0 £2.99
❑ BLACK LACE QUICKIES 4 Various ISBN 978 0 352 34129 7 £2.99
❑ BLACK LACE QUICKIES 5 Various ISBN 978 0 352 34130 3 £2.99
❑ BLACK LACE QUICKIES 6 Various ISBN 978 0 352 34133 4 £2.99
❑ BLACK LACE QUICKIES 7 Various ISBN 978 0 352 34146 4 £2.99
❑ BLACK LACE QUICKIES 8 Various ISBN 978 0 352 34147 1 £2.99
❑ BLACK LACE QUICKIES 9 Various ISBN 978 0 352 34155 6 £2.99
❑ MORE WICKED WORDS Various ISBN 978 0 352 33487 9 £6.99
❑ WICKED WORDS 3 Various ISBN ISBN 978 0 352 33522 7 £6.99
❑ WICKED WORDS 4 Various ISBN 978 0 352 33603 3 £6.99
❑ WICKED WORDS 5 Various ISBN 978 0 352 33642 2 £6.99
❑ WICKED WORDS 6 Various ISBN 978 0 352 33690 3 £6.99
❑ WICKED WORDS 7 Various ISBN 978 0 352 33743 6 £6.99
❑ WICKED WORDS 8 Various ISBN 978 0 352 33787 0 £6.99
❑ WICKED WORDS 9 Various ISBN 978 0 352 33860 0
❑ WICKED WORDS 10 Various ISBN 978 0 352 33893 8
❑ THE BEST OF BLACK LACE 2 Various ISBN 978 0 352 33718 4
❑ WICKED WORDS: SEX IN THE OFFICE Various ISBN 978 0 352 33944 7
❑ WICKED WORDS: SEX AT THE SPORTS CLUB Various ISBN 978 0 352 33991 1
❑ WICKED WORDS: SEX ON HOLIDAY Various ISBN 978 0 352 33961 4
❑ WICKED WORDS: SEX IN UNIFORM Various ISBN 978 0 352 34002 3
❑ WICKED WORDS: SEX IN THE KITCHEN Various ISBN 978 0 352 34018 4
❑ WICKED WORDS: SEX ON THE MOVE Various ISBN 978 0 352 34034 4
❑ WICKED WORDS: SEX AND MUSIC Various ISBN 978 0 352 34061 0
❑ WICKED WORDS: SEX AND SHOPPING Various ISBN 978 0 352 34076 4

To find out the latest information about Black Lace titles, check out the website: www.black-lace-books.com or send for a booklist with complete synopses by writing to:

Black Lace Booklist, Virgin Books Ltd
Thames Wharf Studios
Rainville Road
London W6 9HA

Please include an SAE of decent size. Please note only British stamps are valid.

Our privacy policy
We will not disclose information you supply us to any other parties. We will not disclose any information which identifies you personally to any person without your express consent.

From time to time we may send out information about Black Lace books and special offers. Please tick here if you do <u>not</u> wish to receive Black Lace information.   ❏

Please send me the books I have ticked above.

Name ....

Address ....

....

....

....

Post Code ....

Send to: Virgin Books Cash Sales, Thames Wharf Studios, Rainville Road, London W6 9HA.

US customers: for prices and details of how to order books for delivery by mail, call 888-330-8477.

Please enclose a cheque or postal order, made payable to Virgin Books Ltd, to the value of the books you have ordered plus postage and packing costs as follows:

UK and BFPO – £1.00 for the first book, 50p for each subsequent book.

Overseas (including Republic of Ireland) – £2.00 for the first book, £1.00 for each subsequent book.

If you would prefer to pay by VISA, ACCESS/MASTERCARD, DINERS CLUB, AMEX or SWITCH, please write your card number and expiry date here:

....

Signature ....

Please allow up to 28 days for delivery.